I0576122

Who Unplugged the Stars?

A Tale of Two Cowards

L. K. Lawrence

Who Unplugged the Stars?

DEDICATION

To my parents for instilling in me the love of reading. To my brother Nate for listening when I read my chapters aloud. To the kindred spirits who remember their first crush with all its ups and downs. And to the shadows that formerly filled the recesses of my mind, but now fill these pages instead.

.

What Happened?

In January of my Junior year, after a basketball game that we'd won I answered a question that would forever change my life.

A group of us were leaving the gym when a girl approached me who's known as Hoppy, a moniker she'd earned in grade school because she always seemed on the verge of jumping out of her shoes with excitement so much so that she seemed to bounce rather than walk.

"Hey Grace, do you have a second?" she asked as she motioned me back into the gym away from the others.

"Sure, what's up?"

"Um . . . I was wondering if there was anything between you and

Sam." I looked at her curiously. *Why was she asking? Had she heard something?*

I tried to mask any emotion as I asked, "Why?"

"If there is nothing between you two, I'd like to go after him."

I looked at her wondering how to answer the question. I *thought* there was something between us, but neither of us had verbalized what our feelings were, or what the relationship was, so I wasn't sure how to explain it. It was nice of her to ask me before she acted, but I couldn't imagine he'd want a little critter like Hoppy. He was such a tall guy, that even though I was awkward and just ordinary-looking, wouldn't he prefer a tall girl over the Cottontail? A girl, that if he should ever desire to kiss her, wouldn't cause him backache from having to bend down so far to do so? He'd always seemed fine with me and my height before, or was he? Maybe he preferred back pain?

What do I say?

I agonized over my answer. I couldn't say there was something going on between us when we'd never discussed it. What if I said yes, we were in a relationship, but he thought otherwise and then hated me for him missing an opportunity with that woodland creature? Or, what if I said no, yet he thought there was and gets mad at me for that? I couldn't win and I couldn't lie. After a quick contemplation of my options, I said, "No, we're friends, go ahead."

I couldn't fathom that he'd choose her over me. We had a history; we were good together. *Surely, he wasn't that big of an animal lover.* And even though I was still anxious about it, I returned to the group and dismissed the whole conversation from my mind. Little did I know.

Two weeks later, while standing in the hall during lunch, I saw Sam and Hoppy walking with their arms about each other. I couldn't believe it and I stared after them in shock. *He picked her?! When did this happen? Is this why I haven't seen him around? How can they be this close in such a short time,* I asked myself, dazed at the speed with which both must have moved. Why hadn't he moved at that speed with me? Were they still a new enough couple that I could pull him back to me?

It was a new semester, and Sam and I had two classes together, so I figured I could try and reclaim my chance at romance during those hours. I proceeded to our first class determined to get him back only to find he was no longer in that class, nor was he in the second class. He'd changed his schedule and we had *no* classes together. Why would his being with Hoppy cause him to change his class schedule? It seemed odd, but I still wasn't too concerned. I still felt confident that I could charm him back, because maybe he changed his schedule around for work or sports or something and it was just a coincidence that he was with Hoppy at the same time. *I'll get him at lunchtime.*

As soon as the lunch bell rang, I began to look for Sam. I found him sitting alone on his usual bench in Senior Hall. I plopped down beside him.

"How ya doin', Sam?" I asked, with a big smile as I bumped my shoulder against his. Without a word, he stood and walked away. I was so stunned and confused by this, that I didn't know what to do.

"Sam! Wait," I called as I rose to follow him.

"Hey Gracie, what's shakin'?" Trevor asked, stopping in front of me.

"Nothing," I mindlessly said as I watched Sam walk down the hall away from me.

From that moment on, the life I'd grown to love had changed. Sam and Hoppy were always together. If he was alone in a group and I came along, he'd walk away, even if it was mid-sentence. I hoped no one else noticed his reaction to me or the embarrassment I felt each time it happened. *What have I done?* I asked myself.

Nothing was the same. Within a week of seeing him and Hoppy together he transferred out of our Seminary class to the same class that Hoppy attended. There was no longer a reason for me to come to church early with dad. Instead I would come at the regular time with my mom. For months now the bench I'd rushed to church early to find him sitting on in the foyer was empty. Only once did I see him sitting on his bench when I entered the foyer at church; our eyes met briefly before I quickly looked away to avoid giving him the opportunity to reject me once more. I even began using a different entrance to avoid any more accidental sightings. It was as if we'd never been friends.

My heart was breaking. No, not just breaking, but imploding and the pain I felt was almost palpable. I'd experienced nothing like this before; I couldn't breathe, and out of self-imposed fear of being ridiculed I couldn't tell anyone about my agony. I had to suffer in silence, crying only in private and hiding all emotions in public.

When Hoppy's friend, Roberta would gloat in front of me with stories about Hoppy and Sam her words scraped my already tortured heart. The very mention or view of them left me believing that I would die from the rawness of emotions I hadn't even known I could feel.

I decided my only revenge was to show him how much fun he was missing and that I had moved on. Perhaps this would make him want to be my friend again, at the very least. But first, I had to let my heart scab over, and the pain subside to a dull ache. So I buried myself in my studies, worked every shift I could at the popcorn shop, and let time pass.

Once I was confident that I could show that I didn't care about them, I began to be more outgoing at school again. Soon I was everyone's friend, everyone knew me, and I was always happy and having fun. My plan to get revenge had now begun.

Even though the revenge felt good, I missed him. Once upon a time, we were inseparable. His smile contained all my hopes and dreams and I knew nothing about crush-break. There's so much that went on between us, and I desperately wanted to go back to that time—to go back to the very beginning . . .

Home at Last!

Everyone says that you can never go back, but here I was. I was back!

It was the winter of 1978, and I'd just returned to my beloved hometown, Ashbury. The year had started out rather dismal, with my brother Nate, graduating early and taking off for college leaving me with my two little brothers and parents. However, it started looking up when my parents made an announcement at dinner one night.

"Your father and I have made a decision that we think you'll all be happy about," my mom said. My brothers and I looked at her expectantly. "We've decided to move back to

Ashbury." I couldn't believe my ears.

"We're moving back to Ashbury?" I asked, bubbling with excitement. "When?"

"In six weeks or so. It'll be mid-semester for you," Mom said looking at me.

"I don't care."

"Well, we're concerned that the credits here might not be enough for Ashbury. With all the missed days of school here due to weather, it just concerns us a little."

"I don't care, I wanna go home."

"We think if you'll finish all your courses here before we move, then if you're missing any that would stop you from becoming a Sophomore, you'll have some time to make them up."

I thought for a moment, before I said, "I'll do whatever I gotta do to go home."

"It'll be a lot of hard work for you and Michael, but we know you can do it."

"What about Wayne, won't he need to do extra too?"

"He'll be staying here to help your dad finish build a couple of homes on our property to sell before they both come home," said Mom.

"How long will that take?" asked Michael.

"Six months or so," said dad, speaking for the first time.

This was the best news I could ever imagine receiving, we were going home! I was so busy for the next couple of months between packing and school, I had no extra time, but it was worth it when we drove into our driveway on the farm.

When we got home and the phone was hooked up, I immediately called my best friend since first grade, Sabrina. When we moved to Ferron, I was too young to realize that I could write her a letter or that we might ever move back, so we'd lost touch with one another. You can imagine her surprise when she heard my voice on the phone. I could barely contain my own excitement.

"I can't believe you're back," she said.

"I know! It's great to be home! I've missed it," I replied as I looked around our kitchen. It wasn't large, but Dad had built the addition to make room for the huge dining table our family needed long before we had moved to Ferron, and when combined with the new window he installed, it no longer seemed small.

"When did you get back?"

"Just this week. We got the phone hooked up today."

"Are you glad to be home?"

"More than you know. I can't wait to see everyone."

"When will you be coming to school?"

"Not until Monday."

"Not until Monday. Can you go to a movie tonight?"

"I'd love that, but I better not. Since dad's still in Ferron, Mom needs me to help unpack."

"Well, then I won't see ya 'til Monday."

"Yeah, sounds like it. I'm excited for school, but I hate being the new girl."

"You're not really the new girl," Sabrina said trying to reassure me. "You know a lot of the kids at school already."

"I did know them. But I've been gone for three years, and I'm just nervous about my first day.

"Don't be. I'll be there and I'll show ya 'round."

"Oh, that'd be great! But where should we meet?"

Sabrina thought for a moment, "Meet me near my locker in the Freshman hall. Then I'll take you to the office to get registered," she said. "Oh, and try to be there by eight, that'll give us enough time."

"Perfect! Where's the Freshman hall?"

Sabrina laughed, then said, "It's the first set of double doors in the back-parking lot. And, before you ask, the parking lot is the one between the stadium and the school building."

"Great. I can't wait! I'll see you Monday."

Hanging up the phone I knew I needed to make sure and wear my best outfit so I could make a good first impression. I wanted them to remember me, but not as a junior high throwback; I wanted to look like a high schooler. So, I had to pick my clothes carefully.

I was excited for this next adventure in my life as I got closer and closer to graduating and being able to follow my dream of being an award-winning actress. Go Eagles!

And it Begins

It was a beautiful spring morning when Mom pulled into the back-parking lot of the Ashbury high school, as Sabrina had instructed. It was at a side entrance, which was at the end of what they called the "Freshman Hall". Our bright yellowish-green family van's reflection in the windows of the classroom in front of us, reminded me that I was leaving the safety of the past three years to enter a future that was exciting and unknown.

Excitement, nervousness, hope, and dread bubbled through me as I sat in the front passenger seat. No one wants to be the "new girl".

When news got out in Ferron that we were moving back to

our beloved Ashbury, the friends I'd made told me that my friendships in Ashbury wouldn't be what they had been before we moved away. I refused to believe that—not with my friends. Granted it had been three years since I'd seen anyone, and of course we'd changed a bit, but they'd still be my friends. Wouldn't they? Yet, what if we'd all changed so much in these past three years that I had nothing in common with my old friends?

Still sitting in the van, my mom had to prod me, "You better get going. You still need to go to the office and register."

"I know, I'm nervous about being the new girl, Mom."

"Why're you nervous? You'll see a lot of your old friends."

"Gee, Mom. I never expected us to move back. I'm glad we did, but I wish I could've come back *pretty*, instead of *me*," I said looking in the passenger-side visor mirror.

"You are pretty."

"No, I'm not Mom. Not like Sylvia and Katie."

"You look like your dad, what's wrong with that? He's very handsome."

"Handsome for a *guy*, Mom."

"You're being silly. What's brought all this on now?"

"This is high school, Mom," I said with a sigh. "The pretty girls are the popular ones, not girls that look like me."

"Why are you so concerned about being popular? Your sisters weren't cheerleaders, on a homecoming court, or whatever you think one needs to be popular in school, and it never changed the fact they were pretty girls. You need to be more concerned about your grades and less about your popularity."

"I just wanna be pretty," I said with a pout as I shrugged my shoulders.

With a heavy sigh, she said, "You're gonna be fine, and you *are* pretty. Just go register for school, and don't forget to give them your transcripts from Ferron."

"Okay," I said with a nervous sigh. I grabbed my purse and notebook and stepped out of the van onto the sidewalk and began the first day of the rest of my high school career.

I checked that my red floral print blouse was still nicely tucked into my yellow pleated pants; it was my favorite outfit, accentuating my long legs. Perfect for a first day of school.

I opened the door to an almost empty Freshman Hall, I'd expected a ton of kids to be milling about only to find a few and no sign of Sabrina. I leaned against one of the walls hoping she'd appear at any moment, but as time passed with still no sign of her, I decided I should try and find the office myself.

I walked down the hall not knowing anyone and fighting the shyness that my family and friends didn't believe I possessed. But despite everything, I persevered because I felt like I was home again and that gave me the courage to follow my nose down the "Senior" hall.

At the end of it was a trophy case that displayed all the awards from years past. I looked at the case, trying to appear as if I knew what I was doing while I decided what I should do next when I heard my name.

"Gracie!"

I turned to find my childhood friend. "Sabrina!"

We embraced, and I looked at her for the first time since our move. She still looked like the girl I knew three years ago: shorter than me except with some make-up. "Did you find the freshman hall okay?"

"I did, and I waited. But when I didn't see you, I thought I should try and find the office myself."

"Sorry, the bus was late this morning," she said.

"Wow, you look great. When did you cut your hair?" I asked. Her hair barely reached her shoulders.

"Back in Junior High," said Sabrina as she reached up and raked her fingers through it.

"Gosh, it was so long. Do you like it better this length?"

"It's so much easier to take care of, and you don't find that much of it on the floor, which makes my dad happy," she said with a snicker. "You're still taller than me, even with my wedges."

Laughing, "I've got wedges on too," I said, lifting my wedged foot. "So, I might seem a little taller than I am."

"Have you been to the office yet?" she asked.

"Not sure where it is," I said, and Sabrina giggled and turn me around. There it was right behind me. I rolled my eyes in embarrassment. Sabrina chuckled as she pulled me into the office and introduced me to the office Secretary Mrs. Cook.

"Hi, Mrs. Cook. This is Grace Kaye and she needs to register for school."

"Good morning and welcome," said Mrs. Cook, looking very professional in her teal sheath dress. She adjusted her skinny black belt, and the curls in her short, salt and pepper hair moved as she tilted her head and smiled.

"Good morning," I said.

Lifting the glasses that hung around her neck on a chain she placed them midway down her nose and straightened the loose papers by tapping them down on the counter. "We don't have much time, so let's get you registered," she said while turning the papers towards me.

"I need to go put my stuff away in my locker and get ready for class," said Sabrina backing out the office door. "Once you get your schedule come back to the Freshman Hall, I'll take you to your first period."

"Okay, thanks," I said to her back as she left the office.

"Did your last school send your transcripts with you by any chance?" asked Mrs. Cook.

"Oh, yeah," I said, suddenly remembering the envelope in my purse. I pulled it out and handed it to her. "Here ya go," I told her.

Mrs. Cook took a moment to look over the papers in the envelope, "By the look of it, you've already completed your freshman year." she said laying the papers down on the counter.

"Yeah?"

"Why'd you do that?" she asked.

"Ferron had a different type of school system, and my mom was concerned as to whether I'd have enough credits to complete my Freshman year here at Ashbury."

"That's a lot of work," said Mrs. Cook.

"I know," I said, "So, will everything transfer from Ferron to here then?"

"Of course," she said looking at me. "You don't even need to be here for the remainder of this semester."

"I don't?" I asked, surprised.

"No. You completed all the necessary credits as a freshman. Anything else you do will be considered extra credit."

"Wow, that's great," I said with a sigh of relief.

"So, do you want to choose some courses to take? It'll only be for a few weeks until school ends."

"Sure."

"Okay then," she said placing the list of courses in front of me. "Pick which class you'd like to take."

After completing my registration with only a couple minutes left before the first bell rang, I didn't have time to find Sabrina, so Mrs. Cook directed me to my class down "Sophomore" hall.

My first class was English with Mrs. Garcia. It was my second time taking it, since there wasn't a big variety of courses available. This time it couldn't hurt my grade and would be considered extra credit.

Walking into class, my eyes darted in all directions, looking for a seat. All I knew was that I didn't want a seat in the front for everyone to stare at; I was the new girl and didn't want to be on exhibit. I clutched the notebook to my chest while I approached Mrs. Garcia's desk. To my great disappointment, she assigned me a seat in the front row.

As soon as the bell rang, she stood in front of the room, "Good morning class. We have a new student today, Grace Kaye."

"No way," I heard a male voice exclaim. Surprised I looked for whoever said it.

"Do you have something to say, Mr. Jeffries?" asked Mrs. Garcia.

"No. I just know Gracie," he responded leaning forward from his desk against the wall, a couple rows to the right of mine. I turned to see Trey waving with a big, bright smile.

I never imagined it would be a friend I'd known since I was four years old. "Hi Trey," I quietly said in response.

"Are you here for good?" Trey asked.

"Yeah," I smiled and nodded. I hadn't expected to see Trey so soon. He no longer sported the buzz cut as he had in grade school; his hair had grown out. I'd always loved Trey; he was like a brother to me.

"Okay, quiet down you two. You can talk after class," Mrs. Garcia said.

We'd always sat next to each other in school because of alphabetical seating, and he was always getting me in trouble for talking. And today was no different. Class hadn't even started, and he was already doing it again. Some things never change. I scowled at him hoping he'd be quiet, he only chuckled in response. He was someone who accepted me for me, and that I could always make laugh. I couldn't wait for class to end so I could talk to him.

As the bell rung all the kids jumped up to leave, and Trey

came over and gave me a hug. It amazed me how I reverted to the silly schoolgirl I'd been before we moved to Ferron.

"When did you move back?" Trey asked as we left the class.

"Wednesday," I said. "Do you know where this class is?" I asked showing him my schedule.

He frowned. "We only have English together," he said to me as he handed my schedule back. "I need to stop at my locker first, then I'll take you to your next class."

There was a small cluster of guys standing around the lockers as we approached. "Gracie?" I heard and spanned the group to find another of my grade school friends, Skyler. He'd always been a little guy but had grown a bit in the three years I'd been gone. Trey introduced me to Chuck and Allan before walking me to my next class. Each hour after that, I saw old friends who either directed me or walked me to my next class as we caught up.

At lunch, I headed for Sabrina's locker. When I caught up with her, she introduced me to a few of her friends; Sabrina had found those that best suited who she was—a brainiac. Yup, they were all brainiacs—nice, but still brainiacs. I didn't think I'd ever blend in with that crowd.

After lunch, it came time for the most exciting class of all: drama. I lived for acting. In my drama class in Ferron, I'd garnered most of the awards given out each year even those intended for the upper classmen. I'd also won top statewide honors two years in a row. This gave me the confidence to walk into class and take part my first day, if possible, rather than hold back and observe.

It was a typical drama class with no structure; instead of desks there were only some chairs and a couple of long tables on one end, and a small stage at the other.

Students were already sitting around chatting; some at the tables and a few gathered around the teacher's desk. Because of the casualness of the class, I wasn't sure who the teacher was. I finally spotted a student with a receding hairline and a wedding ring. He was sitting on his desk laughing surrounded by other students; this was a giveaway to me. So, I approached him and introduced myself.

"Hi Mr. Hearst, my name is Gracie Kaye. I'm new."

"I'm sorry, you said your name is Gracie Kaye?" he asked moving around his desk. "Do you have any experience acting?"

"Yes, I—" I began, but before I could brag about myself, he'd already moved on.

"Well, that's great. Welcome to class," he said turning toward the class, "Okay, class. Quiet down. We have a new thespian with us today," and he turned to me. "What was your name again?"

"Gracie Kaye."

"Take a seat anywhere and we'll get started."

Once class started, I ended up sitting back and observing the talent in the room, which, as far as comedy went, was immense. Since we were almost to the end of the school year, there was nothing to prepare for regarding performances, so we did a ton of improv. This was both good and bad; good because I'd get comfortable with the other class members, and bad, because most were Seniors and would graduate and leave. But I loved Mr. Hearst and his casual approach to releasing our creativity and helping the class to have such a positive atmosphere. I couldn't imagine what the future would bring in this class.

At the end of this wonderful first day, it all came crashing down when I remembered that I had to take the bus home. Luckily,

I wasn't the only one; Sabrina had to take it too. So together we walked to the parking lot where my day had started and sat down on the curb to wait for the buses to arrive.

As we sat there resigned to our fate, a bright red truck drove up and began to idle right in front of us. I, for one, was too humiliated about having to ride the bus at such the lofty station as a freshman, to look up to see who it was, when I heard someone calling my name.

"Hey Gracie, what're you doing back here?" asked Trey, before showing that beautiful smile of his.

"Hi Trey," I said, as I stood and walked up to his truck. "I didn't know you had your driver's license."

"I had to get it early since I help my dad on the farm."

"They do that?" I asked, amazed.

"Obviously."

"Wow. I don't get to drive for a while yet, so I have to ride the bus." I grimaced. By this time Sabrina was standing next to me.

"You want a ride?" Trey asked.

"Both of us?" I raised my eyebrows in anticipation.

"Of course."

"We don't have to ride the bus," I said turning to Sabrina as we both did a quick jig, before running and getting our stuff and climbing into Trey's truck. I got in first and sat next to Trey.

"Thanks for giving us a ride," said Sabrina.

"Yeah, you are aaah-maaaay-zing, for saving us," I said

"I can give you guys a ride home any day I don't have practice," he told us. Sabrina and I looked at each other and quietly squealed with glee. Trey chuckled.

Walking into the kitchen when I got home, the first thing out of my mom's mouth was, "How was your day?"

"It was great! Trey gave me a ride home today, so I didn't have to ride the bus."

"He did?" Mom asked smiling. "Wasn't that nice of him."

Trey's in my English class. It was so good to see him!"

"I bet."

"He walked me to my next class and we laughed the whole way."

"You and your twin." Mom always referred to Trey and me that way since we'd always acted like siblings.

"Did you see all your friends?"

"A lot of them."

"That's really great, and you were so worried this morning."

"Oh Mom, it was such a great day." I smiled. "It was as if I just picked up from where I left off." I was on cloud nine. It felt so good to be back with the people I'd known most of my life, that I had grown up with, and that knew my family. The people in Ferron were very nice and friendly, but I just never felt that it was a "permanent" place for me. It never felt like home.

I've Arrived

Sabrina had turned sixteen over the summer and now had her license, and true to form she offered me a ride the first day of school. It was great not having to ride the bus, but to arrive in styyyle, I'd seen it in movies, and I knew in my head how I wanted to look as I stepped out of the old blue Chrysler that Sabrina had inherited from her grandparents. My head was so deep into my fantasy that Rod Stewart was singing in my ear, 'Do You Think I'm Sexy' while exiting the car.

"*This* will be a great year," I told Sabrina with Rod Stewart still playing in my head.

"For what?" she asked.

"I turn the big one-five in November, and I'm a sophomore. Making me that much closer to graduating."

As we walked down to Sophomore Hall to find our lockers, we ran into Joni. She had attended the same grade school we had, and like me had just moved back to Ashbury after a year's absence.

"Hey!" she said, and we hugged. She stepped back to look at me. "Wow, you look great Gracie."

"Thanks," I said, beaming.

"She spent all summer riding her bike and swimming," Sabrina said, with envy.

"That's about all there is to do." I stopped at the end of the Sophomore Hall. "I can't find my locker number. Where would it be?" I asked, looking at Sabrina.

"What number do you have?"

"718."

"No wonder you can't find it here," said Joni. "Your locker's in Junior Hall."

"Junior Hall? How do you know that?"

"Because my locker number is 728." Joni smiled.

"That's a prime location," Sabrina said with a knowing look.

"Really? Why?" I asked, furrowing my brow.

"You're with the Juniors! There's some cute boys in that class," Sabrina said with a giggle. Joni nodded in agreement. Just then, the first bell rang.

"I guess I'll have to wait to find out until after this first class." I waved at both Sabrina and Joni as I turned towards my class while they headed down the hall to theirs.

In first-period English, I found a desk towards the back of the room and was relieved when I saw Trey and Chuck come into class.

"Hey guys," I called to them. Both turned to look.

"Hey," said Chuck as they chose their desks. They set their notebooks down and walked over to mine.

"How was your summer?" I asked.

"Uneventful," said Chuck.

"Busy," said Trey.

"On the farm?" I asked him.

"Yeah."

"What'd you do all summer?" Trey asked me.

"Swam and rode my bike, nuthin' exciting."

Just then, Mr. Foyle came into class. "All right everyone, find your seats and let's get started."

I felt more at ease this year than the previous year. I was no longer the new girl; it wasn't just my old friends that I knew, but I'd made new ones. I may have still needed to remind my new friends of my name or me of theirs, but that was a small price to pay for not being the new girl anymore.

Drama class was second period. I was really excited to begin rehearsals for Tartuffe, as it would be my debut play at this high school. Also, it would be the first time that I'd be doing a play written in rhyme, but not the same type of rhyme as Shakespeare.

Mr. H had given us the script in the middle of summer break so we could get used to the rhythm of the words and memorize them. But because this was such a new style for me, I was unable to learn it the way Mr. H. wanted me to. It wasn't until he showed me how to break it down in a way that would avoid drawing attention to the rhyme that I was finally able to begin the memorization process. Then it was a race for me to memorize my lines before we started blocking it. I had to be off book as we called it.

Looking around the room, I saw many familiar faces, along with some new ones, yet I knew from previous experience that by the end of this production it would be as if we'd known each other forever. It was while I was doing this play that I met Monica, another actress.

Rehearsals were not only during class but after school as well. My character was a rich dowager who had a maid by the name of Flipote, and Monica, whose nickname was Beans, played that part. Who knows how she got that nickname; it sure didn't match who she was: She was a beautiful girl with long auburn hair, big green eyes, and a beautiful smile. Add in the fact that she was smart and had a good sense of humor, and she was definitely a catch. It always amazed me how she didn't have guys lining up to date her. As the rehearsal hours grew, and we spent more and more time together we began to develop a friendship.

I was in the more advanced drama class which was comprised of only sophomores through seniors.

"Who's that?" I asked Beans when I saw Barry walk into

class.

"That's Barry, he's a freshman," Beans said as we watched the tall lanky guy choose a seat at one of the tables and sit to doodle on his notebook.

"I thought this class was only for sophomores through seniors?"

"It is," Beans said as we watched him.

Since I was tall and Barry was tall, I found myself attracted to him. Then again, being a teenage girl, I liked most any boy, but really preferred the tall ones. I didn't look to him as dating material, but he was so funny when he got up on stage to perform, and we worked so often together in skits, it was inevitable I'd get a crush on him. Yet, I never noticed Barry outside of class. He was only someone for me to crush on while in class and rehearsals, which made the time spent rehearsing pass quickly, and a little exciting.

Since I had one of the lead parts, Madame Purnelle, my costume was made to my specific measurements and was very authentic for the time of the play. Because of this I was given my own dressing room so as to accommodate all the pieces that comprised a dress of that time, and rightfully so, as the ruffles and petticoats took more room than any other costume in the play, I even had a specific person to help dress me each performance. This type of attention made me feel special. I couldn't help hearing Donna Summer singing "Hot Stuff" in my head.

Tartuffe was a blast. I had the opening line as I descended the stairs: "Come come Flipote, it's time we left this place!" With my huge authentic-looking dress made of rich brocade fabric and a beautiful lace fan I'd carried with me for weeks—so I could get used to using it—followed by a timid Beans as my maid. And, the make-up that was needed to make me age-appropriate made the audience erupt with applause at our entrance, on opening night. Not even a pound of chocolate could give me the rush I experienced from the audience's response to me when I entered. It was a wonderful two-night run with a full house each night. That was the beauty of living in a small farming community: they supported the arts.

After my debut, everyone in the high school knew who I was and were more inclusive of me, even the seniors now looked at me as an equal. I was now in the midst of building my reputation.

A Glimpse of Heaven

My sophomore year was two-thirds of the way through and was proving to be another great year. I hung out more with Beans than Sabrina. Even though Beans was a brainiac, we had so much in common with our love of theater and musicals, our favorite being Man of La Mancha starring Peter O'Toole. Beans had the complete musical on an eight-track tape that she kept in her car, so whenever we drove anywhere, we'd repeatedly play that musical and sing along with all the characters.

With the completion of the big production of Tartuffe and our budget for the year all used up, we spent the last few weeks in drama class performing in a couple of pep rallies and old folk's homes visits, brandishing our irreverent humor which was well-received by most everyone. And because of our popularity, I felt more confident to interact with one and all, even those I'd thought better than myself before that point.

One day, Beans and I walked down the main hall, laughing.

"Oh Gracie, that's so funny," said Beans.

"You should've seen Barry's face when I started tap dancing in the scene. It was priceless; he didn't expect it at all and had to just go with it," I laughed again. "I wish I had a picture of his face at that moment."

"Do you tap dance?" Beans asked.

"No." I said, still laughing.

"Then how'd ya do it?"

"Like this." I said, showing her my attempt to tap dance right there in the hall, causing Beans to laugh at my effort. I had just started my version of an airplane turn when I saw a vision before my eyes. It seemed as though the crowd parted before us like the Red Sea for Moses and there he stood. I'd never seen him before . . . he was gorgeous! Was he an angel, a god, or just a guy?

I couldn't tell. Time stopped as I gazed upon his beauty. It was as if Michelangelo's David statue came to life and stepped down from his pedestal—but wearing clothes. He moved as if he were on the catwalk, the wind blowing his dark mane back from his face, his piercing dark eyes, and pouty come-hither lips. With every step, his shirt opened wider exposing the shiny gold chains that hung around his neck and laid against his masculine, hairy chest. Angels were singing. Or, maybe it was the Bee Gees? Whoever it was I could hear the song 'Too Much Heaven'.

Okay, maybe it wasn't like that, but he walked towards me in all his gorgeous glory, and then . . . walked right past me as if I didn't exist. He took no notice of me standing in the middle of Senior Hall with my mouth open, drooling.

Where had this guy been all year? Why was I just seeing him now? If I had a class with him, I would have noticed him. But I knew it was the first time the veil had been lifted from my eyes and I had seen this god-like creature walking amongst us mere mortals. I felt as if I'd forgotten how to breathe as I watched him walk away.

Then . . . time was moving again, and I could hear the other students in the hall walking and talking as they passed by me, oblivious of what I'd just experienced. Even Beans was unaware of the apparition I'd just seen.

I rushed to catch up with her. "Beans!" I called. I cleared my throat and tried to come off as casual while still catching my breath, "Beans, wh-who was that guy?"

"Which guy, Gracie?" she asked, looking up and down the hall. By this time, he'd turned the corner and disappeared.

"H-he was just here. He's tall, with dark hair and eyes . . . I've never seen him before."

"Gee, Grace, that description could be a lot of the guys in school." She laughed, "You're gonna need to be more specific." She began walking again as I followed her in a trance, reliving that angelic sighting again and again in my mind.

Who was that guy? I couldn't get him out of my head. *He was beautiful!* At least, I thought so. Why hadn't I seen him before? Where did he hide? Was he new? Or, were the iron pills I took this morning causing me to hallucinate? I had so many questions. But caution and a low self-esteem where romance was concerned made me keep these questions to myself.

I loved mysteries and I loved romance novels. And there I was at the start of what could be a new Barbara Cartland novel: me as the sweet, innocent Heroine with the tall, dark, and ever brooding Hero whose passion for me smoldered beneath his cool devil-may-care personae. *It could happen.* That was the romance portion, while the mystery part was *Who the heck was this Adonis?*

As my sophomore year ended, what started out as an amazing year had turned into days of not only internal frustration but of motivation as well. I put more effort into my appearance in case I saw him again.

I couldn't ask any of my friends about this guy in case he found out about my crush on him and was repulsed by it. So, this life-changing vision remained a secret with me.

Can a fifteen-and-a-half-year-old girl survive this kind of torture: to only see a glimpse of the guy who could be "the one"?" Where was he? Where did he go to feed? Who were his friends? And, the most important of all questions: *Did he have a girlfriend?* Would this passion be forever confined within my tortured soul because he has a girlfriend? After having seen him I was always on the lookout for another sighting, but to no avail.

He **Reappears**

The teachers couldn't get us to do any work, let alone listen in class, we were so ready for our summer vacation to begin. It was the last day of school and we were here 'til noon. And, I still hadn't seen my Adonis guy since the initial sighting.

One day at lunch, I thought I saw him. "I'll be right back," I told Beans as I jumped up from the bench where we ate our lunch, to catch up with this apparition. "Excuse me," I said as I pushed my way through the lunchtime crowd, "'scuse me." I continued pushing forward at a quicker pace. I'd almost caught up with him, when another student tried to stop me.

"Gracie are you going to be-," Shelly started.

"Can't talk now," I said, forging ahead. I was so close to him. He'd stopped at the drinking fountain and I rushed up to him.

"Oooh, it's you," I said in total disappointment.

"Gee, thanks," said Alfredo as he straightened up from getting his drink. "Good to see you too."

"Ah, sorry. I thought you were someone else." Disappointed, I returned to where Beans was still sitting watching my stuff.

"Where'd ya go?" Beans asked.

"I thought I saw someone I've been looking for. Turned out to only be Alfredo," I said glumly, still looking down the hall.

Where is he?

It had been weeks, school was ending, and it left me doubting if I even saw him at all the first time.

Maybe he'd just been visiting? Lost? Or, maybe he'd returned to Heaven. Who knew?

I would never know because I couldn't ask anyone about him. Not just because I was too stinkin' chicken to risk ridicule, but I didn't know his name. I couldn't ask anyone about who the angel or Adonis was, unless I wanted to commit social suicide. So

I marked him down as my first Urban myth.

The school bell rang at twelve noon sharp and by twelve o five, Trey, Sabrina, Beans, Chuck, Brian and I had gathered in a circle by the double doors at the front of the school. We laughed and talked over one another, ready to start our summer, and I was doing silly dance moves, making Trey and Chuck laugh when we heard a guy trying to get Trey's attention.

"Trey! Hey Trey!"

Just then, Brian spilled chocolate milk on the floor.

"Darn it," Brian said as we all jumped to avoid being splashed. Somehow the milk had encased me into a little circle that left me having to stretch my legs to step over it.

"Kaye, what are you doing?" Trey laughed at my Chaplinesque attempt to step over the mess. Then turning he said, "Hey Sam. Where ya been?"

We'd all stopped, even me mid-step as I looked up to see who Sam was, and I froze. *It was HIM!* At this realization, my heart began beating so fast against my ribs I thought it would break through. My mouth became dry; my breathing was shallow. *It was HIM!* His name was Sam and he was friends with Trey. It was irrevocable proof that God loved me, and all was right with the world!

My Adonis had reappeared holding a basketball. He wore shorts and a tank top, and he looked un-beeeeliev-ably gorgeous. I stared in admiration at how the shorts showed off his long muscular legs, while his tank top exhibited the two guns hanging from his shoulders. I was so lost in my appreciation of Sam that I almost missed the moment Trey introduced me.

"Do you know Gracie?" Trey asked, pointing his thumb at me over his shoulder. "She's one of the funniest girls you'll ever know." I quietly groaned at his comment. *"Great, thanks to Trey, now he'll see me as a clown. Thank you for that . . . thank you very much."*

"Uuuuh, no," Sam said, looking at me with a smile. "Are you new?" he asked.

I wanted to answer, but my mind was too busy screaming *"He's talking to me!!!"* On the outside I stood on one leg over a puddle of chocolate milk with a stupid grin on my face, and before I could answer, Brian did it for me.

"New? She's been here all year," he said from below as he

wiped up the milk.

"Gracie was in the play we saw earlier this year," Trey said. "What was the name of it again?" he asked, turning to me.

"Tartuffe," Beans answered, as I stood there unable to respond fast enough.

"She was the old lady that kept hitting Beans with her fan," Trey said and chuckled.

Laughing, Sam looked at me. "Oh yeah. You were brutal to her."

Brian spoke before I could respond, "You weren't in class today. Where'd ya go?" he asked Sam.

"Shootin' hoops," Sam responded as he pushed one of the double doors open to leave. Then turning as if an afterthought, he asked, "Anyone wanna get lunch?" This question was directed at *all* of us. I lowered my leg and followed him as if on a leash, I had no will of my own any longer. I was willing to follow this god-like creature anywhere.

"We can't," said Sabrina. "I've gotta get home." It was as if someone had yanked the leash, pulling me away from Sam and back to reality. Sabrina was my ride home.

"Oh, okay. Gracie, ya coming?" asked Trey as they headed to Sam's truck.

"Nah," I said with a quivering voice. "Sab-Sabrina's . . . Sabrina's my ride. See ya." And they were gone. None of them even looked back.

I walked as if in a trance towards Sabrina's car and somehow took part in the stream of conversation with her and Beans. Still in a dreamlike state, I climbed into the back seat so I could take a moment to think and relive what had just occurred: His name was Sam and when he smiled his eyes became like crescent moons, his pouty lips encased beautiful white teeth, he had beautiful arms and legs that went on forever, and his voice sounded like the amplified purr of a contented cat. His name was Sam. He was real. He was friends with Trey. He'd seen me act. And he knew my name.

Get Me to Church on Time

As far as most teenage girls are concerned, the words "love" and "crush" are synonymous. I wasn't one of those girls. I believed this was a big crush and not love. But I felt I was standing on the precipice and all I needed was that one big push and I would fall face-first into the ever-burning flames of love. To do that I just needed to talk to Sam and get to know him.

Because it was summer vacation, I didn't expect to see him again until school started. I had three months to dream and fantasize and attempt to learn more about my brooding hero.

Since I was only fifteen-and-a-half, I was still too young to get a job, so I spent my summer riding my bike, swimming, and reading romance novels and dreaming that I would soon experience my *own* romance novel. The strength it took for me to keep my head out of the clouds and inside reality was herculean, with all the fantasizing that took place in my mind. I was becoming a regular Walter Mitty as I imagined Sam in all these different situations that always ended with him declaring his love for me.

One day when Sabrina had invited me to go into town with her, we ran into Beans and Jolie at the mall, and decided to grab some lunch. The conversation was rather humdrum and had lost my attention, until it took a turn for the better.

"Did you hear about Sam's dad?" Asked Jolie. *Sam?* This got my attention. Now I was listening.

"Yeah, isn't that sad news?" asked Beans.

"It happened so suddenly," said Jolie.

"Wait, what happened?" asked Sabrina. "What about his dad?" *Yeah, what happened? What about Sam?*

"They had to do open heart surgery," said Jolie. *On Sam or his dad?*

"Wow, is he okay?"

"I think he's home now." Jolie said taking a bite of her sandwich.

"How's Sam doing?" asked Sabrina.

"My mom and I took some food over for his family; he answered the door. He seemed fiiine. He is so cute," said Beans with a wistful grin. *Does Beans like Sam?* I asked myself.

"You are sooo bad," said Jolie at Beans, laughing, "lusting after Sam in his hour of need.

"Who doesn't lust after Sam, whatever hour it is?" asked Sabrina as she took a bite of a fry.

I sat there in amazement, listening to all the chatter between these girls. These girls were talking about my dreamboat, and they all seemed to like him. Maybe this was my chance to get more information. So, I decided to dip my big toe into the water to see what would happen. "Has Sam lived here long?" I timidly asked.

"Oh yeah. His family has been here for generations," Beans said, picking at the bread left over from her sandwich.

"Was it stress from work that caused his dad's heart attack?" I asked. "What does he do?"

"He works at the post office."

The water seemed warm, so I put in my whole foot. "Oh," I said, taking mental notes. Now I dove into the water as I asked, "Does Sam only play basketball?"

Laughing, Jolie said, "He's like the resident stud. He does everything: track, basketball, football, and baseball. He does it all and he's good at it, too."

"He's so good-looking," Sabrina said.

"So, why don't one of you chase him or does this guy have a girlfriend?" I asked. I had no idea how this question would be received. I was carefully treading water.

"In Junior High he had one, but no one since we started high school," Beans said.

"I wish it were me," Sabrina said, confiding in all of us. "But when I'm around him I get all tongue-tied," she said with a giggle, then the others began to giggle. I sat there deep in thought.

"So, why aren't you chasin' him?" I asked, looking around the table.

"Have you talked to him?" Jolie asked, looking at me.

"Who, Sam?"

"Sam," she said to me. "Do you even know who he is?"

"Yeah. I met him the last day of school," I said.

"Remember?" I asked, looking from Sabrina to Beans.

"Oh, yeah," said Beans.

"That's right," said Sabrina. "I was so bummed I couldn't go to lunch with them, but I had to get home."

"I remember that," I said, in a loud mumble.

"Then you know how hot he is," said Jolie

Boy, do I. "If he's so hot, then there's gotta be a ton of girls after him, right?" I asked.

"Right," they all responded in unison. This zombie-like response concerned me. If there were so many girls after Sam, I'd never have a chance.

However, it seemed as if little pearls from Heaven were dropping into my lap from this lunch, giving me even more fodder for my daydreams.

At the end of lunch as Sabrina and I walked out to her car, I went over in my mind the fun facts I garnered from this very, although unexpected, informative lunch: his last name was Reed, he didn't have a girlfriend, he was born and raised in this area, he didn't have a girlfriend, his dad is recuperating from a heart attack, he participates in track, basketball, football, and baseball, and last but definitely not least, no girlfriend!

I kept repeating the wonderful news that, he didn't have a girlfriend over and over in my mind. The strings of my heart sang with that news and my daydreams were relentless. Yet, all I could do was bide my time until school started again, which seemed eons away. However, come September it would be "Operation-Try-and-Get-His-Attention-Make-Him-Laugh-Love-and-Succumb-to-My-Charms" time. Little did I know that I wouldn't need to wait until September to put my little plan into operation.

Now that we were attending church in town, instead of across the bridge which put us in a different state, I got to see many of my high school friends during the summer. In the building where we met, there were two other wards—our local group or parish—that held their meetings there as well. So, between meetings, it was crowded, and since I didn't know anyone in the other wards, I concentrated more on seeing my girlfriends than worrying about seeing or being seen by any boys.

My ward had a huge deficit in boys my age; we only had one and that was Brian. Brian was another friend I'd known since I was four, and not a candidate for crush-hood. So, since there were no guys to impress in my ward, I didn't obsess about getting ready. I looked nice but stress-free. I just had to get up, go to the meetings and come home, no stress of trying to impress anyone. At least it started out that way.

On one particular Sunday towards the end of summer, I rode in early with my dad for a meeting I needed to attend before church. Since Dad was in the Sunday School Presidency, he always had an early meeting on Sundays. My mom and little brothers would come later.

Being so early, none of my friends were there for church yet. So, after the meeting, I meandered around the building trying to find something to pass the time. I walked up the stairs from where the Bishop's office was, just about to step up onto the final stair, looked across the foyer, and who should I see on a bench

outside of the Chapel but none other than Sam! *What the heck?!*
What was he doing here?

I backed up against the wall and retreated down the steps,
frozen in shock and disbelief. This was one thing no one had
thought to tell me. Sam was a member of my church! *How the heck*
did I miss that one? My heart was pounding in my chest; I looked
down to see if it was noticeable to others, but it wasn't. I had to
think about what I should do; did I look all right? Was today a
good day for him to see me? Or should I run and hide? A million
questions raced through my mind. I knew that I couldn't stay on
the stairwell forever. I would need to either go up or go down.

I had to think it through before I made a move; he'd only
met me once and probably didn't remember me. So if I sat on the
bench opposite him, acting as if I was unaware of him, then I could
sit there and still be able to watch him out of the corner of my eye.
Besides, he was sitting with his little brother, so he was probably
too busy to even notice me.

I ascended the stairs to the foyer and didn't dare look in his
direction. Instead, I attempted to look as if I was very preoccupied
and only had eyes for the bench in front of me. I walked over, sat

down, and without so much as a glance in his direction, opened my

scriptures with trembling hands and pretended to read. *I mean, if*

he thought I was spiritual would that be such a bad thing? I stayed

like that until his ward Sacrament meeting ended and it was time

for my meeting to start. When I stood after twenty minutes of very

tense sitting, I felt the sweat cooling behind my knees. I hadn't

even realized I'd been so tense. Since he was still sitting on the

bench, I walked past him, only looking at him once out of the side

of my eye, which almost caused me to run into the chapel door.

Never had I been so glad to sit down and let my body relax.

Sitting through Sacrament meeting, I thought of nothing

else but the previous twenty minutes and how I would get it to

work to my advantage. It was a chance for me to get to know him

and maybe charm him with my wily womanly ways, provided I

had any wily womanly ways. I wasn't sure how I would do that,

but one thing I knew for sure was that I was coming early to

church with Dad every week.

Operation Charm

The next Sunday I rode in with Dad, and once I got to church, I scoped out the foyer. He wasn't there. I sat on the same bench as last week, opened my scriptures and pretended to read. I was way too nervous to pay attention to the words on the page to actually read. The chapel doors were closed, so I didn't know if I would see him or not, but I was ready if I did. And, it was perfect.

Sitting on the bench, I tried to look deeply involved in my scripture study, all the while nervously checking the chapel doors. Then my bishop approached me.

"Good to see you here so early," said Bishop Ford.

"I came in with Dad today."

"How's it going at school?

"It's okay."

"Are you glad to be back?"

"Ooooh man . . . more than you know," I answered, animated by my passion. "It's great being home." Bishop Ford quietly laughed.

"Any boys on your radar?" he asked.

That was the moment one of the chapel doors opened, revealing Sam and his little sister. He walked past my bench and down the stairs to the drinking fountain. I only had time for a quick glance Sam's way, before I returned my attention to the bishop who was laughing at what I said. Or was it me? It was all I could do to maintain eye contact with the bishop when an Adonis was on the loose, but I did the best I could to hide my ardor.

"Noooo," I replied as my face turned red.

"Are you sure?" he teased. I loved Bishop Ford I'd know him all my life. But before I was able to deny anything in this slight inquisition, another ward member unknowingly came to my rescue and pulled the bishop away. Relieved, I returned to my reading, very aware of Sam as he sat on his bench. *Was he even aware of me?*

The foyer was kinda busy that morning, hence it was never just the three of us as it had been the previous week. I had just returned to my scriptures when Sister Patrick walked up.

"Did you have a good time at the activity Wednesday night?" she asked.

Laughing, I said, "Yeah. Once we brought out the water balloons."

"You girls are so crazy," Sister Patrick said, laughing with me. "That little trick brought in all the other girls. I think everyone had a great time. Even if we hadn't planned that portion of the activity."

"Haha! It was a blast. I think we should do that more often."

"It might be too wild for me. I'll let you girls handle that," she responded still laughing as Sister Williams approached, giving her a questioning look. "At the activity on Wednesday, Gracie and Cynthia brought out water balloons at the last minute. It was pandemonium, and no one remained dry," she explained with a laugh.

"Even you?" Sister Williams asked Sister Patrick.

"Especially me; those girls were relentless, but it was fun." Sister Patrick said, then looked at her watch. "Oh! I better go, I need to get some supplies before church starts. I'll see you guys later."

"Okay," I said, watching her walk away.

"Grace, I was wondering if you'd like to participate in the talent show next month?" Sister Williams asked sitting next to me.

I scrunched up my face at the question. "I don't know," I said.

"Oh c'mon, we need your talent."

"I don't know if I'll have time. I'll have to let ya know."

"Well, let me know by Tuesday," she said as she tried to wrangle in her small son who was trying to pull her away. "I know you're dying to do it," she said with a wink as she finally allowed him to pull her down the stairs towards the drinking fountain.

"Not really," I called after her good-naturedly. I looked out of the corner of my eye to see if Sam had at all noticed these interactions. I couldn't have planned it better with all those people approaching to speak with me, laughing and teasing me, all showing me in a favorable light. I would continue with the plan next week to see if there was any progress before I'd make any changes, if needed.

"Hey Gracie." Cynthia plopped down on the bench next to me. "Did you see Sister Williams? She loved our water balloon fight."

"I know," I chuckled. "She already mentioned it to me this morning."

"We're gonna have to come up with more ideas like that, to make these activities they plan fun. Otherwise, I'll die of boredom," said Cynthia. I liked Cynthia; she was the first girl my age to befriend me when we started attending this ward. She was always quick to laugh at my jokes and it didn't hurt that she had a mischievous streak, either.

"Yeah, that was way too much fun."

"Gracie, Mom says you need to come in for Sacrament meeting now," said my little brother Michael, coming up to me.

"Okay," I said. "Just a minute."

"You have to come now," he insisted.

"All riiiiiiiiight," I said, a bit annoyed. "Guess we better go."

"Yeah," said Cynthia. We both stood and walked towards the doors.

We had to pass the bench that Sam was still sitting on with his little sister. I figured I could get one more look at him before he was gone for the day.

"Hey, Sam," said Cynthia casually as we walked past. I almost stumbled in my steps when I heard her so casually speak to him. *Hey, Sam.* Just like that, as if he were a normal human being and not an angel that had fallen from the heavens. Why can't I be that casual with him? *Hey Sam.* He smiled at Cynthia in return. Our eyes met, but only for a moment before I entered the chapel. *Were those angels voices I heard singing?*

****

They, whoever *they* were, say that three times is a charm and unbeknownst to me, that third Sunday would prove that theory. I arrived at the same time I had the previous week, and again, the foyer was empty. I rushed to the bench and assumed my position.

Like clockwork, twenty minutes later there came Sam, alone, out the chapel door. And the kicker: instead of sitting on *his* bench he came over and sat on *mine*! I couldn't believe it!

"How are ya, Gracie?" he asked as if he had been asking me that for years.

"Great. You?" I said, turning towards him as I calmly smiled, while inside I was screaming with excitement. He nodded. "Are you ready for school?"

"We're gonna be Juniors," Sam said.

"I know! Loving it!"

Sam laughed as he casually placed his arm on the back of the bench towards me, looking so cool and relaxed. I never wanted the moment to end.

"So, what'd you do all summer?" Sam asked.

"Just swam and rode my bike. You?"

"I worked."

"Where?"

"My grandfather's plant."

"Doing what?" I asked.

"All the grunt work. They're training me to take on more

responsibility eventually."

"Do ya like it?"

"Not really, but it gives me extra money. I'll have to stop when school starts though," he said.

"Why?"

"Won't have time with all the sports I play."

"Oooh, makes sense."

"How 'bout you? Think you'll be in any more plays this year?"

"I hope so. Think you'll come?"

Chuckling, he said, "Sure. Especially if you're beating on Beans again."

"Poor Beans," I said as I laughed. "That was a fun part for me."

"I bet," he said.

I loved how his eyes twinkled as they turned into crescent-moons, and when he smiled I could see his beautiful white teeth.

"How's your dad doing?" I asked. "I heard he had open heart surgery."

He did a slight double take. "You heard that?"

"Yeah. Is that a bad thing?" I pinched my brow.

He chuckled. "No, not at all. Just surprised."

"Well?"

"He's doing good; thanks for asking," he said with his glorious smile.

"That's good," was all I could manage to get out as I teetered on the brink of falling into the two-deep bowls of chocolate pudding that were his eyes.

"Didn't your bishop say that you'd moved back? Where from?" he asked. So lost was I in the glow of his gorgeousness that I almost missed his question. I was about to answer when suddenly it hit me. *Wait! Did he just say that the bishop had said I moved back?* He had been listening last week! He'd heard our conversation! He was paying attention to me! If this were a musical, I'd be up dancing all over the foyer I was so ecstatic with this revelation. "Gracie?" he raised a brow.

"Wha-what?" I asked, pulling myself out of his dreaminess. "Did you say something?"

"I lost ya there for a minute."

"No . . . no, no, no. I'm right here. What did you say?"

"I asked, did your bishop say that you'd moved back? And, from where?"

"Oh, sorry." I chuckled. "Yeah, we lived here before. Dad worked for the government and they tried to get him to accept a transfer for years, to places all over the world. He kept turning them down, so they made him take this one to Ferron. We were only there for three years though before dad retired and we moved back."

"What does—did—he do?"

"He was a Soil Conservationist."

"Did you like Ferron?"

"It was all right. The town was small, and the people were nice."

"Did ya like it better than Ashbury?"

"No way! I missed this place and all my friends."

We'd been so deep in conversation that neither of us noticed his ward had exited the chapel, until my mom passed by and motioned to me that it was time for mine to start. The time had flown by.

"Well, I better go," I said gesturing towards the chapel.

"It's my turn." I hated leaving the wonderful moment, but Mom would've killed me if I missed church. Reluctantly, I stood to leave.

"Yeah, okay," Sam said without looking at me. I thought I'd lost him as I willed my feet to move, but as I stepped away, he asked, "Are you gonna be early next week?"

"Of course," I said, backing towards the doors. I should have turned around sooner because when I did, I ran right into the door, making a loud bang as my temple and the edge of it connected with one another, which caused everyone to stop and turn to look. One older guy even grabbed my elbow to steady me as I shook my head to try and clear the stars that had appeared. I was so embarrassed. I turned and weakly smiled at Sam who covered his mouth with his hand in an effort to hide his laughter. With a very red face and a smile, I floated into the Sacrament meeting.

I didn't remember walking that morning or for the rest of the day, as far as that goes. I was on cloud nine remembering my conversation with Sam, being in such close proximity with him, being able to look into the deep velvety recesses of his eyes. But I did carry a large, red welt that turned in to an angry bruise on my right temple for a week reminding me that it had happened.

It would become our routine. Each Sunday I would arrive, sit on my bench, and Sam would come out of his meeting early so we could sit and talk. I was experiencing a life I had only fantasized about; I couldn't believe it was *my* life.

Soon it wasn't just on Sundays, but at church events as well. If it was an activity where both of us would be in attendance, he would come looking for me. It was like a dream.

Doink!

Even though I wasn't able to take part in the talent show that Sister Williams had urged me to do, I still planned on supporting the nine different wards that would be participating.

The night of the talent show I followed my family into the church building, and then onward into the cultural hall, which also served as a basketball court, a theater, and a dining hall. I quickly scanned the crowd that had already gathered in anticipation for the promised entertainment, for Sam and his family. With a sigh of relief, I saw no sign of them yet.

Although I loved getting Sam's attention, I still struggled with the fear that one day he'd realize that I wasn't pretty enough for him and I'd be left alone to suffer the slings and arrows of mockery from others, while they laughed at me for my audacity to think I could win his heart. So, there were times when it was a relief to attend these types of events alone, allowing me to comfortably relax into my mediocrity.

Because the Cultural Hall could be used for ward dinners, there was a full kitchen over at the side of the room, near the stage. The common wall between the two had a serving window with a corrugated curtain that could be opened or closed over it.

Tonight, the curtain was closed, but there was still room for the youth to sit on the counter instead of chairs to watch the performances. Already, a group of kids I knew were gathered there. I could see Cynthia and Jessica sitting on the counter, so I headed over to join my friends. As I approached, Cynthia motioned that there was room for me next to her.

"Thanks for saving me a spot," I said, pulling myself up on the counter.

"Sure. Is Sam coming?" asked Cynthia. "Do we need to save him a spot?"

"I don't know." I said, as I smiled, despite myself, and

shrugged my shoulders.

"Hey guys," said Chuck as he moved to stand next to Cynthia, pushing Jessica further down the counter. "Is Sam here yet?"

"Haven't seen him," Cynthia said.

"Oh. He said he was coming tonight," Chuck said, looking at the exit.

As a group we quietly talked and laughed with one another, not paying that much attention to the performances on the stage. With Chuck stating that Sam said he was coming, I found myself sporadically looking for him.

Through the darkness of the room, I saw Sam approach. He was unaware that he had a certain way of walking as if he was a cat on the prowl, but boy, was I aware of it. Once I noticed him, I looked back towards the stage, acting as if I didn't care whether this hunk o' burnin' love was not only comin' my way, but would be sitting next to me. All the while holding my breath that he would never realize that I was an odd-looking girl and lose interest in whatever it was that was going on between us. I couldn't help but feel awkward, having never had not just a boy, but a boy so incredibly handsome, give me this much attention before. I wasn't

sure how to respond at times.

As Sam approached, my friends automatically cleared a

space next to me on the counter.

"Hi, Grace," he said, as he pulled himself up to sit next to

me.

"Hey."

"This any good?" Sam asked, tilting his head towards the

stage.

"Eh, it's okay," I responded as I turned to look at him

sitting next to me in his brown leather jacket and scarf that

complimented his magnificent coloring. "Did you have to work

today?" I asked, watching him turn and unlatch the curtain behind

him, opening it wide enough for him to lie back on the counter that

continued into the kitchen.

"I'm so tired," he yawned as he stretched. *How is he still on

this earth? He's so perfect.* I dreamily watched him stretch.

"Doink. Doink. Doink," Roberta had appeared from

nowhere and was standing near the end of the counter next to Sam.

She chuckled as she poked Sam in his side which caused an

involuntary crunch back to a sitting position.

"Oh, you're ticklish," I said and watched in amazement. Finally, a weakness.

"Doink," Roberta poked him again.

"Sto-op." Sam grimaced at Roberta.

"You kids need to get off this counter. We need to set up the refreshments." A lady from one of the other wards said as she shooed us off the counter and set paper cups filled with punch in our place.

"Wanna go for a walk?" Sam asked, grabbing two cups.

"Yeah," I said, following his lead, hoping one of the cups was for me.

"She's nice, but she can be so obnoxious." He handed me a cup as we walked out of the Cultural Hall.

At school we had four classes together that semester; we sat next to each other, walked to our classes together, always laughing and flirting with each other. We were together every free moment we had, yet he still didn't do anything to change our status from just friends. *Why didn't he ask me out?* I wondered. I wasn't sixteen yet, so I couldn't date, but he should've still asked me out, dang it!

One day while I was studying for an algebra test in the library, Beans came bouncing up with a huge smile on her face. "You'll never guess who asked me when you'll be sixteen?"

"Who?" I asked. I couldn't imagine anyone caring how old I was.

"Sam," she said sitting next to me at my table.

"No way, serious?" I asked, stunned, yet excited.

"Yup," she said with a big grin.

My mind was exploding with this news, "Do you think he's waiting for me to turn sixteen?" I asked, squinting my eyes at her. "I wonder if that's why he was asking?"

"I don't know why he asked, but I told him when you'd be sixteen," Beans said with a big smile as she gave me a big hug.

Only time would tell. For now, I had to be satisfied with seeing him at church and school. But I wasn't sure what our relationship was; it felt like we were more than just friends, yet we didn't hold hands or hug. He never even touched me. But I knew that I liked him. I hoped he liked me. Why would he spend so much time with me if he didn't? We just never verbalized it.

Perhaps it was assumed?

"Gracie," Sabrina said, approaching me one day. "When did you and Sam get so friendly?"

Surprised by the question, I said, "At church, I guess."

"Oh, that's right. I forgot," she said. "How'd it happen?"

"He just came and sat on a bench I was sitting on waiting for church to start and we began to chat," I said, nonchalantly. She didn't need to know about my conniving and planning. This way it seemed more effortless. And besides, that was the truth: he did come to me.

"I'm so jealous," she said with a dreamy smile. "Are you dating?"

"Sam? Not that I know of," I said casually. *But, boy how I wanted to.*

Sam and I were in the same early morning seminary class and on the very first day, when he walked into class, he sat right next to me. What a great way for me to start off my day. My year!

Then one day I came later than Sam. I figured I'd have to sit in the back away from him, but to my wondrous surprise when upon entering the class I saw an empty chair next to him. He'd set his scriptures on the chair as an unspoken sign that it was taken. He only moved them when he saw me. No guy had ever treated me that way, especially a guy like Sam. If this was a dream, I never wanted to wake.

One particular morning as Sam and I were heading to our cars after seminary Chuck called to us, "Wait up." We stopped and turned towards him. "Can you believe that Brother Barter left like that?" he asked.

"That surprised me to see him leave, and almost in tears too," I said. "I didn't realize he'd take it so seriously. We were just playin'." That morning, our Seminary teacher had left right during class due to our relentless teasing.

"Me too," Sam admitted.

"You guys are way too funny though. Too bad he didn't get the jokes," said Chuck.

"We may have gone overboard today," said Sam.

"Yeah. I wonder if he'll show up tomorrow?" I asked. I wasn't proud of causing the teacher to leave class. But gee, get me around a boy I liked, and I was in full performance mode. I'd do almost anything to entertain him. I took no prisoners when I was in a battle of wits.

"Are you guys coming to Brian's party on Friday?" Chuck asked.

"I don't know," I said, looking at Sam. "Are you gonna go?"

Shrugging his shoulders, he said, "If you are, I guess."

"I'll have to check with my mom."

"Well, you guys should come; it'll be fun." Chuck said.

I liked that people saw us as a couple, but still, neither of us had ever verbalized what we felt or what our relationship was yet. This cowardice on my part, proved the undoing of my dreams and the wrenching of my heart.

Itsy Bitsy Spider

"Why is Sam with Hoppy?" Beans asked as we waited in line to see the newest Star Wars movie.

"I've no idea. Maybe she's the only pet he's allowed to have," I said as stoically as I could. "Why?"

"I saw them at school hugging in front of her locker, then she was sitting on his lap at lunch yesterday." Beans looked as if she would throw up. "I thought he liked you?"

"So did I."

"Are you okay?" Beans asked, looking into my face.

"It's killing me," I said, trying to stop my lip from

quivering. *I thought I was past this.*

"Oh Gracie," she said, putting her arm around me. "I didn't know." That was all I needed for the first tear to fall, which I quickly wiped away. They always seemed so near now.

"I'm okay," I said, gaining control. "I just don't understand why he won't speak to me."

"He won't speak to you? You were such good friends."

"I know. I ju . . . I don't know what happened."

"What are ya gonna do?"

"What can I do? I can't force him to talk to me."

"There's got to be something you can do to win him back," Beans said, in deep reflection. "I'm sure you'll think of something."

"To be honest, I may have come up with a plan," I told her tentatively.

"A plan? A plan to do what?" Beans asked.

"To make him want to be my friend again." I said, sitting in the theater seat.

"How're you gonna do that?"

"I'm hoping when he sees how everyone else likes me . . .,"

I stopped there.

"Oh, Gracie," she said with a sigh. "Want some?" She asked, as she passed the box of popcorn to me. We ate in silence, waiting for the previews. Then with a sympathetic look, she said, "I'm so sorry. Do you know how many girls were envious of you?"

"Why?"

"Because you had Sam's attention. It was like he came to life when you were around."

"He did?" I asked. Beans nodded her head as she munched on popcorn. "Then why'd he choose her?" I asked, rapidly blinking to make the tears that had again appeared in my eyes disappear. "I really miss having so much access to his gorgeousness. Now Hoppy gets it all."

"Sam and Hoppy. I would've never believed it until I saw it," said Beans. "Have you put your plan into action yet?" she asked. I nodded my head.

"I call it my *revenge* plan." I turned to her.

"Why a revenge plan? What are you getting revenge on?

"Well, nothing really. But a revenge plan sounded better

than just saying a plan." I confessed to her. "But ya' know what? I'm so busy trying to be happy and friendly with everyone that I forget to think about him," I said, chuckling at the thought. "It's like if I don't see him, I don't think about him." I began to laugh out loud. It was the first time I'd realized it.

Laughing, Beans said, "Oh Gracie, only you'd have such a quandary. You're so busy becoming popular that you don't have time to worry about your heart."

"I think that's a good thing," I said to her. "It hurts too much when I remember."

One project I was working on that was keeping me busy was finishing up a new comedy production called 'My Three Angels,' and thankfully, it took most of my time. That, and working.

I was the female lead, not the ingenue, but the female lead married to Barry's character. I enjoyed working with Barry; he was fun and clever, and we seemed to have good chemistry onstage. Missing the adrenaline I felt when I had a crush and trying to solidify the scab that was growing on my heart, I amped up my infatuation with Barry. It still wasn't the crush, but it helped me to exchange the amazing, colorful dreams I had about Sam with these new, not as vivid and not in color daydreams that included Barry. I guess Barry was the rebound band-aid for my heart right now.

After my performance in "My Three Angels," I was more well known. When I'd walk around school many students felt they knew me and would walk with me to class or sit next to me and talk. All except Sam and Hoppy, though. However, I soon learned that there were those who didn't like me, who felt they needed to try and make me look bad in front of my classmates. I'd never had anyone dislike me that way before.

One morning as I walked down the main hall, I saw Sam without Hoppy talking to Meg and Roberta at Meg's locker. Meg was one of the senior girls who seemed nice and music-minded, but with an odd sense of humor. I knew her well enough to chat with if I saw her at a party, but I wouldn't have said we were friends.

She, Roberta, and Sam laughed together as I walked up the hall. I knew Sam wouldn't want to speak with me, so I planned on just walking past them, until Meg, upon seeing me, stopped mid-sentence and blocked my way, stopping me in my tracks.

"Hey Gracie, I have something for you," she said pulling me towards her locker where Sam and Roberta stood. I didn't bother looking at him or saying anything so I could avoid the cold shoulder.

"Why?" I asked. It would be one thing if it were Beans or Sabrina giving me a gift, but someone I hardly knew? It didn't feel right.

Giggling, she said, "It's just something I saw and thought of you." My suspicion grew and I began to back away. Why would she be giving me a gift? It didn't make sense. "Let me get it out of my locker for you. Stay right there. Don't move," she ordered before turning back to her locker. She rummaged through its contents, giggling along with Roberta. When she stepped back, she held a little silver cardboard box you get when you purchase cheap jewelry with a little, shiny silver bow attached to the lid which she'd taped shut.

"Thanks." I said, as I cautiously took it from her. "I'll open it later."

"No, no," she said raising her voice and giggling, "You have to open it here. Now."

"Why here? I'll open it later. I've got to get to class." I began to walk away, but she pulled me back.

"No. Open it *here*. I want everyone to see your face when you open it." She gave me a devilish grin as she looked around at the crowded hall. The little box was wrapped so prettily that I couldn't imagine what she'd given me.

"You can open it and still get to class on time," Roberta said with a smirk while looking at Sam.

"O-okay," I stuttered. If ten was the highest on a suspicious meter, then mine was at a seventy-five. *Why'd she want me to open it here, in front of everyone?* I wondered. It was awkward holding my books and trying to open the little box that she'd taped shut, but I did. What I saw inside disgusted me: underneath the little sheet of cotton she'd set as a cover, was a huge spider she had somehow covered in wax.

I suffer from arachnophobia, so it was horrifying to me. As a look of repulsion and hurt covered my face, I gasped and dropped the box. I looked at Meg, then Roberta, and then Sam, wondering if he'd been in on it. Before I turned and walked down the hall away from her, my cheeks burned red from the embarrassment. *Did Sam hate me that much that he'd be in on such a sickening trick?* Turning the corner, I heard the conversations taking place as her cackle followed me. I stopped to listen. The hall had gone silent.

"What is it?" Sam asked her.

Through her and Roberta's laughter, Meg said, "It's a spider."

"Doesn't look like it," someone said.

"Why does it look so strange?" asked another.

"It's covered with wax," she said.

"How'd you do that?"

"I followed it as it walked and dripped melted wax on it until it died. The wax makes it keep its shape."

"Does Gracie like spiders?" asked Sam.

"Why'd you give it to her?" asked another person.

"No, she's afraid of spiders," said Beans, my hero. "Meg, that was an awful thing to do. What's wrong with you?"

"I thought it was funny," answered Meg. "I thought everyone would laugh."

I'd heard enough, so I continued on to the library. Why

would she try to put me in that type of situation? That wasn't funny.

Later when Beans found me in the library to see if I was okay, she told me about Sam's conversation with Meg.

"So yeah, after I told her off in front of everyone," she began.

"Yeah, I heard,' I interrupted. "Thanks for doing that. I was so creeped out by what she did. Did you see the size of that spider?"

"It was so gross. But anyway, after you left and I finished telling her off, Sam, who was standing next to her locker, stepped up in your defense."

"He did?" My eyes widened.

"He told her, 'that's not cool,' to which she responded, 'Why not? Then he said, 'So, that's why you wanted me to meet you at your locker this morning?' And she responded, 'Doncha love it?' And Sam said, 'Why? Why would I love it?' Then he turned to Roberta and asked, 'Did you know about this?' She tried to laugh it off and said, 'It was just a little joke. You don't seem to like her anymore, so I thought you'd get a kick out of seeing her look stupid.' But Sam told her, 'Whether or not I like her doesn't give you the right to humiliate her like that,' and he walked off. Everyone stood looking at her and Roberta, not laughing." Beans gave a little chuckle. "It was so awkward. That's when I left."

It was such good news to hear the Sam had stood up for me. Especially since he hadn't been speaking to me for so long. I'd never had anyone do such a cruel act towards me before. *Why would she do that? Why would Roberta?* I asked myself. I'd never been mean to Meg; I didn't even know her that well. Yet she tried to embarrass me in front of the school with such a repulsive trick.

By giving me something like that, and the time it took her to prepare it, I knew she had some serious issues with me. I resolved to stay as far away from her as possible. But I'd never forget Sam standing up to her for me. That was very unexpected. *Was my angel returning?*

Prom? Me?

Finally, I was sixteen years old and able to date! I thought it would never happen, but after fifteen years, it finally came.

I worked at the popcorn shop in the mall where we sold different types of popcorn, hot dogs, candy, and sodas. It was right at the main entrance of the mall, so we saw most everyone that came in and out. About six other girls worked in the shop and we all got along.

It was on Friday night a week before prom and I was alone doing the clean up before closing when in walked Johnny Boone and Trey. It surprised me to see Johnny since he'd never been to the shop before. We weren't close friends, but I knew he was a good guy and hung out with Trey sometimes.

"Hey, Gracie," he said, leaning next to Trey against the glass on the counter.

"Hey, guys. You want something? I've put most everything away for the night."

"Do you have a date to prom?" asked Johnny, getting right to the point.

"Nah. Why?" I continued sweeping the floor.

"I was wondering if you'd like to go with me?"

"Yeah, right," I said, laughing as I continued sweeping.

"No, I'm serious," Johnny said.

"Prom's a week away," I said and stopped sweeping to look at him. "You're kidding me, right?" I studied his face to see if he was joking. Then I looked at Trey for confirmation. "You guys *are* kidding, right?"

"Honest Gracie, he wants to take you to prom."

"Why are you asking so late, everyone else turn ya down?"
I asked, laughing to reduce the embarrassment in case it was a
joke. I still didn't believe he was asking me to prom.

"Nah, I wasn't gonna go. Trey talked me into it and you
were the only person I thought I would have fun with."

Shrugging my shoulders, still in disbelief, I said, "Sure,
okay. That would be fun." I never thought in a million years that
I'd go to prom. I mean, c'mon, the crush of my life had just kicked
me to the curb, who could blame me?

"It'll be fun, Gracie," chimed in Trey, "We're going as a
group: you guys, me and my date, and Chuck and his date."

"Okay," I said, but inwardly I prayed it was not a joke.

They walked out the door. "We'll give you more
information once we figure it all out," Trey said over his shoulder.

I called Mom on the shop phone before I closed the doors,
just to let her know. It was such exciting news for me. As pretty as

my older sisters were, they had never gone to prom. Yet there I was, a gangly girl that looked like my dad, and I was going to prom.

"That is great news, Grace," said Mom. I could hear how pleased she was in her voice. "Is this Johnny a nice boy?" Mom asked. She had never heard me speak of him before.

"Yeah, he is. At least what I know of him."

"Well, Trey takes such good care of you, I'm sure he is."

"But Mom, what are we gonna do about my dress? I have nothing to wear."

"We can call Sylvia and see if she has any ideas tomorrow," Mom said.

The next day when I got home from school, I found Mom in her sewing room. "Mom, can we call Sylvia about the dress?" I asked.

"I already spoke with her this morning. She has an old bridesmaid dress she thinks will work," Mom said. Hearing this news I sighed with relief.

"Is she gonna mail it?" I asked.

"She's coming home for the weekend and will bring it then."

My oldest sister, Sylvia, majored in Fashion Merchandising at school; she was an amazing seamstress. Often, she would send me clothes to wear that she'd designed and sewn. Okay . . . not often; once. *Once* she sent me a dress she'd designed and made.

The week before prom went by so quickly that before I knew it, the *day* of the prom had arrived. And, Sylvia was right about the dress; it was perfect.

Standing in front of the mirror, I looked at myself from all different angles. I remembered what my sister had looked like when she wore the dress. I remembered how pretty the light blue had looked against her olive skin. *So* not the case with me and my Celtic complexion, but I was still happy with it. I trusted Sylvia's sense of style, so I felt good about how I looked.

It was my first date, and it was to prom no less. I was ready and waiting for my date to come—nerves and all.

I would be the last stop before we headed to Pilson, an hour away, for a steak dinner. How that worked since I lived out near Trey and the other members of our party lived in Ashbury, I wasn't quite sure. It seemed odd to me that they'd go into town, pick up everyone, then come out and pick me up. But who was I to know their thought process? I was still learning the ropes.

Most people, when coming to pick us up, stopped at our front steps, but when Trey arrived driving his mom's boat-sized car, he drove to the back of the house out of habit. Then Johnny jumped out of the car and came knockin' on the back door. My sisters' dates would always come to the front door, not mine, they came to get me through the kitchen.

I opened the door to see him standing there in his burgundy tux and ruffled shirt, smiling and without saying a word, held out the plastic floral box that contained my corsage. *Thank heavens he's nervous too*, I thought to myself with relief.

"Mom, Johnny's here!" I said, re-entering the kitchen where my sister and she stood. I led him in and after making introductions all around, I handed the plastic box to Mom and asked, "Will you put my corsage on, please?" Mom pinned on my corsage as all three of us commented on how pretty it was, and Sylvia got Johnny's boutonniere out of the fridge.

"Would you like me to pin this on for you?" Mom asked Johnny.

"Sure."

Now that both our flowers were pinned on our clothes, we headed out to the car. There would be three couples or six people, in the car: Beans was Trey's date and she sat in the back seat with Chuck and his date which turned out to be Roberta—Hoppy's friend. That left Johnny, Trey and me in the front seat. To my surprise, Johnny got in before me and sat in the middle. I stood there confused, not knowing if it was the norm. I didn't know if I should say anything, or just get in so we could be on our way?

"Maybe Gracie should sit in the middle," Beans suggested

from the back seat, saving the day.

"Yeah," Trey responded, laughing as he pushed Johnny away, who began to blush. "What are ya doin'?"

"I just want to be close to you," Johnny teased Trey as he recovered from the embarrassment.

"That is unless you *want* to sit next to Trey," I continued. But Johnny scooched out of the bench seat and made room for me before getting back in.

The correction in the seating arrangement had broken the ice for all of us and we seemed to relax. Trey backed out of my driveway, and I could see my mom and sister through the window laughing, having watched us figure out the seating.

It would take an hour for us to drive to the restaurant for dinner. As we began the journey, I felt a poke on my shoulder.

"Hi, Gracie." I heard a voice that made me cringe. I'd forgotten for a moment that she was in the car.

"Oh . . . hi Roberta." I would now spend, what was already a stressful night, with Hoppy's friend. Yeah.

"Hey, Beans," I said, having not had a chance to greet my friend yet.

"You look great, Gracie," said Beans.

"You, too." It said a lot about the dating life of all three of us girls. These boys had all asked us at the last minute to the biggest dance of the year, and we were all available.

Having Beans and Trey in the car helped relieve some discomfort, as I sat in the middle listening, pushing my shyness down. I racked my brain trying to think of something funny to say, something that would help me take part in the conversation, but I wasn't as quick as normal; my game was off.

When we arrived at the restaurant there were five other couples waiting for us, which made it even easier on me as I focused on the girls' conversations, and Johnny paid more attention to the boys'—out of his own nervousness. *Boy, are we a pair.*

On the way back from the restaurant after a great meal, all of us were looking forward to the dance.

"Did everyone help with the decorations for this dance?" asked Roberta from the backseat.

"I did," I said. "It was fun seeing it come together."

"Me, too," said Beans.

"No," answered the boys at different times.

"Why'd we want to do that?" said Johnny as all three guys laughed as if sharing a private joke.

I sat in the front seat, willing myself to talk and laugh, as it was a night of many firsts: my first formal, my first date, my first dinner a boy paid for . . . it was almost sensory overload

My personality began to rear its head on the drive to the dance though. Whether or not that was a good thing, only my companions could say, but as for me . . . I couldn't wait to see Sam . . . uh, I meant dance. I knew Sam would be there with Hoppy; Roberta had made that very clear to me. I had to be happy and fun, in case he looked my way. I still wanted to win him back. I forgot my nervousness once we got to the dance and began to perform.

The dance proved to be a lot of fun because I didn't just dance with Johnny but also danced with Trey, Chuck, and some of the other guys. Everyone seemed to dance with everyone except for those couples who were exclusive, which of course included Hoppy and Sam. Even though prom was only for the juniors and seniors, there were many sophomores in attendance since they were dating someone in the upper classes.

I would've loved to dance with Sam. He looked heavenly in his black tux with a white ruffle shirt, cummerbund, and a black bowtie. Pure class. I envied Hoppy in his arms, having his eyes on her and the smiles that parted his luscious lips, exposing his pearly whites.

As fun as the night had been, I was glad when Trey dropped Roberta off first, which allowed me to relax and not be as self-conscious. It was tough to be nice to someone who, I felt, went out of her way to hurt me and would report back to Hoppy anything I said or did. Or, was I just being paranoid?

"Thanks for having Johnny ask me to prom," I told Trey as

he drove me home, having dropped everyone else off. He looked at me and gave me that beautiful smile of his.

"Sure. Did you have fun?"

"I did for a first date."

"This was your first date?"

"Yeeeeah," I said, looking at him as if he should know. "It made it so much easier to be with friends."

"I'm glad you came. I know it was last minute, but none of us were planning to go. By that time, we didn't know who was available to ask."

I rolled my eyes. "I see."

"I didn't mean it like that," Trey said, laughing.

"Uh-huh," I said, feeling a little hurt at the recognition that I had no dating life.

"No, no . . . c'mon Gracie. I didn't mean it like that," he said, still laughing, trying to get me to laugh as he pushed my shoulder.

"You're lucky I love ya. Boy, if I told my mom this, you'd be in soooo much trouble." This only made Trey laugh harder. In grade school, Trey would tease me so much that I'd go home crying and Mom would have to call his mom and tell her to have Trey stop teasing me. This would only last until he saw me the next day.

Still laughing, he said, "C'mon, don't do that." By that time, I was laughing, too. I loved having all of Trey's attention. "I'm glad you guys moved back."

"Yeah, me too," I said as Trey drove into my driveway and, true to form, drove me to the back door. "Again, thanks. I had a great time. Goodnight."

"Goodnight. See ya on Monday."

As I was preparing for bed, I replayed the night's events over in my head. With the replay came the memory of Sam and Hoppy, but mostly Sam. I'd only seen them on the dance floor once, then not again until the end of the dance, when they were sitting over by themselves on the sideline, alone. They just sat there, not talking, just watching. That's the moment I knew I had the upper hand in their freeze-out towards me. It was the two of them, unless Roberta counted, then the three of them against me and the rest of the school. I thought it would be more work to not talk to someone than to be friends with that person, especially when that person was me.

I had to pat myself on the back at the realization that I got through most of the night without thinking of them. Now I thought about them for a different reason: the oddness of their relationship. *Does being in love mean you have to be boring?* I wondered.

Going forward, whenever I'd see Sam and Hoppy in the halls, I was more aware that they never laughed or took part in any of the antics that happened during the breaks. They just sat together, quietly observing. I didn't know if it was self-imposed or if Hoppy demanded it, but Sam didn't hang out with the guys anymore as he used to pre-Hoppy. They probably laughed and had fun I just never saw it. But this made me wonder: did I dodge a bullet? Who would ever want to be in a relationship like that? I'd rather have fun and be around friends than suffocate in the cloister of love.

Roberta and Hoppy were nice, cute girls, but they just weren't as funny as they thought themselves to be. I mean, granted there were many times that Trey would laugh and tell me—with love, I'm sure—"Gracie *you're* so weird". As opposed to the times Roberta would try to be funny and we ended up looking at her with a "you're so *weird*" expression. I imagined what it was like for Sam when he hung out with Hoppy and Roberta at the same time. That may have been punishment enough for kicking me to the curb, or had his sense of humor changed to fit the times?

A Crack in the Ice?

When the school year ended, it was much sadder than the previous year to see the seniors go, as I had now known most of them for two years. But, once they were gone, we became the seniors. I had waited all my life to be a senior and I was gonna enjoy every moment. So, it was more of a "Here's your hat, what's your hurry?" type situation regarding our friends from the graduating class.

On the last day of school. I didn't think any of us made it to class. The seniors had graduated the week before, so we were the acting seniors, and there was excitement in the air.

After a couple of hours, many of us left and headed over to

Taco Time for an early lunch and to begin our summer. The guys

went in their cars, Beans drove her and Zelda over, and since I had

to work that day, I drove over in Brutus to avoid inconveniencing

anyone when I left early for work.

When Zelda, Beans and I entered Taco Time, we saw the

guys were already occupying a booth and had pulled a table over

for more seats. We motioned to them that we'd order our food first.

We should've looked where we were going, though. While we'd

been looking at the guys, I bumped into Beans, who bumped into

Zelda, who bumped right into the back of Sam, who was still

ordering his food.

I stopped, frozen in my steps. I recognized the dark brown

hair, the broad shoulders, and those long legs. I'd watched him

walk away just as much as when he approached. He looked great

in his clothes both coming and going. Again, I-I was only being

honest.

My knees felt like jelly and I couldn't move. As much as I

wanted to leave to avoid giving him the opportunity to ignore me

in front of my friends, I just stood there. I needed to disappear, but

he turned around before I moved.

"Sorry Sammy! I almost didn't recognize you without Hoppy," Zelda snorted as she laughed.

"Ha ha, hilarious," Sam responded, turning back towards the counter to pay for his food.

Shoot! Of all the people to run into when I wanted to eat, I thought to myself. I quickly stole a glance of his handsome, smiling face before making a retreat towards where the other guys were seated. I didn't want to witness the expression change on his face upon seeing me.

"Did you already order your food?" asked Trey

"Um . . . no. I don't think I'll have enough time to have lunch before I gotta get to work," I lied as I slid in next to Chuck on the booth bench.

"Aaaah, c'mon Gracie. You're always working."

"I know Brian, but I gotta get money for college," I explained, then Zelda, Beans, and Sam came up, claiming chairs around the table.

"Just eat something quick," suggested Trey

"Gracie," said Beans, "you said you'd go to lunch with us today. You said you had time."

Zelda started chanting, "Graaaacie! Graaaacie! Graaaacie," and soon most everyone in our group was chanting.

I didn't dare look at Sam. Instead, I fell into my gracious celebrity character, feigning embarrassment. I covered my eyes and clutched my chest. "Oh! Dear . . . stooooop! Oooooh, yoouuuu! Aaaaaalriiiiight! I'll staaaaaay. I gotta give my fans what they want," I said as most everyone laughed. Sam used to love when I'd play that way, but I wasn't gonna take the chance and look his way only to be disappointed by him ignoring me. At that moment, everyone's food arrived. "Oh crap!" I exclaimed. "I forgot to order food!" I slid out of the booth and headed to the counter with everyone laughing behind me.

"She's so crazy," said Brian.

"Oooh, Grace," said Beans.

"Some things never change," said Trey.

"I heard that," I called as I stepped up to the counter.

"Good," Zelda called from the table.

I ordered some taco fries, which were just deep-fried tater tots, and returned to the group. Everyone was telling each other their plans for the summer. But I wasn't paying attention. Sam had chosen a chair on the opposite side of the table that was very visible to me from where I sat in the booth. To evade eye contact I had to pretend I had a blinder on my left eye so as to not look at him, in fear of the reception that look might get.

"Gracie! Gracie," Chuck said as he nudged me.

"Wha-what?" I asked, looking from one person to the other. I'd been sitting there obsessing in my mind over the close proximity of Sam after so many months, and him without Hoppy.

"We were asking you what you're doing this summer," Zelda informed me.

Just as I opened my mouth to respond, the whole group chimed in, "Work," and then began to laugh at their creativity.

"Ha ha ha! You're so funny." I grimaced at the group, except for Sam.

"Oh, c'mon Gracie, that's funny," Beans said.

"Yeah, whatever." I rolled my eyes as I looked at my watch, and sighed. "I really gotta go," I said, and slid, once again, out of the booth and turned to leave. "Catch ya on the flip side," I called glibly over my shoulder with a quick wave, pleased with my slick exit.

Once outside the double doors, I stopped for only a moment to take some deep breaths to gather myself from the residual effect of being in Sam's presence after so long. I really didn't have to be at work yet, but it was so tough being around Sam and not knowing when he would shut me down in front of everyone. I really thought it was better that I leave before he had the chance to do it.

I walked over to Brutus and paused, closing my eyes to mourn the loss of Sam's friendship for only a second. *He is soooo dang handsome!* I thought. *What had I done to lose it?* Then I shook my head to clear those thoughts from my mind. I wouldn't dwell on what I couldn't fix. With that resolved for the day, I got into Brutus and turned the key . . . nothing. I tried once more . . . nothing.

"Oh, craaaap," I said to myself as I got out of the truck and looked around for some help. Not a soul in sight. I'd have to return to the gang inside, where I'd just made such a slick exit and get the guys to come out and push me to start up the old boy. My perfect exit was now ruined.

With a roll of my eyes, I entered Taco Time again, "Hi

guys," I called, trying to sound cheerful and charming.

"Thought you had to go to work?" said Zelda before taking a bite out of her taco.

"I do," I said as I gave an overly dramatic deflated sob and lowered my head while pouting. "Brutus won't start. I need a push," I said, looking at Trey. Giving him the sweetest smile, I could muster, and begged, "Pleeeeeeeeeease."

"Aaaaalright," said Trey with an exaggerated sigh. "C'mon guys, Gracie's in distress." I smiled and batted my eyelashes in gratitude as I lead them out the door to my beloved chariot.

"Thank you," I said. Once we got to Brutus, I jumped inside, pushed down the clutch, moved the gearshift to neutral, and readied the truck for the push, "Okay guys! Push." I looked in my rearview mirror so I would know when to pop the clutch. I couldn't believe my eyes; Sam was right in the middle of the others helping push. I was so stunned I almost missed the moment to pop the clutch to get Brutus' engine to turn over.

"Gracie!" yelled Brian. "Pop the clutch!"

"Okay! Okay," I said, popping the clutch and putting the truck in gear. I couldn't stop, so I waved out my window as I drove out of the parking lot. "Thank you!" I called. In my rearview

mirror, I saw all had turned to go back in to finish lunch, except

Sam, who stood with one hand tossing a rock in the air, looking

after me. *What was going on?* I wondered. *Did he regret helping?*

Or, was he fighting the urge to throw the rock at me?

Spilling My Guts, Again

Now that summer had started, I tried to get more shifts at the

popcorn shop, but there were still a couple of girls who'd just

graduated that were trying to get a few more weeks of work before

they left for school, as well. My favorite was Sonya who was one

of the coolest girls: quiet, smart and nice. I was lucky enough to

work multiple shifts with her which gave us many times to chat

and get to know one another better.

By that time, I had only told Beans about Sam. It seemed as

if with all things, time was healing all the angst crush-ache I'd felt.

I began to believe that it had all been a hallucination in my heat-oppressed mind and there had been nothing between us to begin with. That was until the day that Sam came into the shop.

Luckily, we were busy, so one of the other girls helped him. Contrary to popular belief, I was not a glutton for punishment. I'd been burned multiple times when I'd approached him at school. So there was no way I'd willingly approach him and have the same thing happen there at work. Through tenacity and stealth, I avoided him every time he came to buy dinner.

It turned out he'd gotten a job in the bookstore and came to the shop on his dinner breaks. One would think he'd avoid coming there on the nights I worked. Even though I felt my heart had healed, I wasn't ready for any more rejection. For months, I avoided being around him as much as possible. It helped with the healing process. There were even times I forgot he existed. *Hahaha, not really.*

Anyway, I didn't want to give him that power; my self-esteem couldn't handle it. But, now that he was coming into the shop, my place of work . . . uh oh . . . here comes the angst again. Breathe in . . . breathe out.

I knew my luck would run out one of these times and I'd

have to wait on him. I hoped not for a while, though. I'd been lucky so far, until I had a close call on the last Saturday of June.

It was almost closing time and I was helping a customer when out of the corner of my eye I saw Sam. He sat on the wall outside the shop and I felt the bats in my stomach begin to stir in panic at the thought of helping him. You'd think he'd leave seeing me behind the counter, but he didn't. While helping my customer I assessed my situation and how best to handle it with no embarrassment to me. When it looked like I was about to finish, Sam stood and moved next to the counter, waiting his turn.

"Miss, we don't have the fudge yet," the client said to me.

"Oh, I'm sorry," I said, as my heartbeat began to increase. *What was I gonna do?* "Give me one second and I'll get your fudge," I told them and passed through the curtain that separated the front from the back.

Sonya was cleaning up so we could get out of there as soon as we closed the doors.

"Hey Sonya, can you come out and help Sam while I finish with this other couple, please?" I quietly asked.

"Sure," she said, putting down the wire brush she'd been

using to scrape the grill. She came out, wiping her hands on the front of her uniform, and walked to where Sam stood. This gave me the time I needed to finish with the couple I was helping and escape into the back room, allowing my heartbeat to return to normal. I stayed back there until she came looking for me, which let me know he had left.

"Why didn't you want to wait on Sam? I thought you were friends."

"I thought so too until he started dating Hoppy."

"Hoppy?"

"Yeah, you know, Sara Jane."

"She's dating Sam?" Sonya asked with a look of disbelief.

"Yeah."

"When did that happen?" she asked.

I had never spilled my guts like this to anyone but Beans before, but I felt I could trust her. So, while we cleaned up the shop, I told her the whole story. I told her everything with my stomach doing somersaults forwards, backward, and sideways the whole time. *What would she think?* I wondered. *Do I sound like a total idiot?* As I came to the end of my purge, the butterflies had subsided to a slight twitch. She didn't judge me, but listened to my tale of crush-break, then only spoke when I'd finished.

"I always wondered why you two weren't hanging out anymore. You were always together. I think everyone thought you guys were dating."

"Nah, I wasn't sixteen," I answered.

"I don't pay much attention to Sam, but I think I have seen him and Hoppy together. But I didn't think anything of it."

"That's why I asked you to wait on him tonight."

"Gee Grace, I think he really wanted you to wait on him. He kept looking at the curtain."

"Yeah, I doubt that. The guy hasn't spoken to me for almost a year. I don't want to give him the chance to reject me by walking away when I approach him. He did that enough when this first started."

"Well, when he comes in, I'll wait on him for ya, if I'm here. But, I'm only here for a few more weeks. After that it's all you," she said while locking the shop door.

As we walked to our cars I asked, "Does he come in on nights I'm not working?"

"I never see him when I'm working alone." She shrugged and got into her car.

The Big Thaw?

For the next couple of weeks whenever Sam came to the shop, I'd always disappear into the back and let one of the other girls help him. Only Sonya knew the reason for my sudden disappearance, and I kept this up until all the senior girls had quit. After they had all left, a week and a half had passed with no sign of Sam, so I began to relax.

The summer was almost over, and I was looking forward to school starting. I was that much closer to leaving home, going to college, being my own boss, and leaving all this drama behind. I just had one more year. Besides, there were so many more guys outside of Ashbury for me to see and flirt with, guys from all over the world, even. *Sam was not the only fish in the sea*, I reminded myself time and time again. *Oh, but what a fish.*

Just before closing on Friday night, I'd begun the preliminary cleaning. Another shift was ending and thankfully no Sam. *Maybe he'd gone elsewhere for his food now that I was the only one here at night*, I told myself.

Whenever I was in the back-room cleaning, I'd look through the curtain to see if there were any customers. I'd just finished and was drying my hands to head back out when I looked through the curtain to see none other than Sam standing at the counter. I jumped back away from the curtain, hoping he hadn't seen me. *Why am I always jumping to hide from him?* What was I going to do? Stay back there until he gave up and left? What if he doesn't leave? I had to close sometime. Then again, he only had so much time for his dinner break. Could I wait him out? As I stood there contemplating what to do, a young family walked into the shop.

"Aaargh," I muttered to myself. Now I had to go deal with Sam.

Emerging from behind the curtain drying my hands, I

asked, "Who's first?" and looked from Sam to the family, never acknowledging that I knew Sam any better than the other customers. I hoped that Sam would say it was him so I could wait on him and he'd go. I looked from one to the other waiting, when the man from the family pointed to Sam indicating that he was before them, and with a sigh of relief I walked toward Sam when—God bless the little dear—he pointed towards the family.

"No, go ahead. I'm not in a hurry. I can wait," he told the family.

"Are you sure?" The lady asked as she held her little girl who was whining and trying to reach over the glass to the candy. "No, Em. Stop," she said, setting her down.

"Really?!" I thought, I don't swear, but if I did—this would have been a good time to do it. Inwardly I rolled my eyes as I walked over to the small family.

"How can I help you?" I asked with a welcoming smile, standing in front of the candy counter. I could now see the second child standing on the other side of the glass hungrily staring at the candy that was eye level. I laughed at the little boy's expression. "Hi there," I said, leaning over the glass shelf so he'd see me. "Do you see something you'd like?"

"We would like to get a pound of the peanut clusters, please," the mother said, pulling my attention away from the little boy.

"Which would you prefer, the white chocolate or milk chocolate?" I asked.

"Why don't w—" the mom started but was interrupted by the little boy tapping his little finger on the pane of glass pointing at the stars made of pure white chocolate with colored sprinkles.

"Mommy, can we get these?" he asked.

"Get these," said his little sister.

"No. We'll only get some candy to take to Grandma's tomorrow. You can have some of that." The little girl started to cry; you could see that she was tired, as were her parents. The dad picked her up to console her and divert her attention away from the candy so the mother could continue with her order. "Why don't we take half a pound of the white chocolate and half a pound of the milk chocolate."

"And two stars Mommy."

"Would you like this in a box or a bag?" I asked.

"Box please," she said before turning to the little boy, "I said no, Roy. You can have some of Grandma's candy." Roy's bottom lip began to quiver, and his big brown eyes filled with tears.

"Mommy, I want it. I'll share with Sissy," he promised, but his mother ignored him.

The boxes were kept under the counter, as was the excess candy, so when I knelt to get the box, I dropped four of the star candies into a small bag and placed it in the box after including the clusters. Then, as I kept the mother engaged in conversation, I closed the lid and put the box in a bag, all the while hoping the mom hadn't seen what I'd done. I rang up the total owed and handed her the bag. By this time the father had the little girl out in the hallway quietly sitting on his lap as they waited.

I watched the family leave hoping that perhaps, Sam had run out of time on his dinner break and left. But when I turned, he was still there standing next to the caramel corn bin. I grudgingly walked towards him and felt a flinch coming in anticipation of our interaction. Yet, I couldn't help but admire how handsome he looked dressed in a shirt and tie leaning against the bin, smiling. I had to be strong and not allow his wicked good looks to weaken my resolve to stay aloof. I refused to smile. So, I bit my inner lip and tried to think of things I didn't like as in rats, spiders, and Hoppy. This helped a bit with masking any expression or emotion.

I asked, "What would you like?"

"Y'know, that was really a nice thing you did," said Sam, smiling.

"Hmm . . . not sure the mom will think that, but what can I say, I'm a rebel," I responded, still thinking of spiders, dead rats, and Hoppy. "What would you like?" I asked, changing the subject and frowning as those gorgeous eyes twinkled at me.

He chuckled, "I'll take a hot dog if you still have any."

I looked over at the single, shriveled hot dog going around in the carousel. "You really want that? It's been in there for about five hours."

"Sure."

Shaking my head in disbelief, I said, "You must have a gut of iron." Sam only chuckled. "Normally, I'd just throw it away. But I'll give it to you *this* time, no charge," I stated as I walked over to the carousel by the register with Sam following on the other side of the counter.

"I'll pay for it," he said, reaching into his pants pocket.

"Okay then, that'll be fifty cents," I said. "And don't think you can come back here when you get sick from this ol' thing." Holding my nose, I took it from the carousel with a pair of long tongs, put it in the bun, and handed it to him, all to the musical sound of him laughing at my antics, once more.

"I won't. I'm telling ya," he said, patting his stomach. "Gut of iron." He dropped two quarters on the counter.

Walking around the end of the counter, I gave him a bored looked, and said, "Whatever." He laughed as he walked out of the shop, shaking his head, still keeping eye contact with me as he took a big bite of the hot dog. There was no mistaking that twinkle in his eye. I sighed to myself as I felt my knees begin to weaken. Outwardly, I maintained the bored look on my face while I followed and closed one side of the glass doors after him.

"Mmm," he said as he headed back to his store.

While closing the shop, I couldn't stop thinking about what had just occurred. *How did I suddenly get into his good graces? Or, was this a "one-off"?* Only time would tell, I guess. But I had to admit I loved seeing that twinkle in his eyes and hearing him laugh in response to me or as he teased me. I wondered what Hoppy would say if she knew about all his attempts at speaking with me again. *Boy, I'd love to be a fly on the wall when she found that out*, I thought, snickering to myself.

As summer passed by, Sam would wave to me on his way to work, and I would coolly nod back, which only made him laugh. Why? I had no idea. He continued coming to the shop on his dinner breaks on the nights I was there alone, wearing me down, making it harder and harder to think of dead rats, spiders, and Hoppy. Instead, I found myself thinking of romantic, star-filled moonlit nights, holding hands, and getting lost in the dark abyss of his eyes.

I knew he was still with Hoppy, so I'd do or say anything I wanted without worry. I had nothing to lose. I loved how free I felt. I didn't care; he got the Gracie that everyone else got. I think he liked it, maybe even preferred it. I mean c'mon he kept coming back.

As time progressed, when he came for dinner he would stick around and we'd discuss everything. Everything except why he'd stopped speaking to me. As happy as I was with the new version of our friendship, I was curious as to what had caused our old friendship to stop. And, if truth were told, my heart would beat a little faster when he came in and the embers of my crush were beginning to warm.

Seniors In Da House!

Aaaah, the first day of my senior year. *We* were now the big kids on campus. Probably everyone who has been a senior experience that surge of power—even though nobody really has any—that first day walking into high school.

Walking down Senior Hall, I was determined to have an absolutely, incredibly, fabulous year. I had so many dreams for my future: fantasizing about all the Academy Awards I would win, all the travel, all the men that would be at my feet, all the money, and all the good acts I would do in the world with that money. I was confident that life would just get better and better after my amazing senior year.

Being a senior, my locker was in Senior Hall and was near Trey's, as usual. With all the excitement everyone was feeling that first day, you couldn't have a conversation with one person before another would come up and interrupt with some greeting. Guys would grab each other from behind and wrestle, while the girls would laugh and egg them on. The excitement was almost tangible.

The beauty of our high school was the friendship everyone seemed to have for one another no matter their grade or interests. Could it be credited to our farming background? The size of our school? Or, that time of our life? Whatever it was, I was glad we had it there.

Soon, the morning bell rang, signaling all of us to go to our first class. Again, English was my first period and the teacher's name this year was Mrs. Sawyer, a very classy lady who had taught at our high school for many years. She'd even taught my oldest brother and sister who were *nothing* like me. Where they were quiet, I was, hm . . . how to say it . . . not. Much to my mother's chagrin.

I walked into class and chose a desk four rows back from the front and was talking to the person in front of me when I felt the desk behind me move. I turned around to see Sam's gloriously handsome and smiling face as he took ownership of that desk.

"Really?" I asked, and he chuckled. I turned back around to see Trey setting his notebook on a desk in the front row, Chuck a couple of rows to my left between Trey and myself. I laughed thinking of the fun we'd have in class. After choosing their desks, they came over to speak with Sam and myself. But once Mrs. Sawyer stood, we all knew it was time to be quiet and listen as she told us what to expect for the coming year.

With it being the first day, most of the teachers only used the beginning of class time to welcome us and discuss what to expect, while passing out the syllabus and the textbook needed for the class. After they finished, they told us we could talk for the rest of the time but be prepared to get to work the next day.

As soon as Mrs. Sawyer gave the all clear sign to talk, Trey, Chuck, and Allan came over to where Sam and I sat. We compared our schedules; with us being seniors, many left school after the fourth period to go to work. Unfortunately, that would not be me as I was co-editor of the yearbook with Sabrina and yearbook took the two periods after lunch. I only had two classes with Sam: English and economics, which I was surprised at. As Sam and I left class that day I wondered to myself how long Hoppy would allow this. How long would she allow Sam to walk alone in the halls where at any moment I might pounce on him and make him smile and laugh?

How could a relationship that changes your personality so much work? What if they got married? And it was twenty-four seven of just sitting, not laughing, no fun outside your family allowed . . . could that relationship last or would the monotony tear it apart?

Second period was drama and were we ever in for a surprise. Our beloved Mr. H. was no longer teaching the class. *Would class be as good this year as it had been last year?* Only time would tell. Luckily, along with some new students, there were also some of the old such as Barry, Zelda, and Beans.

The new teacher's name was Ms. Budapest and she was a small woman with dark, short hair and a dancer's build. She sat in the window with one leg bent and the other straight out on the ledge, with a feather boa draped around her neck as if she were doing a modern version of Rodin's Thinker statue. A bit dramatic, but weren't we in "drama"? The whole situation was so new to us we just stared in curiosity.

As Ms. Budapest turned her head towards us, it was as if we had surprised her in the midst of very deep thoughts. She began to spew a nonsensical monologue about her approach to theater:

"Theater, like dance, is an expression of the soul. It lets the actor transport emotions through the airwaves to the audience; it is a chance for the actor to enter another dimension. To be a successful actor one must open oneself up to whatever the Universe . . ." aaand she lost me, and I think the rest of the class as well. We all looked at one another, speechless as we realized we had just boarded the crazy train. Yes, Mr. H. had allowed us free reign in class, but there was still structure, which from the sound of Ms. Budapest's monologue left me wondering if the inmates were now running the asylum.

"Now class, I will begin casting for our fall production next week," she announced.

"Great," Zelda said. "When do we audition?"

"That won't be necessary," she informed us. "I will cast each part from the aura you transmit to me." We all looked at each other in silent confusion.

"Have you already chosen a play?" I asked.

"Yes, it is a sweet little English ditty. The name escapes me right now."

"A ditty?" I asked, confused. "Is it a song?"

"No! Oh, heavens no," she said, followed by what might be construed as a musical laugh. "We will discuss this more next week."

"Oh great," I said, seeing my acting career go down the drain. I'd had such aspirations for this year. Now what would I do?

My third period was algebra. My fourth period was economics, or econ, as we called it, which was the second class I had with Sam. None of my other guy friends were in the class, and once again upon entering the room Sam, came and grabbed the desk behind me. *This guy is nothin' but trouble*, I thought. And, I loved it!

After lunch was Yearbook Committee, and since Sabrina and I were co-editors we had to decide the design and layout of the pages so we could begin work as soon as possible. That was exciting for me. I loved the fact that I would know what the yearbook would look like and wouldn't have to wait like everyone else when it was distributed. *Oooh, the power!*

He Touched Me!

Ms. Budapest told us on the first day of school that she'd be casting our fall production within the week. Well . . . that didn't happen. Neither did it happen the second week. Instead, she informed us that because of unforeseen issues with the play she'd chosen she would now have to replace it with another play, one she hadn't found yet. In the meantime, while she searched for a new one, she wanted the class to read the play, *Our Town*, which I absolutely hated.

Before I realized I had even said anything, I groaned out loud, "Nooooooo!"

"What do you mean, no?" she asked, surprised by my outburst.

"Ugh! I hate Our Town."

"And why is that? Have you even read the play?"

"Yes, I have. I have taken part in two productions of the play. It is sooooo boring!"

"Because of that alone, you *should* be in it."

"Sorry. I won't do that play again." I was not budging on my opinion.

"Ya' feel strongly there, Gracie?" Zelda teased.

"I hate it."

"Well, while I am searching for another play, I want all of you to take part in the reading of Our Town. This play is a staple of any Dramatic curriculum," she said, and I moaned. "Everyone will take part except for Grace." Ms. Budapest gave me a stern look as she continued. "But she will sit quietly and not comment while the play is being read." I inwardly groaned again at the thought of having to sit and listen to these people, who weren't really actors, read this awful play, but at least I didn't have to take part in the torture.

So, that is what I did—the first day anyway: I sat and listened—or tried to. I decided that the next day I would ask to be excused to go to the restroom just to get away from the torment of listening to the class read the play. Once out of the class I would wander the halls searching for anyone to help pass the time.

A few days later as I escaped the classroom, I headed to the library to see if there was anyone that I would want to speak with in there, but it was empty, so I left. While walking down the hall I heard my name called.

"Gracie!" Turning, I saw Trevor Baxter walk towards me.

"Did you call?" I asked, perking up.

"Yeah. Do you have a second?" Little did he know that I had the whole class period to chat.

"Sure. What's up?"

"Do you have any interest in being in the Student Body Presidency?"

"As what and with who?" I asked.

"Secretary, with Karl as President and me as VP."

"Sure, I'm in!" *Are you kiddin' me?! They were asking me. I was riding the popular train. Of course, I'm gonna play!* "Who are we runnin' against?"

"No one yet."

"I hope someone does run against us, although we are a formidable team." I said, giving Trevor an over exaggerated wink.

"Yeah, me too." He laughed.

This gave me the courage to head back to class, but a sudden thought stopped me: "Trevor! Wait! What do we do next?"

Shrugging his shoulders, he said, "Wait and see who we have to run against, then campaign, I guess," he said, and I nodded. "Come into the cafeteria at lunchtime; we should have everyone there."

"Okay. I better get back to my class of pain."

"Whaaaat?" Trevor asked, laughing. I waved him off and returned to my class.

When it was time for lunch, I told Zelda and Beans about my conversation with Trevor, and Zelda started razzing me.

"Madame Secretary! May I speak with you, Madame Secretary?"

"I am not a crook," I said, holding both hands up with the peace sign while impersonating Richard Nixon. They laughed as we headed into the cafeteria as instructed by Trevor. Inside were a group of guys standing around one of the long tables next to the windows.

"Hey, guys!" I called, walking up to the group.

I was met with "Graaaaacieeeeee!" and other good-natured jeers from the group. When the guys parted, I saw Karl sitting at the head of the table as if he were holding court.

"Okay, so we have the core positions filled," Karl stated, which turned out to be the reason all those guys were there; they would all fill one position or another.

"Do we know who we're running against yet?" Doug asked.

"So far it's only one other group," said Karl as he listed the members of the opposing team which included, none other than, Roberta. I laughed to myself as I thought, *Seriously?! Does that group think they can win against this power team?*

I was the only girl in the ASB Presidency, and we had the smart, popular people in our group. *Did I just include myself in the "smart" kids' group?* As we were discussing the campaign, the opposing candidates approached us.

And in typical Roberta style, she tried to cozy up to my group. "What are you guys doing? Ready for a battle?" she said, then brayed like donkey. We just looked at her—no one said a word.

After a few moments of silence, Karl responded flatly, "If that is what you want."

Giving an uncomfortable laugh, Roberta said, "Oh, lighten up, I was just kidding. No one wants a battle. We just want a fair chance at the presidency." Her team's eyes were as big as saucers as they came face to face with the formidable administration that Karl had pulled together.

"Come on, Roberta. We should get back to our campaign planning," Fred Barnes said, pulling her away.

"May the best man or woman win!" Roberta raised her arm in the air as if she were declaring something great, then began to chortle with laughter as Fred pulled her away.

It felt so good to be on a "winning" team, especially opposite Roberta.

Unfortunately, it only lasted a day before Roberta's team withdrew their hat from the ring and my team won uncontested. It kinda threw a wet blanket on the whole experience for me; it would have been fun to campaign and win by vote. Oh yes, and to see Roberta and her team fail. Maybe that was bad to say, but I could sure think it.

When Mr. Baxter announced that Karl, Trevor, and I had won, we were in English. Sam, sitting behind me, put both his hands on my shoulders and gave them a squeeze. He had never touched me like that before or really even touched me at all.

When I was eight years old, we had a handsome missionary in our ward and, of course, I had a crush on him (even at eight I was boy crazy). One Sunday evening as he was leaving our home, he tapped the top of my head as he walked out and I inadvertently said, "Ooh la la," which made everyone laugh. I was in heaven and insisted that Sylvia put toothpicks around the spot in my hair so I could remember where he touched me and preserve it. I planned to never wash my hair again. I wanted to do that with Sam's touch; I wanted to put toothpicks around the spots on my shoulders where his hands had been so I would never forget the glorious moment.

Hut! Hut! Homecoming!

For both homecomings and prom, all senior girls were listed as candidates to give everyone a shot at being on the court. Then all the students voted for the five senior girls they'd like to see on the court. When those spots were filled, the school voted again on those five to pick the Queen.

We were right in the middle of drama class when we were interrupted by an announcement over the loudspeaker that the results were in for the five princesses of Fall Homecoming Court. Beans and I were sure that Zelda was a shoo-in for being one of the princesses, so we stopped to listen. Mr. Baxter began,

"Congratulations to the following senior girls who will comprise our Fall Homecoming Court. They are Shannon Collins (cheerleader), Donna Smith (cheerleader), Zelda Potter (cheerleader), Sally Washington (cheerleader), and the final princess is Gracie Kaye (*not* a cheerleader). Be sure and congratulate all our princesses . . ." I became deaf after that. When Mr. Baxter announced my name, the class erupted.

"Congratulations, Gracie!"

"Gracie, you're on Homecoming Court!"

"You're a princess!" and on and on. I was so stunned and humbled at having been nominated that I really had no smart remark to all the comments. What really surprised me was that people were more excited about *me* being nominated than Zelda.

For the rest of the day, I walked around in shock. *"How could I be on homecoming court?!"* I kept thinking over and over. *"This must be a fluke. Perhaps Mr. Baxter made a mistake."* I mean, seriously, the other girls on this court reminded me of that old song from the kids show Electric Company—about one of the things not belonging—and it kept running through my mind. Yeah, one of us didn't belong there—me. All these cute, bubbly cheerleaders and then . . . *me? Oy vey!*

Homecoming was not for a few weeks; I imagined that it would be all tiaras, flowers, and slaps on the back being on the court. Unfortunately, I hadn't really thought it through. Two weeks before the big game, they requested the homecoming court to attend a committee meeting to let us know the agenda for the week of homecoming and the game.

Going into the meeting I was already aware that I'd need to get a new dress and shoes, but boy, was I in for a surprise.

"Okay, quiet down so we can get this meeting started. We've got a lot to do," said Mrs. Boynton the teacher who would supervise the Homecoming Committee. We all looked at her expectantly. "I'll let Sara Jane take it from here."

Standing in front of the group, she stood and said, "Just a reminder of what the agenda will be the week of the game: the tiaras will be handed to each of you on Monday for you to wear all week and we'll have the student body vote for who should be crowned queen, the court will be presented to the school Friday morning, and we'll crown the queen. Then the court can leave after that for the day, if you'd like."

"Heck yeah," said Zelda. We all chimed in.

"Who wouldn't want to leave?" Asked Donna.

"Alright, alright. That's enough," said Mrs. Boynton, smiling.

"Anyway, Friday night we will present the court to the crowd during halftime. We'd like all the fathers to be your escorts at that time. So, please talk to them and let us know if they'll participate." Sara Jane continued speaking for a few minutes more, but I didn't hear it. I was already in my head wondering if my dad would escort me. This was so out of the box for him. Would he be willing to be in front of the crowd like that?

"Will the dads need to stay for the whole game?" Sally asked.

"Only if they want to," Mrs. Boynton said before Sara Jane could respond.

"At the dance, we're going to need you to pose for pictures in the cafeteria for about . . . ten minutes so the pictures can be taken for the yearbook and any parents that wish to do so, right Gracie?"

I looked around, surprised to hear my name singled out.

"Uh, yeah. Especially for the yearbook. I'll have the photographer get ours done as soon as possible," I said. I heard nothing else in the meeting. My mind was going a hundred miles an hour. I couldn't believe I'd forgotten about the *Dance*! And that I needed a *date*. I was so caught up in just being *on* the court, I'd forgotten about it. The elation I had earlier felt was now totally deflated. *Now I'm screwed.*

All the girls on the court had boyfriends but me. I didn't have a boyfriend, and I didn't have a date. Thus far I'd only been on one. Question: do Homecoming Princesses still need to attend the dance if they don't have a date? Or, would I need to resign from the court due to impending spinsterhood? Can one "resign" from the court or does one abdicate since, technically, they are a princess? I had so many questions and I didn't know what I was gonna do.

I decided I wouldn't say anything until we got down to the wire. If I still didn't have a date, *then* I would resign from the court, although I really didn't want to. I didn't want to think about that right then. Being on homecoming court was something I hadn't expected, and I was gonna keep basking in the glow of this compliment from my friends if it killed me.

There were other issues I'd have to deal with before the big day:

"Hey Dad, would you be willing to escort me Friday night?" I asked while we sat at dinner. Dad stopped mid bite and looked at me.

"Your father needs to escort you? Where? At the game?" Mom asked.

"At halftime, yeah. They want the father's to be our escorts then while they introduce the court."

"Ah, they don't need me there," Dad said.

Rolling my eyes, I said, "Yes they do, Dad. All the dads will be there. That includes you."

"That reminds me," Mom said. "You're going to need to wear a dress you already own. We don't have time to make one and we don't have the money to buy one."

"Seriously?" I was almost in tears.

"I'm sorry, but we can't throw money away like that. Have you been asked to Homecoming yet?

"No," I said glumly.

"That is another reason we don't need to buy you a new dress. If you had a date, it would be different."

The next day as Beans, Zelda, and I were lounging around Beans' bedroom, I brought up the issue of not having a date for Homecoming and how I wouldn't go if I didn't have one.

"What are ya gonna do, Grace?" Beans asked.

Laying on Beans' bed, between bites of gummy bears Zelda added her two cents, "Gracie, you'll get a date. I know you will." Zelda was always upbeat and a lot of fun to spend time with. She'd transferred into drama mid-year and, even though she was a cheerleader and popular, she seemed to enjoy spending time with Beans and myself.

"What if I don't?" I whined. "I will *not* go to the dance alone. That's just embarrassing."

"Gracie, you can always go with Ricky and me," Zelda teased and then snorted.

I laughed. "That's never gonna happen."

"C'mon Gracie, you know you'll get a date," said Beans, forever my cheerleader.

"If I was pretty, yeah. But I doubt I will with my looks."

"Why do you say that?" asked Zelda.

"I'm just so plain looking. I wish I was pretty, like you."

"You are!"

"Zelda, *look* at me."

"I am. You are cute! And, that swimming and biking has really paid off —you've got a great figure."

"Thanks. I just wish I was prettier."

With an exasperated roll of her eyes, Beans said, "If you're not happy with the way you look, then do something about it. Maybe wear more make-up. You're on Homecoming Court for heavens sake! That should tell you something."

"You're being silly," Zelda said, standing. "But I've got cheer practice, so I gotta go."

After Zelda was gone, Beans looked at me and asked, "Gracie . . . what is this *really* about?"

"Gee Beans, you know those girls that have a pretty face but not a great body, or the girls that have a great body but not a great face?"

"Yeah."

"I know I have a nice shape. I just wonder if I had a better face if Sam might've chosen me instead. I'd love to have him as my date to homecoming."

"Ah Gracie. I wish I knew the answer."

The very next day as Beans, Zelda, and I sat in drama class, the heavens opened, and a miracle occurred: we were all sitting around a long table chatting about Homecoming, when out of the blue Zelda says, "Barry, you should take Gracie to Homecoming." My heart stopped; I wasn't sure whether it was from the embarrassment that she said it in front of everyone, fearing the rejection when Barry said he couldn't because he was taking someone else, or the mortification that she had put Barry on the spot. Yet, through all these mixed emotions, the truest and strongest emotion was the hope that he'd say yes and take me.

"I thought I already had," responded Barry without even looking up from his drawing. Zelda looked at me with her beautiful rubbery face contorted into an expression of joy that only she could get away with. Beans beamed and silently clapped her hands, and I released the breath I'd been holding. I could have kissed him I was so relieved. I shuffled through all my memories to find when Barry had asked me to the dance . . . *and I got nuttin'*, and that was fine with me—beggars cannot be choosers. I had a date!

There was a feeling of relief to know that I now had a date and wouldn't need to resign or abdicate my little princess crown. Now I just needed to get Dad to agree to escort me at halftime and get my Mom to reconsider a new dress for me. How I would go about doing that I had no idea. But I was gonna pray like crazy for more miracles.

That night at dinner as Mom and I discussed homecoming, my date, and what I'd wear, Dad interjected between bites of food, "I got a call at work from a Mrs. Boynton who wanted to speak with me about escorting you at halftime."

"You did? Are you going to?" I asked.

"Yes," Mom responded before Dad could say anything. "Of course, he will."

"Well, your teacher called to remind me what a great girl you are and how I should be honored to escort you. What made her think I wouldn't do it?" Dad asked.

"*You.* You kept saying you wouldn't do it," I said, leaning towards him. Dad was not a tyrant. He was the kindest, sweetest, most humble man I knew, but he was stubborn at times. I just didn't want to tip the boat and have him change his mind.

"He was just teasing you," Mom reassured me.

The stars began to align for me again. *Gee, why does it always have to be a double-edged sword?* Life gave me this great pat on the back with one hand while the other was trying to pull the rug out and trip me.

The next day when Beans, Zelda, and I drove over to Zelda's home for lunch there was a message for me to call Mom.

"Hi, Mom. You wanted me to call?" *This had never happened before.*

"Hi Grace, I spoke with your dad and we decided that you could buy a new dress for homecoming. Take Monica and Zelda with you and when you find a dress you like; buy it and I'll pay you back." I listened to my mother in amazement. She was telling me to go *buy* a dress. I'd never had a store-bought dress before in my life unless I'd inherited it from someone else. Mom had always sewn my clothes for me until I could sew them myself.

"Grace?" Mom asked. When I didn't respond she asked again, "Grace? Are you there?"

"Uh . . . yeah," I responded, pulling the receiver away from my ear in disbelief, before replacing it, "I'll go tonight after school." Then I mouthed the words "new dress" to Beans and Zelda. "Thanks, Mom!"

"Okay. Bye," she said and hung up. Phone conversations with my mom never really lingered; when she was done, she was done.

"What'd she want, Gracie?" Beans and Zelda asked in unison.

"She wants me to go buy a dress for homecoming. Can you guys come with me?"

"That's so cool, Grace!"

"Of course, we can," Zelda said.

"We need to go tonight since this is the only night I don't work," I said, grabbing my keys off the counter and following Zelda and Beans out the door.

Princess Grace

It was Homecoming week and there were many events scheduled. I had my first store-bought dress, thanks to Zelda and Beans helping me shop. It was a nice dress: a wrap-around style a little past my knees with a mandarin collar, a small brown floral print on a tan background. It wasn't perfect, but hey, it was store-bought.

On Monday they gave us our princess tiaras to wear for the week. At first, it was really fun wearing them, but after I'd worn it for about an hour, the combs that held it in place began to really hurt my head, so I took mine off and put it in my locker until Friday. I privately worried that I'd come across as an ungrateful rebel by not wearing it, but when I noticed that the other "Princesses" had removed theirs as well, I didn't feel so bad.

"Where's your tiara?" Beans asked as we walked to our class.

Rubbing a spot on my head, I said, "I put it in my locker."

"Why'd ya do that?" she asked.

"It was hurting my head. Besides, I still feel like I don't belong on this court, and maybe if no one sees me wearing it, then they won't question it."

"Oh Gracie, you are so funny," Beans said, followed by her lyrical laugh. "The office would have double checked all the votes before announcing the names. Face it, you are a princess!"

"It just seems so surreal."

"If I were you, I'd just enjoy the moment. You won't be on another Homecoming Court," Beans said with a smile as we sat at our desks just in time for class to start.

Before I knew it, Friday had arrived. I wore the crown, my new dress, and new shoes to school. There would be a pep rally mid-morning where they would present the court and announce the Homecoming Queen in the auditorium rather than the gym. Being in a court with four cheerleaders, I was confident I wouldn't be the queen, and that was fine. Not to sound redundant, but I truly was just glad to be nominated.

When it was time for the crowning of the queen, and all the student body had gathered in the auditorium, the five of us princesses lined up outside the auditorium waiting to be announced. We stood with the senior football player assigned to escort each one of us when we were presented to the student body. My escort was Danny Kyle, who was a funny, well-liked guy I had a very mini crush on. There were so many guys in my graduating class that I had mini crushes on; I didn't want to date them, but I enjoyed their attention when I got it. My sister Katie was always teased about being very boy crazy and here I was just as boy crazy, if not more. I guess I was more successful at keeping it secret than Katie had been. However, none of my mini crushes could compete with Sam.

After what seemed an eternity, the doors to the auditorium opened, and each couple entered when the princess's name was announced. I was second to last.

"Please welcome Princess Grace!" Mr. Baxter announced

from the stage. *Princess Grace? I like it.*

"That's us. Ready?" Danny asked. I nodded as I squeezed his arm.

Entering the auditorium with all the students clapping and cheering, I felt like such an imposter. I couldn't keep from thinking at any moment someone was gonna yell "April Fools!" and this charade would be over, and instead of applauding all the students would point and laugh. I still didn't feel as if I fit into the group. All these girls were cute cheerleaders and I was an actress wannabe. *How did this happen?* It was so dreamlike.

The aisle in the auditorium had never seemed as long as it did that day. As Danny and I proceeded down the aisle, I saw the students' faces turn to watch me pass, as they cheered. Halfway down, Sam stood with his hands in his pockets next to the aisle, watching me. Our eyes locked and I couldn't look away until I saw the little paw of Hoppy snake around his waist, pulling him towards her as I continued toward the stage with the other princesses.

In all honesty, I had to admit it was both exciting and nerve-wracking standing on the stage in anticipation of who would be the queen. The same stage I'd played Madame Pernell where I'd felt in such command of it all. Yet there, I stood as me, not some character, as I waited to hear my fate. I knew I wasn't going be the queen, but deep down I kinda hoped I'd be surprised. I mean, it surprised me to even be on the Homecoming Court. So really anything could've happened. But it didn't happen.

They crowned Shannon Collins Queen. No surprise there. Even though I didn't expect to win, I was still very self-conscious about having lost in front of the whole student body, especially after seeing Sam. However, the fact that I wasn't the lone loser softened the blow a little. Yet, as I stood on the stage under the bright lights, I couldn't help but feel self-conscious. I desperately wanted to leave.

Finally, the court could get out of the spotlight and exit the auditorium ahead of everyone else. I was thankful to have a moment to get used to the fact that I'd lost. I was surprised at the disappointment I felt. After the crowning, the court could leave for the day and prepare for the game that night, so I had the rest of the day to get used to being a mere princess.

"How'd it go?" Asked Mom when I walked in the house.

"They crowned Shannon Collins queen."

"Oh. Is she a nice girl?"

"Yeah," I said as I bit the inside of my cheek.

"Are you glad she was crowned queen?" Mom asked, curiously.

"Gee Mom, I really didn't expect to be queen, but I am surprised at the disappointment I feel having lost."

"Did you want to be queen?"

"No, not really. I guess I kinda hoped that I'd be surprised just like I was when I was nominated onto the court. I don't know how those girls that compete in pageants handle standing in front of an audience and losing. That was tough."

"Losing?"

"No. Just being in front of everyone and trying to look happy that Shannon won. I wasn't angry I'd lost, but I was so self-conscious once I did. But it helped that I wasn't the only one up there," I said with a chuckle

I couldn't tell Mom that my biggest concern about losing was doing it in front of Sam. I worried that all my effort to come across as the happy-go-lucky-everyone's-friend was just smudged in front of him. But my day wasn't over; I had another chance to impress him at the game, and I needed to look my very best. So, with the better part of the day still ahead of me, I hoped that I would accomplish that task.

Since Barry would play in the game, we decided to just meet at the dance. I hadn't seen him all day, and now wouldn't until after the game, making Brutus my chariot for the night.

It was a cold night to be sitting in the little convertible MGs, in my dress and sandals. Never had I been so thankful for my nice wool dress coat my parents had bought me. The JV cheerleaders, which included Hoppy, were cheering the Varsity game since most of the Varsity cheerleaders were on the court. That meant I would have a clear view as the little bunny jumped around cheering while I was seated in the stands, in the section set aside for the court. The upside? I would have a better view of Sam on the field.

The plan for halftime was that the court would arrive sitting on the back seat of the little MG convertibles and when each car arrived at its designated spot, each girl's father would come down the bleacher stairs, help his daughter out of the car, and stand beside her as she was presented to the crowd. So, there we all sat, in our designated car waiting for the buzzer.

When the buzzer sounded signaling halftime, both teams ran into their respective locker rooms. As they jogged off the field the chain-linked gates opened and our little cars slowly entered onto the track that circled the field, and I was in car number three ahead of the queen. I observed how the two previous cars drove up to the designated stop and waited while each girl's dad walked down the steps, helped her out of the car, and stood in line, as planned.

Soon it was my turn. My car pulled up to the same spot as the others.

I heard the announcer say, "Princess Grace!" I stayed seated on the back of the car and waited for Dad, shivering from the cold. I watched with pride as within seconds I saw my sweet wonderful dad—my hero—coming down the steps, and onto the track. He walked up to my little car and helped me navigate successfully out of my car. He had come just like all the other fathers and did something that was way out of his comfort zone. I was so proud to show him off.

After they'd introduced us, our fathers walked us up into the bleachers to our selected bench and left to either go back to their seats or leave for home as my dad would. We stayed and froze, huddled together in the stands with our tiaras sparkling in the stadium lights. But, even with all the pageantry, I was so glad when the game finally ended so we could go inside and get out of the cold.

The Homecoming Committee, which Hoppy was the chairperson, had decorated the cafeteria for the dance with streamers, balloons, and a strobe light. They'd covered all the windows with construction paper, which helped to keep the lights out as cars came and left for the night.

By the time I got there, many other couples had already arrived and were beginning to dance out on the floor. Standing in the doorway, it took a few minutes before I was able to see anyone specific, but I could see that the court was already in place at one end of the room where the queen sat in a big fan-backed styled wicker chair with three of the princesses standing on either side of her. Lights had been arranged so that parents and any students that wished to do so could take pictures of the court.

As I approached the stage, the yearbook photographer stopped me

"So, Gracie," Brandon said, stepping into my path. "Do you have any specific shots you want from tonight?" I looked around the room.

"The norm, I guess. You know, pictures of the court, people dancing having a good time, stuff like that."

"Do you want a picture of the homecoming committee, so we know who put this all together?"

"No. I don't think so."

"So, then just pictures of the court, people dancing, etc," he said repeating my earlier statement.

"Yeah, just a few shots. Then put your camera away and enjoy the rest of the night."

"Thanks," Brandon said smiling really big.

"Do you have a date here?" I asked, curious.

Brandon smiled bashfully, then said, "Yeah. She's on the homecoming committee."

I laughed out loud before I could stop myself. "Aaah, now I understand." Brandon turned twenty shades of red from his neck to his hairline. "Take whatever pictures you want. I trust ya." I was in way too good of a mood tonight. "I better get up on the stage."

"Oh yeah, sure." Brandon said. I took my place next to the other princesses. I was now much more comfortable with my place in the court and I was grateful not to be the queen.

Once the yearbook pictures were out of the way, they required us to remain on display for another ten minutes before we could disperse and join our dates. All the other girls' dates were waiting for them, but I couldn't find Barry anywhere, so I stood on the side of the room waiting for him to show up. I could see Hoppy and Sam out on the floor but hadn't realized I'd been so lost in my thoughts until Sam came walking towards me, alone.

"Where's your date?" Sam asked.

"Who knows. I hope he shows up," I said with a sardonic laugh. "Where's *your* date?" I asked, hoping she'd become ill, they'd broken up, or something that meant I had a chance with him again on this night that I was Princess.

"Something to do with the food for the dance. She's the person in charge, so she had to go take care of it." He said as he stood beside me

"Ah," I said, then turning to him, I asked, "So, tell me, how do you manage to get showered and here so much quicker than Barry? It seems to always take him forever."

Shrugging, he said, "I guess I don't play around as much as he does. He spends a lot of time joking with everyone."

"Sounds about right," I said.

"How d'ya like being a princess?"

"Not bad. Except this tiara hurts my head." I reached up to take it off my head and rubbed the spots where the combs had been. "Wanna try it on?" I moved to put it on his head and he tried to brush my hands away. I chuckled. "C'mon, I know you wanna."

"Get outta here," he laughed and ducked, holding my wrists to stop me from putting the tiara on his head. As we kept up our playful exchange, Barry appeared out of the dark.

"What're you doin' with my date?" Barry asked Sam as he held out my wrist corsage that he'd already removed from the florist container.

"Thanks." I held out my one free arm for Barry to place the corsage, the other one still in Sam's grasp.

"She's trying to put that thing on my head," Sam told him,

motioning to my trapped hand that grasped the tiara.

"Don't believe him," I said, pulling my wrist away. "He was curious as to what it's like to be a princess, so I was gonna let him wear the tiara."

"Liar! I only asked you how *you* liked it," said Sam, laughing. "You need to control your date, Barry." Sam said, putting his hands on my shoulders to push me towards Barry. As if on cue, Hoppy appeared with a sneer on her face, glaring at me.

"Hi babe, what's goin' on here?" she asked, changing to an angelic smile when she gazed at Sam and Barry.

"Nothin'," Sam responded. His hands dropped from my shoulders and into his pockets, "Just waiting for you."

"I'm here now. Let's go dance." Hoppy grabbed Sam's arm and pulled him out on the floor as he gave me and Barry an apologetic smile.

"Gee, what did you do to her?" asked Barry. "She really doesn't like you."

"I have no idea. But it amazes me how big her shadow is over Sam when she is so little."

Barry only raised his eyebrows, then putting his arm around

my shoulders, he directed me towards the refreshment tables at the other end of the cafeteria. "I'm starving. Let's check out the food then go get our picture taken." And as we walked, he took the tiara off my head and put it on his.

"Barry." I laughed, attempting to grab it and take it back.

"What'dya think?" he asked, striking a pose. He was so tall I had to stand back so I could see it, and as I did so, I bumped into Danny and Trevor who were walking past.

"Hey, sor--," Trevor said, but stopped when he saw Barry. "Very pretty. You should wear that to the next game," he suggested while Danny gave a shrill whistle that got the attention of the other guys nearby, who then started to do catcalls at Barry. Embarrassed, Barry took off the tiara and handed it back to me as he played off all the attention.

Just before it was our turn to get our picture taken, I realized that I hadn't given Barry his boutonniere.

"Oh no!"

"What's the matter?" Barry asked.

"I'll be right back," I said as I backed away, ready to run out the side door of the cafeteria.

"Where ya going?" Barry asked, following me.

"I left your boutonniere in Brutus; I need to go get it." As I pushed the door open, I was hit with a blast of cold air that stopped me in my tracks, causing Barry to bump into me, which pushed me further into the cold. Barry grabbed my hand and we trotted over to Brutus. I opened the door and grabbed the little, clear plastic container that held his small ivory-colored rose boutonniere, and we rushed back towards the side door, which was locked. We tried banging on it, but with the music inside, no one noticed us, so we had to make a quick dash to the front of the building.

There were three sets of double doors at the front of the high school, and we pulled on the first two only to find them locked as well. It worried me that we'd have to run all the way around to the back by the stadium to get back in the building, but as luck would have it, when we tried the third set of doors, voila! They opened.

"Oooh, it feels so good in here," I told Barry.

"Oh, quit being such a sissy. It wasn't that cold," Barry teased.

"Says the guy dressed in a suit. What is that, three layers?

I'm only wearing my new dress that was *not* made as winter wear."

We laughed as Barry rubbed my arms with his hands to warm me.

Once inside, we stepped away from the doors as other couples began to enter and I pinned his boutonniere on his jacket the way Mom had shown me earlier in the day. Then we went to get our picture taken before going back into the dance.

In the small room, we watched as Zelda and Ricky posed for their picture in front of the Woodsy background. After they left, we did the typical pose of standing with one arm around each other's waist and holding hands in front. As Barry and I waited for the photographer to take the shot, the guy did a double take and asked, "Are you two brother and sister?" *Really?!*

"Ew!" Barry and I said in unison just as the flash went off. *This'll be a keeper, I'm sure.*

It felt much better walking into the dance this time with Barry. As we walked in, Beans and Johnny came up to us.

"It's about time you got here, Barry." Beans playfully frowned at him.

"I know." Barry feigned contrition, "But I'm here now!" He laughed. "Let's go dance!" Before we could hit the dance floor, a couple of his teammates came up and began to discuss the game, stopping us from getting there. As I stood a couple of steps away from the football summit, lost in my thoughts, a familiar voice spoke in my ear.

"Wanna dance?" I looked around to see Sam with his hands in his pockets, leaning towards me in a conspiratorial way.

"Where is your date?"

"Eh, another emergency," he said, then grabbing my hand, he pulled me toward the floor, "C'mon!"

I dug my heels in and pulled back with the hand that he held as I shook my head in false despair, and said, "She's not gonna like this." He gave my hand another tug and I willingly followed him onto the floor.

"All we're doing is dancing. Besides, it's too dark for her to see us in this crowd. But when she comes into the room, we gotta split up until she leaves," he said, twirling me as we danced to Chantilly Lace.

"Chicken," I said. We laughed and he twirled me again and again, and I tried to keep a smidgen of modesty as my wrap-around dress tried to unwrap.

When Hoppy was in view, we'd stop and pretend to be dancing with someone else, then return to dancing with one another when she was gone.

We danced through two songs, but in between them, I looked at Sam and asked, "Why didn't you applaud for me when I was introduced earlier today?"

"Why should I?" he asked watching other couples.

"Because I'm royalty," I said, causing him to turn to look at me and then laugh. "C'mon, I'm the princess of the people."

"I voted for ya, wasn't that enough?" he asked as he began to dance again.

Wait, what? Did he say he voted for me?

After that, the music was too loud for any type of conversation, so we finished the second dance before going our separate ways, Sam back to wherever Hoppy was and me to Barry who was still talking about the game with a bigger group. He was none the wiser that I'd even been gone. The only tell-tale sign that I'd moved was my damp forehead and the rapid beating of my heart. That was the most fun I had all night. Not even being crowned Queen could have topped that!

Barry and I never made it to the dance floor what with the dance not starting until about 9:30 p.m. and Barry not getting there until about 10 p.m., and with my curfew being at 11:00 p.m., we didn't stand a chance. But that was okay; I had my dances with Sam.

At 11:00 p.m., I begrudgingly told Barry that I needed to go home.

"Already?" he asked

"Yeah. My parents are strict about my curfew, and I'm late now as it is. Sorry." I felt bad for ending the night so soon, especially when it had been such a great game and Barry had played so well. "You can stay if you want, but I gotta get home," I told him, hoping he'd choose to leave with me.

"Nah. It's been a long day, and I'm kinda tired. Besides, what would I do here without my date?"

"Good answer." I smiled. "Do you want a lift home?"

"If you don't mind," he said. Since we were leaving for the night, we had to stop by my locker to get my coat and purse. It amazed me how many couples had chosen the dark hallways to either lean against the lockers or sit on the benches and make out. I would never look at these hallways the same way again.

Pulling up in front of Barry's home, I turned to him. "Thank you for taking me to the dance tonight, I really appreciate it."

"Aaah, no big deal."

"Gee, thanks."

"C'mon, you know what I mean," Barry said, reaching over to gently tap my arm.

"Not really, but that's okay. I just have to consider the source, hehehe," I said, trying to make light of the moment. Barry got out of Brutus and I called out my window. "Thanks again."

As I drove home, I thought about the evening. I wasn't sure what I'd expected to happen, but dancing with Sam while Hoppy was so near wasn't even on the radar. The dances reminded me of our time together Pre-Hoppy: Besides the fact that he was otherworldly gorgeous, he was also fun to hang out with, a good dancer, and a bit adventurous.

"I really miss that guy," I said aloud.

Blondie

Soon it would be time for Spring Homecoming and picking

another court. Barry and I had gone out a few times since Fall

Homecoming and in my, what turned out to be, delusional mind I

thought that we were an "item" and assumed he'd ask me to Spring

Homecoming. But, he hadn't yet, so I put his lateness of asking

down to the fact that I was in the midst of rehearsals and he was

busy with track and basketball.

Since he'd transferred out of drama, I didn't really see him

around the school as often. But his method of operation seemed to

be to wait until the last minute to ask, so I figured I just needed to be patient. I was sure he'd ask, I mean, we were a couple, right? Who else would he ask?

I waited, and waited, and waited, and waited—that's all I could do. I couldn't force him to ask me and as far as my "spies" could find out, he wasn't going to the dance with anyone else. But Spring Homecoming came and left, and I didn't hear a word from Barry.

A couple of weeks later while sitting on the bench outside of the office, Zelda and Milly came up and sat next to me. "Hi Gracie," they said in unison.

"Has anyone ever told you that you should be a model in Seventeen magazine?" I asked Milly.

"Shut up," she said, embarrassed.

"You should. You're perfect for that." Milly had the short cropped hair, perfect tan, and beautiful smile that often graced the magazine's cover.

"Yeah, you should." Zelda said.

Totally red-faced, Milly said, "Thanks, but shut up."

"We have to get to practice, but we have some bad news . . . or, well Milly does, that we thought you should know," Zelda said in a sympathetic voice.

"Bad news?" I questioned. "What bad news? About me?"

Zelda looked at Milly. "You need to tell her. We don't have much time." Hearing that, I could feel the ever-ready butterfly wings twitch. I looked at Milly in expectation. "Wha . . . what's the news?"

Taking a deep breath before she started, she said, "One of my friends goes to high school in Yellowwood and she said that she saw Barry at their Spring Homecoming with a girl from that school." My heart dropped into my stomach when I heard those words.

"It . . . it was Barry? Is she sure?" I stuttered as the butterflies became bats and began to viciously beat against my stomach walls.

"Yeah, she knows Barry."

"I thought you two were dating," Zelda said.

"I thought so too. We've been seeing each other almost weekly since the homecoming dance."

"Gee, I'm sorry Grace," Zelda said as she put her arm around my shoulders.

I hate pity. I hate this feeling. All I want was to be like the other girls with their boyfriends. "Well, I shouldn't expect too much. It's not like I'm gonna marry him." I said hoping they would go to the track meet so I could think. I tried to ask very little of him, but for him to cheat on me . . . that was low. *Maybe we weren't an "item" after all?* "Do you know the girl's name?" I asked Milly.

"I don't. I'm so sorry."

"Um . . . do you know what she looks like?" I stammered.

"All I know is that she's tall with blonde frizzy hair and runs track."

"She's on their track team? Is that how they met?" Feeling the indignation that was overwhelming the hurt that encompassed me. "Well, she can have Barry." I rose from the bench ready to leave when Zelda and Milly stopped me.

"If you wanna see what she looks like, she's here today for the track meet," Milly told me. I stopped. Those words extinguished the indignation, the hurt, and humiliation. I felt overwhelmed.

"I . . . I . . . don't know if I want to. It would be too obvious if I went to the track meet now."

"But Gracie, you always go to his meets. You *not* being there will seem obvious and Barry will know that you know."

"I don't care what Barry thinks." Both girls just looked at me. "Thanks for telling me about this." I weakly smiled at Milly and Zelda. "I gotta get to work," I said.

"We're so sorry Gracie, but we thought you should know."

"Thanks." *I mustn't cry*, I thought.

"No one is gonna be nice to that girl if we see her, Gracie. I promise." Milly crossed her heart.

I tried to laugh. "Good!" I said and watched them walk away, wishing that they hadn't told me about that girl and Barry. *This is déjà vu all over again.*

As I sat there deep in thought about the news I'd just heard, I began to focus on three girls walking towards me from the other end of the hall, dressed in Yellowwood's track uniforms: there were two short brunettes and one tall blonde. I blinked my eyes twice; *this can't be, it's only a mirage*, I told myself. But after blinking one more time it was true. There she was, like a gift from the gods. A tall, skinny girl with yellow over-processed blonde hair and a perm that had gone to frizz. She was holding a blue Jolly Rancher stick candy in her hand, sucking on the exposed portion that made her mouth and teeth blue.

I watched my competition as she continued walking towards me, having no idea who I was or that I even existed. I noted that she was barefoot, and the bottom of her feet were black. *This is who he's cheating on me with?* I thought. *This girl with terrible hair and filthy feet? Was there really a competition?* I stopped myself before going any further along that line of thought. That had been my belief with Sam, and where had that gotten me? She was much closer now, and I could see that she circled her eyes with a thin line of black eyeliner, giving them a very harsh, cheap look. S*o not my style, but obviously Barry's,* I told myself jealously.

Just as the girl was almost standing in front of me, all three turned right and headed down Junior Hall toward the stadium. I watched her walk away for a moment before I grabbed my bag and headed out the opposite way to where Brutus was parked.

As I drove the few minutes from the high school over to the mall, I contemplated this new development. I'd never thought

Barry and I would get married; I wasn't in love with him, but he was as close to a boyfriend as it seemed I'd get. In all reality, he really was my rebound crush after losing Sam to Hoppy. If Barry preferred blondie there was nothing I could do. Once again, I'd lost out to another woman. *Would I never be someone's first choice?* Although the pain wasn't what it had been with Sam, there was still humiliation and a hurt ego for me. At least now I understood why he hadn't asked me to Spring Homecoming.

I thought about my situation throughout my shift that night at the popcorn shop, wondering how I should deal with Barry the next time I saw him. *Should I let him know that I know, or should I pretend ignorance and continue as we are, or as I thought we were?* Deep in my thoughts, as I swept the floor, I began to have a pity party for myself. When I thought I couldn't feel any worse, in walked Sam and Hoppy. I pasted on a fake smile and approached them. "What would you like?" I asked, looking at both.

"Uuuuhm," said Hoppy, gazing with love at Sam. "Gee babe, what would you like for your lunch? I'm buying." She looked at me with a victorious expression. "Give him whatever he wants."

This was the last thing I needed tonight. I looked at Sam and waited for him to decide.

"Just a hot dog and coke, please," responded Sam, avoiding my gaze. That was the Sam I didn't like: the one that had no personality. I couldn't help but wonder if he would have acted differently with me.

Giggling, she said, "You're so cute, babe. Why don't you sit over here, and I'll bring it to you." Hoppy pointed to the wall outside the shop.

Trying to not throw up or dry heave from this act she was putting on for my benefit, I worked quickly getting the drink and placing the last wiener, *besides the one sitting on the wall*, from the rotisserie in a bun, then put both items on the counter by the register instead of delivering it to them like I normally would. As she hopped over, the little bunny continued to give me that victorious smile. I bit my tongue to stop myself from telling Sam we didn't allow animals in the shop.

"That will be one dollar and thirty-nine cents please," I said, still sporting the pasted smile. I couldn't let her know that seeing them together still stung a little.

In a condescending tone, she said, "You're so good at your job. I don't have time to have a job, what with being a cheerleader and having a boyfriend." She dropped the money onto the counter and walked back to Sam.

"Enjoy!" I said as pleasantly as I could muster. I only briefly watched as Hoppy handed Sam her gift of food and leaned forward to receive a kiss. *Why didn't she just wiggle her nose?* I cynically thought before walking behind the curtain to the back where I stayed until they left. I couldn't bear to watch Hoppy's Sam when I preferred the Sam that I knew him to be without her. Did she know that Sam? If not, did she know what she was missing? Did she care?

Seeing those two together helped me decide something regarding Barry: I would do my best to hold onto him until prom. Then perhaps I could leave with my head held high, since as far as relationships I'd be one for two, which was better than *none* for two.

The next day I wore my most flattering dress: a seafoam green number that buttoned down to the waist with a tie belt and mid-thigh slits. It fit my slight frame and showed what curves I had to their best advantage. My thought was that if Barry saw me, maybe he would decide that I looked classier than Ol' Blondie and would choose me over her. This dress gave me the confidence I needed.

Sitting in the first period, which happened to be advanced Algebra taught by Mr. Douchet, I was feeling a million bucks in that dress.

Mr. Douchet had been a football player in college, so he was a big guy that gave the impression that he'd been hit in the head one too many times. Yet, how he got into math I always wondered, and that morning was a perfect example of his teaching skill.

Mr. Douchet was talking about the circumference of a circle, yet he kept calling it the circumcision of the circle. At first, I didn't catch it, but when he said it a second time, I couldn't help myself. "Mr. Douchet," I called, raising my hand.

"What, Kaye?" he said. I got called by my last name so much by the teachers who'd coached my older brother, that it actually surprised me when they called me by my first name.

"Are you sure that it's the circum*cision* of the circle?" I asked, trying to keep a straight face.

"Yes, the circumcision of the circle."

"The circum*cision* of the circle," I repeated. My friend
Danny started to snicker, as did the rest of the class, which made
Mr. Douchet look around. "Don't you mean the cir*cumference* of
the circle?" I innocently asked, causing the class to break out in
laughter and Mr. Douchet to turn beet red with what I thought was
embarrassment mixed with a bit of anger.

"Kaye," he yelled. "Go to the office!"

"Why?"

"Go to the office! Now!" he yelled as he pulled the door
open. I gathered my books and walked to the door.

"But, Mr. D—" He let the door slam shut behind me,
cutting me off. I laughed as I headed to the office.

When I opened the door, I saw the Principal, Mr. Brooks,
standing at the front counter with the office secretary, Mrs. Cook.

"Ooooh!" exclaimed Mrs. Cook. "Don't you look nice."

"Thank you," I said with a big smile.

"Why aren't you in class, Grace?" asked Mr. Brooks.

With a sigh, I said, "Mr. Douchet kicked me out of class

and sent me here."

"Oh dear," said Mrs. Cook.

"What did you do?" asked Mr. Baxter in his deep voice, stepping out of his office.

"Nothing," I said in defense. "He kept calling the "cir*cumfer*ence of the circle" the "circum*cision* of the circle," and I was only trying to get some clarification," I stated, beginning to giggle to myself. All three of them looked at one another. Mrs. Cook turned away and covered her mouth with her hand, and both Mr. Brooks and Mr. Baxter burst out laughing. "You can ask Danny Kyle what happened. All I did was ask Mr. D if he really meant the circumcision of the circle." I wasn't rude about it." Taking a deep breath to stop laughing, both Mr. Brooks and Mr. Baxter looked at me. Mrs. Cook walked out of the room unable to contain her laughter.

"All right, Grace. Go back to class," directed Mr. Brooks.

"Make sure you're back here later for the ASB meeting!" Mr. Baxter hollered after me. As the office door closed, I heard all three laughing. I was glad they saw the humor of the situation. I stood outside the office deciding whether I'd go back to class or not, and it didn't take me long to decide. I didn't go back to class; I had a dress to show off.

After the second period, Mr. Douchet stood in the hall next to his door talking to Trevor Baxter and Sam. I walked past, hoping that Mr. D. wouldn't notice me, but I overheard a little of their conversation,

"Wow, Gracie looks really nice today," commented Trevor

"Yeah, but she's such a smart ass," retorted Mr. D., with a sigh. "Kaye, get over here," he yelled at me over the heads of the other students in the hall. I clenched my teeth thinking I had been that close to a clean get away, then turned and smiled as I walked towards the trio, "Look, Kaye, sorry about sending you to the office."

"I'm sorry I asked for clarification on the circumcision of the circle," I responded with a straight face.

Looking at me, Sam asked incredulously, "You called it the *circumcision* of the circle?!" He laughed.

"Not me." I fought the urge to smile and hurried away.

"Kaye! Dammit!" shouted Mr. D while both Sam and Trevor continued to laugh. I hoped they'd be able to calm Mr. D down. I stayed clear of him for the rest of the day.

The next couple of periods were going by without incident until halfway through the fourth period when Mr. Baxter's voice boomed through the intercom, "Could all the ASB presidency and council please come to the office." That was my cue to get out of Econ early. I grabbed my books and with a quick wave to Sam, I headed towards my locker to leave my books, since I wouldn't need them for the rest of the day. Then I made a quick stop at the restroom to make sure I looked okay and that my makeup wasn't smeared. After that I continued down the hall, surprised to find Sam standing at his locker. Giving him a confused look, I walked towards him asking, "What are—" when I heard,

"Dogpile on Gracie!"

My last thought before I found myself on the floor was, *"They wouldn't dare."* They dared.

Danny Kyle started the dogpile, so he was on top of me, but had braced himself so that I didn't feel the weight of everyone on top of me. The pile comprised of the rest of the presidency and council, who were mostly football players (I was the only girl). As I pretended to be appalled by such behavior and attempted to get out from under all those smelly guys, I looked over at Sam

standing by his locker observing.

"Help," I called out to him, but all he did was shrug his

shoulders in a helpless gesture and laugh.

That's when I heard Mr. Baxter's booming voice, "Gracie,

we can't have you causing so much commotion and trouble in the

hallway."

"But Mr. Baxter," I began as I struggled to get free, "they

jumped on me." The guys just laughed.

Mr. Baxter ordered over his shoulder, "Get off Gracie and

let's get this meeting started. With those instructions, the guys

carefully removed themselves from the pile and pulled me to my

feet, laughing. I loved those guys and I *loved* the attention.

It had to be the dress. The dress was *magic*! I especially

loved that Sam had seen this whole fun episode while standing in

the hallway as we left for the meeting. Did he now see just how

popular I was and how everyone liked me? *Does he regret*

choosing Hoppy yet?

At lunchtime, I saw Barry for the first time since I'd been

told the news of the "other" woman. I'd concluded that I needed to act as though I knew nothing and continue on as we were. I mean, once again, nothing had been stated between us that we were exclusive, so I really had no authority to make any kind of claim on his time. *I've got to start getting these guys to state their intentions,* I told myself.

"You look really nice today," Barry said, sitting next to me on the bench in Senior Hall and placing his hand on my knee.

"Thank you. What have you been up to?" I asked, acting the epitome of sweetness.

"Just busy with track."

"Track, huh?" I asked. I couldn't let my hurt show.

"Why haven't I seen you at any of the meets?" he asked, oblivious to my hurt feelings.

Shaking my head, I said, "Just been too busy myself."

As Barry got up to leave, he turned and asked, "Hey, will I see you at the game on Friday?"

"Of course."

"Wanna meet at the dance after?"

Surprised I answered, "Sure. Like a date?"

Barry chuckled, "Yes, a date, you knucklehead." Ah, this

was a term of endearment from him. Perhaps Blondie had only been a fluke and, once again, my imagination had over-reacted?

"That would be fun." Sitting on the bench basking in the warm glow I felt thinking I had a boyfriend, again. I watched him walk down the hallway, and I looked at my dress, *"This dress was mmmagic!!" I really need to wear it more often.*

Friday came and I was in very high spirits; Barry and I seemed to be good. He'd been stopping by the shop at night after practice again. I kept imagining how nice it would be to show up at the school tonight now that I was sure Blondie had only been a one-time thing and that it was me he really liked. My self-esteem was inflating to normal again.

At the basketball game I watched Sam . . . uh, I meant Barry play and was pleased to think I had a "date" with him after the game. I sat in the Pep Club section and took part hoping Sam—again, I meant Barry—would notice me when he wasn't playing. Sam—I still meant Barry (*This was getting embarrassing, darn it!*)—must see how much spirit I had at these games. But in all truth, Sam, and I meant Sam this time, looked so good in his basketball uniform, running up and down the court or even just sitting on the bench, that I struggled to remember Barry at all. *Why did he choose Hoppy over me?*

Not Again

I came to the game to watch Barry not Sam. I'd watched the game and Sam—grrr!, Barry! Barry! Barry! Barry! We won the game and Barry had played great, making over half the points. Beans and I stayed afterward to help Zelda and the other cheerleaders, including Hoppy, clean up our section in the bleachers. I monitored the locker room door, hoping that Barry would come out and we could walk to the dance together instead of me going to the dance alone and waiting for him.

As we exited the gym into the area near the front doors, out of the corner of my eye I thought I saw Blondie walking down the hall. But when I turned to look, I couldn't see her or anyone that looked like her. The crowd was still leaving the building out all the doors, depending on where they'd parked, so it could've just been someone with her hair perhaps.

Before I could stop myself, I asked, "Beans, did you see Blondie here?"

"Where?"

"Down that hallway to the cafeteria," I said, "I thought it was her. Do ya think Barry invited her?"

"He better not; he has a date with you at the dance!"

Laughing in relief, I said, "You're right. He has a date with me. Why would he invite her?" I shook my head to rid my mind of the self-doubt flooding in. Just then Zelda came up to see if we wanted to go grab a taco before heading to the dance. As we walked to Beans' car I kept looking around for any sign of Blondie, but maybe I'd only imagined her. I kept telling myself it didn't matter if she was there. Barry had made a date with me for the dance, not her.

Having taken our time getting dinner, we arrived back at the cafeteria a little over an hour later.

"Do you see Barry anywhere?" I asked Beans.

"No," she said. "And, he isn't someone you can easily miss."

"Maybe he went to grab some food." I suggested and I resigned myself to standing on the sideline waiting for him, as usual.

Since he wasn't at the dance yet, Beans and I stood near the wall waiting and Zelda and her boyfriend headed to the dance floor. They'd only been on the dance floor a couple of minutes when Zelda came over and said, "Ricky just told me that Barry left to get some food after the game and will be here soon."

I smiled. "Thanks, Zel. I need to go wash my hands, wanna come with me?" I asked turning to Beans. She nodded and followed me out of the cafeteria.

"Do you see Barry here yet?" I asked Beans as we returned to the dance.

"No."

"I hope he remembers," I said

"You guys wanna dance?" asked Trey and Chuck.

"Sure," responded Beans.

"Yeah," I said, and we both followed them out to the floor.

"Where's Barry? I thought you'd be here with him." Trey said as we danced.

"I'm not sure. He asked me to meet him here, but Ricky said he went to get food, so hopefully he'll be here soon—before I have to leave." We continued to dance a couple more dances.

The song had just ended and we were walking off the dance floor when the crowd suddenly got louder.

"There's Barry," Beans said pointing towards the middle of the dance floor.

"It's about time!" I felt a wave of relief seeing him and his friends and headed towards him. When the strobe light passed over his group, there was Blondie standing right next to Barry. He was with Blondie! She had been at the game. I hadn't imagined it. I'd waited all this time and he came to the dance with Blondie, and both were holding the same large cup from the same restaurant.

I stood frozen at the edge of the dance floor and stared at them in disbelief unaware that a new song had begun. I watched as they started dancing in the middle of the floor, laughing and talking loud to one another. I felt as if someone had punched me in the gut and I was deflating beyond my control. I was sure all the lights were shining down on me and everyone could see the humiliation I felt. I tried to not cry as I stood there and looked at him and Blondie dancing together oblivious of me. Then he looked over my way, our eyes locked for a moment before I turned away.

"Beans, I can't do this, I gotta go." And I walked as fast as I could out of the room, with her following.

"Do you want me to go with you?" she asked, always the good friend.

"No, you stay and have fun. I gotta go." I walked down the dark hall as quickly as I could, not seeing Sam and Hoppy until I ran into Sam.

"Sorry," I said, wiping a tear so he wouldn't see.

"Are you okay?" he asked, grabbing my arm to stop me.

"Yeah," I responded without looking at him.

"She's fine, Sam. Let her go," Hoppy demanded in a bored tone.

I couldn't let him see me crying, especially over someone like Barry. "Yeah, I'm fine." Still not looking at him, I pulled my arm out of his grasp and ran out the door, heading to Brutus.

Once I got in Brutus, I sat in the dark and cried as I dealt with my bruised ego. *Why did guys always choose the other girl?* I kept asking myself as I sat alone. When I'd finished my cry and feeling totally dejected, I drove home, I realized that it was past my curfew and I'd be in trouble when I got there. On top of everything that had happened, I didn't feel like being yelled at by mom for getting home late so I decided I'd have to use this incident to my benefit. As I walked through the back door into the kitchen, I could see Mom get up from the couch and walk straight towards me with a very cross look on her face, that was my cue to let the tears flow again.

Sobbing, I cried, "Mom, Barry came to the dance with another girl." I stood in front of her and let it flow.

"With another girl?" she echoed, "But he asked you to the dance."

"I know." I blew my nose, "but I had to wait for him and then he showed up with another girl and was dancing with her as if he'd forgotten about me." I sniffled.

"What a puke," my Momma bear said, putting her arm about me. "You go to bed and don't worry about him. He doesn't deserve you," she said, walking me towards my room.

I sniffled. "Thanks, Mom. It just hurts."

"I know. Go to bed." She left me alone as I sat on my bed, quietly crying.

Okay . . . okay, I shouldn't have played my mother like that, but the tears *were* real. I couldn't handle her yelling at me for being fifteen minutes over my curfew when I'd just been humiliated, for the second time, by Barry. And, this time, most of the school and all my friends had witnessed it. He'd made it clear who he chose, and it wasn't me. I'd been stood up for a girl with yellow, frizzy hair.

Saturday morning Beans called to see how I was doing after what happened at the dance, "Are you okay?"

"Yeeeeah," I responded half-heartedly.

"I'll never speak to Barry again."

"I don't think I will either," I said, seeing any hope of going to prom disappear. With a heavy sigh, I sat there in miserable silence, which really wasn't good during a phone conversation.

"Graaaaaace . . . c'mon, cheer up."

194

"I know." I groaned and sighed again.

"Grace?"

"Yeah?"

"Did you see Sam and Hoppy when you were leaving last night?"

"Yeah, I bumped into them."

"Did you tell them what happened?"

"No." I responded, "I'd just begun to cry when I ran into them, but I don't think they noticed. Why?"

"Well, after you'd left Barry came looking for you, and just as he was asking where you'd gone, Sam approached us asking what had happened . . . why you were crying. So, I told him how Barry had asked you to meet him at the dance after the game and then showed up with another girl."

"No way!" This news caused me to sit up in my chair. "You told Sam that, in front of Barry? What happened? What did Barry do? Did Sam say anything?" Beans laughed at the other end of the line.

"Oh Grace, I wish you could've been there. It was great!

"Wh-what happened?" I asked.

Still laughing, she said, "Sam gave Barry this disgusted look and said, 'Not cool.' And Barry was all apologetic saying that Blondie met him and his friends at the restaurant, and Sam repeated that it wasn't cool hurting Gracie. Then he said, 'I like you Barry, but don't make it so I have to teach you how to treat a girl like Gracie.' You could see in Sam's eyes that he wasn't playing."

"What was Hoppy doing while this was going on?"

"Ho ho ho! Oh, Gracie, that was the most beautiful part! She was turning purple she was so pissed at Sam and she kept trying to pull him away. But Sam wouldn't leave until he'd made it clear to Barry that he had to treat you better or else."

"Or else what?" I asked curiously.

"That's what Barry asked."

"No way!"

"Yeah. And by this time, they are standing almost nose to nose."

"Oh, I wish I could've seen this," I whined. "Then what happened?"

"Don't know, but I swear, Sam was on the verge of fighting

Barry."

"You don't know what happened?" I asked.

"No! Hoppy pushed Sam away and Barry got pulled back on the floor with his friends and that girl."

I rolled my eyes. "Oh gee, I can see he really felt bad."

"I'm sorry, Gracie," Beans said trying to console me, "But, gee . . . Sam was sure in your corner. I've never seen him like that before and I've known him since grade school. And Gracie, ya gotta remember that Barry's only sixteen. He's too immature to see the great girl you are."

"Yeah, you're right. I do forget that," I sighed.

It felt good to hear about what happened after I left. Barry might not have been too affected by my taking off, but Sam had stepped up as my protector. No one had ever done that for me before that wasn't my brother. *What was he doing?*

THE Production

Since Mr. H's departure and Ms. Budapest's mental breakdown, my aspirations for my senior year in drama hadn't really panned out as I'd hoped. Yet, once the school hired the new drama teacher, Mrs. Amalfi—who seemed to have all her wits about her— everything started looking up.

Mrs. Amalfi had decided that the drama class would perform the play "Harvey", a play about a seven-foot-tall invisible rabbit who was made famous when Jimmy Stewart played the part of Elwood P. Dowd on both stage and screen. I'd seen the movie a few times and could hardly wait to do the play.

By the time Mrs. Amalfi began teaching, most everyone from the original class had already jumped ship: Zelda, Beans, and Barry to be specific. People I'd never performed with before surrounded me, many who'd never been in a production of any kind but felt that drama would be "fun" and decided to "give it a shot." Just the thought of it made me roll my eyes.

I was cast as the female lead, Veta Louise Simmons, opposite Larry Bronson as Elwood. This was the first time Larry had been in the drama class in high school, but he'd taken it in Junior High. Although he wasn't Barry, I didn't mind his rendition of Elwood. Larry always came ready for rehearsal with his lines memorized, which was more than I could say for the rest of the cast.

Opening night was two days away and we were in the midst of dress rehearsals, correcting all the bugs that other cast members were intent on including in the performance. Specifically, a scene towards the end of the play where Veta and her daughter, Myrtle-Mae, played by Marge Briemer, were in their living room and Veta couldn't find her purse.

"Marge, please do not mention the purse on the table. Let

Gracie find it," Mrs. Amalfi told Marge for the hundredth time.

"Why can't I have it and just give it to her?" Marge asked.

"Because, her character needs to be able to credit finding the purse to Harvey, which shows that she is believing he exists."

"I don't get it."

With a heavy sigh, our teacher said, "Please just do it that way, ok?" The exhaustion she must have felt having to deal with Marge was becoming obvious. "Let's run through that portion once more," she said.

I entered the stage and began to look around for my purse. While I searched, I recited my line asking where the purse was, to which Marge quickly said, "It's right here," and she picked up the purse from off the little side table, and victoriously said, "You just put it there." Then she laughed her stupid laugh.

"Mrs. Amalfi," I bellowed.

"I know, Gracie," said Mrs. Amalfi, walking down and stopping in front of the stage.

"This isn't going to work," I said. "If she can't get this line, or even the whole concept of this scene, it'll be ruined." I was exhausted and out of patience from dealing with this person.

"Let's stop here and everyone can go home," instructed Mrs. Amalfi. "Marge, I'd like you to stay after and we will work on this scene some more." I felt bad for Mrs. A, but she was the one who cast Marge, so it was her responsibility to make sure her performance was up to par. The last thing I heard as I was leaving was, "Now let's start at the beginning. Why do you think we need to hide the purse on the table?"

It was opening night, which is kinda funny to say since with only two nights to perform the play, the next night was closing night. Anyway, here it was opening night and you could feel the excitement in the air, mingled with my nervousness since I'd be performing with so many novices. I knew that Larry was ready, and I could depend on him to help carry the performance; it was Marge that concerned me.

Standing in the wings waiting for the curtain to go up, I could feel the butterflies gently fluttering in my stomach. Being nervous before a performance was always a good sign to me; it gave me the confidence that it would be a great show. Soon, the lights went down in the house, the curtain went up and everyone quietly waited in the wings as Elwood opened the play with his first line.

We were off! Everyone hit their marks, entered on their cues, and the audience laughed in all the right places. That is, until we got to the scene with Myrtle-Mae, played by Marge. I'd just told Elwood that I want nothing to happen to him and I moved downstage while waiting for Marge to enter. As I stood there feeling confident, I did something I hadn't done for a long time—I dropped the "fourth wall" so that I could see past the footlights who was in the audience. And who should I see sitting in the front row? None other but Sam and Hoppy.

In theater, there's something we call the "fourth wall" which is just an imaginary wall between actors and the audience. This fourth wall makes it so I could look out at the audience, but never see them. This was a protection for me when I'd perform; it kept me in the imaginary world and my nerves at bay. In the past, I'd learned that if I looked at the audience, then I got too nervous and would end up in my head and lose my character. Especially if I saw someone I knew in the audience. Therefore, I *never* dropped the fourth wall. *So why'd I do it tonight?!*

Once I saw Sam, my butterflies went crazy. I immediately

moved inside my head and began obsessing that he was right there, watching me. However, before my confidence crashed through the floor, I realized that I was wearing a very grown-up fabulous, form-fitting, sparkly, brown dress that the director had lent me for the play, and this dress looked good on my naturally thin frame.

Seeing Sam at the play was a small victory, and in the front row no less, but that would have to wait. It was time for Marge to enter onto the stage, and she did, with her hands in her pockets, as usual, and plopped down on the couch. She wasn't Myrtle-Mae, but Marge on stage. Crossing my fingers and hoping for a miracle, I moved back upstage and said my line regarding the whereabouts of my purse, then began the motions of hunting for it, still very aware that Sam was in the front row. *Make sure your tummy's flat,* I told myself since he'd see my profile. *I may not be the prettiest girl, but I had a good shape—that I know.*

"Here it is," said Marge pulling the purse out of her pocket and holding it up triumphantly. Her actions shocked me out of my head. She continued, "I put it in my pocket so we wouldn't lose it." This blew my mind. I stood there stunned. It was as if we'd never rehearsed this bit before.

"Thank you, Myrtle-Mae," came out of my mouth before I realized it, and Marge sat there laughing like a loon. I couldn't believe she could take it so lightly. I was furious! There had been so many people who'd put so much time into building sets, sewing costumes, the make-up, selling tickets, buying tickets, etc. *How could she be so disrespectful?* But we carried on and continued to the end and received a standing ovation, no thanks to Marge. But the night wasn't over yet.

Earlier in the week, I'd received some fan mail.

"Here's something I found in my box addressed to you," Mrs. Amalfi said, holding out a letter.

"For me? What is it?" I asked, taking it from her.

"Open it and see." It was a letter from a drama class in a neighboring town. They were coming to see 'Harvey' and wanted to meet me after the show. In the letter, the teacher wrote that she'd been bringing her students to all of my other performances and since this would be my last one in the area, she thought it would be nice if her students met me.

"Wow. I've never gotten a fan letter before," I said, handing the letter to Mrs. A.

"It looks like they want to meet you after the play on closing night," she said.

"I can't do that. What would I say? What would I do?"

"Well, we can't disappoint them since they've already bought tickets."

"I know that, but what if they are disappointed after meeting *me*? Isn't there something else we could do?" I asked, desperate for help.

"Well . . . why don't we have a 'meet and greet' after the show with some snacks and they can meet the whole cast, taking the stress off of you?"

"That's a brilliant idea!" I said with relief.

So, that's what we did. We set up a meet and greet in the cafeteria for after the show with the visiting drama class. I was more nervous about this than the performance. *What if they were disappointed with my performance and regretted making the trip?*

In the beginning, the students were shy, but soon they warmed up and began to pepper the cast with questions: about our characters in the play like if we wanted to be professional actors, stuff like that. It ended up being a fun event and the visiting students seemed to really enjoy meeting all the cast members. All in all, it was a good night. Hopefully, the closing night would be as successful.

On the closing night, we had standing room only and it seemed most of the student body was in attendance. As always, they were very receptive to our performance and laughed willingly and often. Tonight, at my first opportunity I dropped the fourth wall again and I wasn't disappointed. Sitting in the front row, sans his little carrot muncher, was Sam. *What is he doing?* It might've been wishful thinking, but I believed our eyes met for only a moment, and it was enough to throw off the rest of that scene.

The energy that passed between the audience and the cast was tangible. It was an astounding night! We were feeding off each other. Mrs. Amalfi had spoken with Marge the previous night, and for this last performance, during our scene, she actually sat quietly while I did my search, found the purse and said my lines—that was another small victory. Two victories in two nights, who could ask for more?

One thing I noticed both nights though, was no Barry. I didn't know if he came and left or if he didn't even bother coming at all. I was still not talking to him, but I would've loved to have known that he'd come to the play and had seen me in the dress.

And, yes it was a good production, but if we could have done the show together with him playing Elwood, then it would have been a *GREAT* production. As it was, it was *THE* Production: the only one for the year and Sam had been to both performances and didn't say one word to me either after the show or in the classes we had together. Even after our eyes locked each night, not one word—that is until our econ class the day after the closing night.

"Hey Gracie, great show last night," called Allan as he walked over to his desk.

"You came?"

"Yeah. That is a really fun play."

"Thanks! Did you come alone?

"Nah, Brian and Chuck were with me."

"Well thanks for coming, I'm glad you enjoyed it," I said. Now was my chance to bring it up with Sam, who had taken his seat behind me. So, turning to him, I asked, "Did you see the play?"

"Nah."

"Liar! I saw you there." I sat looking at him, amazed, not only at his supreme gorgeosity, but at the twinkle in his eye which let me know he was teasing me. *Why wouldn't he admit to seeing the play, not just once but twice?* But I couldn't say anything else because Mr. Fremont had started the class. I only gave Sam one last glare before turning around in my seat.

It wasn't the great year for my drama class that I had hoped for. But it was a great way to end the year, with a little Harvey as an homage to my favorite actor. And, just like Elwood and Harvey at the end in the Hollywood movie, my senior year and I would walk into the sunset together.

Seven?!

Monday

This year was going by so fast! There it was, already time for the Senior Prom and choosing a court. Every Senior girl was nominated for Prom Court and, like Homecoming, the whole school would vote on five girls that would comprise the court. Like Fall Homecoming, I didn't expect to be nominated to the court, nor did I want to be this time. I didn't want to go through the stress I had felt at Homecoming of getting a date.

Those who can easily get a date should be the ones on the court. With me not speaking to Barry there was zilch to none chance of me going to prom. I couldn't think of anyone who would want to ask me, so I expected to be sitting at home with my parents. *Maybe I'll ask to work that night.*

It was with a sigh of relief when they announced the court and I was not on it. True, it would have been flattering to be on the court, but only if I had a date. I was okay with four of the nominees, but the fifth I didn't really get: Janice was a cute girl that had moved to Ashbury this year, and it surprised me that enough people knew who she was to vote her on the court. But obviously there were.

The day after they announced the Prom Court, I was sitting on the bench at the end of Junior Hall learning a monologue Mrs. Sawyer had assigned all her students to memorize and recite in class.

"Hi, Grace."

Looking up from my book, there stood Ms. Hoppity herself—Hoppy. "Hi Sara Jane," I said. She hadn't spoken to me since she purchased that sumptuous feast at the shop for Sam.

She sat next to me. "Did you know that I'm on the Prom Committee?" she asked, a bit too cheerful.

I shook my head. "Nope. I didn't know that. How'd you get on that committee?" I asked, not really caring to hear her answer.

"Sam thought it would be fun for me to do."

"Did he." I turned back to my book.

"What do you think of the girls that got on the court?"

I glanced up from my book. "It's fine, I guess. Makes no difference to me."

"It should. You were almost on it."

"All of the senior girls were almost on it," I said sarcastically.

Hoppy gave a condescending snort, "No, that's not what I meant. *You* were almost on it."

"What do y'mean?"

"It was a tie between you and Janice. I had the deciding vote." She smiled at me as if to say "gotcha!" and walked away. It stunned me that she'd go out of her way to tell me that. I didn't think I'd ever understand why she disliked me so much. She got the guy, not me.

Prom was three weeks away and I had not yet spoken to Barry; he'd tried to talk to me a couple of times, but I'd pull a Sam and just walk away. Besides, I was too busy to worry about him. We were down to the wire on getting the yearbook ready for printing. We just needed the pictures of the Prom Court, then we could turn it in. I was excited for all the different ideas that Sabrina and I had put into the book; hopefully, the school would feel the same way. Unbeknownst to me, this coming week would prove way more interesting than finishing the yearbook or anything else that had happened that year that didn't include Sam.

The day Hoppy informed me that I was not on the court because of her, I was in the art class working on the yearbook when I looked into the hallway and saw Hal Sampson sitting on the bench opposite the classroom door and acting rather nervous. Hal was known in the school as a wild boy and doing drugs, but he was a nice guy and harmless, so I walked out to sit next to him and chat.

"Hey Hal, how's it going?" I asked with a smile.

Nodding his head but not looking at me, he said, "Good."

"I haven't seen you around much this year, where ya been?" I asked, even though rumor had it that he was down behind the bleachers getting high.

"Working." He didn't seem to really want to talk so I got up to go back in my class. "Wait a sec, would ya?" he asked, looking at me.

"Sure. What's up?" I said, sitting back down on the bench.

"Um . . . would you like to go to prom with me?" He was so nervous; I felt bad for him. But there was no way I wanted to deal with that mess on my last prom. I had to think fast so that I wouldn't hurt his feelings.

"Oh, I'm sorry, I've already been asked. But, thanks for asking." *This is lie number one.*

"Sure." He stood up from the bench. "If your date doesn't work out, will you let me know? I'd really like to take ya." He smiled.

"Sure." I smiled back.

I watched as Hal walked away and silently prayed that Barry or someone not as wild would ask me to prom. Yes, I knew I wasn't talking to Barry, but it wasn't like that couldn't change.

Tuesday

I'd arrived at school fifteen minutes earlier than normal to finish some homework in the Library. I stopped at my locker to get my books and paper, and when I closed the locker door, there stood Fred, which scared the crap out of me. I hadn't even heard him approach.

"Hey, Gracie."

"Oh, hi, Fred. Ya scared me." Fred Barnes was about an inch shorter than me and was a rather quirky redhead, and someone I didn't see around the halls that often.

"Sorry 'bout that. Didn't mean to. I wanted to ask ya something."

"Sure," I said. "I need to go to the library." I motioned for him to follow.

"Do you have a date to prom yet?" he asked

I sighed, then gave him a smile. "Why do you ask?" I said, holding my breath. I had *no* interest in this guy. *Please don't ask me to prom. Please don't ask me to prom.* I repeated over and over in my head as I smiled and walked, waiting.

"I was wondering if you'd go with me?" He stopped in front of me and gave me the sweetest smile he could muster. *If only I was interested in gingers.*

"I'm so sorry Fred, but I already have a date," I lied. *Oh, I was going to hell. Two lies in two days.* I inwardly moaned. I stepped around Fred and entered into the library. He followed me in. "Please go with me," he begged.

I didn't even know what to say to this. "I-I-I'm sorry, I can't. I've got a date already." I said, turning from him and walking towards an empty table.

Again, he begged, "Pleeeeease go with me. Pleeeeeease." He sat down at the table before I could. I looked at him, stunned.

"Fred I'm sorry, but I really can't," I sternly responded, embarrassed for him. Now I really didn't care about being polite. Why was he begging? Didn't he realize how pathetic it made him look? I turned and left the library, horrified by his actions. *I'll have to avoid him for the rest of the year if he doesn't avoid me on his own*, I told myself.

The rest of the day was uneventful, and I began to forget the morning's Fred episode. When I walked out to Brutus to head to work, I heard my name called, so I turned around and saw George doing a light jog in my direction. George was my height, a member of Future Farmers of America, and was on the wrestling team. He was a super nice guy and we'd probably chatted twice this year, and both times he had some chewin' tobacco in his lip— major turn-off, especially when he turned his head and spat into a cup he carried with him. I hoped he didn't have it in his lip this time, but as he walked towards me, he lifted the cup to his mouth and spit. *Grrross!*

"Hey, Grace."

"Hi, George."

"Grace, I know we've only talked a couple of times, but I was hopin' you'd go to prom with me." *You've got to be kiddin' me! He was asking me to prom.*

Feeling exasperated, I responded, "Gee George, thanks for thinking of me, but I've already been asked." I wasn't lying this time; I had been asked twice before.

Shrugging his shoulders, he said, "Well, it was worth a try. You're one of the funniest girls. I thought it'd be a hoot hanging out with you; maybe some other time." He spat into his cup and smiled.

"Sure." I inwardly cringed as I opened Brutus' door and quickly got in and drove away. *What in the heck was going on?!*

I'd been asked to prom three times in two days, and not by one person I wanted. Barry or someone that I actually liked needed to ask me. This was crazy!

Wednesday

I told no one about this sudden flurry of guys I wasn't interested in asking me to prom. I couldn't understand what was going on; it was so not normal. Was someone putting them up to it? They were all so random. What made them decide to ask me? I just needed to wait and hope someone else would ask, otherwise I wouldn't be going to prom.

I'd been having a good day; so far I'd made it through with no more invitations to prom and my shift at work was rather humdrum. No one seemed to be shopping. I'd just handed Sam his hot dog and soda and was standing by the popcorn bin with my back to the main entrance when Sam motioned to me that there was someone standing by the candy section of the counter. Looking over my shoulder, I saw Ted, a sophomore who I'd seen in the halls a couple of times and who played on the JV Football team.

"I'll be right back," I told Sam and walked over to the guy. I smiled as I asked, "Can I help you?"

Giving me a huge grin, he said, "Can I get a large Sprite, please?"

"Sure," I walked back to where the soda machine was, then asked, "Anything else?" I said, putting the cup under the soda spout.

"Yeah, will you go to prom with me?"

This startled me enough that I jerked the cup to the side, spilling Sprite all over my uniform and the floor. "Whoops! Sorry, just hold on a sec. S—sorry."

After gaining my composure, I wiped off what I could with a moist towel I had nearby to avoid the stickiness, before dropping the towel on the floor and using my foot to wipe up the spilled soda.

"All right there?" asked Sam

"Yup," I responded. Since my back was to Ted, he didn't see me roll my eyes at his question, but Sam had stopped in mid-chew watching my reaction. "You're kidding," I said, looking over my shoulder at Ted.

"No, I really want to go with you," Ted nodded, his eyes bright.

Half turning in disbelief, I said, "You want me to go to prom with you?"

"Yeah, will you go with me?"

While searching for words, I walked to the counter and set the cup of soda down in front of him. "I don't think you can go to the prom, Ted, it's just for juniors and seniors."

"I can if I go with you."

I looked at him as I bit the inside of my lip in thought, and asked, "So, you're just asking me because you wanna go to prom?" *This was a new approach.*

"No, that's not the reason."

"Do you have your license? Can you drive?" I asked, wondering what to say to avoid hurting him.

"I have my learner's permit. I'll be sixteen in two months," he said with pride.

"Gee, Ted, prom isn't in two months, more like three weeks."

"Then you can drive. I don't mind."

I laughed before I could stop myself. "It's really sweet of you to ask, but I'd prefer to go with someone who can drive *me*. I'm sorry."

Gone was the smile. "Okay. It didn't hurt to ask. You could've always said yes."

"I'm sorry, but thanks for asking," I said as Ted walked away. Turning to Sam I held my hands out, giving him a confused look questioning what had just happened.

He chuckled, then asked, "Have you been asked to prom before tonight?"

"Would you believe that's the fourth time," I told him as I walked back to where he stood eating his hot dog.

"Fourth?" he asked in disbelief.

"Is that so hard to believe?" I raised my eyebrows.

"Well, no . . . of course not," he stuttered. "I mean . . . four? Have you accepted any?"

"No one I wanna go with has asked me yet."

Thursday

I talked Beans and Zelda into eating lunch in the cafeteria

because it was fish sticks day, and I loved fish sandwiches. As we progressed forward in the line to get our food, somehow a younger student had stepped in front of me, separating us. So, after Zelda and Beans paid for their food, they motioned to me they'd find a table. I stood in line waiting for the student in front of me—who was digging in her bag the size of Mary Poppins'—to get enough money to buy lunch. I looked over at Beans and Zelda who were laughing at me and made faces at them, trying to communicate my frustration.

Finally, it was my turn. I paid my two dollars and as I headed towards our table, Johnny, who took me to prom last year, crossed in front of me and bumped my tray out of my hands where it crashed on the floor.

I groaned. "Great!"

"Oh man, I'm sorry," he said, "I wasn't watchin' where I was going."

"What're you doing here?" I asked as I began picking up fish sticks, bun, and using my napkin to wipe tartar sauce off the floor.

"It's fish sticks day; love fish sticks."

221

"A man after my own heart. They're the best, right?" We laughed as we piled all the food from the floor back onto my tray.

"Hey, has Barry asked you to prom yet?" he asked, picking up my tray as we both stood.

"No, but just about everyone else has."

"What?"

I shook my head. "Nothing. I'm hoping he will, but I'm still kinda hurt about what happened at the dance."

"Yeah, that was a jerk move." Then he laughed. "When Mr. D heard about it, he made Barry run stairs."

"Hahaha! Perfect." I couldn't help but show my glee at this news.

"If he doesn't ask you to prom, after we beat the crap out of him, I'll take you if you'd like," he said, making me laugh.

"Gee thanks Johnny, that's hilarious! I might just avoid him for that very reason."

"Gracie, we don't like seein' ya hurt. Guys can be jerks. I know, I am one." He pointed at himself, laughing.

"You're sweet Johnny, and honestly the only one I'd go with if Barry didn't ask. I'll let you know."

222

"Okay." Johnny grinned at me and walked away after that leaving me in the lunch line to attempt getting my fish sticks fix again. With my mind spinning, I couldn't believe that there were now five guys willing to take me to prom. This had to be a first for someone like me.

Walking up to the table where Beans and Zelda were just finishing their lunch, I set my tray down. "You won't believe what Johnny just told me." I said, laughing.

"What'd he say?" they asked in unison. I relayed the whole conversation. When I told them that Johnny had said the guys were gonna beat Barry up if he didn't ask me to prom, we began to laugh and joke about it. We knew he wouldn't get beat up, but it was nice to imagine revenge that sweet. I still hadn't told either of them about the four other guys who'd asked me to prom—that I'd keep to myself.

Friday

It was the last day of the week and still Barry had not asked me to prom. I'd seen him around but hadn't stopped to talk to him because I wanted him to know that he hurt me by his showing up at the dance with another girl. Maybe we weren't "exclusive," but he'd asked me to meet him there after the game. I couldn't imagine that he'd intentionally tried to hurt me that way, but maybe I had it all wrong.

Sitting on the bench near the lockers in Senior Hall, I'd all but resigned myself to missing my final prom when to my utter surprise, Barry plopped down on the bench about the width of three other people away from me. I said nothing, but I knew I needed to talk to him if I wanted him to ask me to prom. If I kept freezing him out then it was no one's fault but mine that I missed the dance, so I stayed put and waited to hear what he had to say. After a few beats, he broke the silence.

"So, are you going with me to the prom?" he asked.

"Are you asking?"

"Yes."

Relief flooded my soul, but I still had to pout, a little. "You aren't taking your girlfriend?"

"I'm asking my girlfriend, but she hasn't said yes yet."

Inside my body I was doing somersaults, *he called me his girlfriend!!!* yet outside I remained calm.

"Why didn't you ask me sooner?"

"Are you going to go or not?"

"Yeah, I guess," I responded, trying not to smile.

"You guess, huh?" He pulled me over next to him and hugged me, releasing all the pent-up stress.

"Why'd you ask me to the dance and then show up with Blondie?" I asked.

"I didn't show up with her, she just happened to be in the group."

"Then why'd you immediately start dancing with her when you got there? Why didn't you come to look for me, since you'd asked *me* to meet you there?"

"I came looking for you, but you'd run out of the room and Beans stopped me from following you."

"She did?"

"Yeah, she said that I'd made you cry and how dare I treat you that way."

"She did?" I asked, smiling. *She was so my hero.*

"She stood in front of me and pointed her finger at me and really let me have it. I felt so bad."

"If you felt so bad, then why didn't you call and apologize?" I asked, beginning to smell a rat.

"I don't know." He shrugged. I had to keep reminding myself that Barry was only sixteen, even though he was very tall, he was still immature. And, since I really didn't plan on marrying him, I needed to let it go. Only a few more weeks and I would be outta there! "Besides," he said, "I thought I'd catch you at school, but you wouldn't even look at me."

"Barry, I was so embarrassed. I thought you liked me until you walked in with that skank."

"She's not a skank. Look," he said, turning to me, "the guys and I got some food after the game, and she was there. We started talking and said we were coming to the dance and she and her friends came with us."

"That doesn't explain why you immediately started dancing with her and would've continued if you hadn't seen me." We both sat in silence for many long moments until I said, "You don't have to take me to the dance if you'd prefer to go with *her*. I've been asked by five other guys to go to prom; maybe one of them are still available." I couldn't help it—even though this would end soon, I was still jealous and a little hurt. Or maybe I was just being petty?

With a deep sigh, he said, "Look, Gracie, if I didn't want to take you, I wouldn't ask. There's no one else I'd rather go with to prom. Okay?" he looked at me impatiently.

I hesitated, then finally said, "Okay, I'm glad you asked." I began to get up from the bench when he grabbed me and pulled me onto his lap.

"Are we okay?" he asked.

"Yeah." I rose from his lap and began to walk away.

"Wait, what do ya mean five other guys asked you to prom?" He asked behind me.

Now that Barry had asked me, I had to figure out how to tell Mom so that she would be happy I was going with him. My mom was a little 5'4" woman who was very protective when someone hurt her kids. She wasn't happy with Barry after I told her about the dance. So, I would need to approach this carefully and really reason with her. All the way home from school I rehearsed telling Mom I was going to prom with Barry.

When I got home I found Mom in the kitchen putting the finishing touches on a roast for dinner.

"Hi Mom, I'm home," I called. All my life, my siblings and I always yelled to tell Mom we were home.

"You don't need to yell. I'm right here," she responded, not looking up from putting the roast in the oven.

"Hahaha, sorry, habit." Taking a deep breath, I said, "Guess who I'm going to prom with?"

"Who?"

"Barry." I held my breath.

Disappointment flashed across her face. "Oooh Gracie. Why are you going with him after what he did?"

"He and I talked today, and he apologized for the dance. He said he was really sorry."

"I don't think you should go with him."

"I know. But . . . I really want to go to the prom, and I like Barry."

"Even after what he did to you?" She stood with her hands on her hips, looking at me.

"Mom, I can't miss my Senior Prom." I frowned. "And I only have a few weeks before I leave. So, I decided to go with him. I mean, I'm not gonna marry him, so what the heck?"

"Well, it's your prom so you can do what you want," she said reluctantly. "Sylvia will be home that same weekend, so you better see if she has time to make you a dress."

"Oh yeah, I need a dress. Can I call and tell her before she gets here?"

"You better do it now before your dad gets home." Dad didn't like us making long-distance calls.

I immediately called my oldest sister and told her about the date. She said she'd been working on a dress for one of her fashion design classes that she thought would work. With a great sense of relief, I thanked God for giving me such a talented sister and for her willingness to clothe me.

Monday

Only two weeks before prom; and I had a date and a new dress. *Life is good,* I thought as I walked into English class earlier than normal. Trey and a few others were the only ones in class; not even Mrs. Sawyer had shown up yet. Waving at Trey, I dropped my books on my desk then walked over to his. I hadn't seen him to speak with most of last week.

"Hey, Trey! What's shaking?" I asked, stressing the

question as I moved my shoulders back and forth with my best imitation of Steve Martin.

Laughing, he said, "You're so weird."

"Eeeeh, you still love me," I told him as I danced around in front of his desk, making him laugh more.

"Why are you in such a good mood?"

I stopped dancing, and said, "Barry asked me to prom."

"He did?" His shoulders slumped.

"Yeah, finally." I answered, confused at his reaction.

"I was going to ask you."

"No, you weren't!"

"I was too. Ever since you moved back, I've been waiting to ask you to Senior Prom.

"Really?" I asked in disbelief.

"You're one of my oldest friends and I thought it would be fun to go to our last prom together."

"Why'd you wait 'til the last minute then?" I asked.

"I thought I'd have time."

Suddenly it was all clear to me. "You didn't think anyone else would ask me, did you? I can't believe you. You thought no one else would ask me and that I'd be so desperate that you could ask me at the last minute." I turned to walk away but stopped and placed my hands on my hips. "For your information, you're the seventh person to ask me to prom! I went with number six." The reality of what he thought of my social life totally deflated my ego.

I hardly remembered what class was about that day, my thoughts were so concentrated on my conversation with Trey. I wasn't mad, but it humbled me. *If your best friends won't tell ya, who will?*

The remaining days leading up to prom were a blur of excitement and a little stress. Barry had a big track meet out of town the day of prom so I wasn't even sure if I'd get to go anymore because he didn't know what time the meet would end or if he'd get back in time. So, after all the drama of getting him to ask, it might all be moot. Since neither of us really knew what would

happen Saturday, all I could do was proceed as if we were going and be ready when he picked me up. *If* he picked me up.

What Was That?

Sylvia came home with my dress, and she'd done such an amazing job: it was a floor-length formal with small floral print on a lavender-colored background fabric with a chiffon overlay. I hoped that Barry had gotten a tux that would look good with my dress. *It's all about the dress.*

All day I waited to hear from Barry. I didn't know if I should eat dinner with my family or wait and eat with Barry, or *if* we would even make it to prom. However, at 7:30 p.m., Barry called to tell me he was home and would be out to pick me up as soon as he got cleaned up. *Yeeess!* I quickly put on both my make-up and my dress then stood around and waited for Barry. And yes,

I *stood* around—I couldn't sit since that would wrinkle my dress. I wanted to look perfect for him.

Barry showed up around 8:30 p.m. in his family's brown sedan. I made Mom answer the door so I could make what I hoped would be a grand entrance. I imagined that upon seeing me he'd be in awe of my beauty or maybe have an intake of breath or some reaction that showed he liked what he saw, but . . . nuttin'! He just gave me a blank look, not a widening of his eyes—not even a smile. But he did seem a bit nervous.

"Hey Barry, did you meet my mom?"

Barry nodded his head, not looking straight at my mom, and said, "Yeah, sorry I'm so late." He handed me my corsage.

"Thanks," I said, taking the plastic floral box. I smiled at his silvery gray tux and ruffle shirt. "You look nice." I paused for a moment hoping he'd return the compliment to me, but he didn't. Disappointed, I said, "Let me get your boutonniere," and walked into the kitchen to retrieve it from the fridge. This gave me a moment to think of another approach in my attempt to squeeze a compliment out of the guy. I sounded needy, but gee, I wanted to hear that he appreciated the effort I'd put forth.

As I exited the kitchen with his boutonniere I said, "I really like the color of your tux; it goes with my dress." I paused again, waiting for him to respond with a compliment—still nothing. *Really, Barry?* I tried to pin his boutonniere into the lapel of his tux without success. "Mom, will you pin his boutonniere, please? It won't stay for me." I was too nervous to handle that skinny pin—besides, I thought I might stab him. And, I wasn't sure if that "stab" would be by accident or on purpose.

Handing her the pin and flower bud, my vertically challenged mom stood in front of Barry and reached for the lapel. "Oh Barry, you're gonna need to slouch so I can pin this. I'm not that tall," she said, and laughed as she pulled his lapel down towards her. This made him laugh which broke the ice between them, and he slouched down. Then she pinned on my corsage, being careful not to mess up the nice material. Standing back, she surveyed her work. "You two look really nice together."

"Thanks, Mom." I beamed. Still nothin' from Barry. *Boy, this guy's tough*, I thought.

"We better go," Barry said, moving to the door and holding it open.

"Bye Mom, see ya later," I said as I walked out the front door, with Mom following.

"Have fun," she called after us. Within seconds, we were on our way to prom and drove in silence.

"How'd the track meet go?" I finally asked.

Great. I'm State Champion," he said flexing his free arm in mock bravado.

"Wow, congrats! That's really cool!"

"Thanks! Every time I'd win a race, one of my little sisters would run down to get the medal and take it up to my dad in the bleachers. I kept winning so many races that Dad finally came down and stood next to the fence between the bleachers and the track," he said, pleased with his day. Barry was very close to his dad since his mom left. "Hey, my stepmom wants to see us before we go to the dance, are you okay with that?"

"Sure." I was a bit nervous having never met his family before. Barry pulled into his drive and walked around the sedan to open my door. Once we were inside his home and I'd met his family, his dad began to take picture after picture of us. While his dad put new film in his camera, his little sisters—who'd been standing off to the side—began to warm up to me being there.

"You're so pretty," his little seven-year-old sister gushed.

"You look like you're getting married," came from his five-year-old sister. We both laughed in nervous embarrassment.

"Barb!" Barry called to his stepmother.

"Alright you two, that's enough," his stepmother said, coming to our rescue.

"Okay kids, just a couple more pictures." Barry's dad said as we posed for the millionth picture.

"Dad, that's enough. We gotta get to the dance before it ends." Barry reasoned with his dad.

"Just a couple more," and he clicked away.

"Ed, give Barry a break. This isn't the last time he'll go to a dance. There'll be more." His stepmother said with a laugh as she pulled the camera down from Ed's eye. All the while his sisters looked on adoringly. But still not one compliment from Barry. *Did he even notice my dress?* I questioned myself.

Even though the high school parking lot was full as we drove in, we were able to find a spot close to the front. Barry pulled into the spot and turned off the engine. I sat waiting for him to get out and open my door. He turned to me and said, "I'm gonna kiss you." When I heard those words, my heart leapt with excitement. He'd never kissed me before. All the times we went out or did things together—they'd never ended in a kiss. *I'm finally getting my first kiss—and it only took me seventeen years.*

Barry took my hand and pulled me toward him slowly—the suspense was killing me. I was curious as to how it would feel to kiss someone I actually liked. Softly our lips met, and I was just beginning to enjoy the new sensation when he plunged his tongue into my mouth. I recoiled in shock.

"Ew," I exclaimed before I could stop myself, totally surprised. "What was *that*?"

"I was kissing you."

"No," I said, grimacing, "That thing you did at the end there?" I pointed at his mouth while scraping my tongue against my teeth to rid it of the taste.

Barry laughed. "It was my tongue. That was a French kiss." . . . and the moment was gone. I had just blown what could've been a very romantic moment by my over-reaction.

"Oh." I searched my mind for something to do or say that

might recover the moment. I didn't want my naivete to ruin the night, but I'd been so surprised by his tongue, I was at a loss for words. *Who does that?* There I'd expected a chaste little kiss as you see in the movies, not one with his slimy tongue. I thought a "French" kiss was something French people did, not a farmgirl from Ashbury. Barry got out of the car and came over to open my door. I watched him, worried that he now regretted asking me to prom because I was so naïve. *Had I ruined this date?*

As he opened the door, I apologized. "Barry, I'm sorry about my reaction to your kiss, it just surprised me."

Barry laughed. "It's okay," he said, taking my hand. We began walking towards the main doors until Barry heard some of his friends gathered by a car across the parking lot from where we were, and instead led me towards them.

"Hey Barry, want some?" Ricky asked, holding out a can of beer to him.

"Sure," he said, taking a drink from the can. "Gracie, do you want one?"

"No. I don't drink."

"Have you ever tasted beer?" asked Ricky.

"No."

Barry grabbed me close to him and gave me a lingering kiss, minus the tongue. "Now ya have," he said, pulling away. Everyone laughed, and I smiled trying to hide my bashfulness at being kissed in front of everyone. But secretly I hoped this meant Barry and I were okay.

"Ooh, Gracie got a ki-iiiss," Zelda said, stepping out of the back seat of Ricky's car. I was so embarrassed she'd seen that.

"I didn't know you were in there," I said, mortified. Zelda laughed and took a drink from the beer she held. Most of the people in this small group were drinking. How long or how many beers they'd drunk I couldn't tell, but they were all feeling good.

I was impatient to get into the dance and didn't want to waste time watching those guys drink, so I walked towards the school. "Are you coming, Barry? I wanna dance," I said over my shoulder.

"Here, take this. I gotta go, man," said Barry handing the beer to Ricky. "My girl is leaving." Followed by catcalls and laughter, soon I felt Barry's hand on my back as we approached the door.

Eight Minutes in Heaven

Standing at the threshold to the gym, it was so dark we couldn't
see anything, but once we'd walked through the blackout curtains
and our eyes adjusted, it was like walking into the heavens:
everything was dark with what must've been a million white lights
twinkling as though they were stars both above and below from
their reflection on the floor. In the middle of the room stood a
circular staircase and an arrow-shaped sign with the word
HEAVEN on it pointing up the stairs. Yet, a chain across the
stairway blocked it off. The theme of the dance was "Heaven Can
Wait."

Couples were out on the dance floor, with their arms about each other, rocking back and forth and gradually turning in a circle.

We immediately entered the dance floor and began to slow dance,

"Great job today, Barry," Allan patted Barry on the back as he passed by.

"Thanks man," Barry replied.

"Yeah, great job today. You represented the school well," Mr. Smith, an assistant basketball coach said as he smacked Barry on the butt.

"Why do you guys do that?" I asked.

"Do what?" asked Barry.

"Smack each other on the butt instead of just patting each other on the back."

Shrugging, he said, "I don't know. We just do." I rolled my eyes.

"Let's go get our picture taken and get that out of the way, k?" I grabbed Barry's hand and led him over to the spot designated for pictures in a corner of the gym. Moments later, we were back on the dance floor next to Trey and Beans.

"Hey, guys!" I said as I pulled Barry towards them. "You came together?" I gave Trey a meaningful look before smiling at Beans. She'd been Trey's prom date last year and it seemed like he'd asked her at the last minute after I'd turned him down. *They make such a cute couple; why didn't they date?* I wondered, but I didn't like that he always asked her at the last minute. "Have you been here long?"

"No," they said in unison.

"We went to dinner first with Chuck and Joan," Beans continued. "How 'bout you guys?"

"We got here a little bit ago. Barry had a track meet out of town," I said.

"How'd ya do?" asked Trey.

Posing as if he were on a trophy, Barry answered, "State Champion!"

Trey laughed at Barry's pose. "You are?"

At that moment, Trevor and Danny came over and bumped into Barry to congratulate him.

"Great job man." Said Danny.

"Yeah, you were on fire," Trevor said as he patted Barry's butt. I just rolled my eyes.

"State Champion.

The rest of the night was the same. Everyone was so happy that when the DJ played Cheap Tricks', *I Want You to Want Me*, all couples were abandoned and instead we danced as a group on the floor laughing and teasing one another. Everyone that is, except Sam and Hoppy. They stayed to themselves over to the side. When the DJ announced, "last dance," we all broke into couples again, a little more solemn as we realized this really was our last dance in high school.

The DJ chose Foreigner's song, *Waiting for A Girl Like You*. As Barry and I began to dance to the melancholy tune, I noticed Sam and Hoppy still dancing on the opposite side of the room. I felt sorry for how boring their romance must be; to be so serious about one another that you have no fun with anyone else. But I couldn't ignore the longing I felt when I saw how handsome Sam looked in his tux.

"I feel bad for Sam and Hoppy," I said, voicing my thoughts before I could stop myself.

"Why?" asked Barry.

"They're always so serious; they never seem to have any fun." I nodded my head in their direction. "I think romance should be fun, not boring."

"Like this?" He grabbed my sides and tickled me.

"Stoooop," I said, laughing, and broke free of his grip. "Stop that." I hit him on his arm. Once I'd regained my composure, he put his arms around my waist and mine went around his neck, and I continued, "We're anything but boring; you with your other women, track, French kissing . . . what could be boring?" I said, still looking over his shoulder. In response, Barry tried to tickle me. Again, I wiggled out of his grasp and put both his hands back on my waist and returned to watching Sam and Hoppy.

When I caught Sam's eye, I smiled and waved at him. He stopped dancing and stood there watching me, then said something to Hoppy. Shaking her head no, she put her hands on her hips. Sam nodded his head in my direction and reached for her hand as he began to walk towards us. Hoppy tried to pull Sam back, but he just shook her off and kept walking. She hopped until she caught up with him, then grabbed his hand. He turned to say something to her, then still holding her hand, he pulled a pouty Hoppy behind him as he walked to where Barry and I were dancing. His face was a blank mask. *Uh oh*, I thought and looked the other way, pretending I hadn't seen his approach. I'd only expected him to wave back, not come over.

Sam stood behind Barry and tapped him on the shoulder. "Wanna switch partners?" he said. I didn't move lest I woke and found I was dreaming. For the first time, I noticed that Sam was only an inch shorter than Barry as they stood face to face. *Was he really asking to dance with me?*

"Not really," Barry responded, playfully turning away and making Sam laugh.

Nudging Barry out of the way and giving him Hoppy's hand, he said, "You can dance with Sara Jane." Then he took my hand and pulled me close.

I'd never been in such close of proximity of Sam before. He sat behind me in class, and we'd done the wild dancing at Homecoming as we attempted to hide from Hoppy, but never a slow dance. Never in this intimate of a space before.

He held me differently than Barry. Sam held me as if we actually knew how to dance. He hadn't even held Sara Jane that way. Instead, he held her in the typical slow dance style of all ages. *Was he holding me this way because we were only friends?*

As he held my right hand with his other hand resting on the small of my back, I hesitantly put my left hand on his shoulder. We slowly moved as his hand seemed to direct. I could feel myself melting into his arms; we were Fred Astaire and Cyd Charisse dancing to Foreigner's love ballad instead of Begin the Beguine, just the two of us on a blacked-out stage surrounded by millions of twinkling stars for light, gently enveloping me in the moment's magic. But suddenly, everything stopped: the lights, the music, everything. You couldn't see your hand in front of your face, but I could feel Sam's arm tighten about my waist, all enhanced by the faint intoxicating scent of his cologne. Everyone was silent.

"Who unplugged the stars? I can't see," someone finally called from the crowd.

"Yeah, I liked those," another person said.

The power had gone out, and we all stood around waiting. Even in the darkness Sam and I stood as when we were dancing: with me in his arms. Then the emergency lights came on, giving everyone a soft glow. *I think I like this lighting.*

"You look really nice tonight," he told me in my ear. *Finally.* I finally got the compliment I'd been waiting for all night. I sighed to myself, thankful for the darkness that hid the effect Sam's words had on me. "I hope you don't mind my cutting in like this," Sam said as he leaned back, loosening his arm about my waist.

"You look great too," I responded, a bit too quick. In my attempt to regain my composure, I said, "I'm surprised, Hop . . . Sara Jane agreed to this. She doesn't like me much."

"She likes you," he said. I gave him a disbelieving look, making him chuckle before he continued, "She let me do this."

With a mocking laugh, I said, "Yeah, I saw how she *let* you. From what I saw, it looked like the little hare was fighting you all the way." *Okay, I'm not perfect. I had to make a little jab.*

"You have no idea," he responded with a sigh. Abruptly, the music came on very loud then stopped, then started again. A couple of moments later the stars reappeared and everyone applauded. That was when the DJ announced he was starting the song over, but it wasn't the same song. Instead of Foreigner, he'd put on Eric Clapton's, 'Wonderful Tonight'.

We danced in silence as Sam moved us further into the depths of the dance floor away from Barry and Hoppy's view. The further we moved into the center of the crowd, we were cloaked in darkness, and surrounded by starlight and other couples. With each breath, I became more and more engulfed in this enchantment. *What is he doing to me? He has a girlfriend! I'm not a rubber band that can pull back at will*, I cried inside my mind as I tried to pull myself back to reality. But I never wanted this dance to end.

"Why are you dancing with me?" I asked, leaning back so I could look him in his eyes. Sam didn't respond right away, but continued to dance, looking over my head.

"This is our last high school dance. I couldn't let it pass and not have one dance with you," he stated not looking at me.

"We danced at Homecoming, or did you forget?" I asked, so aware of his body so close to mine that I could feel the strength of his arm when he gently pressed the small of my back.

"I'm gonna miss you," he said.

"Are you going somewhere?" I asked, raising my

eyebrows.

"Not really," he responded, "but you are."

"Hm, that's true."

"When are you leaving?"

"Right after graduation."

He began dancing again, deep in thought as our bodies swayed to the music. It reminded me of part of a poem. Without thinking, I muttered the words under my breath:

"You'll unplug the stars and cover the sun when you finally know you've found the one."

"What did you say?"

"Huh?"

"Just now, about finding the one."

"Oh, sorry. I didn't realize I said it aloud. It's just something Mrs. Sawyer read in class last week that I really liked."

"Hm . . . just promise to always stay in touch. My family'll know where I am," he told me as his arm tightened around my waist, drawing me even closer.

"Sure." With a spurt of bravery, I asked, "Why did you stop talking to me last year?" But, before he could respond—if he was going to respond—Barry and Hoppy were pulling us apart as the song ended. The lights came up, chasing the magic out of the room with the harsh light of reality. We covertly peeked at each other as we separated, pulled in opposite directions. I couldn't imagine being deprived of his beauty forever.

My heart was racing after spending so much time encircled in the warmth of Sam's arms, listening to him reveal, in the cloak of darkness and out of Hoppy's earshot, that he'd miss me. And to think it all started with a wave. I never dreamed that he would hijack the last dance from Barry and give me almost eight minutes in heaven.

As Barry drove me home, I couldn't stop thinking about Sam; I could still smell his scent on my hands and clothes; I could feel his hand holding mine and the pressure of his body as we moved around the floor. It took a superhuman effort on my part to carry on a conversation with Barry when all I wanted to do was relive that last dance.

"Why did Sam need to dance with you?" he asked, still watching the road.

"We're friends. It was the last dance."

"So?"

"So?" I responded. "For your information, I have a lot of good friends here and I will miss them after graduation."

"I know you do. But you'll see them during the summer."

"Uh—no, I won't. I'll be leaving for school right after graduation, with my sister when she leaves." I looked out at the darkness through his sedan window—just saying the words aloud made them more final. The reality that in a couple of weeks I would leave these friends I loved for a place where I had no friends, was crushing.

Reaching over from the driver's seat, Barry put his hand on my knee. "Hey, I'm sorry. I didn't realize you'd be leaving so soon after graduation." His apology made my eyes tear up, and I quickly blinked to make them go away as we pulled into my drive. The night needed to end on a high note, not tears.

Pulling into my driveway, Barry stopped the car and walked around to open my door. I hated that the night had to end. It had been so much fun with so many surprises. Barry walked me up my front steps and then slowly lowered his head to give me a gentle kiss, minus the tongue. *Thank heavens!* Pulling away, he descended a couple of steps and waited for me to go inside before he left.

Watching him drive away, I marveled that guys my age could be so tender: first with Sam cutting in and dancing with me, and now Barry. Yes, this had been a magical night. I think I floated into my parents' room to tell Mom I was home before I went to bed and had the most fantastical dreams.

A Clown?

After prom, the remaining weeks seemed to be flying by as Graduation drew closer. But there were still a few things that needed to be accomplished before I would be done and ready to move away.

We still had to recite the memorized monologue from MacBeth in Mrs. Sawyer's class. It went something like this:

Is this a dagger which I see before me,

The handle toward my hand? Come, let me clutch thee!

I have thee not, and yet I see thee still . . . blah, blah, blah.

I remembered my oldest sister learning this monologue and was so excited when it was my time to learn it. This monologue made me feel like I was a true actor; I was doing Shakespeare after all!!

At school, every classroom door had a window overlooking the hall that let you see who was out there, provided you were standing at the front of the class and were tall enough to see out that window. It had never been an issue for me until today when I had to recite the monologue in front of the class.

All of Mrs. Sawyer's classes were reciting Macbeth, and luckily, I wasn't the first student to do this, so I had a chance to listen to the others to get an idea of what she expected. When it was my turn, I walked up to the front of the class with butterflies in my stomach and stood behind the podium ready to do the best Shakespeare recitation of all the other students. *I am an actress, reciting the Bard for heaven sake!*

While memorizing the monologue, I'd fantasized that my rendition would be so awe inspiring that students would write about it in their journals. This day would go down in history as the day Shakespeare was finally performed as it was written.

I stood at the front of the class, behind the podium, and took a moment to prepare before I started. Unfortunately, I looked out the window in the door and saw Trevor peeking in making faces at me; that was all I needed. Since Mrs. Sawyer was sitting in the back of the class today to watch us recite, she couldn't see Trevor. *I am such a fool for guys I have a mini crush on.* Instead of the magnificent recitation I'd practiced, I began to speed up my recitation, making Trevor laugh, but Mrs. Sawyer immediately stopped me and asked that I do it slower. Old smarty pants me began to recite it reeeeeeally slooooow which made Trevor laugh even more. The whole class laughed, except Mrs. Sawyer, a classy lady who wouldn't be happy with my shenanigans, as she later called them. *Why was I such a goof?* I lamented to myself. *I would do almost anything for a laugh.*

After I finished, I sat back at my desk and found a note from Mrs. Sawyer asking to see me after class. *Uh oh.*

I had four older siblings who, all but one, were good students and didn't get in trouble, but not me. For some reason, I was more of an extrovert than they were and that didn't always work to my favor; case in point my having to stay after class as requested in the note. However, in this class it wasn't always my fault, like when Sam sat behind me and made comments throughout class, and when I turned to tell him to stop, it would be the exact moment Mrs. Sawyer would glance my way and get after me, which would make Sam snicker. I couldn't win.

After everyone had left, Mrs. Sawyer sat in the desk across the aisle from me and said, "I've been meaning to speak with you about your shenanigans in class. I don't think where you're sitting is working." Which I thought was odd since I only had a couple of weeks before I graduated; why move me now? She continued, "So, I would like you to move up to the front row." She pointed to an empty desk.

"But Mrs. Sawyer," I exclaimed, "It's not my fault. You should move Sam; he's always the one talking."

"I don't see him talking. It's always you," she responded. "If this move doesn't work, then the next move will be out the door." I stared in disbelief. Seriously? She was threatening to move me out the door in a couple of weeks if this move didn't work? This made me laugh. It's called Graduation. All the seniors will be moving out the door in a couple of weeks. "You can go." And with that, she dismissed me. It stunned me that I had just been reproached for Sam's antics. She didn't say one word about my recitation. I had never been reprimanded like that before. Yes, he was cute, maybe not even cute—more unearthly, devastatingly handsome—but I wasn't gonna be his fall gal. *Why was she picking on me? She must hate me.*

The next day in class, I set my books on the desk Mrs. Sawyer had told me she wanted me to use for the rest of the year. When Sam came in, he looked over at me in confusion and shrugged his shoulders in a questioning manner. I glared at him and said accusatorially, "You got me in trouble." He laughed and set his books down on his desk.

"Why are you sitting there?" he asked.

"Like I said, *you* got me in trouble. Mrs. Sawyer doesn't appreciate my shenanigans. I tried to tell her they're *your* shenanigans, not *mine,* but she didn't believe me." Sam sat on the desk across from me and laughed. Oh, how I loved to see that twinkle in his eyes and hear his unguarded laughter.

As I sat at my new desk waiting for class to start, in walked Trey and Chuck, who both did a double take when they saw me.

"Why are you sitting there?" Chuck asked.

"I got moved thanks to Mr. Chatty back there," I responded,

pointing at Sam sitting at his desk with my thumb over my shoulder.

"You shouldn't talk so much," said Trey.

"It wasn't me! It was the chatterbox," I said, glaring at Sam.

"What? Me?" Sam responded, feigning shock. Then all three laughed. Trey's seat was across the aisle from me and Chuck's was right behind me. "Don't talk to me, you guys," I told them before Mrs. Sawyer came in. "I don't want to get in trouble again."

"No, talk to her. She loves it," chided Sam. I turned and glared at him. *There is no compassion in this group.*

I thought I was doomed with those two, but they proved to be quite studious and only bothered me when Mrs. Sawyer wasn't looking with Sam egging them on. If Mrs. Sawyer even glanced my way, I was facing front staring straight ahead and would only turn when I knew she wouldn't see; I had two weeks to play the angel.

This was the same week the yearbooks came in and had to be distributed to those who paid for one. It had been a lot of fun putting the yearbook together and having the power to decide what pictures went in and which ones stayed out. That kind of power can be very dangerous for a teenage girl whose heart has been crushed.

By wielding the little power I had, I made sure there were no extra pictures of Hoppy and Sam besides the necessary ones—the ones I couldn't avoid. I knew that was sneaky, but hey, for a whole year he hadn't spoken to me, and he had chosen Hoppy over me. My heart had broke in twain! Besides, nobody was hurt. In fact, they probably didn't even notice, and it made me feel better. I mean, seriously, why have all that power unless you wield it? So, I wielded it. I didn't hurt them, didn't vote to keep them off a court, didn't give them a dead spider covered in wax, I only kept their pictures in the yearbook to the very minimum.

Once all the yearbooks had been handed out, it was time to get everyone to write some sort of note in your yearbook. I loved reading the little notes; any that came from the guys I would quickly peruse to see if anyone had declared their undying love. *At last count, not one.* But, having been voted "Class Clown," I read multiple "you're the funniest girl," or "You make me laugh," or blah, blah, blah. Were there any claims of "I have loved you forever" or something like that? Nope, nada, zilch. Not one declaration of love.

Then I saw it. The one inscription that made all the others palatable: it was from Sam and said, "Who unplugged the stars?" and he didn't even sign it. I knew instantly who it was from. It surprised me that he'd remembered me saying that portion of the poem when we were dancing. *So, he was listening.* I couldn't stop myself from smiling.

The problem with me was that I was an ingénue trapped inside a character actress' body. I had read so many Harlequin and Barbara Cartland romance books that in my head I dreamt of the tall, dark, handsome, brooding man declaring his love to me with his chest bared, holding my waif-like frame in his arms with my cherubic, heart-shaped face and big eyes gazing up at him . . . or however those descriptions go. Unfortunately, the closest I ever got to it was the moment at the dance with Sam. Thusly, I would forever be Pagliacci's clown with the words, "Laugh Clown, laugh!" running through my mind as tears streamed down my painted face. *Too dramatic? Well, I come by it naturally.*

The Escape

It was the last week of school, which ended on Thursday, and we would graduate on Sunday. This final week was chockfull of activities. *Oh, life is good!*

First, on Monday we got our caps and gowns, which were in our school colors: the girls wore green and the guys blue. We needed to make sure they fit and were ready before Sunday.

On Tuesday, the word was being spread that the senior kegger would take place on Thursday night. I didn't drink, so I had no plans to attend. However, I had multiple people approach me and say that I *had* to go as this was the final class party before graduation and everyone was going.

"But I don't drink," I explained.

"That's okay. It's really for us to all be together one last time," explained Trevor and Danny.

"I don't know."

"You have to come," Danny urged. "We want all the fun people there." *How could I say no to that compliment?* I thought.

Still uneasy, I asked, "What if the cops come? I can't go to jail for being at a kegger. There is no way my parents would understand that."

"You won't go to jail," said Danny.

"We'll have a place where you can hide in case the cops show up," Trevor promised me.

"They're not gonna show up," muttered Danny under his breath.

"Okay. I'll come," I said hesitantly, holding my hands up in capitulation. "But ya gotta promise that nothing happens to me if the cops show up." It was like I'd resigned myself to my fate.

"We promise," Danny and Trevor said in unison.

"Scouts honor," added Trevor.

"No cops are going to show up," Danny said, once more in exasperation to Trevor as they walked away.

"I know." Trevor said, calmly.

Yes, it was flattering to have my friends want me with them at the senior drinking party, but having never attended a kegger, as they were called, I was nervous because I didn't know what to expect. It worried me that because we were all underage, the cops would show up and load us into the "paddy" wagon like in the movies, and the next day the headline in the paper would read:

Bishop Kaye's Daughter Arrested!! (gasp!)

News like that would not go over well with my parents. But I loved my friends and was flattered they wanted me there, and it *really* was our last party as a class.

However, the Jury was still out as to whether this was the best decision I'd made up to that point in my life. When Sam came to the popcorn shop for his nightly hot dog, I ran it past him: "Are you going to the senior kegger?"

"I don't drink."

"Neither do I. But it's the last class party."

"I take it you're going, then?"

263

"Well . . . yeah. Danny and Trevor really want everyone there. You should come, but I think you'll need to leave Sara Jane in her burrow." This made Sam laugh.

"Would you stop with all your bunny references? You're the only one that calls her Hoppy," he stated, trying to keep a straight face.

"That you know of. Can you survive without her attached to you and sucking the life out of you?" I asked cynically. Sam only frowned.

"Do you really think it'll be that fun being around a bunch of drunks?" Sam asked, ignoring my question.

"Don't know; never been around a bunch of drunks," I responded. We ended the discussion there, totally undecided.

On Wednesday, we finished up all classwork, that is, for those who even showed up to class. Most of us were ditching school; the weather was so wonderful they couldn't expect us to stay indoors all day.

Thursday, we had a rehearsal for marching into the stadium. We had to gather in the gym and line up, and those girls that had male marching partners were at the beginning of the line followed by those without. Allan Devers had asked me to partner up with him a few weeks ago, so I was towards the front and Trey was a couple of people behind me with his marching partner. I had no idea where Mr. Adonis was or who he was marching with.

We were all so excited that the powers-that-be could hardly control us as we laughed and danced about and walked out of the gym towards the stadium. Finishing the run-through, we marched back into the gym and then into the auditorium one last time.

As we walked into the auditorium, some of the mothers were standing in front of the stage behind tables loaded with donuts and both regular and chocolate milk, along with a couple of bowls of fruit. This meeting was so the mothers could go over the agenda for the senior party that would take place Sunday night at the community college. Once the moms had finished their spiel, we could eat and leave for the day if we so desired. *Oh yeah, we desired.*

In the parking lot, you could hear multiple car stereos playing what should be considered the national anthem for all senior classes: Alice Cooper's *School's Out* with all windows open, and at full volume.

Having given notice at work two weeks earlier, I was free to go home and enjoy the rest of the day. I loved my home during the summer, with the opened big screened-in window at the back of the kitchen, allowing the breeze to come in, always having corn on the cob, tomatoes, and salads for dinner. And remembering the summers past when my brothers and I would run through the fields playing cops and robbers or cowboys and Indians, riding my bike everywhere, swimming—the memories flooded into my mind. And since I knew my days of living at home were coming to an end, I wanted to enjoy my time left.

No matter how slow I moved, time sped by and soon it was time to head to the party. I decided that I'd only make an appearance, and then leave. Beans, and Zelda would meet me there since they might want to stay later than I would. Having never been to a kegger before, I had no idea if or how crazy it could become.

Following the directions that Danny and Trevor had given me, I found the party in an empty section of land on the opposite side of town I wasn't familiar with, hidden off the main thoroughfare. I specifically came late so that I could see most everyone before I left, which meant I had to park a way's down the road as other cars had already taken the spaces closer to the party area. Nervously, I walked up an incline towards the sound of laughter and music.

Once at the top, it opened up into a glen and I could see most everyone that was attending this drunken shindig. Walking towards the picnic table where they seemed to congregate, they greeted me with multiple calls of "Gracie!" It was nice they were so happy I was there, and whether it was heartfelt or beer induced, I didn't care. Most were holding large glasses filled with the golden brew and I could see behind them sitting on the picnic table a large metal barrel with a hose coming out of it.

"Glad you're here Gracie," Danny yelled as he came over to me and put his arm around my neck, having already partaken from the metal barrel. That's when I noticed Sam standing a few feet away from the picnic table talking to Trey and Chuck.

"Hey guys," I called, walking towards them, glad to notice that none of them were drinking.

"Hey, Gracie," said Chuck.

"How long you guys been here?

"Before you," said Trey, "If I'd known you were coming, I would've given you a ride." I looked at Sam with a questioning look.

"Just got here," he stated.

"So, you came after all."

"Only to make sure you don't get arrested," Sam answered.

"Ha ha!" Before I could say any more, Brian came up to our group.

"We have a great place for you to hide," he proudly announced.

"Where?" I asked. With all this land and outside stuff, I was sure there'd be many spiders about, which would make it impossible for me to stay hidden long, if at all.

"Hidden?" asked Trey and Chuck in unison.

"Why do you need to hide?" Trey asked.

"Because she's afraid of getting arrested if the cops come," Brian offered.

"Ooooh," Trey and Chuck again responded in unison.

"Why show up if you're afraid of getting arrested?" asked Chuck

"Because it's the last party for our class and Danny and Trevor asked me to come."

"If they asked you to jump off a bridge, would you?" asked Sam mockingly.

"Maybe," I responded before sticking my tongue out at Sam, who laughed.

"C'mon, I'll show ya," Brian volunteered and led me away from the group with Sam following. We walked for a couple of minutes before the land dipped into a ravine, where Brian's old red Buick was parked. Pointing at the car, he said, "That's my car. We parked it here for you to hide in if the cops come."

"Thanks," I said, touched by their effort.

"Follow me," Brian said as he headed down to the car with Sam and me in tow. Once we reached it, Brian opened the front passenger door for me to get in the front seat, pointing out the case of Coca Cola they'd placed in the middle next to where I'd be sitting. "We got this," he said, pointing to the cans, "in case you had to stay down here for a little while, and the keys are in the ignition in case you need to drive away."

"Wow! Thanks for all this," I said as I got out of the car. I appreciated all the thought that had gone into setting that up.

"*If*, and that's a big if, the cops show up, I'll take you down to the car and wait with you. Watch for me," he instructed as we walked back to the group.

"That's okay, Brian. *I'll* take her to the car if the cops show up," Sam stated with authority.

"Are you happy?" asked Trevor, as we walked up to the picnic table.

"Yes, I feel better," I said with a laugh. Danny came up and put his arm around my shoulders while holding up his beer, and said, "Since this is Gracie's first time at a kegger—"

"And, my last," I interjected.

Danny continued, "I want a picture with her." He handed his camera to one of the other guys to use. One after another picture was taken with different people standing next to me holding up their beer or me holding their beer, most were very careful to not spill any on me.

After having been there for about an hour and those drinking had mellowed, Brian suddenly yelled, "Hide her!! The cops are here!" Hearing that, Sam pushed Brian aside, grabbed me by the elbow and quickly led me to the car in the ravine.

My heart was pounding so fast I thought I was going to have a heart attack. I reprimanded myself that I should have never come there; it was a bad idea. And now I'd be going to jail, I'd be a jailbird, succumbing to a life of crime as I became some gangster's moll. Okay, maybe I was being a little overly dramatic, but it scared me. Sitting in the car, after I calmed my mind down, I did what my parents had taught me to do all my life: I began to silently pray that I would be okay and not get arrested.

"So, you think this was worth it?" Sam asked as he leaned against the driver's side door, cool as a cucumber.

Ignoring his question, I said, "Why are *you* here?" I turned to face him, "Where's Sara Jane?"

"She doesn't know I'm here," he said, I raised my eyebrows at the confession. "She thinks I'm helping my grandparents." His actions were so confusing to me. Why was he doing this? Was he there to protect me? Just as I was about to respond, I thought I heard my name. I stopped to listen, and looked at Sam.

"Did you hear that?"

"What?"

"Someone calling my name?" We both got out of the car to check.

"Graaaaaacie!!! Graaaaaacie!! You can come out now." Beans and Zelda appeared at the top of the ridge, calling my name.

"Where are the cops?" Sam called.

"It was just Luke's dad checking to make sure we're all okay," Zelda informed us. Luke's dad was a cop, so knowing that he knew about this party and was okay with it put me at ease, but I knew it was time for me to go. Once Sam, Beans, Zelda and myself were back amongst the group, it was getting dark, this allowed me to silently escape the adventure and go home, leaving Sam behind. *Would he even notice?*

"How was the party?" Mom asked as I walked into the living room.

"It was okay. I sat in the green rocking chair, appreciating the soft light the table lamps gave off that created an ambiance of warmth, safety, and home.

"You're home early."

"Yeah, I know. I just went because everyone wanted me to

go. I didn't want to stay long." I sat and rocked, thinking about

Sam. *What was he doing?!*

The Graduates

And Sunday was there, just like that. It started when Mom woke me and told me I needed to finish packing before we went to church, because after that there would be no time before I left with my sister. I took a quick shower, which was the norm since Dad didn't want us taking long showers, and I gulped down a bowl of cold cereal before we headed into town.

There were a lot of extra people at church because of graduation; the only out-of-towners I had would be my two sisters: Sylvia, who was already there, and Katie, who lived a couple of towns away. She'd come a little later with her husband and my two-week-old nephew. I was so excited to see that little guy and show him off to my friends after the graduation ceremony that he almost eclipsed the main event.

After church, Mom and I hurried home so I'd have time to eat before I left for the ceremony. I gulped down my food and grabbed my cap and gown to head to the high school. As I drove into town, I reminisced about the past twelve years and all that had happened. It was still difficult to believe that I would finally graduate and be on my own, be my own boss, be able to pursue my acting, and become rich and famous. I had imagined that day for so long, and it was finally there.

Pulling into the high school parking lot, if one went by all the parked cars it seemed as though everyone was already there. Yet, as I entered the school and headed to my locker, there were only a few of my classmates putting their belongings into their lockers one last time before heading into the gym as instructed. Already, as I walked through the sparsely populated hall, it felt as if I were a visitor, even though I hadn't yet graduated. I wondered if anyone else had felt that way, or was it just me?

Entering the gym—where I had participated in so many pep

rallies, watched so many basketball games, and had experienced the dance of a lifetime with Sam—I found the rest of my class. Almost all were congregated in there, standing about in small groups talking and laughing in subdued tones, but it wasn't as noisy as it had been on Friday. We were all excited, yet a little apprehensive in regard to taking our first big step into the world.

They required us to arrive three hours before the graduation ceremony would start. I couldn't imagine why we would need so much extra time; I expected to be spending most of it standing around. But, we really didn't. I'd only been in the gym for about thirty minutes when Mr. Baxter started herding us all towards the bleacher section that had been pulled out of the wall.

"All right class! Let's have everyone move over here to the bleachers so we can take the class picture." We were like sheep going wherever we were directed; it wasn't normal for us to be so compliant, but we did as we were told. "Let's sit alphabetically. This will be the last time for your class picture." Mr. Baxter stood near the bleachers as he continued to direct us, "Let's have the A's here . . . then the b's, etc. You know how to do it."

As usual, because of my name, I sat in the middle of the

bleachers where I could view the faces of the people I'd grown up with, both before my dad's transfer and after, seated on either side of me. As I waited for the others to take their place, I felt hands on my shoulders. Sam was walking on the row above mine, and gently squeezed my shoulders before continuing on to his spot a little further down on the bench. These people were more than friends, they were family and oh how I would miss them. With these thoughts going through my mind I became melancholier than I thought I would, but the reality was really kicking in for me. As soon as we were all quiet, the final class picture was taken. I wished they'd have taken a candid picture of everyone turning around or leaning forward in their space, chatting with one another—that would have shown our true class spirit, instead of just the one that was posed.

It was time for us to line up with our partners and prepare for the march. While I waited to hear my name, I tried to memorize every moment so that I could always remember it. When I took my place in line next to Allan, I held his arm as if the rollercoaster ride of my life was just beginning to click up the track. I could barely keep still and wait for the cue to begin the march, but soon we were given the signal. As each girl approached the exit, she was handed a long stem red rose with ribbons tied about it representing our school colors. No one spoke as we walked toward the entrance to the stadium; there was both an excitement and solemnity felt up and down the line.

As the first couple entered the gate to the stadium, the band began to play 'Pomp and Circumstance'. As we proceeded past the announcer's box, Mr. Baxter instructed the crowd to "Please stand in honor of our graduates," we continued to our chairs below. As I descended the steps, I tried to look for my family in the crowd, but with everyone standing and the fact that I didn't know where they were seated, I could only hope they got a picture or two.

I didn't remember one word that was said during the ceremony. I recalled there were a couple of speakers, the choir singing, and then it was time for us to get our diplomas—another moment I had been waiting for ever since I saw my oldest sister walk across the stage to receive hers. I'd waited eight long years for that walk and now it was minutes away. The first row rose and walked to the steps at the side of the stage.

Trey, the class president, read each person's name, who then received their diploma as they shook hands with the school principal, Mr. Brooks, before continuing across the stage, down the steps and back to their chair. Row by row the names were called, and when it came time for me to walk the stage, the only thought going through my mind was to *not* trip on the stairs or anything else until I got back to my seat.

Trey's voice sounded from the microphone, "Grace Kaye." *This is it!*

I carefully climbed the steps and solemnly walked towards Trey—it was my moment. It was there! As I approached Trey, he began to laugh which caused me to shrug and mouth the word "What?" at him, which caused some chuckles from the audience. After Trey gave me a quick hug, I continued toward Mr. Brooks where I shook his hand, got my diploma and went back to my seat. *"I've done it!"* kept going over in my mind as I watched the rest of my classmates cross the stage.

Now that everyone had their diplomas, Mr. Brooks stood at the podium to give, what I thought, would be the instructions to move our tassels from one side of our cap to the other, showing we were now graduates, but it wasn't so. Instead, he stood to read a list of the students that received scholarships. As he started to list the names and schools, I began to zone out. I'd applied for a scholarship to BYU but was denied, so I felt this part didn't really pertain to me, or so I thought until I heard, "Grace Kaye, full-ride drama scholarship to New York University and a two-year scholarship to the community college."

Turning to Allan, with wide eyes, I said, "Wai . . . wait . . . what did he say?!"

"About what?" asked Allan, trying to listen to Mr. Brooks.

"About my getting scholarships," I said.

"You should know; you have one to NYU and the community college."

Shocked, I sat back in my chair. "That's what I thought he said." I whispered more to myself than anyone else. *Why hadn't anyone told me about these?* I wondered. *This was the first I'd heard about them. NYU? How'd they know about me?* I was totally stunned and taken by surprise. As I sat there in shock going over in my mind how NYU had known anything about me, I almost missed Mr. Brooks instructing all my classmates to move the tassel to the other side.

"Move your tassel," Allan whispered, mere seconds before most everyone threw their caps in the air with a big cheer, followed by a major scramble to retrieve it before we marched out. *We're graduates!* With our caps back on our heads, the band began to play Pomp and Circumstance as we walked, with our partners, out into the parking lot towards the rest of our lives.

Once outside, the line broke up as all the graduates went in search of their families. I hoped to find mine out there, but was unable to see them, so I went back inside the stadium. *So much for a dramatic exit. I love dramatic exits.* But it's anti-climactic when you have to go back into the scene you just left, looking for your family.

And, there they were, still standing in the bleachers where they'd been sitting. I checked for my little nephew and didn't see any sign of him either in someone's arms or in a baby seat nearby. He was nowhere in sight!

"Where's Preston?" I asked.

"Oh, we left him at home with Sylvia. He's just too little to be outside for this long," said my mom as she began to herd everyone out of the row.

Moaning in disappointment, I said, "Oooh. I wanted to show him off." I gave an exaggerated wink to my brother-in-law, then said to Katie, "Even though I haven't seen him, and for all I know he's hideously ugly." Then I ducked to avoid Katie's right hook.

"Well, you can see him when you get home. And you need to hurry so we can get you on the road before it's too late. Your sister needs to be at work tomorrow," my mom instructed in response to my disappointment.

"Okay. I just wanna say goodbye to some of my friends and then I'll come home," I said, and I headed back to the school building, passing all my friends with their families, taking pictures and receiving gifts and flowers. However, upon walking into the gym, a mega wave of nostalgia washed over me as I stood in the middle of the floor, all alone, engraving the moment into my memory.

"Hey!" I turned to find Trevor walking my way, and the tears started to flow. He walked up to me and gave me the biggest hug that lasted for maybe thirty seconds as we rocked back and forth. We separated and standing behind him was Danny, who hugged me, and behind him was Trey, then, Allan, then Johnny, then Doug, then Mark, and finally Chuck; all those guys were my friends. *I guess it is true that men can't ignore a woman in tears.*

"Don't cry, Gracie. You'll see us at the party tonight," said Trevor, trying to comfort me.

"N-n-no," I sniffled, "I-I-I'm l-l-leav ing t-town to-tonight f-f-for school."

"You're not gonna go to the senior party?" asked Trey

Sniffling, I said, "N-n-no. I-I'm leaving with my s-s-sister. Th-i-i-is is the-uh la-ast t-ime I'll s-see you guys." My sorrowful statement started them all hugging me again. Making it through a second round of hugs, and not wanting it to end, I heard my mom calling to me.

"Oh Grace, c'mon," she said, walking over to the group.

"Hi, Mrs. Kaye," said all the guys greeting her, not in unison.

Laughing, she said, "You boys spoil her." Everyone chuckled. "C'mon Grace, we need to go." With one last hug from Trey, Mom and I walked out the door.

"Your sister and Curt already left, so I'll ride home with you," Mom informed me as we walked towards Brutus.

"Gee Mom, I'm so gonna miss my friends," I lamented.

Shaking her head with a small laugh, she said, "You have proven the age-old quote wrong."

"Which quote is that?" I asked.

"That you can never go back."

"I can never go back?" I asked, confused.

"Yes, there is an old quote that says you can never go home after you've left. Remember how we tried to tell you that before we moved back from Ferron? But you've proven everyone wrong with the friendship you have with Trey, Brian, and your new friends." She smiled at me. "Nothing ever changed with you and your friends but time."

"I know. I have the best friends here." I sniffled. As I drove past the main door and observed my friends milling about, I told Mom, "I'll never have better friends than these."

Right then, I saw Sam and Hoppy crossing the front lawn of the school towards the cars, and I realized I hadn't said goodbye to Sam or Barry. As I stopped at the exit of the parking lot, mine and Sam's eyes connected for a moment and we smiled at one another. I took one last look at the high school, all my friends, and pulled out on the street, ready to start a whole new chapter of my life

without Sam.

Where the Boys Are

I couldn't believe how little my nephew was when I held him; it was like a dream come true. This little guy made me an aunt! I had waited all my life to be an aunt and now I was one, and I was gonna be a great one! Once I held him in my arms, I was a gonner. I really hated that I was leaving soon and wouldn't be able to hold him again for quite some time. I needed to be there to spoil and brainwash him that I was not only his favorite aunt but his favorite everything. *How would I do that eight hundred miles away?*

While I was holding Preston, Mom packed my belongings into Sylvia's car; it was almost as if she wanted me out of there more than I wanted to leave. The first clue being that she started packing my stuff in black garbage bags because I wasn't doing it fast enough in suitcases—or maybe we didn't have enough suitcases for me to take. I was the fifth child to leave home, with only my two little brothers remaining. However, I had a hunch that the biggest catalyst for my mother in getting me out of the house was that she would only have to compete with my dad and two little brothers to hold my nephew. *Oooh, she's a sneaky one.*

Living in Provo on my own was great except for the lack of transportation; I'd been driving Brutus at home and that is where he stayed for my little brother to use. There at school, I had to hoof it everywhere I went or ask for a ride from one of my roommates or extended family members.

Most Freshman lived on campus, but I didn't want to live in a dorm and still be accountable to the "Dorm Mother," so I lived in an apartment complex just off-campus. It was the same place my older sisters lived when they attended school. I had spent the summer with them when I was eleven years old and saw how much fun they had, so it was the only place for me to live.

The students in the complex ranged in ages from around

forty to me at seventeen, and —I ended up being the youngest one there. There were so many activities: volleyball in the quad, pool parties, video parties, dances, etc. It was so much fun, and everyone was always outside doing something. Oh, and the boys were pretty great, too. I loved laying out at the pool or playing volleyball and watching all the cute guys. I was in heaven and hadn't thought of Sam for one moment.

By the time I moved in, my sisters had not lived in the apartments for many years. Just my older brother, Nate, lived there. It so happened that the building he lived in was kitty-corner to mine; I could literally step outside my door and see his.

I loved having Nate-the-skate so close by and it made my mom feel better about me not living on campus. But there were cons to having my brother so close. When we were in the quad, I'd yell to him, "Love you, love me?"

"Hell no," he'd answer, which would make everyone around us laugh. The girls who wanted to date Nate because he was so cute with a great sense of humor laughed the hardest. Since they wanted to date my brother, they would be especially nice to me, hoping I would give them an "in" with my brother. *Ha! Like that's gonna happen.*

Having a cute brother meant that he usually had cute friends. I didn't know why that was, but cute guys seem to hang out together, like in a herd. So I thought it would be a perfect way for me to casually meet one of them and *boom!* I'd have the college romance I had dreamed of since leaving home. But something that had never occurred to me was the fact that when people witnessed our banter, they became envious of our relationship. I knew that because a guy that lived across the lawn from me told me so.

"I wish you were my little sister," he confessed.

"Why?"

"You and your brother have so much fun. Most of the guys here wish they had a sister like you." *Oh great, that is just what I wanted for my social life, all these guys looking at me as a little sister,* I thought sarcastically. So much for dating.

As the months began to pass, I adapted to all the changes: I walked to school whether it was raining, sunny, or through twelve feet of snow. Same with grocery shopping—I could only purchase what I could carry home unless one of my roommates were willing to give me a ride in their car. Walking became my way of life.

Soon, it had been a year and I hadn't seen one of my friends from home, so when I got the call from Sam, I was both excited and curious.

"How are you?" I asked.

"Doing pretty good," he said. I could hear his family in the background. "How do you like Provo?"

"I love it! There's so much to do here, and I live in a really fun place.

"I meant to ask you the day we graduated, but I didn't get a chance."

"Ask me what?"

"Why didn't you tell me about your scholarship to NYU?"

"I didn't know about it or the one to the community college. No one had told me."

"But you could still have gone to NYU, all expenses paid. Why'd you choose BYU where you have to pay everything?" he asked with an incredulous tone.

"Well, first of all, I didn't know about NYU. So, by the time I found out I'd already paid my rent for the summer in Provo. And, secondly . . . I paused for a moment, and I quietly said, "it scared me."

"It scared you?!" Sam exclaimed loudly into the receiver, which I instantly pulled away from my ear.

"Yeah," I said, after a slight pause. "It scared me. I'm from Ashbury—Provo's a big city to me. Besides, I spoke with my parents—when Mom wasn't pushing me to pack—about the scholarship, and —they told me they'd known about it but hadn't wanted me to go to New York by myself. They said they felt I wasn't mature enough to be there alone."

"Really. I can't believe you let an opportunity like that pass you by. You chose Provo over New York." Hearing the disappointment in his voice, I relived how stupid I'd been. But I was raised to listen to my parents—I respected and trusted their opinions and advice. However, I should've realized I was almost an adult and should have made up my own mind. That was a mistake I'd never make again.

"I didn't realize how big a deal it was, at the time," I tried to explain to him. But now knowing the opportunity I'd let pass me by, I couldn't deny the disappointment that often washed over me like a wave. Trying to change the subject, I asked, "Are you still living at home?"

"Yeah."

"When do you send in your mission papers?"

"I've already got my call."

"Really? Where are you going? When do you leave?" I asked, very excited to hear his news.

"Paris."

"Paris? No way! That's soooo exciting! Are you happy about the call?"

"Yeah. I think it'll be fun going foreign."

"Is Sara Jane happy or is she sad you'll be leaving?"

"I don't know, probably both," he responded with a sigh.

"Well, I'm really excited for you. When do you leave?"

"Tomorrow," he said.

"Tomorrow! And you're just calling me now?" I wasn't sure whether I should be unhappy that he was just now calling me or flattered that he was calling me at all. Either way, it was great to hear from him. After my question, there was only silence on the other end of the line. So after the long pause, I said, "Well, it's really great to hear your voice and your good news," I said.

"You'll have to call me when you get back—well, you better call me . . . I hope you'll call me?"

Through his wonderful chuckle, he responded, "You'll hear from me. Don't worry." Again, the awkward silence, then he said, "Well, I better go. See ya." And he hung up before I could say bye. I looked at the receiver for a moment before putting it in the cradle on the phone.

I sat on my bed thinking about our conversation and the reality that this past year had sped by without thinking about him once. There was way too much new eye candy for my brain to take in and still think about the old eye candy. Before I could get too melancholy, I heard loud voices and laughter in my living room; we had visitors and it was time to have some fun. So, I quickly pushed any thoughts of Sam to the back of my mind, once again, and went out to enjoy my friends.

I didn't expect to hear from him again unless it was a wedding announcement. I was glad that his mission was so far away and would get him away from le nullard—which meant the rabbit, en Francaise. I truly believed he needed to see the bigger picture of life and learn that there were more lapins—again, rabbit in French—than his little bunny in Ashbury. As for me, in the past year, I felt like I'd moved on. *"Qui n'avance pas, recule."* Which loosely translated, means 'who does not move forward, recedes.'

The Stranger

I only lived in Provo for a couple of years before I moved to Salt Lake City. I had a plan and there was a method to my madness, or should I say my moving. Since I came from a small town, I wanted to gradually move up in the size of cities I lived in so that when I made the shift to Los Angeles, I would be more confident than scared in moving around a big city.

When I first got to Salt Lake, I lived in a condo in the west valley while I worked at a retail store nearby. After two years, all my roommates seemed to be moving so I found another apartment up in the Avenues. My dad had lived in Salt Lake very briefly when he was my age and only paid forty dollars a month for rent, so he challenged me to find a place for the same price, and I did.

Sadly, I learned that with cheap rent comes cockroaches—with that apartment anyway. It wasn't until after I moved in that I experienced my first la Cucaracha and learned what it was like living with them. There were nights when I'd wake up with them crawling all over me and my bed. I would have to run into the shower and try to shake them off (*bluuuck!),* and if it hadn't been for a couple of my roommates that already lived there, that I really liked, I wouldn't have lasted as long as I did. And, it was while I lived in this apartment that I began working in the gift shop at the Hotel Utah.

The Hotel Utah was a very well-known old hotel downtown across from Temple Square, and a preferred hotel of many celebrities that came to town. While working at the hotel, Danny Kaye, Neil Diamond, and President Reagan all stayed there. The Concierge who'd worked there for over forty years told me that Jimmy Stewart and Henry Fonda used to stay there every time they'd come into town. Of course, I didn't get to see any of them.

Working in the gift shop was always a new experience, as I

dealt with the hotel guests that came from all over the world. I often had to remind myself when speaking to a foreign guest that these people weren't deaf, they just spoke a different language.

Now that I'd been living away from home for a few years, I rarely, if ever, thought about the guys from home. There were so many good-looking men everywhere I turned, that it pushed my old crushes deeper and deeper into the recesses in my head. Also, my point of view had morphed a bit since leaving home; yes, I still wanted to be a world-famous actress, but I also wanted the romance of falling in love and getting married. That was as far as my "dream" went, though; I never really thought about life *after* the honeymoon, as I was sure many girls my age didn't.

Most girls get caught up in the excitement of the engagement, then the wedding, and then the honeymoon, not realizing life would take over after those events. It seemed like one could say that marriage was on my "bucket list" of things to accomplish, but my major focus was receiving an Academy Award one day. So, with that in mind, I continued on my merry way working, looking for famous people, and fantasizing about being swept off my feet as described in any romance novel. Yes, I still read romance novels.

I currently had a crush on one guy from church named Rod, and when I was working the evening shift in the gift shop, I'd have time to daydream and imagine this guy falling all over himself to get to me. I would think back on every moment I saw him and would read into any little movement he made as to whether or not he was interested in me. Then I'd reproach myself with how silly I was to think he even knew I existed, especially since he was dating another girl. Ten to one he didn't even know my name or cared whether or not I looked at him. *He was so out of my league.* But that didn't stop my fantasies.

One Sunday in September, the hotel was particularly full due to a big convention happening in town and people were in from all over. My little gift shop was so full, I was grateful for the counter that gave me space from the small crowd of shoppers looking for keepsakes, mementos, film, candy, and tobacco before they went to their next event. Crowds like that helped make the time pass quickly and me to appreciate the quiet moments.

Ever scoping out guys, normally I could wait on a customer and still be aware of any male specimens that might come into buy something; I had turned multitasking into an art. However, one day the crowds in the shop were so thick that I was a bit off my game. So much so that I hadn't noticed a potential stud that at some point had entered and was standing at the far end of the shop, looking at magazines.

What I could tell from the few glances I managed his way, he was tall with a great physique wearing a thick, oatmeal-colored sweater, jeans and had black curly hair. Thus far, he'd kept his back to me so I couldn't decide whether or not he was worth my fantasies. I hoped he'd turn his face towards me before he left. If he was unattractive then no big deal, but if he was cute then I could try and flirt with him. At least my version of flirting which meant to make him laugh before he left and work my magic that way. In my experience, I'd learned that most men like a funny girl. *How many of those men marry the funny girl, I didn't know.*

Finally, the crowd in the shop dissipated, returning to their event in whatever room in the hotel their particular presentation was taking place. It was just me, the faceless stranger, and an older, short, bald man in the shop. I waited behind the counter for the faceless stranger to either choose one magazine to purchase or turn and leave and never darken my doorway again, but either way, I needed him to turn around. I was waiting for that to happen when the older man came up and dropped his purchases on the counter.

"I'd like a roll of film too, please," he said, pointing to the rows of film we kept behind the counter.

"Which one would you like?"

"That one," he pointed to a Kodak box of twenty-four shot film.

"This one?"

"Yes." I handed him the roll and as I turned to the register, I saw the strangers face for the first time.

"Sam!" I exclaimed in surprise. *He* was the mysterious magazine peruser. And boy did he look good with his five o'clock shadow that usually began around two o'clock. And that shawl-collared sweater he wore stressed his physique. Once again, I was in heaven's favor.

My exclamation to Sam made the old man jump. I held up my hand. "Hold on," I said to Sam, then turned to the old man and cringed. "I'm sorry." I said, then pointed towards Sam, "Don't go anywhere. Stay right there."

Sam chuckled to himself. "Some things never change," he muttered low enough for me to hear as he turned away from the counter.

Apologizing to the old man again, I said, "I'm so sorry." I paused, trying to remember where I was. "Oh yeah . . .."

"The film." He motioned towards the little box of film on the counter.

"Uh . . . yeah . . . that'll be four dollars and twenty cents," I said and watched the old man dig into his wallet and count out the money.

"One . . . two . . . " he said at an extremely slow pace, and I looked over at Sam and crossed my eyes, ". . . three . . . four dollars . . . and five . . . ten . . . twenty cents," he finished, dropping the coins on the counter next to the dollar bills.

"Would you like a bag for that?" I asked, wishing he'd just go.

"No thank you. I can put it right in my pocket," he said, patting the side of his coat.

"Thanks. And, sorry again about scaring ya there." He just laughed and walked out.

Once he left the shop, I rushed around the counter and hugged Sam.

"Wow! I can't believe you're here," I said as I stood back and looked at him. "How'd you find me?" I furrowed my brow.

"I called your mom."

"You did?"

Laughing, he said, "Yes. You sound surprised."

"At least *my* mom will give you my information. I called *your* mom and she said she didn't know where you were."

"She did?"

"Did I do something to upset her?"

"Not that I know of. You should've called one of my sisters."

"I did. Or, at least I ran into Martha at the mall and she told me, in not so many words, to leave you alone."

"*She* did?"

"Your family doesn't like me, Sam."

"I don't know why," he responded, confused.

"I do. It's called Sara Jane." Sam didn't comment, just stood with a creased brow, so to lighten the mood, I said, "But that doesn't matter now. You're here! I'm so excited to see you! I can't believe you're here." I gave him another hug. *He looks good, I'm gonna take any opportunity I can while he'll allow it.* Stepping out of the hug, I looked at him again and giving a faint whistle. "Mm-mm-mmm, you look fantastic," I said, looking him up and down. In high school, I would've never dared.

"Shut up," he said all embarrassed and pushed me away, which made me laugh. It felt good to be in control—if only for a moment.

"How long have you been out here?"

"'Bout a week."

"And I am just now hearing from you?!"

"I had to find ya first. I didn't know where you were."

"Yeah, yeah, yeah." I paused and grabbed his bicep. *Goodness gracious,* I thought. "Are you here for good?"

"For now, yeah."

"That is sooooo cool!!" I looked at my watch and frowned. It was four forty-five and we closed at five o'clock on Sundays. "Hmm . . . I gotta close up," I said hesitantly.

"How long will that take?"

"Too long for you to wait." I hated saying anything that would cause him to leave. "Wanna meet me at my apartment? I'll be home in about thirty minutes," I hesitantly asked.

"Okay. What's your address?"

After he left with my address and the directions I gave him, I barely remember closing the shop as my mind was a million miles away. *Was he really here and wanting to spend time with me? I'll get to have him all to myself? And, he looks soooo good.*

Before leaving the hotel, we always changed out of our uniform, so heading home I was already in my street clothes and wouldn't need to waste any time changing. I was still on a high from having him look for me. I guess I'd assumed he'd be married to Hoppy by then. To be honest, I hadn't thought about him since he called me the night before he left on his mission. I felt a little guilty having been so disloyal to my crush. I was embarrassed at how easily my head could be turned by a handsome face.

I drove home still basking in the glow of having seen Sam and knowing that he'd come looking for me. As I approached my street, it was habit for me to locate the home my apartment was in before parking my car. I lived in what I considered a Stepford-like neighborhood with all its duplicate homes. It often caused me to have to drive past it in order to check the address, and then turn around and try and park again.

Once I'd located my apartment, I slowed down to find a place to park on the street, but seeing a good-looking guy sitting on the doorstep threw me, causing me to drive past it. Never before had a good-looking guy sat waiting on the doorstep for any of my roommates before, let alone me. I turned my car around to head back and had every intention of parking. But as I slowly drove by a second time, the sheer enjoyment of knowing that the gorgeous man sitting on the stoop was waiting for *me* caused me to pass it again. I turned around yet again, *determined* I'd pull up to the curb and park, only pausing a moment to appreciate this piece of art framed by my piece-of-crap car window and waved.

"Heeeeeey!" I called to Sam, finding a spot and turning off the engine. "Where'd you park?" I asked.

"Right up there," he said, pointing up the street to a motorcycle. *No way! He rode a motorcycle?! Be still my heart. Can he get any more rugged?* It was like a Windsong perfume commercial.

"You ride a motorcycle?" I asked, trying to keep my cool.

"Ya gotta take me for a ride," I said as I walked towards him.

"Wanna go now?" he asked, standing up from the step.

"Uh . . . yeah! Of course! Just let me put my purse and stuff in the house," I said. He waited outside while I quickly threw my stuff in the living room. "Okay, let's go." I reappeared and shut my apartment door.

As we walked up the sidewalk to his bike, we heard metal hitting metal, a thump, and watched as a motorcyclist flew through the air and landed between the parked cars. I followed Sam as he sprinted towards the accident at the end of the block. Approaching the victim, a flood of relief swept over us when we didn't see any blood. We found him laying with his head on the curb and his body in the street in front of the parked car he'd just hit. He moaned, barely moving.

"Are you all right?" Sam asked, kneeling near the rider's head on the curb.

"I think so," the man responded in a barely audible tone, attempting to sit up. Sam quickly put his hand on his shoulder to stop him.

"You better stay there," he said, then turned to me. "Gracie, go call an ambulance."

"Okay, I'll be right back." I quickly retreated to my apartment to make the call. It probably took me all of two minutes to call 911 and explain the situation. We were told to keep the rider laying still until the ambulance got there and that they had already dispatched the cops. On my way out, I grabbed a blanket from the couch and returned to the scene of the accident. As I approached the end of the block, the cops were just arriving. I handed Sam the blanket.

"We should put this on him to avoid shock, dontcha think?"

"Great idea." He took the blanket and lightly placed it on the rider, who hadn't attempted to move again.

"Did you see what happened?" the first cop asked as the second cop ran over and crouched over the rider.

"All we saw was him flying up in the air and landing as he is," answered Sam.

"We only heard the crash when he hit the car," I quickly added. My adrenaline was pumping.

"Yeah, and he was lying in this position," Sam continued.

The rider was completely still—he seemed to have passed out.

"Sam made him stay down," I offered, and at that moment, the ambulance pulled up, and the EMTs jumped out and came running over.

"Can you folks stick around so we can take your statement?" asked the second cop as Sam and I moved back to give the EMTs room.

"Sure," we said in unison, realizing that this could end up taking most of what time we had left. The plan had been for Sam to give me a ride on his bike, but after seeing the somersault the rider had just done, I wasn't sure I wanted a ride now, especially since he didn't have a second helmet with him.

The whole incident from when the rider hit the car to when the cops left probably took about two hours, including when they took our statements—one at a time. The cops told us that if he hadn't been wearing a helmet his head would have cracked open like a watermelon.

Afterward, we really didn't have time to do anything since we both had to be at work early the next morning. So we settled for walking around my neighborhood.

"This neighborhood might come across as Stepford wife-like-ish with all the same architecture, but it's an old neighborhood and still has a charm all its own," I told Sam as we walked.

"I noticed that."

"I usually have to drive past my house a couple of times before I'm sure it's mine," I confessed with a chuckle.

Laughing, Sam said, "You can't find your house?".

"Well, look at 'em. They all look alike." I waved at the homes in the neighborhood.

"You are too much," Sam said, smiling at me. Then with a big grin, he said, "Some things never change, I guess."

"Hey!" I said, laughing, while playfully pushing him away. We both enjoyed being in each other's company again. We walked in silence for a few minutes before I asked, "How'd you like Paris?"

"It's a beautiful city."

"I bet. I hope to see it myself one day."

"The food was great, and the people were amazing! As much as I love Ashbury, it was hard to come back to the small town after the City of Lights—Paris."

"I know what the City of Lights is," I said. "What have you been doing since your return?"

"Working at my grandfather's plant."

"Did you like that work?"

"No! But there wasn't much else to do."

"That's my thought."

"It was my grandfather that got me my job out here. He knew I was about to explode if I stayed there much longer."

"I'm surprised you lasted that long." Although, I knew why he'd stayed. "Whatever the reason, I'm glad you're here now. It's a nice surprise." I accentuated my remark by slipping my hand through the crook of his arm and hugging it for a moment as we walked. Again, we walked in silence as twilight began to color the evening. It was such a beautiful fall night with the leaves gently falling from the trees and the briskness of the night air.

"Well, if I'm totally honest, it wasn't just the small town or the promise of a job that brought me here," he said as I let go of his arm.

"Oh," I responded, totally unprepared for what he was about to confess. "Then what was it?"

"I missed *you*," he continued, looking ahead of us. "The popcorn shop wasn't the same."

"You have to admit I made a pretty mean shriveled hot dog. Not surprised you missed that," I replied dryly, then gave a sniff that would rival Barney Fife's. *Wow! Sometimes I surprise myself.*

"That, and the girls are so young that work there now."

We continued to talk about everything, except whether or not he was still with Hoppy. I really wanted to ask, but I was afraid of the answer I might hear, so I adopted the policy of "don't ask don't tell." I wasn't ready to give up the fantasy playing in my head yet.

But the true gem of the evening was when Sam confessed that he missed me. After that, nothing else mattered. He missed me!! He . . . missed . . . me! And, I hadn't even thought about him once. Oops!

5, 6, 7, 8!

Now that Sam was in town, if we weren't working, then we were either doing something, attending an activity together, or chatting on the phone. It was so much fun having a friend from home in town.

"I think I'm going to audition for Seven Brides for Seven Brothers," I told Sam while we waited in a booth for our food.

He squinted his eyes at me and asked, "You're going to audition for a musical?"

"Yes. Why are you so skeptical?"

"Do you dance and sing?" he asked, then said, "The only time I've seen you dance was that silly stuff you'd do when we were in high school. Do you seriously sing?"

A waitress appeared with two plates. "Okay, which one of you had the cheeseburger?" We looked at each other with raised eyebrows, then at her.

"We both did," Sam said with a furrowed brow. The waitress looked at him blankly, then at the plates before she broke into grin.

"Ha ha! I'm just messing with ya," she said with a wink and a chuckle, which made me laugh, then set both plates in front of us, and said before walking away, "Enjoy."

"That was really funny. She had us going there." Sam just rolled his eyes as he stuffed a few fries in his mouth.

"Oh, come on. Lighten up, ya old sourpuss." I told him, then proceeded to make silly faces at him until he cracked a smile.

"You're so weird," he said before he could stop the chuckle that escaped his lips.

"Heeeeey!"

"So," he began between bites, "you never sang in a choir, but now you're going to audition for a musical?" He tilted his head.

"Look, I've taken a couple years of tap, and I sing all the time."

"But seriously—for people who don't know you to hear?" He asked, still doubtful.

"Yes," I said before taking a bite.

"What are you going to sing?" Sam asked, eating more fries.

"I'm going to sing "Don't Rain on My Parade," from Funny Girl." I said and smiled.

"Well, the title is very apropos for you."

"Ha ha," I glowered at him.

"I'm sorry, I just don't want you to look foolish. That comes so easy for you," he said, followed by, "Ouch!" as I kicked him under the table and threw some of my fries at his face.

"I've never auditioned for musical theater before, but I can't imagine it being *that* tough," I said, looking over at him. "So, why don't you go with me to the audition and you can protect me from looking foolish. Which I really don't think I will," I said cockily. *This will be a home run; I can't fail*, I reassured myself.

"You got a date. I can't miss an opportunity to see

greatness in the making," he said sarcastically. I rolled my eyes. Then he smiled and winked. *Darn him!* He knew I couldn't stay angry when he did that.

"You'll see. I'll sing as well as Streisand and dance like Gene Kelly. It'll be great and you'll eat your cynical words."

Or, so I thought, until the day before the audition and I woke up with the worst cold that had settled right in my vocal cords. *How could this be happening?* I couldn't believe my luck. *What should I do?* So, I called Sam after he got home from work.

"Hello?" he answered.

"Heelloooo?" I barely croaked out, not sure if he could even hear me. When he didn't answer I croaked again, "Heeellooo?"

"Hello?" Sam asked again, waited for a few seconds and just as I was about to try again, he hung up. I took a couple of swallows of warm tea, cleared my throat, and then called him again.

"Hello, Sam?" I croaked a little louder, "Don't hang up, it's me." I coughed after the effort.

"Me who?"

Even my cough sounded like a squeak. "It's me, Sam . . . Gracie."

"Gracie?" he asked. "You sound awful."

"Thanks," I squeaked. "In all fairness, I sound worse than I feel."

"Uh, what?" He paused. "Never mind. Take care of yourself and I'll call you tomorrow."

"Don't forget my audition tomorrow," I croaked before he hung up. My phone rang seconds later.

"You're still going to audition?" Sam asked before I could even say hello.

"Of course," I responded a bit louder. My voice was warming up with the tea I was drinking, I was actually making noise when I spoke.

"But you sound awful," he repeated.

"I'll be fine."

"Okaaay," Sam relented. "I'll see ya tomorrow." And he hung up before I could say bye. *I wish he'd stop that.*

The next day I awoke and immediately began to speak to see if I had a voice; it wasn't great, but better than the day before.

L. K. Lawrence

316

So I chose to save my voice until the audition and hoped it would be stronger then.

When Sam showed up to go with me to the audition, I had barely said a word the whole day. Hopefully, the tea I'd been drinking all day to warm up my vocal cords would let me perform the singing part of the audition.

I drove my car to the audition since I didn't think it would be a good idea for me to be on a motorcycle where the cold air could get to my throat.

"Are you really sure you wanna do this?" Sam asked as we sat at a light.

"I'm fine," I whispered, accelerating again when the light turned green.

"Yeah, you sound great," Sam responded dryly. I glared at him before slamming on the brakes as the new light turned red. "Nice," was all he said.

The audition was at one of the high schools in the area. Pulling into the near-empty parking lot gave me hope that I'd have a better chance at being cast rather than rejected, cold and all. But Sam wasn't drinking the same Kool-Aid I was that day.

"Not many people here for such a big production," Sam commented as we pulled into a parking spot.

"There's enough," I whispered. We walked into the school through the main entrance and followed the posted signs directing us to the auditorium.

Standing in front of the doors, the butterflies in my stomach were waking up. Before I could grab it, Sam pulled the door open for me, exposing the dark auditorium.

"I don't think you should do this. It's not gonna end well," he told me as he followed me inside.

"Shuuut up! You're not helping."

Being Saturday, there were no students in attendance at the school, but there were probably about thirty actresses sitting in the front of the auditorium waiting for instructions. I left Sam sitting in the back and headed to join the others. I'd brought a bottle of water with me and took sips of it to soothe my throat. I'd just sat in a seat when one of the people in charge stood and began to give us instructions.

"Can I have your attention please," he called. "My name is Pete and I'm the stage manager for this production of Seven Brides for Seven Brothers, and this is Shannon, the choreographer," he said, pointing to the girl standing next to him. "The schedule for today begins with the dance portion—Shannon will break everyone up into groups of four so that you can learn the choreography, then we'll have the singing part after." When he'd finished, Shannon began grouping us together by having us count to seven, divided us into our groups, and we left the auditorium to learn the dance steps.

I was really excited and felt confident that I could do this, I mean how tough could the dance be? So, standing in a portion of the hall designated for our group, the four of us watched our dance instructor's every move. You could tell those girls who had dance experience by their attire: from the sweats they wore to the leotards and tights with the thick stockings that kept their calves warm. Me? I came in jeans and tennis shoes. *Oops!* But I moved forward with confidence—I had this.

I concentrated so hard on the instructor when she executed the steps, and repeated them over and over again: two side-steps to the right, then a glide to the left, airplane turn, touch the floor while kicking the same leg out behind us, then we straightened up with our feet together and kicked our left leg out in front, then posed with our right hip extended and our feet crossed. The four of us practiced until Pete came out and motioned everyone in through the side stage doors, where we were told to line up in the wings.

When we entered the stage, I made sure that I was in the very back line of girls, which wasn't the best choice. The back part of the stage flooring had a foot-wide hole that ran the length of the stage, with strings of wire running alongside. I had only a moment to change where I stood on stage before I had to run through the steps they'd taught us out in the hall. *I should be able to maneuver this fine,* I told myself.

"5, 6, 7, 8!" called the choreographer and we began to move en masse through the routine. I was already off my game after the first run-through, having worn tennis shoes instead of dance shoes that the other girls wore. Tennis shoes aren't at all good for dancing, I quickly found out.

Even with all the commotion that was going on in my area of the stage, I'd made it through the first run of the routine. *This isn't so bad,* I thought, *but I will need to get dance shoes for rehearsals.*

"5, 6, 7, 8!" the choreographer called. Again, the group

moved together with just me and a few others stumbling over the steps as they picked up the tempo. I almost got kicked in the chest, so I had to move during the routine, which threw me off even more than I already was. And as soon as we finished, the choreographer yelled out right away, "5, 6, 7, 8! Make it count, ladies!"

Just as I began the routine, I noticed out of the corner of my eye a stage electrician behind me. He was trying to avoid both the wires, the hole in the floor, and being kicked. But for some reason he stopped right behind me. That was all I needed to throw me off yet again; as I began the airplane turn, I was turning my head when my right contact moved off my eye, throwing my depth perception off, so I quickly closed that eye and continued with one eye.

Unfortunately, now I was half a count off so when I kicked my right leg out behind me, I accidentally kicked the electrician who fell against the wall. I immediately tried to recover, which pushed me forward right into the foot of the girl ahead of me as she kicked up right into my chest, throwing me off balance as my right foot landed right in the midst of the wires on the floor. In an effort to lessen the chance of injury to one of us dancers, an electrician offstage pulled the wires I was already standing on, causing me to lose what little balance I had left. I fell back, bottom first, right into the hole in the floor.

With the help of the electrician I'd accidentally kicked into the wall, I promptly extricated myself up out of the hole—I was mortified. I hoped neither the director nor choreographer had seen the fiasco I'd caused. I limped through the routine once more before they excused us to prepare for the singing part of the audition.

We had a ten-minute break to get water and our music ready. With only a slight limp I made my way around to the back of the auditorium to find Sam doubled over in his seat. At first, I hoped he was in pain, but realized he was convulsed in laughter and was trying not to make a sound. He was laughing so hard that tears were running down his face. I just stood there looking at him. *Really??!!*

Wiping his eyes, he feigned concern as he asked, "You okay?" and began to laugh again.

"Shhh!" I croaked out, my voice a bit more audible.

"Whoo!" he said, trying to gain control. "That was like watching an I Love Lucy episode. I haven't laughed like that in a long time."

"Uh-huh . . . thanks. Gla . . . glad you're entertained," I responded over his laughter. "My hip hurts though," I muttered, rubbing it.

"Oh, sorry." He wiped his eyes. "Are you okay?" He swallowed the laughter bubbling up in his throat.

"Yeah, like you care," I croaked. "Hand me that other bottle of water please," I asked, not looking at him out of embarrassment. Sam handed me my cold water bottle which I thoughtlessly rubbed back and forth on my hip. He turned away from me in his seat to muffle the fit of laughter that hit him again, making his body shake. I grabbed my sheet music and with an exasperated sigh, limped towards the front of the auditorium to wait for the singing part of the audition.

"Attention! Attention please, ladies," called Pete. "Ladies! Please. We need quiet so we can begin the next portion of the audition!" The auditorium quieted down as everyone stopped talking to listen. "So that everyone can warm up without disturbing whoever is on stage, we ask that you all go out into the hallway and we'll call you in when it's your turn." All the girls began to get up and move towards the doors at the side. "Be sure and have your music ready when we call your name," Pete instructed.

Out in the hallway, all the girls went off by themselves to warm up their vocal cords but me. I leaned against the wall and just drank water, trying to make sure that they would be able to even *hear* my voice; but I was really wishing for some warm tea to drink. I wasn't sure the cold water was that great for my throat.

Time seemed to crawl as I waited out in the hall and watched the girls, one-by-one, get called in to sing.

Finally, I heard, "Gracie Kaye," as the assistant director stuck his head around the door, then he called again, "Gracie Ka-" but stopped when he saw me walk towards him. "You're up next. Wait in the wings." I walked past him into the darkness of backstage and waited for my turn to sing.

Listening to the girl before me, I was amazed at her talent and hoped I would impress the director with mine. Although, I couldn't understand why I didn't have any butterflies; was it because I didn't feel well or because I thought I was so well prepared? While contemplating this, I heard my name called. I walked out of the wing, past the accompanist, to the center of the stage.

"Name," I heard from the seats.

Clearing my throat, I strained to croak out, "Hi." I walked closer to the front of the stage. "My name is Gracie Kaye," I said while I looked over the floor lights into the dark, searching to find where the director was seated. Once my vision became acclimated, I could see three people sitting in the seats mid-way up.

"What?" This was more of a demand than a question.

"I said, my name is Gracie Kaye." I strained to speak louder so they could hear me.

"Can't even hear her," I heard one of them say.

"What will you be singing?" someone asked.

"Don't Rain on My Parade," I replied, then walked over to the piano, handing my music to the male accompanist.

"What key?" he asked me, taking my music.

"Wha . . . what key?" I asked, giving him a blank look as I quickly unscrewed the lid on my water bottle to take another swig and to buy some time.

He responded, "Yeah. What key do you sing in?"

"Whatever key *that*'s written in," I said, pointing at the

sheet music. I had no idea what key I sang in.

"Okay," the pianist said with a sigh. "You sing, and I'll make the music work," he told me with a dismissive wave of his hands.

"Great, thank you," I said, and returned to the center of the stage. Then the pianist played an intro that I didn't recognize, so I just stood there.

"That's your cue," he hissed.

Looking at him sheepishly, I said, "Sorry. I'm ready." And just as I took a deep breath, he played the intro, which I missed; he started over and repeatedly hit the first chord for me to start. *It's now or never,* I thought. I took a deep breath and began to sing. The first two lines seemed to go okay, but when I started the third line my voice was gone. Not that it was there to begin with, but now it was really gone. I looked at the accompanist nervously, not sure what I should do.

He mouthed to me, "Louder!"

I tried with all my might, but nothing came out.

"Next!" shouted a voice I hadn't heard before—perhaps the director—and I froze. "Next!!" I gave one last searching look into the darkness of the auditorium and slinked off the stage, mortified.

Sam was waiting for me outside the door. And, lucky for him he wasn't laughing—to my face, anyway. Not that I could've said anything if he were laughing because he wouldn't have heard it, my voice was so badly gone. We drove home in silence, except for the periodic muffled snicker. Every so often I would look at him, but his face was turned towards the window with his hand covering his mouth, and his shoulders shook with suppressed laughter. *It's a good thing he is so gorgeous,* I told myself, *or I'd leave him out on the highway to thumb his way home.* I knew he would not let me forget this.

At work on Monday, I told Sharon, my supervisor, about the audition.

"Sooooo, are you a singer?" Sharon asked.

"Not really. I mean, I sing along with my records, and I love to sing, but . . ."

"When you were in school, did you study singing?"

"No. But I studied tap in college."

Laughing, she said, "Wait . . . wait, wait, wait. You don't consider yourself a singer and you've never studied singing, but you thought you could take a Barbra Streisand song to an audition?"

"Yeeeaaaah," I said.

"A Barbra Streisand song," Sharon said, then repeated her name to me slowly, trying to get it to sink in, "A Baaaaar brrrrrrraaaaa Sttrrrrreisand song." She paused for my reaction. I gave her a blank look, and she continued, "I think it's great you auditioned, but don't ya think that a Barbra Streisand song is a little beyond your capability? I mean, singing along with a record is different from singing at an audition." Still no response from me. "There's a reason *she* wins music awards and you don't."

"Gee thanks. This was just my first audition. I'm sure I'll do better at the next one," I said confidently.

"All I'm saying is that for your next audition maybe you should sing something a little more along your skill level, like The Wheels on the Bus."

"Hilarious," I said, hoping she'd shut up. "I can sing that Barbra Streisand song just fine with my record so why would it be any different with a piano player? The only reason this audition hadn't gone well was because of the awful cold I had," I continued, still in denial.

Later that week as I reported to my acting class about the audition, after everyone gained control and stopped laughing, I was again reprimanded for having tried a Streisand song for my audition piece.

"You really need to do songs that are in your skill level," explained Jean Collette, my acting teacher. Jean had lived in New York in the sixties and had performed in musical theater, so I respected her opinion. If she said Streisand was above my skill level, I needed to listen.

She continued to compare my experience to that of someone who sings in the shower and how the acoustics are better in the shower than in a bigger room. Not unlike when I sang with a record, I couldn't hear myself well enough to judge if I was on key.

"I'll give you the name and number of a vocal coach. You go meet with him and he'll help you choose the right music for your next audition," Jean said with an understanding smile.

Jean's explanation as to the reasons I should avoid any Streisand songs reminded me of a conversation Beans and I had once.

"Hey Beans, do you think I can sing?" I asked her because I knew she would tell me the truth.

Beans thought for a moment then as tactfully as she could, told me, "Well Gracie, you can sing if you're playing a character who thinks they can sing but really can't, or are in the chorus where no one can really hear you."

"Oh," I mumbled, totally deflated. "Thanks." I visualized any chance of a career crashing to the ground. Maybe I wouldn't be one of those triple threats: someone who can sing, dance, and act. So far, I was one out of three. I hoped.

"Gracie, I'm only being honest," apologized Beans. She'd heard me sing many times in her car to the soundtrack of "Man of La Mancha," so if anyone would know she would. From that day on I never attempted to sing in public until the audition.

Frankly My Dear...

Between work and all the activities going on, unless we were working, Sam and I were hanging out together. Soon everyone saw us as a couple—and I did nothing to dissuade them.

It was like high school all over again. I had this gorgeous guy's attention and I loved it. Yet, I avoided the big bunny that was in the room. Having Sam with me in Salt Lake was like having a second chance at what should have been, pre-Hoppy. Except now I was older, more outgoing, and aware of what I thought I'd lost in high school. I gave it my all and I avoided any mention of Hoppy at all cost. But, in all fairness, he wasn't talking about her either.

I pondered whether it was because of our avoidance in discussing her that we never got super close; we still never held hands or kissed. It had only been a few weeks, so maybe I needed to be patient and just enjoy the fun times we were having together. One thing I knew was that I was in full crush mode again. Sam had it all as far as I was concerned: he was tall, gorgeous, in Salt Lake, and enjoyed spending time with me. What more could a girl ask for?

Soon the holiday season was looming in the near distance; Halloween was the first to approach and there was a big dance that most everyone would be attending. It took a lot of talking, but between me and my roommates we finally got Sam to agree to come as a motorcyclist—big stretch there, since he would be wearing the normal attire he wore when he rode his bike. But at least he was coming.

I, on the other hand, was really looking forward to the Halloween dance. I thought I had a great costume lined up: I would dress up as Carol Burnett's version of Scarlett O'Hara. I'd rented a southern belle hoop skirt and purchased loads of green fabric and tried to duplicate the costume she wore to the best of my ability and budget, including the curtain rod through the shoulders.

Sam and I had planned to go together to the dance, but because I had to work overtime, we decided to meet at the dance instead. This proved to be a much better plan, since it would take me longer to get into my costume and I wouldn't have the stress knowing that others were waiting on me. Although I was excited about my costume, I worried no one else would get it.

One thing I hadn't taken into consideration when I decided to attach a curtain rod to my shoulders was driving from my home to the dance in my little car. It took me a good ten minutes to figure out how to maneuver everything in, then prayed that no one went by and side swiped me while the rod stuck out the driver side window. It never crossed my mind to condense the rod down.

The building where the dance was held was dark when I drove up, but I was sure it was the place. Yet, being unfamiliar with it I cautiously walked around inside in search of the ballroom, while trying to avoid dinging any walls with the curtain rod. I gave a sigh of relief when I found the ballroom on the second floor, having followed my ears to the loud music playing.

The ballroom was huge; I could tell there was a large

crowd attending, even in the dark. I could make out what had to be hundreds of singles in costumes, mingling, eating, and dancing. As I maneuvered my way around the sides of the dance floor, I struggled with the extended curtain rod on my shoulders. In the end, and with the help of a kind stranger, I shortened it to avoid putting out any eyes.

I tried to find anyone that I might know, which was hard with all the different costumes. I decided to just stand on the side and hope that someone would ask me to dance until I could find my friends and Sam. First, I danced with a killer bee, then an Elvis look-alike, and while I was on the floor dancing with a Christmas elf, I saw my roommate, Pam, dressed as a mangy cat, four or five couples away.

Pulling the elf behind me, I quickly danced over to her. "Have you seen Sam?" I asked.

"You look great," she said, making me do a turn. "It really turned out cute."

"Thanks. Have you seen Sam?"

"No. He called and told Rosie that he was coming with his roommate."

"Hm." I frowned.

"I'm sure he's here somewhere. You guys'll find each other. You always do." Frowning, I turned and finished the dance with the elf. When that dance ended, he walked me back to the sideline and left to ask another girl. I stood there hoping that I'd dance again, but the song started, and I was one of the few standing on the side. I worried that if Sam saw me standing on the sideline not dancing, he might view me as a wallflower and I wanted him to see me as popular and desired by others. *Why was my self-esteem still so low?* I stood there hiding in my thoughts through the whole song and as everyone came crushing off the dance floor to prepare for the next dance, I put a smile on my face hoping to be asked to dance. But the dance started and ended with me still standing on the side.

I paced the length of the room hoping that I'd find Sam, but I found Stephen and Rosie instead. They were dressed as a doctor and nurse. *How original.*

"Have you guys seen Sam?"

"That is really classic," said Stephen, laughing.

"I love it," Rosie said.

"Thanks. Do you know where Sam is?"

"I don't really look for him," Rosie told me. "That's your job."

"Wanna dance?" Stephen asked Rosie as he pulled her on the floor.

Not knowing what to do, I returned to the sideline and stood there with my hands on my hips searching the dance floor for anything that even closely resembled Sam's costume as a motorcycle rider. Getting Sam to do anything outside of the norm was tough, add dressing up for a dance and you might as well forget about it. But he had agreed to come to this dance—even if it was as himself. Again, beggars can't be choosers. This had become my mantra with him. If he just wasn't so darn gorgeous.

But, as time passed, and I still hadn't found him I began to wonder if he'd even come. I knew he wasn't a fan of dancing or dances, but I hoped he was a fan of me and would show up just because I had asked him to. So I stood there trying to figure out my next move when I heard, "Would you like to dance?"

I turned hoping it was Sam, instead I saw an old friend from Ferron. "Oh my gosh! Leon!" I attempted to hug him, which was a little tough with the curtain rod getting in the way. "How are you?" Leon was a few years older than me and had always made me laugh, which caused me to have a crush on him.

"I love your costume," he told me, laughing.

"Thanks. Where's yours?"

"I don't have one. I'm only here for a couple of weeks then off to New York to start my teaching job. Besides, I wasn't planning on coming to a Halloween dance."

"Wow, New York?" Before he could answer, Roy Orbison's 'Pretty Woman' began to play.

"Let's dance," he said, pulling me out on the floor. Leon was always so much fun to dance with that I just let myself go. Soon I broke out in a sweat as I danced and sang along with old Roy and laughed the whole time. After the song ended, we walked back to the side of the dance floor as we chatted about New York until we heard the beginning strains of Kenny Loggins' 'Footloose.'

"I love this song! Ya gotta dance with me!" I said, as I pulled him back on the floor. Once again, we were dancing and singing until we noticed that someone had started a line dance type of step. We moved near them and tried to learn the steps but were laughing too hard, and my costume kept getting in the way. But we didn't give up until the song ended. It was so good seeing Leon that without thinking I gave him another hug before we parted.

As I stood on the edge of the dance floor again, this time I welcomed it as a time to cool down. It was such a wonderful surprise to see Leon, to dance with him again and to laugh like we used to. I was in a much better frame of mind as I stood there listening to the music and moving to the rhythm.

Before Sam had come to town, this was how most of my dances were spent—on the side, watching. When the DJ announced that we would have a closing prayer and then a couple more dances to finish the night, everyone stopped.

Opening my eyes at the end of the prayer, I looked up to see my Rhett Butler, all six foot four of him in a three-piece suit, with his curly dark hair slicked back, a pencil mustache drawn above his sensuous lips, and his dark eyes that were like pools of molten chocolate. Sam looked more magnificent as Rhett than Clark Gable had. He stood on the dance floor, looking at me.

"Would you like to dance?" someone said. I turned and

Leon stood next to me again.

"You're back!"

"Wanna dance?"

"Of course!" I said, then quickly stole a glance Sam's way; he was already dancing with some cheerleader.

I followed Leon onto the dance floor and we danced to Foreigner's ballad, 'I Want to Know What Love Is.' We danced the same way Sam always danced with me. We swayed back and forth to the notes that floated through the air as he directed me around the floor.

"I thought you were leaving?" I said.

"I was until I saw you standing on the side alone. So I decided I could stay and keep you company—for another dance anyway."

"Thanks. I love to dance."

"Not sure if a guy is supposed to say this, but your makeup is smearing," he said apologetically.

"Where?" I asked, embarrassed. *Was that why Sam was staring at me?*

"Just under your eyes; it's all black." I quickly licked the edge of both my index fingers and rubbed under my lashes.

"Did I get it?" I asked, looking up at him.

"Yeah, that's better. I kinda felt like I was talking to a raccoon there for a minute," he said with a wink.

"Thanks for letting me know. Now you know why I'm still single," I said, and then laughed. I felt so comfortable dancing with Leon that before I knew it, I was singing along.

"You have a good voice," he told me.

I chuckled, and said, "Boy, that's the first time anyone has told me that."

"You do."

"Oh, fiddle dee dee," I told him in my best southern accent. When the dance ended and we were walking back to the side of the dance floor I told him with the sincerest smile I could muster, "That was so much fun. Thanks for coming to my rescue."

"Would you like to dance again?" he asked. I was just about to answer when someone grabbed my arm from behind.

"You promised me this dance, Scarlett." I knew that voice even before I turned around.

"Did I?" I asked. "Why Mr. Butler, I do declare."

"Yes," he said, pulling me on the floor.

"I'm sorry," I called to Leon as Sam pulled me away.

Once we were on the floor waiting for the song to begin, I looked at Sam dressed as Rhett Butler. "You look absolutely gorgeous," I said before I could stop myself.

"Shut up," he said, and I saw the beginning of a blush. "You look like you've had fun tonight. Who was that guy?"

"Just a friend from Ferron."

"Ferron?" he asked with a confused look.

"Remember the place my dad had been transferred for a few years before we moved back to Ashbury?" He nodded. While we waited for the next song to start, I stepped back to look at his costume once more. "Why didn't you tell me you were coming as Rhett?"

He chuckled and said, "I wanted to surprise you."

"I almost didn't see you."

"I saw you."

"Well, if you saw me, then why didn't you come up and say something?" I glowered at him.

"I was busy dancing."

I rolled my eyes. "Too busy to let me know you were here and not as a motorcyclist?" Sam shrugged his shoulders. "I bet you're a big hit with all the girls. Have you been dancing much?"

He shrugged again. "I've had my share, I guess."

"I wish I'd have seen you sooner, but I couldn't find the motorcyclist someone told me to look for," I said as I scowled at him, again.

"You were pretty popular yourself. I'm surprised you remembered I'd be here."

Before I could respond to that, Chicago's 'You're the Inspiration' began to play, "I love this song!" I exclaimed as I started to dance alone.

"Come here," Sam said pulling me into his arms. As much as I loved being there, I couldn't stay. Before I knew it, I was singing the words in his ear

"Are you singing?" he asked.

"Yes." And I continued. Soon we were swaying back and forth to the music as I kept singing in his ear. Over Sam's shoulder I could see Rosie laughing as she watched me over Stephen's shoulder. Soon we were singing at each other. Then they were next to us, by time the chorus began we had pulled away from the guys to strut like Mick Jagger to sing at them and at each other as if we were members of the group Chicago.

Both Sam and Stephen just danced opposite Rosie and I, watching us sing and strut around. It made me laugh how uncomfortable they looked, but we really didn't care.

Eventually, they began to smile and relax. They even surprised to us when the chorus came up and they sang the "ah's,"—in unison, no less. That was when we noticed that many of the other dancers on the floor had been singing with us, Rosie and I laughed and continued singing and by the end we were all laughing as we clapped and cheered. It was like an MGM musical. *I love it! Give me a stage any day.*

The DJ announced into his microphone. "You guys are having so much fun out there that we've decided to do one more song. This should help everyone cool down." Then Eric Clapton's 'Wonderful Tonight' started.

It was the song Sam and I'd danced to at prom. I stayed rooted in my spot—suddenly shy. Sam looked at me, then with his index finger began to motion me to come close. I shook my head no and pointed to the floor that I was staying where I was, yet he looked so handsome dressed as Rhett Butler that all I wanted to do was get lost in his arms. Slowly he approached and without a word brought me into his chest.

I didn't care what anyone else might think or say, but in my limited experience I believed that the dance floor in a darkened room is one of the most romantic places—ever. Sam began to slowly direct me around the dance floor as we melded together.

I loved the emotions that music could pull out of me when I was unable to find the words to express myself. Many a night when I felt melancholy, or needed to sooth my scorched heart, I sat in my room and listened to songs that helped me to cry, to think, or to dream. My soul responded to music no matter the situation and helped me cope with my emotions. I was told by one of my acting coaches that actors feel more and are more sensitive to the moment than most. Whether or not that was true I didn't know, but there with Sam, I chose to believe it.

At that moment, in the arms of Rhett Butler, with only the light from the mirrored ball that hung from the ceiling casting its reflections like stars around us, I let myself get lost in the moment.

My walls melted away. Now I only heard the music, his breathing, and the pressure of his hand on the small of my back as he held me close. I breathed in his musky scent whirling me back to Senior Prom. And this time, I didn't have to worry about Hoppy interrupting us. This dance was ours—or so I thought until I felt a tug on my curtain rod.

"May I cut in?" asked a tall, gorgeous blonde girl with a beautiful smile dressed as a car hop from the '50s. I felt as though a klieg light was focused on us. Unable to look at the brightness of reality, I stepped out of the warmth of Sam's arms to give him the option to dance with her. He wouldn't refuse her, surely. She was gorgeous. I was just a sweaty poor man's version of Scarlett.

"No thanks," was all that Sam said before he pulled me close again and we danced the rest of the song. I no longer heard Eric Clapton singing, instead it was my own voice as it sang,

'God loves me this I know

For this dance tells me so.'

This was way too perfect of a night and one that I didn't expect. *Did he really care for me or was I just a great friend to him? Would I ever have the guts to ask him?* I secretly agonized over.

"Are you okay?" Sam asked.

"Hm? Yeah, why?" I asked, startled out of my thoughts.

"You just dug your nails into my arm."

"Oh, sorry." At that moment the light filled the room and romance fled. Sam and I separated as if we were strangers and walked off the floor; he to find his roommate and me to drive myself home.

"I'll talk to ya tomorrow," I said. He nodded his head and waved. I watched him walk away, but not alone as the car hop and Raggedy Ann that he'd danced with earlier caught up with him. He never looked back.

Slip Slidin'

With November came loads of snow that usually would stick around through the rest of the year, making it very difficult for my lightweight beater of a car to plow through. So, at times like that, it was always iffy as to whether my car would successfully transport Sam and me to our destinations. Especially since it was too cold to ride on his motorcycle. However, the last few days proved different from the norm in that most of the snow was melting with what we Utahns considered warm weather. And, in its wake were puddles of water or residue of the snow that had been there. *I loved that the snow was going away.*

Unfortunately, when I got up one Sunday, I noticed that the temperature had fallen. The yellow-brown dead grass on the lawns was visible, but because of the low temperature, we would have to deal with ice instead of snow. Yes, ice, the leading instigator of cars sliding into cars, and the breaking of human limbs due to slippage.

Ice was death for my little lightweight car, which was unable to gain any traction for going anywhere. If I wanted to experience bumper cars, then my car was perfect for that. There were so many times I'd be driving on ice, unable to steer or stop my car as it slid through traffic, traffic lights, or from lane to lane. Often the only way to stop it was by allowing it to crash into any available bank of snow. Luckily, policemen were very understanding when they pulled up to help dig my car out of the bank they'd just witnessed me crash into. *I don't like driving in the snow.*

"Oh man! I bet there's a ton of ice out there." I groaned to no one in particular as I looked out our living room window.

Rosie laughed as she walked into the kitchen. "What makes you think there's ice?"

"Just look at the puddle next to that bush over there."

"Doesn't mean it's all over the place."

"Oooh, it's all over," I assured her. "Hopefully Sam can get his roommate's truck because my little tin can will be of no use today," I said as I dialed Sam's number.

"Morning, Sam," I said cheerfully when he picked up.

"Hello." It sounded like I had woken him, so I asked the obvious.

"Did I wake you?" I could hear fumbling of objects and then a crash as something fell on something.

"Uh . . . yeah. It's only seven in the morning. Waddya want?"

"Oops, sorry," I said cheerfully.

"Well?" he asked impatiently.

"Okay, okay! There's a lot of ice on the ground; my little car will be useless. Can you get your roo—"

"Gracie," Rosie called from the kitchen. "Gracie," she called again, coming into the living room.

"Hold on," I told Sam and turned towards her. "What?"

"Why don't you guys come with us? Stephen will bring his

jeep."

"Really? Is he—" I started, but heard Sam groan in my ear, so I said to him, "Stop being so grumpy and hold on." I turned back to Rosie. "Will Stephen stop and pick up Sam before he comes over here?"

"I don't see why not, but you'll have to get off the phone so I can call and check."

"That would be great!" I said. "Sam . . . Sam!"

"What?"

"Stephen's gonna pick you up today before coming here. I'll call ya and let you know the time."

"Okay, okay, okay. But church isn't until ten, so don't call back for a couple of hours."

"Whatever . . . sorry to wake you from your *beauty* sleep." Without even saying good-bye I heard the click of his receiver in my ear. *I hate it when he does that!* I turned to Rosie, but she wasn't there; she'd gone back into her room, so I followed her.

"Hey, Rosie?"

"Yeah?"

"If it's okay with Stephen, just let me know the time so I

can call the brat and tell him," I said, laughing. *What a boob!*

"I'm sure he'll be okay with that; besides, he likes Sam," she said.

Knowing that I wouldn't need to drive the icy roads to church, I was able to relax and enjoy my morning. And with the expectation of seeing Sam, as usual, I took extra care in what I wore and how I looked. I chose a white, straight skirt and blousy top with a black belt and suede shoes to match. To avoid wrinkling my outfit, I opted out of wearing my winter coat. I didn't think I'd need it since we wouldn't really be out in the elements for long that day.

However, climbing up to get into the jeep was tricky, due to its oversized tires and elevated body, especially when wearing a straight skirt. It probably wasn't the best outfit to wear, but I looked good if I said so myself. With the help of Sam lifting me onto the seat, I was able to get in with a little bit of dignity intact.

"Whyd'ya wear a skirt like that when ya know you've gotta climb into a jeep?" Sam asked impatiently.

"She looks very nice; leave her alone," Rosie told him.

"Yeah, Sam. You're treading on thin ice," Stephen chimed

in with a chuckle.

"Oh, she looks nice and she knows it," Sam responded as he stepped up to sit on the bench seat next to me.

"Stop being in such a bad mood." I scooted away to make room for him. "And, thank you for the compliment," I said in a perky voice, smiling at him. All he did was shake his head while rolling his eyes. After a couple of minutes I knew he was out of his bad mood when he draped his well-defined arm across the back of the seat and gently pushed me on my shoulder while looking out the window. I couldn't hide the smile on my face.

Once Stephen had parked the jeep near the curb, we had to climb out. I wasn't looking forward to Sam's bad mood returning, so I tried to exit by myself, which was proving difficult with my skirt.

"Hold on," Sam said with a chuckle as he turned and saw my effort. "Let me help ya." And putting his hands around my waist, he lifted me down. *I do love playing the damsel in distress.* Thinking that I would have Sam's help getting back into the jeep, I wasn't too worried as we walked towards the church building.

However, after church, when the four of us arrived at the

Jeep we all went to our respective doors to get in. Then I heard my name called.

"Gracie!"

I turned to see another friend, Mary, approaching me, so I met her halfway, while the others got into the jeep.

"What's up?" I asked.

"Will you be able to help with the talent show next month?" she asked.

"Do I have to perform in it?"

"No, just be on the committee to organize," she said.

Shrugging, I said, "Yeah, sure."

"Great, I'll call you later this week and give you more details."

"Okay. I'll wait to hear from you," I said as we separated— her down the hill and me up the hill to the jeep

My friends were already in the jeep, and none of them saw or heard me approach, they were so involved in their conversation and both the music and the jeep engine were so loud. So I grabbed the handle to open the door and had stepped off the curb onto what looked like a little patch of snow when suddenly my feet slid out from under me and I slid right under the car. The only saving grace was that I was holding onto the door handle which kept me from actually lying on the ground.

"Uh, guys?" I called, "Can someone help me?" My calls for help were drowned out by the engine and music, making my three friends oblivious to my problem. "Uh, guys?" I called again. "Heeelp!" They continued laughing and chatting, and with the music playing, they still couldn't hear me.

I tried to dig my heels into the ice to gain some traction to pull myself up, but I didn't want to ruin my new suede shoes, so I just hung there. I thought about letting myself fall to the ground and get out from under the jeep that way, but I didn't want to ruin my outfit. I thought I could pull myself up by the handle, but regrettably, I didn't have enough upper body strength to accomplish that, so there I hung. I called out again, "Sam? Rosie? Stephen?" and still no response. *Why hadn't Sam remembered that he needed to help me get in the jeep? Why didn't they realize I wasn't in the car with them?* I asked myself in disgust.

Still holding onto the door handle under the car with just my arms and head visible, I looked around and saw three guys, or should I say, angels, walking my way. In desperation, I tried to get their attention by moving my head and called out, "Heeeeelp!" When they saw me, they ran to my aid.

The first angel, dressed in a dark suit, shouted to my friends, "Guys!"

"Don't move the jeep!" called the second angel as he ran up and hit the fender hard a couple of times to get their attention. That was when Sam, Rosie, and Stephen all turned to see what was causing the commotion. And there stood my three angels helping me out from under the car. My friends' laughter died on their lips. *As it should, the bums.*

"There ya go," said the first angel as he helped me onto the sidewalk, while the second angel, who only wore a dress shirt opened at the neck and dress slacks, helped to steady me and make sure I wasn't standing on ice.

"Gracie! Are you okay?" asked Rosie. I only glared at her.

"Thanks, guys. You saved my life—and my shoes, I hope," I said, laughing as I looked at the heel of each shoe for scuff marks. I was so embarrassed it was difficult to look them in the eyes.

"What happened?" asked the first angel.

"I was just opening the door when I stepped on what I thought was snow," I said pointing to the patch of ice. "Luckily I was holding onto the handle when these new shoes slid right out from under me." I said.

"Why didn't you just let go and crawl out?" Asked the second angel, his face scrunched with curiosity.

"I-I didn't want to ruin my outfit or shoes," I said, embarrassed at how silly it sounded. I looked at the guys to see their reaction. Only for a moment did a hint of a smile play on the second angel's lips.

"Oooh," they all said in unison as they nodded their heads in understanding.

Hesitantly I asked, "Can someone help me in the Jeep, so I don't slide under it again, please?" Sam began to get out of the jeep, only to be stopped by the third angel, who up until then had only observed, but then came forward and opened the door, as he took my arm and carefully lifted me up on the bench seat next to where Sam sat. Then he gave me a shy smile as he stepped back and I swear if he'd had a cowboy hat, he would have tipped it to me. I no longer saw his reddish, pock marked face slightly hidden by his glasses and his western wear, but instead a possible Clark Kent.

"Thank you," I said, smiling as sweetly as I could while the first angel stepped forward and closed the door. I was so embarrassed.

"What happened?" asked Stephen.

"I thought I was stepping on snow that turned out to be ice and I slipped under your jeep. Luckily I was holding onto the handle when it happened."

"You should've called for help," said Sam.

"I did."

"Why didn't you just let go of the handle and then crawl out?"

"Stephen," said Rosie. "She's wearing a white skirt and top that would've been ruined. Are your new shoes okay?" Rosie asked.

"Yeah, I think so," I said, again looking at my shoes from different angles. "No thanks to *you*," I accused Sam. "You guys didn't even notice I wasn't in the jeep? What did you think I was doing that was taking so long?" I asked, pouting.

I hardly spoke on the drive home. Of course, it would be me who'd slip on ice and go under the car. *Who does that? Me, obviously.* Once we arrived home Sam made a point of getting out of the car first to open my door and lift me down. "We don't want to lose you under the car again," he joked. "But at least we'll know where to look."

"Ha ha ha, so funny." I smirked at Sam. "I am sooo embarrassed," I said and put my hands up to hide my face.

"Why?" asked Rosie.

"Yeah, it could happen to anyone," chimed in Stephen. I just looked at him in disbelief until Sam came up from behind me, put his hands on both my arms and held them tightly against my chest as he directed me towards the apartment door. *Is he publicly showing some PDA?* I wondered.

"No, it wouldn't happen to anyone, just Gracie. She'll do anything for a laugh," he said.

Now I knew why he held my arms that way—not to show affection, but to protect himself as I tried to swing my forearm back to hit him. "I do not!" I began to laugh. "You're such a jerk."

I pulled away from him and walked into the apartment followed by

the others. *Who'd slide under a car for a laugh?!*

California Here I Come!

With Thanksgiving approaching and since so many of our friends weren't going home, a group of us decided that we'd take a trip to California for Thanksgiving and see the ocean. I'd never been before, so I was really excited and immediately began my preparations for the trip, which included getting a swimsuit and all the accessories that go with it. With the cold weather here and summer gone, I was lucky to find a one-piece, sapphire blue, French-cut swimsuit with two yellow button snaps at the top. I also found some big, round, yellow earrings that looked perfect with the suit, and a big beach towel. I already owned shorts and t-shirts, so I didn't need to buy any. With my purchases complete, all I needed to do was pack and I was ready to go.

Driving to California was the beginning of our adventure. Because of our numbers, the guys took one car while the girls took another, which gave us ten whole hours to talk about those boys.

"Hey Jana, are you sure you know where we're going?" asked Claire from the backseat, chomping on a potato chip. Her green eyes sparkled against her bobbed black hair and she smiled threw her chewing.

"Yes," Jana confirmed. "My parents rented two RVs to use for the week."

"Just two RVs?" asked Claire as she wiped broken chips off her lap.

"Of course. Mom said there is enough sleeping space for all of us, and a heater in each RV if we need it," Jana added.

Leaning towards us, Claire asked in a conspiratorial manner, "Okay, since both Sam and Stephen are taken, which of the guys are you gonna pursue?" She was met with silence. "C'mon, you can tell us, we won't tell the guys," she promised.

Taking a deep breath, Pam dove in. "Okay . . . I really like Cory. Don't know that it'll happen, but I don't mind spending time with him. Besides, he's a good dancer."

Looking from Jana to Claire, Rosie asked, "What about you two? We have two left; who wants who?"

I sat back, relieved that I didn't have to make this choice.

"Okay, okay! I'll take Frank!" Jana blurted out, followed by a squeal of excitement. Frank was short and stocky like she was.

"How apropos!" Rosie said with a gleam in her eyes. "That leaves Johnny for you, Claire," she said with a sly smile. We all started to laugh. For months, Claire had been crushing on Johnny who was a tall, skinny ginger.

"Now that everyone has been coupled up, we need an update on what's going on with you and Stephen?" I asked Rosie.

"What do ya mean?"

Well, it's been a year, right? Or close to it." They were the perfect couple: tall Rosie with her dark auburn hair against her olive skin tone and athletic body, and Stephen, even taller, blonde and with a slender build. Stephen wanted to get into med school and Rosie was studying to be a nurse. It was almost out of a Harlequin.

"Yeah, close to a year, I guess. Why?" Rosie asked.

"D'ya think you'll get married?" I asked.

Rosie shrugged her shoulders. "I'd like to, but don't know. It's up to him," she said. We sat in silent contemplation.

"We've gotta stop in St George to get some gas. This boat goes through gas like it's water," Pam announced. Pam often referred to her Regency 88 as the "boat" because it seemed as big as one and you felt like you were riding on water as it glided over the streets.

"Good," I called from the back, "I need the restroom." I gave a slight laugh in embarrassment. My friends knew that because I drank so much water the restroom was always a must.

"Of course, you do," said Jana sarcastically as she rolled her eyes.

"Weeeell," I said, and gave a look of 'I can't help it.'

Thirty minutes later, we pulled into a Shell station with the guys pulling up behind us. Once the car stopped, we all piled out, and I immediately headed for the store to get to the restroom. Just before I got to the door, I heard Sam ask, "Where's she going in such a rush?" then one of the girls responded, "Restroom." I didn't stop to hear the rest of the conversation.

Since I was the first one to stand in the already long line to use the facilities, I was the first one out and had time to buy a bottle of water. Exiting the store, I saw that Pam and Frank had both pulled their cars into parking spots after filling their tanks and had gone inside to use the facilities and get snacks. As I was leaning against the car waiting, Sam came and stood beside me.

"The sun feels nice," he said, looking out towards the street. I nodded in agreement.

"It's good to be away from the snow," I replied. We stood in silence until the rest came back to the cars and we separated into our respective rides and continued on our way. This time Rosie and I were in the front with Rosie driving. The others were in the back and eventually fell asleep. The lack of snow on the landscape and the warmth of the sun felt so good.

"I'm so excited to go to California and see the ocean for the first time," I blurted out. Rosie, being a California native, smiled at me knowingly.

"I know, I can't wait for some sun and maybe surf."

"I didn't know you surfed."

Rosie shook her head. "I'm not great, but I do love being near the ocean."

"I'm so excited to see the ocean. I can't even imagine what it'll be like . . . it's so massive."

"I think you'll love it, and you can wear that swimsuit of yours." She gave me a wicked smile and a wink, which caused me to blush.

"Do you think Sam will appreciate it?" I cringed, hoping she'd say yes.

"You look great in it. Of course, he will," she assured me, putting my mind at ease. *I really want to impress him.*

"Do you think he *liiikes* me?" I asked, still looking for assurance.

Rosie paused while she contemplated my question, then said, "Well, it's very obvious that you're best friends. Has he kissed you or held your hand yet?"

"The only time he holds my hand is when we slow dance," I answered with a heavy sigh. "I love spending time with him and have liked him for so long that I'm terrified of losing him again."

"I know," she said. Rosie was the only one that knew our

history, "but I don't think you have to worry about losing him; I've seen the way he looks at you."

"You have?" I looked at her. "Is that a good thing?"

"Yes," Rosie answered with a chuckle. "When you two are in the same room he watches every move you make, even if he's talking to someone else."

My eyes widened. "Really?"

"And he always has this smitten smile on his face, or maybe it's an amused smile."

"Or gas."

Laughing, Rosie said, "Whatever it is, no one would look that goofy unless they liked that person."

Her words gave me hope; whether it was true what she said, I didn't know. I'd never seen Sam watching me. But, if what she said was true, why didn't we move beyond just friends? What stopped him from moving us to the next level?

"I wonder what the boys are talking about?" I asked, trying to change the subject.

"Sports," Rosie said.

"Yeah, you're probably right." We drove in silence until

we had to stop to fill the tank again. The girls in the back didn't even wake up until we were back on the road, and the guys didn't stop either, they just waved as they passed us. Thank heavens we knew where we were going.

"Did the guys stop for gas?" Jana said.

"No," Rosie said.

"Do we know where to go?" asked Claire.

"Of course," Pam responded with confidence.

We pulled into San Diego just after dark. Since we didn't know where the guys were, we stopped and had some dinner at In N' Out, which was another new experience.

This particular burger franchise had reached mythical proportions outside of California; whenever a Californian spoke about it, their eyes would glaze over with a faraway look as they reminisced about the fries and burgers. For me, it was just okay; I thought the burger was dry and the fries were cold. But I wouldn't dare say it aloud to avoid making enemies with either Rosie or Pam.

Thirty minutes later, Jana turned off of the freeway into a very large parking lot. "Look at all the RVs and trailers. I sure hope we can find ours," Claire said, amazed as we pulled into the well-lit parking lot.

"Yeah, that's the whole purpose of this lot. These trailers keep people off the beach with their tents," Jana said as she wove the car between each unit. "But Mom said that ours are on the sand—or as close as one can get."

Hey look," said Pam, pointing from the back seat. "Isn't that Frank's car there?"

"Yeah, I think that's his car." Rosie said, leaning over the front seat.

Frank's car was parked behind two of the biggest RVs I'd ever seen. Jana pulled into the parking spot next to Frank's car. She had barely stopped when I opened my door and stepped out.

"Brrr," I said as the cold breeze began to whip around me. "It is so cold."

Rosie laughed and said, "What did you expect? Its November in California just like in Utah."

"I just thought it would be a warmer breeze."

"Let's get our car unpacked and go to bed," Claire said, and yawned.

"Where's the ocean? How close are we to it?" I asked.

"Come get your bags," said Rosie, holding them out to me. "Now take a deep breath."

I did as she instructed. "What is that smell? The ocean?" I asked, then took another lungful of the salty, briny air. Claire laughed.

"That's the ocean you're smelling," Jana said, walking towards our RV as the rest of us followed. It was parked with the door facing the ocean and was only inches from the sand.

Following Jana to the door of our RV, I said in a whiny tone, "I want to see the ocean."

"You can hear it."

"I can?" I asked, looking at Rosie.

"It's right there," she said as she turned and waved her arm the whole expanse of the horizon before me. But it was so dark I couldn't see anything. As I stared into the blackness, I became of aware of a sound.

"It sounds like the muffled cheers from a crowd. Is that it?"

"I've never heard it described like that before, but yeah, that is the ocean," Jana said with a chuckle as she stepped into the

RV. I continued to stare in the direction of the muffled roar.

"Come on, Gracie, we want to go to bed," Pam called from inside the RV. I turned and followed them in.

"I hope I can sleep tonight," I said to no one in particular. And I was out like a light the minute my head hit the pillow.

Sun, Sand, and Sea

The next morning, the sun shone through the blinds right across my eyes as I laid on the sofa bed, which immediately woke me. I looked to see if the other girls were up, but they were still sleeping, so I quickly got dressed in shorts and a t-shirt, pulled my hair back in a ponytail, slipped on my sandals and headed out. As I stepped out the door, a blast of cold air hit me, sending me back inside to change into long pants and a warm long-sleeved pullover sweater, and then I was gone again.

Standing on the little steps that led into the RV, I gazed in awe at the majesty of the ocean; it was more beautiful than I ever imagined, and I felt drawn to it as if hypnotized by its strength. The moment my sandals touched the sand, I knew they had to go. So I stepped out of them, letting my toes sink in the cold sand and feeling all stress leave my body. I was so mesmerized by the ocean and the sound of the waves as they swept in and then out. With each step closer to the water I felt more and more exhilarated by all the elements: the air, water, and sand. I began to walk parallel to the water along the beach—for how long, I didn't know. But eventually, I sat on the sand and watched the water as I felt the sun's rays gradually warm me up. I was in love.

I wasn't sure how long I'd sat there when I heard someone calling my name. I looked around to see Johnny and Claire walking towards me but made no move to get up.

"How long have ya been out here?" Johnny asked as they got closer.

"Don't know. What time is it?" I asked, shielding my eyes from the sun as I looked up at him. He moved to block the sun for me.

"Well, it's almost eleven. Did you put on any sunblock?" Claire asked, and I shook my head. "You look a little pink." Claire handed me a tube of lotion.

"I didn't even think about getting sunburned," I said, squeezing the lotion into my hand and rubbing it on my warm face. "Thanks for bringing this." I handed the bottle back, then took off my sweater and tied it around my waist, loving the warmth of the sun on my bare arms. Claire squeezed more lotion into my hands and I rubbed it on my arms, neck, and legs. "Is everyone else up?"

"Yeah. They're eating breakfast," Johnny said as he tossed the football, he'd brought with him, in the air. "Did you eat breakfast already?" he asked me.

"Nah. I came out here as soon as I woke up. I couldn't wait to see the ocean; it's my first time," I explained and got up.

"Aaah," said Johnny in an understanding tone. "Go long," he told both Claire and me as he stepped back, imitating a quarterback. We ran a little way off and turned to catch the ball Johnny threw, missing it by yards. My brothers and some of the guys I'd known when I lived in Provo had taught me to throw, so I returned it to him, just a little short of where he stood.

"Nice throw," he said with admiration and threw the ball to me. Soon Claire and I were taking turns catching and throwing the ball and the more my arm warmed up, the better my throws became.

"You've got a great arm for someone who rarely plays," he said, boosting my confidence as we continued to play. I even ended up in the water a couple of times just to catch the ball. Eventually, we all collapsed on the sand laughing and exhausted.

While sitting on the sand my stomach grumbled, reminding me that I hadn't eaten or drank anything since last night. I jumped up and announced, "Gotta go."

Looking at me in alarm, Claire asked, 'What's wrong?"

"I need to eat and get a drink of water," I called over my shoulder as I ran in the direction of the RVs.

Frank and Sam were sitting in beach chairs outside their RV, and as I approached, they both said something to me which I ignored. "Gotta go. Talk later." I bounced up the three steps to our RV, pulled open the door and entered. Stephen and Rosie quickly pulled apart, trying to hide the fact that they'd been making out.

"Oops! Sorry! Don't mind me," I said with a chuckle as I walked past them with my hand over my eyes, which made them laugh. I could see through my fingers their faces had turned bright red.

Before I exited the bathroom, I called through the door, "I'm coming out. I hope the coast is clear." I laughed when I saw that Rosie and Stephen were now sitting on opposite sides of the dinette table. "So, what've you guys been up to?" I asked, trying to keep a straight face, but laughed as their blush deepened. "Busted!"

"Shut up," demanded Rosie good-naturedly. I raised my eyebrows as I grabbed a banana and hardboiled egg leftover from their breakfast and left.

"Boy," I said, pointing my thumb at the door over my shoulder and looking at Frank and Sam, "someone needs to monitor these two."

"What were they doin' in there?" Sam asked from his beach chair.

"A post-breakfast make out session I believe."

"Shut up, Gracie," Rosie called from inside the RV, which pushed Frank and Sam to laugh and make catcalls. Finally, both Stephen and Rosie came out of the RV still in full blush mode, snickering through their embarrassment.

Sitting in the empty beach chair next to Frank I asked, "Are we gonna do anything today or just hang out?

"Why don't we go to lunch and then come back to swim and lay out," suggested Rosie.

"Oh, that sounds fun," I said and jumped up. "I need a shower before we go." And I headed back into our RV to prepare for lunch.

"Better hurry," Stephen called after me. "We need to leave in forty minutes." Turning to Rosie he asked, "Does she take a long time to get ready?"

When I heard that, I leaned out the RV door and opened my arms. "Do you think *this* happens by magic?"

Pointing, Stephen said, "Get in the shower." I could hear the others laughing as I closed the door.

I didn't need the full forty minutes, which I wasn't allowed to take anyway as the other girls had to get ready too. After a quick shower, I scrunched my freshly washed hair as I blew it dry, then pulled the sides of my hair up into a barrette on the top of my head and plastered it with hairspray so it would stay put once we were out in the wind. Then I applied a little makeup, put on a pair of jeans, a t-shirt, and a light button-down sweater, and with my ever-trusty sandals on my feet, I was ready.

Leaving the four girls still prepping, I stepped outside to find Frank sitting in a beach chair waiting; most guys didn't take that long to get ready, which was frustrating for us girls, but there I was ready and only one guy was waiting.

Frank and I were sitting chatting about the differences in our RVs when everyone began to emerge all showered and ready.

"Wow, you look really nice, Gracie," Cory said, doing a double take.

"You sound surprised." I laughed.

"You do." Jana smiled. "It must be all the sun you've gotten today."

"I'm sure I'll feel it tomorrow when it turns into a sunburn." I grimaced at the thought.

"If everyone's ready, let's go," directed Stephen, leading us up to the path that ran along the beach. *Who made him the boss?*

The Waitress

The restaurant Stephen and Rosie had in mind was on the beach and close enough that we could walk to it. Since I didn't know where I was going, I hung back and followed. Before we'd gone far, Sam was walking beside me.

"How do you like California so far?"

"I loooove the ocean," I told him. "Have you been here before?"

"Not San Diego, but yes, I've been to California before."

"I just really love the ocean," I said and stopped for a moment to look at it. "I'd love to live closer to it," I told him wistfully.

"I can help you get closer to it." He picked me up and began to carry me to the water.

"Nooooo," I screamed, squirming, while the others stopped walking to watch. They were used to our antics.

"Come on, ya wanna get closer," he teased and continued walking to the water. This made me cling to him even more as I fought to not get wet. Once I wiggled free of his grasp, I began to run back towards the group, but he grabbed me and slung me over his shoulder as we approached the restaurant.

"Sam, put me down," I demanded through my laughter.

"Nope," he said, smacking my bottom.

"Sam!"

We stood in front of a rundown shack that looked like a little Mexican hacienda with some lone cacti placed around it. Over the door hung a beat-up sign that read, 'Guacko Jocko's'.

"Who found this place?" Johnny asked as we approached the door.

"Yeah," echoed Frankie, "who hates us enough to send us here?"

"C'mon guys, my little brother told me it was fantastic," admitted Rosie.

Sometimes a building will look terrible on the outside yet once you step inside it is totally different. Not this one. It looked bad on the outside and even worse inside.

Instead of low lighting, earthy colors, and some mariachi music playing, we were blinded by bright lights that reflected off the dirty white tile floor, and the blaring top forty music playing. The place was empty except for the cook and a cute, dark-haired beauty posing as a waitress. On the walls were a couple of posters of Mexico's coastline and a sombrero. That was the only ambiance in the place. We all stared in disappointed amazement.

"Sam, let me down," I said as I tried to straighten up while still slung over his shoulder. He loosened his hold on me and I slid down the length of his torso as if he were a slide, until my feet touched the tiles.

"Let's grab a table and get our food ordered; I'm starving," said Stephen, pulling two tables together. "We can sit here." We all sat down, with Sam next to me.

"What can I get you?" asked the cute little Latina with

gorgeous dark eyes that lit up when she saw Sam.

"I'll have the deal for two tacos," said Frankie.

"I want the same," said Pam.

"Me too," Rosie chimed in.

"Who all wants this deal?" asked the waitress, looking straight at Sam while the others raised their hands. "Five, six, seven, eight, nine. Got it," she counted and took a moment to write it down. "Does everyone want water?"

"I'd like some pop," said Corey.

"I'm sorry, but the soda machine isn't working." The waitress frowned.

"Then it's water all around." Stephen smiled at her pleasantly.

"What'll you have?" she asked me.

"I'll take the Taquitos plate special, please."

"Sure. I'll be back with your food in a few," she said, walking away. I tried to see Sam's reaction and whether he was watching her or not, but I couldn't tell until he got up from the table and walked over to where she sat behind the counter. I felt my heart falling into my stomach. *Why? Why does he do this to me? Especially after we'd had so much fun walking here.* I looked up to see Rosie watching me with a sympathetic look on her face. I shrugged it off.

Sitting at the table waiting for our food, I heard Sam laughing with the waitress. I wanted to leave so desperately I could barely breathe. What I needed was a good excuse to leave that wouldn't cause alarm: I could've said I was sick, but then I'd have to act it the rest of the day. Or, I forgot something at the RV. That might work. But then they'd want to know what I forgot. Nothing seemed to work. I'd just have to suck it up. I'd dealt with this so many other times, what made today any different?

Sam helped Lucy, the waitress, bring over our food and place it in front of each person, but me.

"Yours is taking a little longer. I'll let you know when you can come get it," Lucy informed me.

"Great, thanks," I said and sat back to wait. The room was quiet with everyone eating and no music playing when I thought I heard the ding of a microwave bell. *You gotta be kidding me,* I thought and headed to the counter.

Looking through the service window, I saw Lucy pulling a

plate of formerly frozen taquitos from the microwave. She looked up in time to see me and quickly pushed the box they'd been in out of sight.

"That mine?" I asked.

"Yes," she said, bringing the plate of food out of the kitchen and setting it on the counter in front of me. "I'm sorry, but that's how it's done here." She cringed. *Great, not only is she cute, but she's nice too.*

I smiled. "Is any of it authentic?"

"No," she said with a chuckle.

"That's okay, thanks for telling me." I smiled and reached for my plate of food.

"Can I ask you something?" she said, stopping me.

"Sure."

"Are any of those girls at your table Sam's girlfriend?"

Nooooooo! Not again. I moaned inside, but outwardly I answered, "No." I took my plate from her.

Walking back to the group, I saw my empty seat next to Sam. And, for the first time, I just didn't have the heart to sit next to him and continue my happy farce. *I'm not doing this today,* I told myself. I set my plate down on the table and said, "Ya know

what? I don't think I'm hungry. I'd rather lay on the beach." And I

walked out of the restaurant and didn't look back.

The Tumble

Once I reached the RV, I quickly changed into my new swimsuit. I didn't bother to take off my makeup but added the earrings I'd bought, some lip gloss, my sunglasses, wrapped my beach towel about me, and headed out the door to go find a place to be alone to lay on the sand and cry.

I didn't know how far I'd walked down the beach before I found an empty spot with a restroom nearby. I'd forgotten to bring any Kleenex in my rush to get out, so I thought it would be a good resource for toilet paper to blow my nose after my cry. I placed my towel on the sand and sat down to watch the ocean. The sound of the waves crashing in and out began to soothe my soul, and the tears spilling down my cheeks were blown away by the breeze.

I needed to cry, to release those emotions so I could be civil with Sam the next time I saw him. This had become my routine ever since Sam entered my life.

I didn't know how long I'd been laying out before I saw my group approaching in swimsuits with towels in hand.

"There she is," called Corey.

"Gracie! We've been looking for ya," called Jana. "And we've got music," she said, holding up the radio.

"Here I am," I answered, raising up on my elbows. I lifted my sunglasses to get a better view of them before lowering them back on the ridge of my nose and asking, "How was the food?"

"Awful! You were smart to not try it," said Stephen before turning to Rosie." That is the last time we take your brother's suggestion."

Rosie laughed. "I'm surprised. He usually has much better taste than that."

As they approached, they began dropping their towels. Johnny had brought his football and soon he and Corey were throwing it back and forth, and I really wanted to play.

"Where's Sam?" asked Stephen, but no one answered; everyone just looked at each other.

"It's okay, guys," I said. "Sam can see anyone he wants. There's nothing between us." I sat on my towel and felt the awkwardness from my friends who didn't know what to say or do, so I jumped up. "Hey Johnny! Can I play with you guys?"

"Sure! C'mon," he answered. "She's got a pretty good arm once it gets warmed up," he told Corey.

I jogged over to where they were, and we began taking turns tossing the ball. Eventually, the others followed and soon we were playing a small game of flag football. As we began to play, someone turned the radio up so that we had a soundtrack for our little game. It felt good to be so active; it was getting a little cool and the activity warmed me up and took my mind off Sam.

Having music while we played made it even more fun for me. Because of my long legs, I usually ran the ball. But it was tough for me to stop singing and dancing when I heard a good song, which was surely very frustrating for whoever's team I was on.

"Get her," yelled Corey at Pam as she chased after me before Rosie tackled me, pulling me into the sand.

"Foul," I called, getting up out of the sand. "Where's a ref when ya need one? That was unnecessary roughness." I wiped off the sand that had collected on my suit and skin. I must have looked a mess but was feeling so much better and had almost forgotten the lunch episode. That is, until I saw Sam approaching with Lucy by his side, who looked adorable in her shorts and top. *Great,* I told myself. Then I had to swerve in time to miss Corey's attempt to tackle me, again.

"Do you guys wanna play?" Stephen asked.

"Ya wanna?" Sam asked Lucy, with hope.

"No. I don't like football. I'd rather just watch, if I have to."

"Nah, we'll just sit here . . . and watch," Sam said. I chuckled to myself since I knew this was killing him. He loved to play football.

So I did what I'd always done: pretend he wasn't there, put up my fourth wall, and have a good time. As we put the next play in motion, the song 'Footloose" came on the radio. I heard the beginning drumbeats and began doing jerky steps towards our end zone.

"Gracie! Don't dance! Run," Johnny yelled. "Run, Gracie! Stop dancing!" But there were so few of us playing that it was easy to avoid being tackled. Soon, the other girls joined in and we were all dancing in the sand. "Gracie! Run!" The other girls got Frankie and Corey dancing too, so there was only Stephen and Rosie to avoid since Johnny hadn't moved since he threw me the ball.

"You're not gonna get anything out of her when she's singing and dancing," Sam yelled at Johnny from over on his blanket with the waitress.

"It's becoming very obvious," Johnny said throwing his hands up in the air.

Still dancing, I kept inching closer and closer to the end zone. Just as the song ended, I crossed over and slammed the football down.

"Ha ha! Touchdown," I yelled with my arms raised in victory. I began to dance when I heard "Here Comes Santa Claus" on the radio and didn't notice Stephen come up and try to put me over his shoulder. I fought and screamed which brought the girls to my aid as we all dog piled on Stephen.

"C'mon guys! It's your ball," yelled Johnny. The other team hiked the ball right as Queen's 'Radio Ga Ga' began to play. It was tough to sing and run but I felt I was getting better at it with each play. Johnny stood there agape.

While looking at Sam, he asked, "Does she ever shut up?"

Sam just laughed and shook his head. "No." He then turned to the waitress and asked, "Are you sure you don't want to play?"

"Ick no!"

Unfortunately, the more I danced the fewer points were made as I included more and more of the players. Finally, Johnny and Stephen called the game due to dancing, singing, and the need for food, then they chased me into the water.

I felt so great in my swimsuit even if I was covered in sand and sweat. I was happy that Sam had seen me having so much fun while sitting next to his pristine date. It gave me the confidence to play in the water to wash off all the sand I had collected on myself, and hopefully entice Sam away from the waitress.

As I stood in the water, I heard Huey Lewis and the News' new song, 'Stuck with You', which was a song I loved, so I sang and danced as I moved further into the water, imagining the song was about Sam and me.

Being the novice that I was with the ocean, I was unaware of just how strong the waves could be, especially when returning to the shore. I was about to learn a lesson I would never forget as I began to make my way back to the shore. I saw that Sam and his petite Latin beauty were walking away, which stopped me in my tracks, ignoring the ocean behind me. Seeing that I forgot about the tide coming *in*, I hadn't prepared myself for the force with which it would hit me. Before I knew it, I was tumbling in the wave.

During my watery chaos, I tried to open my eyes to see without losing my contacts, and for that nanosecond all I saw before the next tumble was a pair of long, white legs sticking up in the air as if they belonged to a mannequin. When my rolling came to a stop, all the girls ran up.

"Are you okay, Gracie?" Pam asked with concern on her face.

I couldn't fully open my eyes due to the mascara and saltwater in them. And still not wanting to lose a contact— supposing they'd survived—I stood and laughed to hide my embarrassment. "Ah, I'm fine. Just can't open my eyes."

"Why not?" asked Jana.

"Don't want to let any more mascara or saltwater in 'em," I explained as I attempted to crack one eye open, but when I did my contact was so dirty, I couldn't see anything. "And I need to wash my contacts." Luckily the other guys were busy tossing a frisbee they'd found on the beach and were oblivious to my tumble, I hoped. Jana handed me her towel to try and wipe off some of the sand from my body and the gunk around my eyes. It helped. I could now open my eyes a little.

Suddenly, all four girls began to laugh. "Look at your suit! What is in there?" Pam asked, pointing. Looking down, I could see many little lumps disfiguring my fit-like-a-glove swimsuit. Pulling the top of my suit away from my chest, I tried to see what it was.

"Ooooh, I need to go empty my suit," I mumbled before walking towards the nearby restroom.

Since I'd forgotten to put on my sandals before heading there, it was my bare feet on the damp sand and whatever disgusting things were mixed into the sand on the floor. In the metal sheet tacked to the wall as a mirror, I barely made out just how horrible I looked: my eyes were round black circles that had smeared to the top of my cheekbones, my hair, due to the hairspray I'd put on it before lunch, was now in the shape of a lopsided triangle, and my swimsuit looked like it was covering a terrible case of boils.

The only cure was to grab the straps and peel the suit off my body. I watched all the sand it had been holding fall to the ground. I quickly wiped down my body with the towel Jana had lent me, shook out my suit before putting it back on and headed back to the group. As I approached the girls, I resolved—once more—that I would no longer try to impress Sam. I had to be me, otherwise I'd always end up looking silly. If he even noticed.

As the group returned to the RVs, we decided to have a weenie roast in the fire pit. Rosie and I trailed behind the others as we walked back.

"Do you think Sam saw my tumble?" I asked.

"Mm, not sure. Wasn't really watching him."

"Never fails; whenever I try to impress him, I make a fool of myself. Did it look bad?"

"It was so quick, we all just kinda laughed," she answered with a chuckle. "Did you hurt yourself?"

"Just my pride," I said with a sigh. "D'ya think we'll see Sam anymore tonight?"

Rosie shrugged. "Don't know, sorry." She put her arm about my shoulders as we passed the guys' RV and entered ours.

Once inside our RV, I showered before dinner, washing all the makeup and hairspray away. I didn't bother to blow-dry my hair but instead, let the natural wave take control.

Later as we all relaxed in front of the fire pit, we laughed while we listened to Frank's attempts to play the guitar he'd brought.

"Have you ever even had a guitar lesson?" Corey asked.

"Nope. Not one," Frank said proudly before he returned to playing.

"Gee, what a surprise," said Stephen as he and Rosie chuckled while cuddling.

"Don't you dare," screamed Pam as Corey chased her with a gooey marshmallow. "I mean it! Don't you dare!" Gracie watched Corey chase Pam down towards the water. Jana sat at

Frank's feet, staring up at him adoringly.

"Play another one," she said, never taking her eyes off him.

What had happened to all these people? Does everyone get bitten by the crush bug except Sam because he's immune to it? At least where I'm concerned? I couldn't deny that I was feeling jealous of everyone as I sat, alone.

"Do you know when Sam will be back?" Rosie asked, lifting her head off Stephen's shoulder. *Really? She's asking me that?* I only shrugged my shoulders in response.

Corey and Pam were done chasing one another and sat on a rock with a blanket wrapped about the two of them; Jana sat at Frank's feet while her head rested on his knee, Johnny was giving Claire a neck massage, Rosie sat on Stephen's lap cuddling in the beach chair, and me? I sat alone. Would it have been any different if Sam was there? We were all tired after a day with so much sun and excitement, at least I was. I was exhausted from both the mental anguish of what Sam and my relationship really was and the physical restraint needed to not fight any girls that he looked at. *Maybe we really are just friends.* He could have any gorgeous woman he met; why would he settle for me?

With those thoughts filling my head, I took the blanket I'd wrapped about me and sat on the sand, close to the water where I could really think and have my pity party without interruption. I needed to face reality and let him go. It wouldn't be easy, but it needed to happen if I wanted to enjoy this vacation. I couldn't spend it wallowing in self-pity or it would be high school all over again. While I sat in the sand and listened to the roar of the ocean, it began to rain.

"Perfect. A perfect end to a perfect day," I mumbled. I stayed out in the rain until I felt my self-pity wash away, then shivering, I jumped up and ran back to the RV.

"Whooo hooo," I said as I entered and dropped the wet blanket on the couch—I was soaked. "Wow, it's really coming down out there." Everyone stopped talking to look at me with only the background music to be heard.

"We wondered when you'd come in," Cory said.

"I just love the ocean," I confessed, taking the towel Claire handed me, before stating the obvious, "It's raining out." I laughed as I pulled my wet t-shirt away from my body, trying to dry it with the towel.

"Can't get nothin' past you," said Cory.

"I better change," I said after glaring at Cory while I closed the partition to the back behind me.

Moments later when I opened the partition, I saw Sam sitting on the couch with his arms resting on the back. I couldn't believe my eyes, so I closed the partition again, counted to three then pulled it open. He was still there in all his glorious coolness.

I gave a sigh of relief when I saw he was alone and sitting near the spot where I'd left the wet blanket that was now draped over a chair near the heater. I reminded myself to try and let go. As if on cue, Huey Lewis and the News' song, 'I Want A New Drug' began to play on the little stereo, so I started to sing and dance along. Soon all the others were up dancing, while Sam sat and watched, laughing with us. I refused to be the one to pull him into the fun, as usual.

"I wonder what anyone passing by thought when they saw this RV rocking?" asked Johnny at the end of the song. We all laughed. I was now warmer and looked for a place to sit and cool off, but the only available spot was next to Sam. Normally I would've jumped at it, but not this time. Tonight, I anchored myself near the sink on the pretext that I was filling a glass with water.

"So, what are the plans for tomorrow?" I asked, not looking at Sam.

"I don't know what you girls are gonna do, but us guys have some errands we need to run," Stephen informed us, while looking at the guys to confirm.

"What errands? You're on vacation. You don't need to do no stinkin' errands." I set the glass of water on the counter and placed my hands on my hips. Stephen ignored me and started talking to the guys.

Feigning indignation, I looked at them then said to the girls, "Notice he doesn't respond? Hm, me thinks there's something rrrrotten here," I said, making the girls laugh. "We'll just have to find something fun to do."

"I wouldn't mind going shopping at the big mall," suggested Jana. Pam, Rosie, and Claire all quickly agreed. That left me out—I didn't come from a wealthy family as the others did so my funds were very limited. I avoided all unnecessary spending but didn't tell them or they'd insist on buying things for me which drove me crazy.

"We're gonna take off," said Frank as all the guys stood to leave.

"Yeah, see ya," echoed Cory.

"Not if we see you first," I said without thinking. That was something my brother, Nate, always said to me. *I must sound so obnoxious at times.*

"Huh?" Cory stopped, causing Sam to bump into him.

"Nothin'," I said, shaking my head.

"You're too much." Sam chuckled as he pushed Cory out the door and winked with a smile at me. I returned the smile with an over exaggerated wink. I wasn't mad at him, just pulling back, if possible. But, gee, he looked so handsome it was gonna be tough. And when he winked and smiled at me like that there had to be angels holding me up so I wouldn't swoon.

"Bye," called the girls after them.

After the guys had left, I glumly dropped on the couch as I went over in my head how I'd acted once he'd reappeared. I groaned to myself. Why could I never stop myself from trying to be funny when my heart hurt? My timing was off and my jokes all fell flat. *Why can't I turn off the clown?*

Beachcombing

Again, I was the first one up. It was only seven, but I knew that I

wouldn't go back to sleep, so I quickly slathered sunscreen all over

my body before pulling on clean shorts, a t-shirt, and a sweater

over my swimsuit. I grabbed a baseball cap one of the guys had left

the previous night, a beach bag we'd purchased in St. George, and

some water—of course. I quickly scribbled a note letting the girls

know I was walking up the beach in search of fun and would be

back later and hoped they had a great time shopping, then left.

Upon exiting the RV, as I closed the door I turned to look

for any sign of life from the guys' RV. I was surprised to see Sam sitting on the RV steps outside their door. I smiled and waved as I walked away.

"Where ya going so early?" he asked. When I didn't turn around, he called again, "Gracie! Where ya going?" I just waved and continued on my quest—my attempt at keeping it casual between us. "Be careful!" he said.

The air was crisp but the day was gorgeous, the sky was blue, the sun was out. Though the day had just started, already a few people had set up their camp for the day.

Since I was in no hurry, I meandered along the beach, exploring the shells I found on the shore, enjoying the waves as they lapped at my feet, feeling the ocean breeze as it whipped my sadness away from the day before. So engrossed in my thoughts, I hadn't noticed a black lab puppy loping towards me.

"Hey there, lil guy." I knelt, softly clapping my hands. "C'mere." The excited puppy greeted me with kisses as I lifted him up while looking for his owner. "Is this your puppy?" I asked an older woman sitting on a blanket in the sand near the water.

"Yeah," she said, leaning her head forward as her hand cupped the flame she held to the cigarette in her mouth.

"What's his name?" I called as I walked towards her.

Taking a long drag on her cigarette, she turned her head away as she released the smoke from her lungs, and said, "*Her* name is Lola."

"Ooh. Sorry. Do you mind if I play with Lola?" I asked.

"Knock yourself out," she said, laying back on her blanket.

Lola had so much energy and was so happy to play, that I couldn't resist running along the beach with her. It felt good to forget all my insecurities and heartache and just play.

Eventually, I decided to let Lola go back to her owner and proceeded down the beach. This proved a little difficult since the adorable puppy wanted to follow me. So, after repeated trips of returning Lola, finally her owner took an interest and held on to her to restrain her from following me.

The morning had warmed up so I took my sweater off, put it in the beach bag, and continued down the beach until a large outcrop of rock stopped me. At first, I thought I would turn around and go back, but then decided to walk around it and explore the other side. I was pleasantly surprised to find a little cove; the sand was so clean, and the colors of the rock were amazing, it was almost like a little hideaway. People walked past but didn't stop—it was like they didn't even notice the little cove. I laid my towel on the white sand to relax for a bit, then I pulled out a book I'd grabbed from the RV and laid back to read.

I awoke with a jolt. *Where was I?* As I began to get my bearings, I remembered where I was, and that I was alone. *I must have fallen asleep, but for how long?* I wondered. Being alone in a secluded spot may not have been my smartest move to date. I quickly put my book and beach towel in the bag and began to retrace my steps.

As I walked back towards the RVs, there were more people out enjoying the sun than when I'd first crossed that way. In the distance a volleyball game was in full swing with probably twenty people gathered around it, so when I approached, I joined up to watch.

The game was four on four with guys and girls on each team, and some of the nicest looking people I'd seen since we got there: they were tan, in shape, and very attractive. I cheered and laughed with the crowd as more people approached to watch the games. Soon, one of the girls sitting in a beach chair nearby with a knee brace on began to chat with me.

"This is a great day for a game, isn't it?" she asked. She was in her mid-thirties, slender, with sun-bleached curly hair and a dark tan. She wore shorts, a bikini top, and an open zip-up sweatshirt.

"It's amazing," I gushed. "I had to take my sweater off it was so nice, but sometimes the breeze is kinda cool."

"Yeah, I know," she said, pulling at her sweatshirt for emphasis. "It is November," she said with a chuckle.

"It's easy to forget that here. I'm from Utah."

"I kinda figured you weren't from around here, with your pale skin."

I rolled my eyes. "I know. A group of us came out here for Thanksgiving. We needed some warmth."

"Gee, I bet. I'm Sandi, by the way. This is Steph." She said pointing to a girl with brown hair cut in a bob and bright green eyes.

"Gracie," I said with a smile.

"Gracie?" she asked. "That's a great name."

"Thanks."

"Do ya wanna play?" she asked, tilting her head towards the volleyball game.

I held up my hands to ward off the suggestion and laughed. "Oh no. I'm no good at volleyball," I said.

"Oh, c'mon. I bet you are." And turning towards the players, she called, "Max! Hey Max! We have a new player." She pointed at me. I gaped at the gorgeous specimen that stopped mid-game and walked over. He looked to be six feet tall, dark hair, eyes as blue as the ocean, skin the color of raw honey, with a mustache that when he smiled revealed a set of beautiful white teeth, like a stage curtain opening. He smiled at Sandi and me as he approached.

"You play volleyball?" he asked.

"Noooo," I said. "I really don't."

Laughing, Sandi said, "She's here on vacation, from Utah."

"Oooh, then just visiting," Max said as he plopped down next to Sandi. "If you want to get the whole experience, ya gotta play beach volleyball." He winked at me. *Man was he gorgeous,* I thought. *He could really give Sam a run for his money.*

"C'mon," Max said as he stood and reached out his hand to

pull me up. "I'll be on your team and teach ya the basics." I grimaced. "It'll be fun." He tried to assure me.

Hesitantly, I took his hand. He lifted me like I weighed nothing and continued holding my hand until we got to the court. Once there, he introduced me to all the players and the game began. I wasn't sure how long I'd played before I saw Claire walking up the beach, just as we were taking a break.

"Claire!" I called, but she didn't hear so I called again, "Claire!" Finally, she stopped and looked around until she saw me waving my arms at her. "Did you already go shopping?" I asked, stepping away from the group of people.

"What are you doing here?"

"Playing volleyball. These are the nicest people," I said as I motioned around the area. "Did you go shopping?" I asked again.

"Yeah. They have some great stores here," Claire answered absentmindedly as she continued to look at the group of people.

"What time is it?" I asked, having lost complete track of time.

"Three. Are you gonna come back? Sam's been looking for ya."

"Well, here I am." I smiled at her. "This is Steph and Sandi," I said, pointing out the two girls sitting closest to where we were standing.

"Hi," they said in unison.

"This is Claire."

"Hi," she responded.

"We're trying to get Cece to play another game," Sandi explained to her. Claire looked at me and mouthed "Cece?" I just smiled at her.

"Will you be out here tomorrow?" I asked Sandi.

"Of course! Don't forget Max wants to take you surfin'."

"If it's okay I'll come back and play . . . and surf, then," I said with a smile.

"You're leaving?" Sandi asked

"Yeah, I should probably spend some time with my friends now that they're done shopping," I told her as I grabbed my stuff.

"Okay," said Sandi, then turned to the players on the court. "Cece is leaving!"

"Aaaaaah," was the chorus from the other players. I smiled and waved.

"Ce CEEE," called Max from the volleyball court. "We better see ya tomorrow. Be ready to surf." He smiled before turning his attention back to the game in time to hit the ball back over the net.

"See ya tomorrow." I waved again as Claire and I began our walk back to the camp.

"Wow, you met some nice people," said Claire.

I chuckled. "I did, didn't I? They are so much fun, too."

"Who's the guy?"

"Max?" I asked and she nodded. "Oh, he's Sandi's boyfriend. Really nice guy."

"And fantastic-looking. You better be careful, or you'll make Sam jealous."

"Ha! Like he'd care."

"Are you two okay?" she asked.

"Who two?" I asked, playing dumb.

"You and Sam."

"Sure, I guess. Why?"

"You've hardly spent any time together since before your tumble."

"Really? Is this how we're measuring time now, pre-tumble and post-tumble?" I asked with a chuckle, making Claire laugh.

"I just mean—"

"Look, I'm giving him space for all other women. Besides, I'm not even sure he's interested in me as more than a friend."

"You gotta be kidding."

"Not really. He gives me no clue that he likes me as more than a friend."

"You just don't see it. You don't see how he watches you from across a room?" She raised her eyebrows. "Or, how he makes a beeline for you if another guy is paying too much attention? What about how relaxed he seems around you? You don't see that?"

I looked at her in disbelief. "He does this with or without the other women?" I asked and rolled my eyes.

"I'm serious. I think he's in love with you. I only wish a guy looked at me the way he looks at you."

It was difficult to believe, due to the fact that he never held my hand or kissed me, and only hugged me when we danced.

I began to laugh. "In love with me?" I doubled over in an

exaggerated fit of laughter. "That is heeee larious."

Shaking her head, Claire said, "Yeah, I think he is."

"I'm sorry, but I just don't see it," I said, stone-faced. "I'd *love* it if he were; he's got everything I want."

"Why dontcha ask him?" Claire asked, turning and stopping in front of me.

I sighed. "I'm afraid to hear the truth. What if he says he isn't into me like that? It'll kill me. I'd just like him to *like* me as more than a friend. Forget the love stuff, that's not even possible."

"But you'll never know unless you ask," she said.

"I'm just too chicken. I'd much rather have him around and not know, than not have him in my life at all," I said, staring out at the ocean, "It's high school all over again."

"I'm sorry. Did you date?"

Shaking my head to pull out of my memories and sadness, I said, "I don't wanna get into it right now." I began to walk again. "I'll tell you about it on the drive home . . . it should take about ten hours," I said, pointing to the group standing around the fire pit.

"Where've you been all day?" Sam called as we approached.

"She's been playing volleyball," Claire called back.

Approaching the pit, I said with animation, "It was so much fun! I'll play more tomorrow after Max takes me out on his surfboard." Everyone looked at me, stunned, "Oh yeah, I said *surfboard.*"

"Wh-who's Max?" Sam asked.

I ignored his question. "I'm going surfing, I'm going surfing, I'm going surfing," I blissfully sang as I danced around the group.

Sam grabbed my arm as I passed him. "Who's *Max*?" he demanded.

"Ooh, I saw Max," said Claire in a tattle-tale tone. "He's a really good-looking guy that made Gracie, or CeCe as he calls her, promise to come back tomorrow."

"Is he a surfing bum?" asked Jana, and I shook my head no.

"What does he do?" asked Corey

"I don't know; he's in the Navy, I think," I said as I warmed my hands over the fire.

"Really?" said Claire. "Your day sounds way more exciting than our shopping trip." I just smiled.

Looking at them over the fire, I mimicked Edward G. Robinson, "I've got skills, see . . . see." Everyone laughed at my lame impersonation but Sam. He'd stayed quiet through the conversation after his question about Max. I snuck a look out of the corner of my eye to see if he was watching me the way Claire had said he did, but I just saw him looking into the fire.

My stomach growled. "What are we doing for dinner? I haven't eaten all day."

"Why don't you go ask your new friends?" Sam asked, sitting in one of the beach chairs.

"Will they know what we're having for dinner? Because all I know is I'm going surfing, I'm going surfing, I'm going surfing," I said and continued my surfing chant as I danced around Sam until he lunged for me, but I eluded him, and the chase was on. Oooh . . . . I loved this kind of attention. He chased me down the beach. and I "allowed" myself to get caught.

Once Sam caught me, he tried to bury my head in the sand, which I wouldn't let him, which caused everyone else to get involved. The tension that was festering between us quickly dissipated with the light-hearted play.

The Big Secret

We only had a few more days before we'd be heading back to our lives in Utah, so I planned on making the most of the remaining time and keep myself busy to avoid obsessing over Sam.

The sky was overcast the next day, so I waited a while before heading down to the volleyball game and surfing. Besides, I needed to spend some time with the group I came with, unless they were going shopping. I tried going back to sleep only to lie on the couch wide awake. It was cold in the RV, so I quickly slathered on the sunscreen, put on some jeans and a t-shirt over my swimsuit with a pullover sweater on top, then tossed some shorts, my beach towel, and water into my beach bag.

Outside in the chilly air, I wrapped a blanket around me and sat in one of the chairs, then noticed the radio/cassette player had been left on the ground next to me. Would it still work after being left outside all night? I was about to turn on the radio when I noticed a tape inside the cassette player, and being the inquisitive person that I am, I pushed the button. The music blared out and I quickly lowered the volume to hear the strains of a romantic ballad emanating from the speakers of the player. I had never heard anything as beautiful before. When the song ended, I quickly rewound the tape and played it again . . . and again . . . and again— it spoke to my romance starved soul. The words spoke of the singer's devotion to a woman and the effect love had on him. Mesmerized I stared out at the ocean and daydreamed of Sam saying those words to me.

"What're you listening to?" asked Sam, making me jump. I hadn't heard his RV door open or him approach. He looked at me curiously. "I've watched you hit rewind a dozen times."

"Have you heard this song?" I asked.

"Why doncha play it?" Sam said. "Again." And he chuckled, pulling a beach chair next to mine and sat down. I looked at him out of the corner of my eye; besides being absolutely gorgeous, this guy was just cool. Everything about him screamed coolness. Was he even aware of how cool he was?

Ignoring his tone, and still looking at him, I hit the play button as he sat in the chair next to mine. I scanned his stunning face for any sign of emotion.

"Isn't it pretty?" I asked, but only silence answered. "I've never heard this before, have you?"

"Mmm, yeah it is."

"Why are you guys listening to such romantic music? Are you in love?" I teased, making Sam laugh and shake his head no—of course not. We listened to the remaining strains in silence.

"I'm gonna tell ya something and you have to promise you won't tell anyone," Sam said, leaning closer to my chair. I hoped that it was him declaring his love for me, but it wasn't.

"I promise; what?" I said, in a conspiratorial tone.

"Stephen is going to propose to Rosie." Sam smirked. "And

this song has something to do with what he has planned."

"No way!" I said. "That's sooo great! When?"

"Shhhh!" Sam said, putting his hand on my arm to stop my animation. "The night before we leave."

"How?"

"Send her on a treasure hunt and the final clue will lead her back to your RV, which will be full of candles, this music, and Stephen holding a ring."

"She'll know what's up as soon as she starts on the hunt if she's all by herself."

"He's hoping that you girls will take part and gradually be disqualified until the end when it'll be only her."

"So, it's more of a game, and she's the winner," I said, stating the obvious. "And, I'm one of the losers." I sighed.

"Well . . . yeah."

"Hm. What are we supposed to do while *they're* inside *our* RV having dinner?" I asked.

Sam just shrugged. "I don't know."

"He can't do that in *your* RV?" Sam shook his head. "Why do we have to be inconvenienced?" I asked.

"Yours is cleaner than ours and doesn't smell," Sam answered. I rolled my eyes.

I pointed to the cassette player. "That really is a romantic song," I admitted before expelling another sigh. "And, it's neat that Stephen feels that way about Rosie."

"Saaam . . . Saaaam!!" We both turned to see Lucy the waitress waving and walking towards us from the parking lot.

Pushing myself up from my chair, I quickly said, "Well, there's your girlfriend, and I'm gonna go surf. It's my date with destiny!" I grabbed my bag and walked away.

"Wait," Sam said as I left, but I didn't turn back.

"Hey, Sam," Lucy called.

"Oh hi," he said, and I heard nothing else, nor did I want to hear any more. *Always the friend never the girlfriend.* As I walked away, that beautiful song continued to play in my mind, making me long for the romance I'd never have.

Catchin' A Wave

Approaching the spot on the beach that I'd pre-arranged to meet Max I resolved to forget about Sam, his woman, romance, and just have fun, again.

"Cece," called Max, standing near the water's edge holding a surfboard underneath each arm. I waved. "Are ya ready to surf?" he asked, setting his boards on the sand next to one another.

"As I'll ever be," I said, hoping I wouldn't look too foolish. I looked out at the water and noticed for the first time how it mirrored the sky; today the sky was gray, and the wind blew, taking away the charm of the previous days. But it didn't seem to make any difference to Max. As soon as I'd set my bag down, he started.

"The first thing you need to do is lay on the board, face down and hold on to the sides like this." He laid on his board with his hands holding the sides. I did the same on the board next to him.

"Like this?" I asked.

"Yeah, except you want to place your hands more in this area." He leaned towards my board and moved my right hand into position. "You need to be able to push yourself up like this. Then grip the board with your toes." He immediately sprang to his feet in a crouch position. "Now you do it."

"Like this?" I asked, awkwardly raising to my feet.

Max chuckled, and said, "Close. Do it again." I laid on the board and pulled myself up. "You need to do it quicker. Like this," he said, showing me the speed.

I blew out some air, then with determination I laid on my board and sprang to my feet. "I did it!"

"Good. Do it again."

"Again?"

"Yes. You'll do it many more times before I'll take you out on the water. It's much more difficult then."

"Okay." I lowered myself to the board. At Max's command I sprang to my feet—repeatedly. The good thing about the exercise was that I no longer shook from cold—or nerves, for that matter— as my body grew warmer from the exertion.

After what seemed an eternity and just when my legs were turning to jelly, Max said, "Let's go in the water."

I looked at him, then at the cold gray water with both excitement and trepidation. I wasn't looking forward to the cold, but I wanted to try surfing.

"Now?" I asked.

"Sure," he said. I gulped in some air. "Better put this on or you'll freeze to death; it's Sandi's, so it should fit you." He handed me a wet suit. I took it and with shaking hands, stripped off my outer clothes and pulled it on with Max's help over my swimsuit, then he got into his suit and handed me a rubbery leash connected to the bottom end of the board. "This'll keep your board from getting washed away."

"Washed away?" I asked nervously. "You mean I could lose this board . . . out there, in the ocean?"

He chuckled, and said, "You won't with this leash. Now hold still while I attach it," he said and wrapped a Velcro strap around my ankle that connected to the leash. He did the same to his ankle, and picking up our boards, we walked towards the water. The closer we came to the water the more I began to shake; I didn't know if it was from the cold, my nerves, or what, but there was no way I was backing out.

"We're going to get on our boards and paddle out into the water. That's where we'll wait for a wave, okay?" Max said as we stepped into the ocean. "Do what I do."

Using just our arms, we paddled further into the ocean—further than I'd ever been. The board rose and fell as the water undulated beneath us. Thankfully, we came to a spot where Max stopped paddling and sat upright on his board. I did the same and let my feet dangle in the water, resting my arms and trying to forget how freezing my feet were.

"Okay Cece, let's try this wave. You need to be ready to spring up in the crouch position," Max coached. I laid on my board and watched the wave approach, and as it drew closer, I paddled like crazy. My adrenaline was pumping so hard and my heart was beating so fast. "Get ready!" Max yelled. The wave reached me, and I felt a push.

"Now!" Max commanded. I sprang up and immediately fell off my board into the freezing water. Thankfully, I only tumbled a little with the wave, yanking my board along with the leash on my ankle. As soon as I resurfaced, Max yelled, "Get back on your board. Quick." I pulled myself back on and paddled back to him.

"It's so cold," I said breathlessly.

"You'll get used to it the more you move," he said, and I nodded. "Here comes another wave; get ready."

I did as he instructed. I looked over my shoulder and watched the wave, paddling hard. Just like before, it softly pushed me forward.

"Get up now!" he yelled. I sprang into the crouch, only standing for a moment before I fell into what I was sure would be my watery grave. I swam to the top, choking on the saltwater that burned in my nostrils, then paddled back to him again. "You almost had it that time," he said with a smile.

"Really?" I asked, hoping I wouldn't disappoint him after all the time he'd spent with me. I pulled myself back on the board, ready for the next wave, then the next wave, and the next. I wasn't sure how long we were in the water before I couldn't feel my toes, making it difficult for me to stand on the board.

"Okay, see that wave? As soon as you feel it take your board, then get in the crouch position. If you don't stand up in time, you'll miss the wave," Max coached. I curled my legs up and watched the wave approach, my arms burning in pain from paddling so much, and the closer it got, the more ready I was to crouch on the board. Then the wave hit, pushing me forward. "Get up now! Now," yelled Max. I tried to do as he said, but my feet were so numb, I couldn't even tell if they were on the board or not. I fell headfirst into the water in only three seconds' time.

As soon as I surfaced, I grabbed my board and tried to pull myself on it when Max paddled over and asked, "Are ya ready to go again?"

My teeth chattered. "I-I-I d-don't th-th-think I c-c-can. I c-c-can't f-feel m-m-my f-f-feet."

Immediately, Max grabbed my board, with me attached, and pulled it closer to his. "We better stop. Can you get back on your board?" he asked. I made a valiant attempt, but my fingers were numb from the cold as well, so he pulled me onto my board. I couldn't believe how strong he was; it was as if he was picking up a piece of cloth. "Just relax," he told me. "We'll get you warm." I observed the look of concern on his beautiful, masculine face and wondered if Sam had ever looked at me that way. Max's eyes seemed to change with the ocean; today they were a greyish blue and almost matched the water. Laying on my board, as he towed it behind his, I felt bad that I'd wimped out, but the water was *so* cold. *I'm okay to die if this is the last face I see*, I thought dreamily as I floated toward the shore.

Finally, we reached the shore and Max helped me off my board into the shallow water, then took both boards under each arm. Slowly, I made it to the sand, and proceeded forward as if my feet were those of a ninety-year-old—they were so numb.

"How'd you like surfing?" asked Sandi, walking toward me. Then, she saw the pained look on my face and my shivering and asked, "Is everything okay?"

"I'd l-l-like t-to s-s-say that I k-killed it, b-b-but m-my fe-e-et are sssooo c-cold I co-couldn't f-f-feel them t-t-o stand up," I chattered. Sandi immediately grabbed a blanket that was set on a chair and wrapped it around me.

"We better get you inside and warm your feet," she said, leading me towards the nearest beach house.

"Ins-s-side where?" I asked, shivering and praying that it was close.

"Here," she said, pointing to the house just ahead as she helped me limp into the little courtyard, up the steps to her porch and into her warm house. The heat felt painfully good after the cold, I couldn't get close enough to the fire. I needed the warmth to engulf me, I was so frozen. Once in front of it, I stayed wrapped in my blanket inside the wet suit until Max brought in my clothes from the beach a minute later.

"Whoo! It just started to rain," he said dropping my clothes on the chair near the fire. "I shouldn't've taken you in the water." Max frowned. He knelt before my chair and began rubbing my feet. "I forgot you aren't used to it."

"Th-tha-that's ooo-k-kay, I w-w-wanted to t-t-try s-s-surf-f-fing. I'm s-s-sorry I was su-su-such a w-w-waste of-f-f y-y-your t-ti-tme th-though." I drew even closer to the fire.

"Let me help you out of the wet suit," Max offered, standing and taking the blanket from around me. I noticed the shaking had calmed down.

"I'll help her," said Steph who had just come down the stairs. She moved Max out of the way. "These can be kinda tricky and difficult to undo unless you know what you're doing." She helped me up, then turned me around and pulled on the zipper in the back. It wouldn't budge; it was stuck. After multiple attempts she called, "Hey Max, I do need your help after all. Can you come get Cece out of this suit, please? I can't get the zipper down." Max came out of the kitchen with a half-eaten roll in his hand, and handing it to Steph, he turned me around again and gave the zipper a good tug, pulling it down the full length to my waist.

"Thanks," I said as I pulled my arms out of the sleeves, making sure my swimming suit straps were firmly placed on my shoulders.

"Thanks, Max." Steph said as she pushed him towards the kitchen. "We need to get Gracie out of her wet swimsuit and you don't need to be in here." With that, Steph held up the blanket that had been wrapped about me, as a shield so I could change in front of the fire. Getting back into my jeans and sweater was a huge relief.

"Do you wanna stay for lunch?" Sandi called from the kitchen as I sat by the fire.

"I'd love to! It smells really good. I'm starved."

"Can I come out now?" Max asked from the kitchen. Steph

and I laughed.

"Of course, you can. Gracie is all dressed now."

"Good," Sandi said. "I can't keep him out of the food." Then we heard a slap and some giggling before Sandi pushed him out.

Sitting in Sandi's warm kitchen eating lunch, the conversation seemed to flow.

"How much longer are you here?" asked Sandi.

"Tomorrow is our last day."

"Got any big plans?" asked Steph, her green eyes sparkling.

"Just the proposal."

"Proposal?" Sandi and Steph said in unison.

"Are you asking someone to marry you?" said Steph.

"No! One of the guys is proposing to my roommate and we all have to help."

"You don't sound too excited about it. Do you like the guy that is proposing?" asked Max.

"He's okay—a bit bossy, but okay."

"But you aren't romantically interested?" questioned Sandi.

"Oh no," I said, unable to hide my disgusted look. "Whose

house is this?" I asked, trying to change the subject.

"Mine," answered Sandi. "My mother left it to me."

"Wow, I'd love living so close to the beach."

"Eh, it has its pros and cons, but luckily Max and Steph are here often enough to help."

"Do you live here all the time?" I asked Steph.

"I wish."

"She lives in Wisconsin but comes to California for the holidays. She's been doing it since she was little," Sandi informed me.

"Are you related?"

"We're cousins," Steph answered. I leaned back and looked at them both: Sandi with her blonde hair with the beach waves, and Steph with her straight as sticks brown hair, not convinced they were related, when they both smiled and there it was. The dimple in the same spot on each girl's face.

"I guess I see it, now."

"Do you like livin' in Utah?" Max paused from shoveling soup into his mouth.

"I think I'd prefer it here."

"Do you like any of the guys in your group?" asked Sandi with a curious look on her face.

I did a quick double-take, then cleared my throat before I answered, "Uh, why do you ask?"

"Ah! She does," exclaimed Sandi. "Which one?" I was unable to stop myself from blushing.

"Ah-ha!" Max pointed at me, chuckling.

"N-n-nooo, not really," I said, avoiding their faces. To change the subject, I quickly said, "So Max, what is it you do with the fish?"

Looking at me confused, he asked, "What fish?"

My brow furrowed. "I thought you told me you trained fish in the Navy?"

Mumbling to himself, he said, "Fishes . . . fish . . . Oh! You mean seals?"

I cringed in embarrassment. "Yeah, I think so."

"I don't *train* fish, I train Navy Seals, sometimes called Seals. I used to be one." Laughing, he turned to Sandi. "Cece thought I trained fish. You're cute."

I cringed again, then hurried on. "So, do seals swim a lot?"

"That, among other things."

"Hmmm."

"So back to you," Steph said, placing her chin on her hand and leaning towards me with intrigue. "Which of those guys do you like?"

I always got so nervous when I was about to spill the beans on my unrequited crush. But looking into the three eager faces focused on me, they all seemed so kind that I couldn't hold back. I told them the whole story. After I'd finished, Sandi leaned back with a curious look on her face.

"Which one is Sam?" she asked.

Taking a dreamy sigh, I said, "He's about six foot four, dark curly hair, great build." I looked at Max. "He could give you a run for your money." All three of them laughed.

"Oooh man, don't tell him that," groaned Sandi. "You'll bruise his ego." We laughed some more. Then Sandi stood and began to remove the empty soup bowls from the table. "I think I saw someone that matches that description sitting over on those rocks near the path that comes down from the road today."

"What was he doing?" I asked.

"Watching you surf. But he had a girl with him."

I looked down and played with the soup left in my bowl.

"Yeah, that's probably him." I rested my face in my hand. "Now ya see why this doesn't go anywhere. Did he stay long?"

"I don't know, I'm sorry. I just noticed him when I was taking out the trash. You're right though: he is good-looking."

"Heeey," said Max, pointing at himself. "I'm right here." We looked at him and couldn't help but laugh.

"I didn't say he was better looking, just good-looking," said Sandi; as she put her arms around Max and kissed him on the cheek.

"Gee Cees, that's really tough," Steph said with a sympathetic look.

"Yeah, but I'm used to it," I said, brushing it off as I stood to take my bowl over to the counter. "I've been living off of the crumbs he throws me for so long, I've developed my own coping skills." I tried to laugh to lighten the mood.

"Are you sure he doesn't like you?" asked Steph.

"Yeah," said Max. "Guys don't go out of their way to watch some girl surf in this kind of cold with another girl along if they're not interested."

"That's right," agreed Sandi. "Have you ever asked him?"

"No . . . no. You saw how good-looking he is. I don't think I'm pretty enough. I'm just a filler between the pretty ones."

"No," said Max. "I think you're wrong."

The Big Game

We would head back to Utah super early the next day, so it was

our last full day in California, and tonight Stephen would propose

to Rosie. I wondered if the other girls knew about the big event yet

or not—I could only ask Sam since he was the one who told me the

news and had sworn me to secrecy.

As usual, I was the first one up, but moved a little slower

this morning. My shoulders, back, and arms were stiff from my

surf adventure. Hopefully they would loosen up as the day passed.

I struggled to pull my jeans and sweater on, went outside, and

dragged one of the beach chairs and a blanket I found near the fire pit closer to the water. I sat captivated by the waves as they swept in and out, lost in thought. It was another beautiful day, a little cold, yet it would probably warm up. As I sat there, I promised myself that I would be back for good someday.

Sitting in my chair, I contemplated the last few days: the ocean, this vacation, and the lack of romance in my life no matter how badly I wanted it. I suddenly became aware of Max and Sandi sitting next to me.

"Hey! Where'd you guys come from?"

Max laughed. "Boy, were you far away. We've been here for a few minutes," he said as he tipped my chair over.

"Hey-ey," I shrieked and scrambled to get unwrapped from the blanket and up before he was on top of me.

"What were you thinking about?" asked Sandi

"How much I hate to leave and go home to the cold weather," I said as Max dove for me. I almost got away, but he caught one leg. I screamed out while struggling to get away, only to have Max pull me back to the point that I was powerless. I groaned aloud as I tried to fight him off, as the stiffness in my shoulders from all the paddling yesterday raised its ugly head stopping my movements.

Sitting on top of me, Max chuckled as he said, "Looks like our little surfer is feeling a bit sore today."

"Shut up." I giggled.

"Wanna go out again? It's warmer," he said with his devilish grin and his bright blue eyes twinkling.

I grinned back. "I wish I—"

"When ya leaving?" Sandi asked, interrupting.

"Tomorrow." I sighed pitifully while trying to escape from Max's weight. "Where's Steph?"

Max and Sandi looked around. "She was just here."

"Oh, there she is," said Sandi, pointing at Steph who stood in front of the RVs talking to the group. "Max, let her go," Sandi ordered. With a sigh, he got up and I backed away from him, both of us smiling like Cheshire cats.

"We better go see what she's doing," muttered Max. As we followed Sandi, Max carried my chair and blanket with one arm, while his other arm rested casually around my neck.

As we approached the group, Steph pointed in our direction. "That's Max and my cousin, Sandi with Ceecee," she said to them. They nodded their heads in recognition. "Sandi, they've all agreed to come play a game of flag football and barbeque."

"Great!" Sandi smiled.

"I'll run and get some meat to barbeque!" Steph said to the group.

"I can go with you," came a random chorus from Frank, Corey, and Sam. *Of course*, I thought. Steph turned pink from the attention, tucking an errant strand of dark brown hair behind her ear in her naturally shy way. You couldn't blame 'em falling prey to her cute smile with the one dimple. Truthfully, it didn't surprise me when the guys hovered around her.

"We might have enough food here," said Rosie. "Let's check the RVs and see what's left. Since this is our last day, we should probably eat as much of it as we can to avoid throwing it out."

"Great idea," said Stephen. Rosie went into the girl's RV while Stephen went into the guys', then both came out about the same time.

We've got enough food to cover lunch," said Stephen,

looking at Rosie for confirmation.

"Yeah, plenty. You won't need to buy anything."

"Good to know," said Sandi. "You wanna come down to my house? I can get the barbeque ready while you guys play flag football."

"You're not gonna play?" asked Johnny.

"No, I'm recovering from knee surgery, still have to be careful." Sandi rubbed her left knee while flexing it. Max picked her up and threw her over his shoulder.

"See you guys at eleven," she called as Max carried her down the beach.

"See ya then," Steph said, following Max and Sandi at a slow jog, laughing.

I observed Sam, Cory, and Frank watching Steph jog away. *Men can be so pathetic.* I shook my head and followed the other girls into the RV.

"Did you see how those three jerks were falling over each other to help that Steph?" Jana pouted as she plopped down in one of the chairs. She looked at me. "How do you handle it, Gracie? Sam does it all the time."

"I have no control over Sam. He does what he wants," I responded.

"None of us do," added Pam as she helped Rosie load all the food into a large box.

"Right. We have no say what they do or who they see unless we're in a committed relationship," said Claire. "The only one close to that is Rosie."

We changed into shorts and t-shirts to play flag football. I was actually looking forward to this group activity.

We headed towards Sandi's a little before eleven, loaded down with enough food to feed twenty people, let alone thirteen. When we were halfway there, I decided I wanted to bring my towel, just in case.

"Hey, guys! I'm gonna run back to the RV for a sec, I'll catch up," I called at them as I turned to head back.

"Whaddya forget?" Sam called, turning to look at me.

"Don't worry, I'll be right behind you," I said and trotted off toward our campsite. Entering our RV, I quickly grabbed my towel, slathered on more sunscreen, then went back out to find Sam standing near the fire pit waiting for me. "You didn't have to come with me," I said with a slight glare.

"Why not?" he asked.

"I'm surprised you're going to the barbeque."

"Why?"

"I figured you'd want to spend the last day with that girl." I couldn't help but roll my eyes the slightest bit.

"What girl?" asked a confused and lying Sam. I just looked at him, then shook my head for him to never mind and walked away from our little campsite.

We walked in silence for a couple of moments before I said, "So, what's happening with the engagement? Is it still on for tonight?"

"Yup."

"Do all the others know about it except Rosie?"

"Yup."

"Great, I can hardly wait. Am I expected to take part?"

"Yes."

"And the other girls?"

"Yes."

"What if the wrong girl ends up at the finish line?" I began to walk backward to look at him and smirked. "Does that mean Stephen will propose to whoever is there?"

"No," Sam said, with a look of disbelief.

We approached the area that the guys were marking off for the game. Bing Crosby singing 'White Christmas' floated towards us.

"I love Christmas music," I declared and ran towards the group on the court, singing along with Bing, causing the others to begin singing.

Within minutes of when Sam and I got there we were choosing teams: Johnny and Max were the captains and each team had three guys and three girls, minus Sandi. As luck would have it, Sam and I were on the same team, but I'd already decided to just ignore him and play. Max talked so much smack at us, he had all my focus.

Thirty minutes into the game we'd lost all the girls but Rosie and me, making it four on each team including a girl. So, while waiting for the ball to be snapped, if it took too long to set up, I would try to talk smack back at Max.

"Hey batta batta batta swwwwing," I'd yell at the top of my

voice.

With a big laugh, Max said, "That's baseball, ya goof!"

"It took your mind off the game," I said with a jig. When the smack talk didn't work, then I'd dance and sing along with whatever Christmas song was playing. Max would laugh and try to sing, but he never knew the words, which made me laugh.

Johnny had me run the ball, and each time Max would try to tackle me instead of just pulling the flag. He was so strong he'd grab me from behind with one arm and pull me to the sand.

"This is flag football, not tackle football," Sam told Max.

"Ah, she doesn't seem to mind." Max shrugged then winked at me, making me laugh. This made the game much more fun for me, and I loved the attention from Max; it made me feel feminine and desired. With each attempt to tackle me we'd end up in the sand laughing with me attempting to escape his hold.

When Johnny moved me to the quarterback position, I threw the ball to Sam, who proceeded to make a touchdown. However, Sam's victory dance ended quickly when he saw Max and I laughing as he threw me on the sand.

"He can't tackle the Quarterback after she's thrown the

ball," Sam said to Johnny, watching me and Max laughing and wrestling each other.

"Unnecessary roughness on the Quarterback," called Corey. "Even though she deserves it." He laughed.

"What?" Max said, feigning innocence.

We continued playing, and whether I played offense or defense, Max was all over me. *I loved it!!* But it seemed as though Sam wasn't enjoying the antics.

By the time we finished the game, on the last tackle, Max carried me over to the water and dunked me, but I didn't go down without a fight and was able to pull him down with me. Everyone cheered when I came out of the water a total mess with sand in my hair and clothes, yet victorious!

Coming out of the water, Sandi met me holding a towel, laughing. "Why don't you use this outdoor shower to get the sand and salt rinsed off, before we eat," Sandi suggested as she led me over to it.

I glanced at her. "You know I'm not flirting with Max, right? We're just having fun." It worried me she'd think I was chasing him, but she only laughed.

"I know, don't worry 'bout it. He's just trying to help," she said, turning on the water.

"Help? Help with what?" I asked, confused as I reached out to test the temperature of the water. It was lukewarm, so I stepped into it.

"Trying to make Sam jealous," she said, which made me laugh.

"Of what? Max?"

"Yeah," she stated, making me laugh even harder. "We thought—"

"We, as in you and Max?" I interrupted.

"Yes, and Steph," she continued. "It was really Steph and me, but Max wanted to help. He really likes you. And after you told us how you felt, we thought we'd try and help."

I laughed. "Thank you. I doubt it will work, but I love that you tried."

"It's a time for giving, and this is our gift to you: making Sam jealous, hopefully," she said with a wink.

"He'd have to care to get jealous." I stopped to look at her. "You've seen how handsome he is, he can have any woman he wants. He's made it pretty clear that he only wants me as a friend," I said with a frown.

"He might surprise you."

The Proposal

As a ploy to get Rosie away from the camp, we girls were instructed to take her to see a movie, thus buying time for the guys to prepare the treasure hunt and set up for the proposal. We found a four o'clock showing of Seven Brides for Seven Brothers at a retro theater near the beach. Needless to say, I was less than thrilled to be so involved in yet another proposal that wasn't mine. *Sigh.* *Always the bridesmaid, never the bride.*

I wasn't against proposals, especially for a great roommate. The problem is that when you live with roommates, proposals seem to happen—a lot. Just not to me. And, the boyfriends always seemed to think I lived for a chance to help make all the arrangements for a proposal. How could I say no to a guy who's so gaga over your roommate that he is willing to look the fool to give her a memorable proposal? Tonight's will be number five. For the record, I preferred hearing about it *after* the fact, rather than being so involved in it.

You could never go wrong with the Seven Brides musical, unless I was auditioning for it. It always lightened the mood and left you wanting to dance with an ax in the snow, or on logs at a barn raising. But, no matter how many times I'd seen it, not once had it inspired me to marry a perfect stranger—even if he looked and sang like Howard Keel. We left the theater in high spirits, singing the songs and attempting to copy the dance steps we'd seen performed as we made our way to Pam's car.

"What's this?" asked Pam, taking an envelope with Jana's name on it from her windshield and handing it to her. We gathered around Jana as she opened it and read aloud:

Our time in Cali is over and done

We've had a great week of sand, ocean, and fun

Since our friendships have grown beyond all measure

The best way to end is with a hunt for treasure.

You'll each get a clue that leads to a prize

To show your value in each of our eyes.

With your prize in hand, your turn is done

You'll then move to the back, leaving room for the next one.

Will you find love, or will you find chance?

Only one will know at the final dance.

With all that said, here's what you do

Go back from whence you came to find the first clue.

It's at the first window just give 'em your name

With prize in hand, let's start this game!

"A Treasure Hunt! How fun," exclaimed Rosie. It was a good thing she was excited to do it, since it was all for her benefit. The rest of us rolled our eyes as we prepared to play our parts as instructed by Stephen. On to the first clue.

Following the note's instructions, we returned to the movie theater and up to the first and only window, "Um . . . excuse me?" began Jana, tapping on the window. "Excuse me!" she repeated, trying to get the elderly lady's attention who sat with her back to us. "Excuse me!" Finally, she turned around and Jana continued, "Do you have a small package back there for a 'Jana'?"

"What's the name?"

"Jana," we all said at once as the lady began to root around under the counter.

"Here it is," she proclaimed, holding it above her head like a prize before handing the envelope to Jana. Taking it, Jana quickly opened it and pulled out a cute pair of dangling earrings with little sombreros, then read the note:

Now you're done, please step aside

It's time for Pam to check her ride.

Heading home, facing the glare,

Thanks to her prize, she won't care.

We followed the clues: at Pam's car, we found a pair of sunglasses under the passenger seat and another note. At the Ramada Inn, Claire got a beaded necklace. Then it was my turn. I was the last one before the finale.

The clue for my prize directed us back to the restroom

where I'd emptied all the sand out of my suit after my tumble in the waves. In the dark, it was a bit tricky finding the trail that would lead us down to the beach near the restroom. Thankfully, Pam had the forethought to grab the flashlight from the emergency kit in her car's trunk, supplying us with the desperately needed light to see.

"Guess I'm last," noted Rosie as we walked down the trail single file. We all ignored her comment since we knew she'd be coming out way ahead of the rest of us that night.

Once inside the dark restroom, we searched together as a group rather than separating to look for my "prize" since I held the flashlight. We found the envelope taped under the sink. Gingerly, I pulled it away from the surface they had taped it to, unsure of what disgusting thing I would pull with it, then we headed back to the car where I read the note:

We started with five and are now down to one
The smaller the number the bigger the fun
Show Miss Rosie the flicker of a candle,
For tonight with her prize, she'll prove too much to handle.

In my envelope was a simple bracelet with a few charms attached: a surfboard, a starfish, the sun, and a heart. As we headed back to the campsite for the long-awaited finale, I fastened the bracelet around my wrist, admiring the charms and wondered who'd chosen this prize for me.

It was close to nine p.m. and we were all hungry, cold, and eager to get this proposal over, or maybe it was just me. Pulling into our parking spot near the RVs, Rosie was uncharacteristically quiet. I wondered if she'd figured out what was happening.

Approaching the RVs from the back we didn't know if we'd see candles, lights or whatever the guys had decided for decorations in the RV. However, as we entered the campsite, we gasped at how beautiful it looked. The guys had decorated outside with votive candles on every available surface in our camping spot: on the table and chairs near the fire pit, and even some on the ground. Romantic music quietly played out of speakers strategically hidden around the area, but no one was around. All but Rosie held back as she cautiously stepped further into the magical glow of the candlelight, unaware that she was alone.

We stood as spectators watching the romantic scene unfold:

Rosie stopped in amazement taking in the beautiful setup, forgetting she was in shorts and her oversized U of U sweatshirt. She willingly followed Frank when he appeared from around the RV to lead her over to the table near the cozy burning fire. Once she was seated, he melted into the dark, replaced by Stephen in a suit and tie, taking his place opposite Rosie at the table.

"What's going on here?" she asked Stephen with a nervous laugh.

"Your treasure hunt prize."

Looking around, she said with an embarrassed giggle, "But none of the other girls got this big of a prize." Stephen laughed and smiled. At that moment, Johnny walked out from behind the RV holding high above his head a tray, and with much ceremony placed two paper plates of food before them, causing Rosie to nervously giggle again.

"What's on the plates?" Claire whispered.

"PB&Js," I answered.

"Ooooooh," Claire, Pam, and Jana all whispered in unison. Rosie loved those sandwiches. She didn't care whether it was jelly, jam, or honey that was used, as long as it was mixed with peanut butter.

Still undetected, we watched Sam enter the scene holding a bottle wrapped in a towel. After he carefully set two paper cups on the table and poured the liquid into each cup, with a flourish he removed the towel and set the bottle down on the table, exposing the words 'Root Beer'.

"This was a very good year," he said and like Frank, he retreated into the dark.

Watching them eat, my stomach grumbled, reminding me that I was hungry. I motioned to the other girls to follow me as we made our way around the back of the RV, hoping to find the guys and food. Sure enough, at the front end of the RV sat all four guys munching on sandwiches.

"Why haven't you come out yet?" I whispered to Cory.

"I'm in charge of the music," he said and pointed to the system that had been set up, quite ingeniously, for the night. "See, the cassette player is attached by a couple of wires that run under the RV and attach to speakers hidden by the tires, to hear the music better."

"Very nice." I nodded my head in admiration. "Did you

choose the music too?”

"Nah, that's all Stephen," he said. As a group, we gathered into a small circle to whisper without the two love birds hearing us while eating our sandwiches.

"Thanks for the bracelet, by the way," I said, holding up my wrist as I shook it for all to see.

"Yeah, who picked all the gifts?" Pam asked.

"We all did," stated Frank. "Stephen thought it was the least we could do for all your help with this."

"Wow! You guys bought us these gifts?" asked Jana quietly.

"We picked them out, but Stephen paid for them," Cory informed us while giving a sly laugh. "We all picked the girl we wanted to get the gift for, wrote the clue for that gift, and gave Stephen the bill."

"Aren't you the cheap, clever ones," Claire said with a soft laugh.

"What happens next? Does anyone know?" Jana asked between bites of her PB&J, which Frank began to mock by talking with his mouth filled with food. Jana quietly laughed, causing her to choke a little on her last bite.

"Sorry," Jana said as she patted her chest and drank some water to stop her cough. We ate in silence. "Do we know when he's actually gonna ask her or are we gonna be waiting here 'til morning?"

"Now, now, retract your claws before someone gets hurt," teased Cory.

"We've been working this proposal since early this afternoon: with the movie, the treasure hunt, and now this," Claire informed the guys.

"Us too," Frank said.

"I thought this was supposed to take place in our RV?" Pam asked.

"Not enough room," Sam said matter-of-factly.

"Can someone look to see what the lovebirds are doing now?" asked Cory. "I still have another song to play."

"Oh yeah," said Johnny as he pushed his way through the little circle to look around the corner at Stephen and Rosie. He quickly turned back, waving his arm. "Start the next song! Start the next song," he hissed, and we all scrambled to get a spot to observe

Stephen make the big move. Claire, Sam, and I ended up where we had started at the far end of the RV. Standing there, I couldn't help but be affected by the ambiance from the scene in front of me: the soft glow from all the little candles, the romantic music, the roses that Johnny brought out with the dessert, the anticipation that a proposal was gonna take place, and having my crush so close behind me. My romantic barometer was in the red zone.

Neither had started on the dessert, which I knew was chocolate and would now go to waste. *Seriously?* The music got a little louder as Stephen stood and held his hand out to Rosie. While gazing into his eyes, Rosie stood, placed her hand in his and without a word they began to dance. *Where do these guys learn these moves?* I wondered. *From the movies?* It wasn't the song I'd previously heard and fallen in love with, but a new one, almost as gorgeous.

"This isn't the song I heard," I leaned back and whispered to Sam. The whiff of his musky scent was overwhelming and awakened my, already very sensitive, romantic emotions even more.

"That tape busted, probably from all the times you played

it," he said in my ear before gasping as my elbow connected with his rib, causing him to laugh as he moved to protect himself from any further hits.

"Shh," both Claire and I mouthed to him.

"Very pretty song," Claire said in a whisper as we stood watching them dance, then Stephen stepped back and knelt on one knee, holding out an opened small box that held the ring.

The diamond caught what light was available and sparkled in the dark. I didn't hear what he said, but I'm sure whatever it was included the words "Will you marry me" in there somewhere, and he barely stood before Rosie was in his arms. That was our cue to come out of the darkness and congratulate them.

Rosie was on cloud nine as she held out the magnificent diamond Stephen had placed on her ring finger. I swallowed hard, pushing the jealousy I felt back down as I hugged them both, and tried to mirror their happiness.

"Congratulations!" I said.

"I'm so happy for you."

"It's about time," I heard one of the guys say.

"Wanna go for one last walk on the beach?" asked Sam,

quietly in my ear.

"Give me a sec," I said with a sigh of relief. I quietly left the congratulatory group to go into the RV. Seconds later I emerged, having changed into warmer clothes, to see Sam standing off from the excitement wearing a sweatshirt, waiting for me. We quietly walked away from the group along the water's edge in silence.

Back to Reality

Once back in Salt Lake, it was only a matter of days before the little amount of color I'd gained from my time in the sun had disappeared and I was back to looking pasty white as usual. Oh, but the memories I had at my fingertips; they were mine alone and kept me warm as I waited for the snow to melt.

I was so glad that my last walk on the beach had been with Sam after the proposal. I played it over and over in my mind and relived the feelings of the moment:

"Boy, I'm glad that's over," Sam said.

"Really? You don't like romantic proposals?"

"If ya gotta do it," he said, shrugging his shoulders.

"Sheesh, aren't you Mr. Romance." I rolled my eyes. "Now the mystery's solved."

"What mystery?"

"Why, with all these women, you're still single." I stopped and turned to him.

"Oh, ya think so, eh?" he said with a devilish grin. "You don't think I can be romantic?"

"I just call it like I see it," I said, raising my hands as I backed away. Then smiling, I turned and ran with Sam chasing me.

"I'll show you romance," he said, lifting me from behind and carrying me towards the water. I kicked and shrieked in desperation.

"Nooo! Sam." I laughed and struggled to get away. We fell on the sand and I quickly scrambled to my feet. Sam grabbed my foot and held on as I attempted to drag him.

"Gotcha," he said, laughing. I fell to the sand, as if I gave up. Once he relaxed his hold on my foot I jumped up and began to run again. Sam rose to his feet and chased me towards the water.

"No Sam!" I couldn't stop my laughter as he feigned to

tackle me but instead lifted me over his shoulder and ran towards the incoming wave. As the wave crashed into him and the spray from the wave hit my face, I could taste the salt on my lips. "Sam! Don't put me in the water!"

"Do you think I'm romantic now?" he asked as he took me from over his shoulder into his arms and held me above the escaping wave. When I didn't answer, he held me away from him in pretense of dropping me in the water.

"Yes! Yes! I think your romantic," I agreed in an effort to appease him and avoid the cold water. "Now put me down!"

"Okay," He laughed and acted as if he'd drop me in the water.

"No!" I screamed. "Not here. On the sand." I vigorously kicked my legs trying to get him to move in that direction. He laughed and turned towards the sand, holding me in his arms. For the first time, I noticed that my arms had gone around his neck and were holding on for dear life. He dropped to his knees and let me softly fall on the sand with a chuckle.

"I knew you'd change your mind," Sam said with a grin.

"Only under duress." I laughed.

"Duress, huh?" He grabbed my wrists and pinned me on the sand as he straddled my body and began to tickle me. "Stop! Stop," I choked out through laughter. He let me push him off me so I could sit up and catch my breath.

He fell back on the sand behind me. We sat in silence, exhausted as we listened to the roar of the ocean. It had been a long day with all the activities and the elaborate proposal. Sighing, I pushed my sleeves up and rested my hands in the cool sand, exposing the bracelet.

"Do you like my heart?" Sam gently tugged on the heart charm on my bracelet.

"I love it," I said, looking over my shoulder at him. I hesitated. "So, you chose that for me?"

"Yeah. I chose all of them."

Our eyes met. "I like your choice of charms."

"So do I," he said as his warm hand rested on mine. I hoped we'd stay that way for hours, but it was only moments before he pulled his hand away. A sudden gust of cold air whipped through me.

"We should probably go back; I'm getting cold," I said

with a shiver. Sam immediately stood, offering his hand.

"Thanks." I grasped it and let him pull me up. However, once I was standing, he didn't let go of my hand but continued to hold it as we began to walk back. I was grateful for the darkness that hid my face as it turned forty shades of red. I fought the urge to giggle as I walked next to him relishing in the warm strength of his strong hand as it held mine and willing my body to stop reacting to his touch so feverishly. *This is so crazy. Do not giggle!*

"I know you're confused by this whole thing," he stated without looking at me.

"What whole thing?" I asked as casually as I could muster.

"You and me."

I paused, unsure of how to answer this question. The last time I'd answered a question like that I'd lost him to Sara Jane. If I said the wrong thing, would it scare him away? Being the smooth operator that I was, I immediately began to trip over my words, "Well . . .I . . . uhm," then I decided to ask a more pointed question. "When you say you and me: is it 'you and me and the waitress?' or 'you and me and Sara Jane?' or 'you and me and all the other women?' I tried to make light of the moment and began to feel my face cool as I gave him what I hoped was a witty smile that hid the bitterness in my tone.

"Just you and me," Sam said, pulling me to a stop.

"Oh Sammy," I said with a heavy sigh, looking down at the sand. My heart was so tired of playing stupid and hiding my feelings for so long. I was worn out from waiting in the shadows for him to tire of the other women before shining his spotlight back on me. I looked at him from the corner of my eye. "You're such a goofy guy. I'm exhausted from wondering about you and me. After all this time, I have no idea how to read you." I couldn't believe I had just said all that. But, as soon as those words came out of my mouth, I felt my shoulders lift and square up.

"You've never called me that before," Sam said with a pleased look.

"What, goofy? Well ya are," I said, obstinately.

Involuntarily, Sam threw his head back and laughed. "Nohoo. Sammy. You've never called me Sammy before."

"Oh, well . . . " I said and looked out at the water.

"Look, Gracie," he said, moving in front of me so he blocked my view. "You're my best friend."

"*I'm* your best friend? Shouldn't Sara Jane be your best friend?"

"No one can make me laugh as much as you do."

My hope sank. A best friend isn't someone you're romantic about. I didn't need to hear him say what a great buddy I was—not tonight. I could feel my mood darken a bit, so I gave a half-hearted attempt to lighten it, "Aaah, so you think of me as a clown, do you?" With a condescending smile I turned to leave, but Sam gently caught hold of my arm.

"Nooo! I'm trying to say you make me very happy." Sam pulled me to him until we were facing each other. He stood there smiling at me, his eyes twinkling in their crescent moons. I found myself smiling back. Gone were the clouds from a moment ago. *How does he do that? How does he make me so happy?* I just stood there, barely breathing, waiting for him to do something, anticipating the moment that had eluded me for so long; was it finally gonna happen? *Was he finally gonna kiss me?* A million questions raced through my mind: *Should I close my eyes when he kisses me? Do I lean in? Will he use his tongue like Barry did?* I inwardly grimaced at that one. *Does my breath smell okay or does it smell like peanut butter? I should have brushed my teeth before we left the camp.* But he didn't kiss me, he just stood there looking at me, not saying a word.

"So . . . what are we?" I asked, trying to stop my teeth from chattering as the cold sea breeze penetrated my sweats. Subconsciously I hugged myself and began to rub my hands on my arms.

Sam noticed this and pulled me into his arms; the warmth from his body permeated mine, easing my shivers as it banished the cold from within. Speaking over my head, he told me, "Be patient. There are things I need to clear up." Hearing these words, that spark of anticipation continued to sputter. I took a big sigh and tried to burrow further into his warmth as we stood together against the cold looking towards the ocean. He was barely audible as he murmured to himself, "You'll unplug the stars and cover the sun when you finally know you've found the one."

"What'd you say?" I asked, knowing what I'd heard, but wanting him to repeat it.

"Nothing," was all he said before he let me go from his arms and started walking again.

But before I let the moment pass, I had one more question, "One more thing," I grabbed his arm, causing him to turn and face me again. "*Why* did you stop talking to me in high school?"

"What are you talking about?" he asked.

"Our Junior year, when you started dating Hoppy . . . I mean, Sara Jane. You didn't talk to me that whole year. Why?"

Without answering, he stepped around me and began walking.

"We better head back," he said quickly, not looking at me. I stood there stunned. *How could he not remember that?* Without looking at one another, we returned to the RVs, walking with our hands in our pockets. Something had changed.

That last night on the beach played on a continual loop through my head whenever I had a moment alone. Why would he deny giving me the silent treatment? But since that had caused such a strong reaction from him, I never asked that question again. Nor did I bring up the conversation we had on the beach. I didn't want to come across as desperate, obnoxious, or have him think I was impatient. I didn't want to do anything that would turn him away from me. So, I stayed quiet and kept my thoughts to myself.

While inwardly, I bathed in the warmth of his wonderful, promising words.

The Apocalypse

Once we were back, Sam and I still spent as much time together as we had available, going to parties, attending church, dinners, and movies. Yet through all these activities he never again held my hand. The only time he'd hug me was if we were dancing—I could barely wait for the next dance. He seemed to have pulled back from me. And he never referred to our conversation on the beach either when we were alone—it was as if it hadn't happened.

With the approach of Christmas, a whole new problem reared its ugly head. *Do I give him a gift or not? What if he gave me one and I didn't have one to give him in return? Better to be safe than sorry.* I couldn't really get Rosie's opinion on this decision since she was so busy planning her January wedding. So, I decided to go ahead and get him new gloves to wear when he rode his motorcycle. I justified the gift as not too personal and something he really needed.

Two weeks before Christmas, Rosie and Stephen had an engagement party that Sam and I attended. I wasn't sure about Sam, but I had so many people quietly asking me if he and I were next.

"When are you and Sam gonna announce your engagement?" one person asked.

"We're not engaged, so that would be difficult to do," I dryly responded.

"You're such a perfect couple. Has he asked you yet?" asked Celia, another friend. "I bet he does over Christmas."

"I really don't think so," I said, but secretly I hoped he would, as I remembered the conversation we had the last night on the beach.

"You might as well admit it. It's obvious the way he looks at you," said Sharon.

"With what?" I asked. "Disinterest?"

"Aren't you funny! I bet you're already engaged," Sharon said and dismissed my comments with the wave of her hand.

As flattering as it was to have people think we were engaged or close to it, all I had was what he had told me on the beach, and that wasn't for publication.

With all the romance in the air and the happy lovebirds excited about their next step, you couldn't help but be happy, nor stop yourself from wishing the same would happen to you.

Since I'd driven us to the party, I had to drop Sam off before heading home.

"Wanna come up?" Sam asked when we stopped in front of his place. These were the first words he'd uttered since we left the party.

"Sure," I said and pulled into an available spot.

It was lightly snowing as we walked from my beat-up, piece-o-crap car to the front entrance of his apartment building.

All his roommates were gone when we entered his apartment, but we still went into his bedroom. Right away he began to pace between his closet and dresser. Reluctantly, I sat on the end of his bed; I could sense that something wasn't right, but until he told me what it was, I sat there clueless. So I waited, watching as he struggled with whatever he needed to say.

"Tonight was so much fun," I said, breaking the silence. He didn't respond. I furrowed my brow and tried something else: "Don't forget we have that reception to go to the week of Christmas." He still wouldn't look at me. I began to chew on my lip and I followed him with my eyes as he continued to pace, all the while searching his handsome, brooding face for some sign as to what the problem was. The longer I had to wait the more rapidly the butterflies fluttered in my stomach. I remained silent when he again stopped and pretended to concentrate on outlining something on his dresser top.

"I can't go to that reception with you," Sam blurted out. "I'm going home."

"Oh. You're going home for Christmas? When will you be back?"

"I won't be back." Sam looked at me for the first time since we entered his bedroom. "I'm moving home." I sat frozen on his bed, unable to breathe. It felt as if all the oxygen had escaped my lungs.

"You won't ever be back?" I said quietly, grasping for any hope.

"No," he told me gruffly, trying to mask his emotions. My heart wrenched into a knot when I heard those words. It took all the acting I could muster to respond as a friend and not a wannabe girlfriend. I sat on his bed, unable to move. I desperately wanted to hold onto him and never let him go, but my arms were like lead and wouldn't move.

"Why?"

"I've gotta go back," he said, avoiding any eye contact. "Sara Jane calls me crying, or her mother, or my family call to tell me how upset she is and that I need to come home." Sam attempted to return to his pretense of tracing on his dresser top, but I could sense his misery.

"But, why? Wh-why can't you just go home for Christmas, see Sara Jane and come back?"

Shaking his head, he said, "I can't take the calls anymore. I need to go home. I . . ."

"What about your job?" I asked, grasping at any straw.

He shrugged and said, "It doesn't matter. I'll work in my family's plant."

"But you hate that job. You hate that town. Why . . ." I stopped myself. I knew exactly what was happening: Sara Jane knew that Sam was spending time with me and would use any trick in her arsenal to pull him back. It would do me no good to argue with him about going home; he'd already decided, and he didn't seem happy about his choice. She'd won again.

Totally deflated, I asked, "How long before you leave?"

"Tomorrow."

"Tomorrow? How long have you known you were moving back?"

"A couple days."

Fighting the desire to collapse in a puddle of tears, I stood up and said in a flat voice, "Well, I guess I should go so you can get ready." I had to leave while I could keep the tears at bay. "Give me a hug," I said, turning towards him. Sam walked over and without saying a word, took me in his arms for what could be the last time. I so desperately wanted to linger there and to breathe in the familiar scent as I had when we'd danced in the past, but before

I knew it, he let go.

"Are you flying home?" I asked, trying to recover my poise and prolong the moment.

"No. Gotta take my bike home."

"You're gonna ride your bike all the way home?"

"That's how I got here," he said matter-of-factly.

Then I asked the question that scared me the most: "Are you gonna marry her?"

"Probably," he said, not looking at me. If he'd said anything else, I wouldn't have heard it anyway. All I could hear was the crash of my heart, my hopes, my dreams all breaking into a million pieces, like glass shattering over, and over, and over again.

"Well . . . drive safe," I finally mustered the strength to say.

"Give me another hug," Sam said, to which I willingly melted into his arms for the last time.

"Who unplugged the stars?" I asked with a tremor in my voice. As soon as I said that, Sam hugged me tighter for only a moment before releasing me from his arms. I walked out the door.

I wasn't sure how long I stood in the hallway outside his

apartment listening, hoping that he'd come running after me before I was able to make it to the stairs. I forced my legs to move and myself to continue to breathe as I fought the pain that was exploding in my chest. *Right . . . left . . . right . . . left . . . right . . . left* I repeated to get my legs to move. *Now go down the stairs*, I told myself as I felt the tears raging behind my lids. But I didn't move. Instead I stood there grasping the rail, desperately wanting to go back to his apartment and fight for him to stay. But why would he want to stay with me? What did I have to offer? What if he rejected me completely? What if all my dreams about us were just that—my dreams and only my imagination, and I meant nothing to him? What if he laughed at me?

When I reached the bottom of the stairs and walked outside, I welcomed the blast of cold air that pushed me back against the fear that propelled me forward. The snow was coming down harder, but I didn't notice. I wanted the numbness of the cold to stop the hurt that was ripping me apart inside. All I could think was, *I had lost him again!! I'd had a second chance and I had lost him again!!*

I sat in my car staring out the snow-covered windshield. At

one point I got out, determined to fight for him. I returned to his building and pulled the door open but stopped as I thought I heard the daunting cackle of fear laughing at me for thinking I was good enough for him. I quickly turned to go back to my car when I stepped on a patch of ice and fell flat on my back. I didn't move. I just laid there looking up at the dark sky and allowed myself to float in my pity as the tears flowed.

"Are you okay?" A stranger asked, as he ran towards where I laid.

"She might be hurt, don't move her," his female companion said. I looked up into their concerned faces.

"Are you okay? Can you hear me?" The stranger asked, again. I nodded my head, feeling the snow and gravel crunch underneath each movement.

"I'm fine." I managed to say as I struggled to stand. I wasn't sure how long I'd been lying there, but I could feel the cold through my bones and began to shiver.

"Are you sure?" the female stranger asked.

"Yeah. I just slipped on that patch of ice. I'll be okay." I told them flatly, welcoming the physical pain.

"Where's your car? Let me walk you to it." The stranger offered, gently placing his hand on my elbow as we walked, in silence to my piece-o-crap car.

I don't remember driving, but I made it home. I'd driven through the snow, parked my car, and entered the apartment to find Rosie and Stephen cuddled up on the couch watching TV. This was more than I could bear. With a herculean effort, I walked through the living room with a smile on my face.

"Sit and watch TV with us," Stephen cheerfully invited me from the couch, stopping my progress for a moment.

"Oh . . . um . . . no thanks. I'm exhausted. I'm going to bed." I said, avoiding eye contact.

"Did you and Sam have a good time?" asked Rosie.

"Yeah," I quickly responded wanting to escape this torture.

"You guys are next," added Stephen, cheerfully. I looked down half expecting to see a knife twisting in my heart.

"Good night," I said, with a forced-smile and small wave, then quickly escaped into my room where I collapsed on my bed, buried my head in my pillow and quietly sobbed, again.

The weeks that followed seemed so empty without Sam

around. I would think of something funny to tell him or to invite him to and would pick up my phone to call him only to remember that he wasn't there. My mind burned knowing that he had gone home to marry someone else.

In my daydreams, I held onto the possibility that he would show up out of the blue, on his motorcycle, declaring his love and we would ride into the sunset like you see in all the good old movies.

However, on Christmas Eve I received his and Hoppy's wedding invitation, complete with a picture. I tossed it into the trash on top of his Christmas present.

Survival

Ten plus years passed and I'd survived the loss of Sam and his decision to marry Sara Jane. I'd accepted the fact that he was no longer available to me.

I also survived the loss of my dear friend Trey in a car accident. While at his funeral, the gang from high school stood in a somber group at his graveside.

"Gee, almost everyone showed up," Sabrina said as she dabbed a kleenex under her eyes.

"Everyone but Sam. Did anyone call and tell him about Trey?" Chuck asked. We all shook our heads.

"I can't believe he's gone," said Beans, his widow, as the tears began to flow again. "How am I going to live without him? What about the kids?" Chuck put his arm about her shoulders and hugged her as she hid her face in his chest.

"I didn't even think about Sam," Zelda said. I stood silently by, afraid to say anything that would cause my tears to flow again. Right now, Beans needed all of us to be strong and help her through this horrible loss.

"Well, somebody should let him know," Sabrina said, looking at me.

"Right. Gracie, you should call him," Zelda said.

"Why me? Why not Brian or Chuck?" I asked and felt the slight tremble of butterflies in my stomach at the thought of speaking to him.

"You probably know him the best," said Sabrina.

"We all knew him. Anyone could call him. I haven't talked to him for years. I don't even know where to find him," I said, hoping they'd choose someone else.

"Call his mom; that's how I found all of you." Brian's voice broke as he looked down at his feet.

"Why don't you want to talk to him? Did you guys have a falling out or something?" Sabrina asked.

I avoided her question. "I'm just not sure I am the best choice to tell him this news."

"Would you do it for me?" Beans asked, sniffling as she pulled her head away from Chuck's chest.

I sighed. Looking into her tear stained face and eyes red from crying I acquiesced, "Of course, I will. I'll try to find him and let him know." I hated being the bearer of news like this. I hated having to tell Sam that a friend we all loved had left us. However, when I got his phone number—begrudgingly from his mother— and called it, it wasn't Sara Jane who answered the phone.

"Hi, is Sam there?"

"No, he isn't right now. May I take a message?" asked a guarded female voice I didn't recognize.

"Yeah. I'm a friend of his from high school and I wanted to let him know that one of our good friends, Trey, died. Can you have him call Gracie, please?"

"Sure, what's your number?" she asked, then hung up right after I gave it. It was only a couple of minutes before my phone rang. I picked it up, confident it would be Sam.

"Hello?"

"Is Gracie there?" Sam said. I quietly sighed, it was so good to hear his voice again. I couldn't deny the old feelings that began to stir. I was astonished that the sound of his voice could still cause a short intake of breath and put a smile on my face.

Stop it! I told myself before answering, "Hi Sam. Thanks for calling back."

"Did Trey really die?"

"Yeah.

"How?"

"Car accident outside of Denver. It was one of those big pile ups."

"Was he alone?" Sam asked.

"Yeah. Beans and the kids were home." We sat in silence for a couple minutes as Sam took in the news.

"When's the funeral?" he finally asked.

"It was a couple of weeks ago. I'm sorry no one told you sooner," I said with a cringe.

"He was such a great guy." I could hear the sadness in

Sam's voice.

"Yeah, he was." We sat in silence again.

"How are you doing?" he asked.

"I-I'm good. It took a few days before I could cry, but . . ." My voice trailed off as I fought the sorrow that often welled up in my throat.

"You two were close."

"Yeah, we were. I'd known him most of my life and I'd see him every time I went home. After he married Beans, it was even easier to stay in touch. Did you know I was godmother to their oldest?"

"No, I didn't. I didn't know they had kids. I guess I've been out of touch with everyone."

"Yeah. Three little girls." Again, the silence entered our conversation until I tried to change the subject, and asked, "Are you still married to Sara Jane?" I couldn't help myself, I *had* to ask.

"No. Not for a long time."

I gasped. "Wow, you two were so in love, what happened?" I asked, then caught myself and said, "Oops, sorry to be so nosy."

He chuckled. "Like that's ever stopped you before." I heard him give the sigh I'd heard a million times before, and knew he was smiling. "I'd made a mistake," he said.

"You made a mistake," I repeated, stunned at this news. "So . . . who answered your phone?" I asked. I couldn't help it—others may call it being nosy, but I liked to think of it as gathering information. I mean, he didn't have to tell me, so if he did who was I to stop him?

He answered, "My wife, Luann."

"Do you have any kids?"

"Five."

I involuntarily gasped. "Five?"

"Yup. Three girls and two boys." I could hear the pride in his voice.

"Did you have any kids with Sara Jane?"

"Just one."

I imagined that he was a good dad. The longer we spoke, the butterflies that had emerged began to subside and become dormant as I realized he was definitely out of my grasp being married with kids.

"Wow, that's really great." We sat in awkward silence.

"Well, I better let you go. I really just wanted to let you know about Trey."

"Do you ever make it to my area?" he asked just as I pulled the receiver from my ear.

"What?" I brought it back to my ear.

"I was asking if you ever make it to my area."

"Where's that?"

"Near Vegas."

"When I see my parents—they live around there now." *Why did I tell him that?* I couldn't stop myself; it just came out. Does hope truly spring eternal with me? Would I ever let him go? He's married! With a lot of kids! *Hellooooo?*

"Maybe you could come by and we could play golf," he suggested. *Why was he doing this?* There came the butterflies of hope. *He's married—with kids,* I kept telling myself as I pushed my fist into my stomach to stop the flutter.

"Does Luann play golf?"

"Nah, she hates it."

"I don't know how to play," I admitted.

"That's okay. I'll teach ya," *He's married!* the little voice in my head yelled at me.

"That sounds like fun. Would Luann be okay with it just being you and me?"

"Sure. Just call me when you're in the area and we'll go play."

"Okay . . . I'll call you. See ya." That time, I hung up first. Although it had been good to hear his voice, I already knew that I could never call him again. I had to forget about him, and continue on with the life I'd created post-Sam.

I'd had a crush on the guy for years. I'd fantasized about him; I'd waited on the side for him. He had given me hope time and time again and played on my desire for love over and over. These were all tricks and games to him. I knew that now, and I didn't want to play any longer.

For years I'd considered him my Mr. Darcy; I had measured every man I'd dated by him, until he married Sara Jane, then his hold on me began to fade with the realization that he was a married man. My life had moved far beyond the shadows of Ashbury and the ghosts that played there and I was happy.

L. K. Lawrence

The Final Goodbye

I had been so lost in my memories that I hadn't been aware of reaching my destination until the GPS voice announced that I'd arrived. I looked out the passenger side window at the gray, gloomy day as I saw the end of the driveway that ascended upward at a steep incline to who knows where. Going by the GPS on my phone, I was at the correct address, but I could not see the home from the street.

I stepped out of my rental car and closed the door. I paused for only a moment before I began my ascent and I didn't stop until

I was standing on the front step. Looking at my reflection in the glass door, at first I saw that awkward fifteen-year-old girl staring back, but when I blinked, she was gone. She'd been replaced by the reflection of a woman in her fifties. *Who is that?* I thought. Taking a deep breath, I paused—was I ready to face Sam again? Had I really compartmentalized my feelings for him from so long ago? I rang the doorbell and waited for what seemed hours, but I'm sure was only seconds.

I'd never seen the lady that opened the door before, but she knew me. "You must be Gracie," she said, and I nodded. "Please come in. I'm Sam's wife, Greta." She was a beautiful younger woman with blonde hair, an olive complexion, and a smile that lit up her face, belying the pain she felt. "Why don't you come in here with everyone else," she suggested, leading me into the living room, only to find Sam's mother and sisters seated on the couch and chairs. Entering the room, I could hear their whispers as though I'd just entered a den of vipers hissing to one another.

"What does she want?" Martha hissed.

"Why's she here?" his other sister, Miranda hissed in return.

"Will she never leave him alone?" His mother scowled. These comments surprised me since I hadn't spoken to him for over fifteen years. I didn't understand why they so disliked me; I'd never dated Sam or divorced him. I only attempted to reach out to him because he was my friend—nothing more.

"Sam asked her to come," Greta sternly stated, silencing the flickering tongues of venom. I was thankful for Greta's intervention. I turned away so they couldn't see my discomfort, especially at a time like this. "Please ignore them," Greta apologized, "I know he'll be glad to see you." I smiled.

"How is he doing?" I carefully inquired of Greta.

"I'm glad you could come now instead of later as you'd thought," she said, weighing her words, which alarmed me. "He's asked repeatedly for you. Let me tell him you're here."

After Greta left, I stood near the entrance to the living room wondering who would greet me. Would it be the Sam I'd adored so long ago? Or only the shell of what he used to be?

I'd been surprised to receive the Facebook message from Greta asking me to come see Sam. But the brevity of the situation never really sunk in until I told my sister, Katie, about it.

"You're not going to believe who I heard from today," I told Katie while watching her cut out quilt squares at her kitchen table.

"Who?" she asked without looking up from the task.

"Greta Read."

"Who's that?"

"Sam Read's wife."

"Wow! That's a name from your past. How long has it been since you've seen him?"

"Years. I haven't spoken to him since Trey died." I paused for a moment, then continued, "I haven't even thought of him, if I'm really honest."

Katie looked up, surprised. "You haven't? Really?"

"I haven't."

"Good for you. It was such a mess the way he ended things with you." Katie frowned as she looked down at the fabric before her.

"I know."

"Why'd she call you?" Katie asked, looking up again.

"She didn't call, she contacted me on Facebook."

"Why?"

"I guess Sam isn't doing well. He's asked me to come see him." I shrugged, still trying to wrap my mind around the situation.

"Oh. Are you gonna go?"

"Originally, I'd declined her request. I told her that my schedule was too busy."

"But . . ."

Sam was so long ago. I have no desire to—" I said, avoiding eye contact.

"Gracie . . ." Katie said cautiously. "What are you thinking?"

"I don't . . . I don't know," I said. Katie watched as sadness engulfed Gracie's face. "You know, he made me feel so much without even touching me. The passion I had for life then was all encompassing: The highs were heaven and the lows were hell. But looking back I'm thankful for all that I learned. It was a wonderful fantasy come true, for a teenage girl like me to have a guy like him in my life. It just came down to the fact that he didn't want me romantically, he just wanted a friend. And, th-that's fine. I was the one that wanted more. He was always my friend." I finally made eye contact with Katie. "And, I miss that friendship."

"So, you are going to go?" Katie asked, tenting her brows.

"I hadn't planned to until she wrote me that he was dying of pancreatic cancer." The news still shocked me to my core, even more when I said it aloud.

"Are you okay?" Katie asked, looking at me with concern. She set her scissors down. She was the one who picked up the pieces of me after he left to marry Sara Jane. She knew the whole story.

"It's just difficult to wrap my mind around the fact that I'll spend the rest of my life without him."

Katie rolled her eyes, then frowned and said, "You've been living without him since he left to marry that girl."

"I know. But, as stupid as this sounds, I always felt we were meant to be together," I said. "But . . . you know, he's on his third wife now, so . . . there's that."

"His third?" Katie asked, incredulously.

I nodded my head, and said, "Third."

"Wow, that could've been you."

"True . . . true, but it's kinda like the lotto, you can't win it if you don't play it."

"Thank heavens you don't' gamble then." Katie made a goofy face and chortled. I didn't respond. Katie became serious, and asked, "You are over him, right?"

"Yes," I answered, irritated. "But he was a good friend, and I still care for him." Katie continued to scowl at me. "He's got stage four pancreatic cancer and is in hospice care." I gave her an incredulous look. "Nothing is going to happen."

"Let's hope nothing happens." Katie said sternly, lowering her head as she looked at me over her glasses. "Just don't forget his track record."

"Give me some credit here."

Katie sighed, then said, "So it's just because he's dying that you're going?" Katie waited for me to answer. "Gracie?"

"Yeah . . . yeah, of course. Greta told me that his dying wish was to see me. I can't ignore that."

"Will you be okay? Do you want me to go with you?" Katie asked with a sympathetic smile.

I shook my head no. "How much more damage could he do that he didn't do years ago?" I told her as I got up from the table.

"When do you leave?"

"I'll leave tomorrow." *Would it hurt to see him again?* I wondered. It astonished me that my heart still skipped a beat at the thought of seeing him. He'd played with it for decades, until I could no longer allow any type of contact with him in order for me to heal and move on. And, now, he was dying, and wanted to see me. I had to close this chapter for good, and I had to forgive and let go.

I was in Utah visiting family when she reached out to me, so I knew I could easily get to his home within hours. Now that I was there and saw the seriousness of the situation, I was glad I'd come.

Greta appeared from the hallway. "Gracie, why don't you come with me," she suggested and put her hand on my back, directing me towards the bedroom door. I stopped just outside the door, afraid. Greta gave a slight push on my back and a nod of her head. "Go on. He's waiting," she whispered.

I was unprepared for the scene before me: gone was the rugged man I'd known. Instead, lying on his back in the hospital bed that took most of the space in the room, was a shrunken skeletal figure, only a shell of his former self. Gone were the dark, thick curls due to the chemo treatments and the ravages of that horrible disease. His eyes were sunken in and half-closed as if he were sleeping.

I looked at Greta and whispered, "He's sleeping. Should I go?" She raised her hand for me to stay and moved to the head of the bed and gently touched Sam's shoulder. At her touch, his eyes opened, and he slightly turned his head towards her. "Gracie is here to see you," she gently told him, then motioned me over to the side of the bed where I took her place and stood in his line of vision. She turned to me, "He doesn't say much. Stay as long as you like, I'll be in the kitchen if you need me." She sadly smiled and walked out of the room leaving Sam and me alone.

I'd never been that close to someone so near death before. Especially someone that I'd cared about so deeply, and for so long. Standing next to his bed I looked at my dear friend, who laid there with his eyes closed. I quietly sat in the chair next to his bed and put my arm through the rail and gently took his fragile hand in mine. The coolness of it shocked me as I remembered the many slow dances when I'd felt his warm strength as he held my hand

and moved us about the floor. Or especially the last night on the beach when I held the strong warm hand that I'd thought held my future.

Quickly, I brushed the tear that had escaped my eye away before it got to my cheek, surprised at the rush of emotions I felt. Looking up, I saw Sam watching me. I looked into his eyes, and I thought I could see a faint spark of the old Sam. Or, did I imagine the twinkle in his eyes? That ever-present twinkle when he laughed or teased me. We sat in silence as I warmly smiled at him while holding his hand. I attempted to communicate my affection for him through my eyes and to quell the beating of my pulse. But my heart began to beat as if it was waking after lying dormant for so long and I could feel the blood coursing through my veins again. This can't be! I've moved on! I've been happy. But I couldn't deny it.

I was afraid to try and put into words what I felt, words that I'd never been brave enough to utter before. Did those words really matter now? We sat quietly until he tried to say something that came out as more of a raspy whisper than words.

"What, Sam?" I asked. "What'd you say?" I stood so I could lean over and put my ear close to his chapped lips.

"It . . . was . . . you," he labored to say in a raspy whisper

"It was me? Is that what you said?" I quietly asked, straightening enough to look in his eyes better. Yet, I cried in my heart, *You can't say this to me now, Sam.*

"Always . . . you," he said with an almost imperceptible nod of his head.

This can't be happening! I could feel the anger begin to rise from all the suppressed longing from years ago, from the love he'd denied me. And now with so little time left, he decides to come clean?! *It's not fair!* Every fiber of my soul cried out; every tear I'd held inside pushed to escape the confines that held them. But standing next to his bed and knowing there was nothing I could do to change our history or time, I blinked away the tears that seethed against my lids and tried to calm my soul.

"Di-did you say, *always me*?" I asked in a whisper that quivered with emotion.

"Always you," he replied with an almost imperceptible nod of his head.

Hearing those words, I closed my eyes in grief. *How can he tell me this now?* I cried inside. When I felt I could trust myself, I opened my tear-filled eyes and before I could stop myself, I choked back a sob and whispered, "Don't you dare do this to me. Not now. Not after all this time. It's not fair, Sam!" Then, I stopped. I'd never seen such pain in his eyes before. I never knew he cared enough to be affected by my words. I wanted to stop, but I continued, spurred on by the bravery I'd never had before with him. "I have adored you from the first moment I saw you. It shattered my heart when you chose Hoppy over me, then the next girl, and the next—never me. Yet you repeatedly sought me out. Why?" I stopped myself again as I saw the distress in his eyes. I took a deep breath to gather myself, swallowed my emotions, then I revealed to him with a slight smile, "Yet, despite the pain, I wouldn't change one second of the time we spent together." Leaning over his bed rail, I gently put my hands on either side of his face and looked into his eyes. "*You* made my world better, the moon bigger, and the stars brighter. You brought the passion to my life." I could see the tears fill his eyes. I knew I couldn't leave him like this, not my friend. So with a small chuckle, I said, "I just wish I could've caught you between wives." He made what sounded like a slight laugh.

I smiled and winked before leaning over to give him a tender kiss on his cold, chapped lips and a final hug, and only then did I allow my tears to escape and fall on his pillow. Tears he'd never see. *How will I survive this loss? First Trey and now him.* Out of habit, I deeply inhaled expecting his musky scent that had been replaced by the smell of disinfectant. I whispered in his ear, "Who unplugged the stars?" then I lingered as I gave him a soft kiss on his cheek. I felt the light feather touch of his hand on my back as he tried to return the hug.

Straightening up, I stood back and looked in his eyes for the last time. A single tear escaped the outer corner of his eye and slid down the side of his face. I gently wiped it away. Holding his hands, I lifted each to my lips and lightly kissed them. No longer could I deny the feelings I'd had for this man so long ago. "It was always you too," I whispered, then gave him one last smile before turning to leave. I left the room, unable to see clearly through the tears that filled my eyes. Twice before this man had shattered my heart. And this time, he took it with him.

I leaned against the wall just outside his door to pull myself together, gulping down my emotions. *Why? Why did I have to lose the only man I'd ever loved? Yes, loved.* So desperately I wanted to sob aloud, to fall to my knees and howl out my grief to the heavens. But I knew I had to be strong, especially before entering back into the vipers' den. I could already hear their hissings in my direction. But I ignored them.

I wiped the tears away as I walked into the kitchen to find Greta staring out the window.

"Greta," I said, and she turned around and looked at me, I continued, "Thank you for letting me see him one last time. I hope it wasn't too much of an imposition."

"Nonsense," she said coolly, her voice full of unvented emotion as she wiped an already clean counter. "He's always spoken of you with such affection. I-I-I knew it was very important to *him*, that I find you." Greta stopped wiping the counter and looked me in my eyes. "Did you know you were the other woman in our marriage, and probably his other marriages as well?" I was taken aback by the flash of anger I saw in her eyes that replaced the hurt I'd seen earlier with this disclosure.

Surprised, I asked, "How can that be? I haven't seen or spoken to him for over fifteen years."

"That doesn't matter. He was consumed by you. You were a poison that was killing our marriage." I stood there in silence, stunned. She continued, "We have a beautiful little girl, and he insisted we name her Gracie."

"Gracie?" I whispered, shocked.

"Gracie." She looked at me, and the anger had been replaced with hurt, again. "After the one and only girl he ever loved." Turning away from me to look out the window, she said, "I've known about you from the beginning. But I loved him so much I thought that my love could erase you from his mind. And when it didn't—I grew to hate you." She turned back to me. "I've hated the mention of your name and the way his voice changed when he spoke of you. And now every time I call for my beautiful daughter, I'll think of you and how you possessed his heart, leaving no room for us."

"Then why'd you invite me to come see him?" I asked, puzzled.

"Because I love *him* the way he loves *you*." Her voice choked with emotion. "If seeing you will help him sleep better and make the time he has left easier, I'd have come picked you up

502

myself." With a tear trailing down her cheek, she choked out, "I *love* that man. He is my world."

I stood in front of her, dazed. I finally said, "I-I'm sorry, I-I didn't, I didn't know. But, it's you he married, not me. You have nothing to be jealous of. He married who he wanted." I didn't know what to else to say. I wasn't going tell her what I thought he'd said to me in his room. She didn't need to hear that— ever. We stood in uncomfortable silence looking at one another. I tried to wrap my mind around what she had said. How could that be true? We'd lived different lives. I'd been so busy with my life and career I hadn't even thought of him.

Before I turned to leave, I said, "I'm so sorry." Then I walked toward the door followed by Greta, who wiped tears from her cheeks. "Thank you again for letting me see him. Please, let me know if you need anything," I offered. She tersely nodded her head as she opened the door, once again the gracious host.

"Of course," she said, although I knew I'd never hear from her again. "Oh! I almost forgot. He asked me to give you this," she said, pulling a sealed, white envelope out of her sweater pocket and handing it to me.

I crinkled my brow. "What is this?"

"I don't know. You'll have to open it to see. Hopefully, he hasn't given you our home," she said curtly. Then catching herself, she said, "Sorry." Without another word, she closed the door.

"Thanks," I said to the door. What could this possibly be?

Who Unplugged the Stars?

Truth Shall Set You Free

Standing on the front step with my back to the door that literally closed on the final chapter of my friendship with Sam, I knew in my heart that despite everything, Sam and I had been and always would be friends.

I stood on the step and looked down at the white sealed envelope Greta had handed me. With a bit of trepidation, I put my finger beneath the flap and carefully pulled along, tearing an opening while trying to avoid any papercuts. Once I had it open, I pulled out two sheets of plain notebook paper. As I unfolded them, I could see Sam's sloppy cursive filling both front and back. *What did he have to say to me? Did Greta know?* I asked myself. I found

an Adirondack chair set over to the side on the lawn next to a small

table; I thought that would be a good place to sit and read his

epistle to me. Once I was comfortably situated, I began to read:

Dear Gracie,

If you're reading this, then Greta

found you, and I'm either already gone or

very close to it.

When the doctor told me I had cancer,

at first, I was in shock. Then I was angry, then

scared. I spent hours sitting in the dark feeling

sorry for myself and asking why me? I went

over my life again, and again and the one

consistent bright spot, was you. I didn't know

whether or not I'd see you again so I thought

I'd write a letter to tell you what I should have

told you long ago. I'm sorry it's not under

better circumstances.

I've had a wonderful life with three

wonderful women. But my biggest regret was

that I didn't follow my heart—which was you.

From the moment I met you my life was so

much better: the sun was warmer, the stars

twinkled brighter, and I laughed so much

harder.

When Trey introduced us that last day

of our sophomore year, as you stood on one

leg over a puddle of chocolate milk. I knew

you differed from all the others. And getting to

know you, I realized it was the difference I

wanted in my life.

I longed to be so much more than just

friends, yet you couldn't date until you were

sixteen, so I waited. I put my heart on hold,

slowing its beats when I saw you, keeping a

distance when all I wanted was to encircle you

in my arms and gorge myself on everything

about you. I thought you felt that too.

Yet, when Sara Jane told me you only

saw us as friends and had given her your

blessing to pursue me. I couldn't deny the hurt

I felt or my surprise that I'd read you so

wrong. So, I tried my life without you, but I

missed you too much. Even though I cared for

Sara Jane, my heart still ached for you. I

needed my best friend—I needed you.

Then there were the dances, and as

much as I disliked dancing, it became an

opportunity to hold you in my arms and feel

the warmth of your world, your laughter, and

put up with your singing, when necessary

(LOL). I didn't care how ridiculous I looked

because it was the closest I could get to you in

those moments.

After high school, you were never far

from my mind. When I was in Paris I wished

you were there with me, or in Ashbury, I

longed for the talks we had on my dinner

breaks. But I needed to know if what I thought

was between us was real or just kids flirting.

That's why I came to Salt Lake to find you.

The moment I saw you in that little gift shop I

couldn't deny what I felt. You had no idea I'd

been in the hotel for hours that day, working

up the courage to surprise you. For hours I

sat and watched you with the customers as

you laughed and waited on them—unaware

that you were being admired from afar. I

wasn't sure if I'd be welcome or not, but I

wanted back in your world.

I loved every moment we spent

together. I'm sorry that you were hurt and

confused by the other women. My only excuse

is that I was selfish: I wanted you, but I

wanted my family's money more. I was afraid

to be poor. Sara Jane's family ran in the same

circles as mine, so our marriage was more

palatable to my family. I was too scared to go

against their wishes, to follow my heart. I kept

telling myself that you weren't that special to

me, but everything else proved the opposite.

I know you wanted more from me and I

longed to give it. That night on the beach in

California, when I held you in my arms, I

wanted to propose to you right then and there

and stop playing all the games. But it scared

me. I'm ashamed I wasn't stronger against the

forces that assaulted me from home.

Or that night in my apartment when I

told you I was going home. After you left, it

took all my strength to not run after you, but it

had already been decided. And I knew when I

left Salt Lake that I'd made the wrong choice,

but it was too late.

After all these years, I need to tell you

that you made me happy. It was always you.

I've only wanted you—just you. Which

probably wasn't fair to my wives, but it's the

truth.

I'm so sorry, Gracie. All these years I wasted because I was a coward. Instead of following my heart, I followed my family's money. It didn't make me happy like I could've been with you. I'll regret that forever.

I often think about our dance at Prom and that poem you quoted. At the time, I didn't get it, but I understand it now. When you have the "one" you no longer need the sun or stars for light, and it still applies:

You'll unplug the stars

And cover the sun

When you finally know

You've found the one.

You'll forever be my "one", Gracie.

Sam

I sat with tears sliding down my face as I held my hand to my mouth to muffle the sobs that racked my body. I was overwhelmed with a myriad of emotions that I didn't know I still had. Emotions that had laid dormant for years: with regret and sorrow fighting the hardest to be heard.

In the letter, he'd answered so many questions I'd had through the decades that we'd known one another. Finally, he'd put in writing what I'd have given my right arm to hear him say so long ago. He chose to do it now, when there was no future. Yet with this letter he silenced all the angst I'd always felt with him. When the sobs had dissolved to mere sniffles, I read through it once more, and this time there were no tears, only a warmth that felt like a hug squeezing out any doubts or hidden insecurities still locked within my soul. This was his gift to me—peace.

I sat in the chair and contemplated his love that I'd never known I had. I carefully organized the pages and returned Sam's declaration back into the envelope. My mind was spinning with the revelation that he had loved me. My "angel" . . . my "Adonis" had seen me for *who* I was not *what* I was. I alone had judged myself for *what* I thought I was, and not *who* he saw me to be, thus allowing myself to be tossed aside because I didn't think I was good enough to fight for him. He never asked me to change, nor did he have the courage to ask me for anything else. And I in my cowardice had allowed it.

I marveled that this man, who had left me with a heart scarred beyond recognition, had loved me. My soul sang with the truth that it hadn't been my imagination all those years. He had loved me. I regretted the sentence we'd both served because of our cowardice. Now it was too late—for him. But me? I was going to live my life, love freely and bravely, and never let cowardice decide my future again.

I stood, and carefully placed the envelope in my purse. I couldn't help but smile with the freedom his words gave me. He might be physically gone but I had my memories and his last words now engraved in my heart to keep me warm on those cold, lonely winter nights of self-doubt. No one could ever keep us apart now, nor take away, or spoil those memories with their harsh words again. They were mine. Mine to lock away or sift through. But that is all they were—memories.

I had a life to live, and a heart ready for love. Who knew, maybe one day I'd tell this story and have my own happy ending?

I looked up to see that the sun had burned away the gray skies. And with a deep breath, a spring in my step, and Sam in my heart I descended his driveway, knowing that I would never doubt my worth or be a coward in love again.

THE END

ABOUT THE AUTHOR

L. K. Lawrence is a West Coast author that has finally found a way to share her imaginations with others. Whether it is a bittersweet love story, a romance, thriller, or cozy mystery.

www.ingramcontent.com/pod-product-compliance
Lightning Source LLC
Chambersburg PA
CBHW071729110726
47908CB00006B/1543

* 9 7 8 1 7 3 4 5 4 8 6 0 0 *